Y0-BDG-024

A THIN COLD SMILE TOUCHED THE STRANGER'S MOUTH.

"Its power is of no value to me. But it is of great value to a creature such as yourself. It is called the Commanding Stone. It is ancient beyond measure. I will not bore you with a lengthy recounting of its history. None of it matters now. What does matter is that you can use the Stone to summon and control the dragons of which you dream."

Tyne was startled to realize this being could peer into his sleeping mind. *Who knows what a divine being can do?* he thought.

"How do I control them? I've dreamed of them, and I can feel a . . . *connection* between me and them, something binding us together. But I don't know how to make them do what I want."

"Are you asking for my help?"

"Yes."

"And in return, will you kill Gerin Atreyano?"

Tyne answered without hesitation. "He deserves to die."

GILL MEMORIAL LIBRARY
145 E. BROAD STREET
PAULSBORO, NJ 08066
(856) 423-5155

By David Forbes

The Osserian Saga

Book One
THE AMBER WIZARD

Book Two
THE WORDS OF MAKING

Book Three
THE COMMANDING STONE

ATTENTION: ORGANIZATIONS AND CORPORATIONS
Most Eos paperbacks are available at special quantity discounts for
bulk purchases for sales promotions, premiums, or fund raising.
For information, please call or write:

Special Markets Department, HarperCollins Publishers,
10 East 53rd Street, New York, New York 10022-5299.
Telephone: (212) 207-7528.   Fax: (212) 207-7222.

THE COMMANDING STONE

THE OSSERIAN SAGA
BOOK THREE

DAVID FORBES

GILL MEMORIAL LIBRARY
145 E. BROAD STREET
PAULSBORO, NJ 08066
(856) 423-5155

An Imprint of HarperCollinsPublishers

This is a work of fiction. Names, characters, places, and incidents are products of the author's imagination or are used fictitiously and are not to be construed as real. Any resemblance to actual events, locales, organizations, or persons, living or dead, is entirely coincidental.

EOS
An Imprint of HarperCollins*Publishers*
10 East 53rd Street
New York, New York 10022-5299

Copyright © 2009 by David Forbes
ISBN 978-0-06-082044-2
Cover art by Keith Birdsong
www.eosbooks.com

All rights reserved. No part of this book may be used or reproduced in any manner whatsoever without written permission, except in the case of brief quotations embodied in critical articles and reviews. For more information, address Eos, an Imprint of HarperCollins Publishers.

First Eos paperback printing: October 2009

HarperCollins® and Eos® are registered trademarks of HarperCollins Publishers.

Printed in the U.S.A.

10 9 8 7 6 5 4 3 2 1

If you purchased this book without a cover, you should be aware that this book is stolen property. It was reported as "unsold and destroyed" to the publisher, and neither the author nor the publisher has received any payment for this "stripped book."

This one is for Alex, my Little Man.

THE
COMMANDING
STONE

Sontel *Girding Mountains*

Arlosan Uplands

Horon

Kaldas Highlands

Farad

Soharel River

Ferondril R.

rill R.

Url-Azgish (ruins)

The Long Sea

Heart River

Irinil

Igrin Hills

Pellur

HELCAREA

Neiyes   Mt. Kail

Graymantle Mountains

Plains of Drommon

Moriteri

Kirosi River

Nirovai Deep

Kalemnon

ELLOHAR

Avelnur   Serel

Gap of Ellohar

Withered Hills

Wa

Redhor

Gap of Ellohar

Br
F

HUNZAR

Mendan Mountains

DOREL

Rhosa
Mespa

Samaro River

The Sunder

Ghesevaras

H

Tumlaren R.

NEDDAR

Scale in miles

0   100   200   300

o by David Forbes

OSSERIA

Fourteenth Century
of the Common Age

Maurelian Sea

Uplands
of Eithos

*Cape
Igaz*

Hazi

*Brendis
Bay*

Tieren's Fence

*Bay of
Tassair*

MALAGAR

Theril River

Lingul

Faranwood

Faillian River

Darron

KERYA

Muros

Roumael River

*Hallas
Bay*

Strait of Sechel

HARLAD

Londros

*Cape
Veilas*

Marcarax

Hanadi

Saros R.

Brindal
Haro

Athram

Landwall Mountains

TAGEREA

Tappan R.

Pomman R.

Brangaran

Valesh Peninsula

ARMENOS

THRENDELLEN

Taldos

Turen

Winding R.

Trothmar

Candago R.

*Gedsengard
Isle*

*Gulf
of
Gedsuel*

Urkein

vos

Ailethon

Neldemarien

Almaris

Cressan

The Seawall

Pelkland
Islands

an's
air

Agdenor

KHEDESH

Tan
Orech

Edonia

Tolthean

Istameth

Azren R.

Halir
Barellen

Lormenien

Orech R.

Indis R.

Orleth

Khedesh's March

Haranwaith

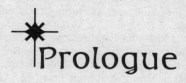

Prologue

The small coffin swayed gently as it descended into the grave. *The earth is swallowing him up.* The grave looked like a raw, open wound, a physical reminder of the pain Tyne Fedron felt in his soul at the loss of his youngest brother.

Tremmel's grave was next to his brother Rukee's, who had died less than a year earlier. Anger and outrage roiled through Tyne's guts as he thought about Tremmel's death at the hands of the thing that had risen from the Bronze Demon Hills. Tyne himself had not seen the demon, but Tremmel had witnessed the crimson lightning that had opened a hole in the ground, out of which the demon had come. Tremmel had fled at the sight, frightened out of his mind, but for some reason Rukee had stayed. And died for it. When they found him, there was no wound upon his body, but dead he was, cold and stiff, his eyes open and staring.

It had taken a long time to get the full story from Tremmel. The youngest of the Fedron boys was so frightened he could not speak; when he finally found his voice a day later, all that emerged was a terrible keening sound mixed with Rukee's name.

Tyne had gone in search of Rukee before Tremmel recovered. He found his brother's body just off the road that led past the Bronze Demon Hills, near old man Hilagren's farm.

Tyne had dimly taken note of the smoldering hole in the side of one of the hills, but in his grief he gave it no more thought. With the help of his friends Marchus and Draen, who had accompanied him on his search, he brought Rukee's body back to their mother.

Loesta Fedron had lost a husband four years past, but had managed to keep the family farm going with the help of her sons and a gift of gold coins from her brother Brulchee, a merchant who dealt in furs throughout Formale. After her husband's drowning death in the Uron River, Loesta refused a number of suitors who pursued her hand. She confided to her oldest son Tyne that they wanted either her land, a woman for their beds, or both, and she would be damned if she would spit on her husband's memory by giving such weak men what they wanted.

"We are Helcareans," she told him. "The blood of Helca flows in our veins. We're descended from mighty warriors of old, men who placed their boot heels on every kingdom in Osseria and forged an empire from the struggling, kicking lot of them. Never forget that. We are a strong people, the strongest in the world. We can't act weak. We can't *be* weak. That's why the empire fell. Because weak men with no vision, no purpose, came to rule it. Mark my words, Tyne, the empire will rise again one day, but only if we are strong enough to show we are worthy of it."

When Tremmel recovered enough to tell them what had happened to Rukee, Tyne immediately led a group of men from the nearby homesteads and the town of Konfatine to the Bronze Demon Hills. The hole in the hillside was still there, mocking him. He'd marched to it without hesitation while the others faltered, fearing the hills and the legends surrounding them. Weak men, he realized. Weak and unworthy of their heritage, their birthright.

His own display of courage—he reached the hole alone, carrying only a long hunting knife—shamed the other men into following. When they reached him, they spread out around the yawning pit, a shaft into the hill so deep its bottom was swallowed in inky blackness. Twilight was settling over the land, and none of them wanted to be there when night came.

"Marchus, light a torch," he said. He dropped the flaming brand into the opening. It fell twenty feet through charred dirt, rock, and clay before coming to rest on the stone floor of a tunnel.

"Gods preserve us," muttered Draen. "What is that down there?"

"We're going to find out," said Tyne. "Give me some rope."

"You're not going . . . " Marchus could not finish. In that moment, Tyne despised his friend for his cowardice.

"Of course I am," said Tyne. "Whatever killed Rukee came from there. And now it's up here, with *us*. Maybe there's something down there that can tell us what it is or how to kill it. Someone stay up here to keep watch and help with the rope. The rest are coming with me." His tone made it clear there would be no discussion or debate.

He expected half of them to turn and run home like whipped dogs, but to his surprise they obeyed him. Even Marchus. The youngest of them, a wide-eyed boy of thirteen named Iskarea, remained above ground.

After securing a rope to the black, twisted trunk of a nearby tree, they followed Tyne into the pit.

Later, Tyne could recall little of what they found underground, as if something in the very air prevented him from retaining what he saw. The others suffered from a similar lack of memory. What remained were impressions punctuated with vivid images, some of which made little sense to them. Tyne's memory of that time was very much like a dream.

He remembered long tunnels that twisted throughout the hills like a labyrinth, broken at regular intervals by stairs that led deeper and deeper into the earth. Smaller tunnels branched off into a blackness so deep, so impenetrable, that even he dared not enter them. The very air in those passages seemed to emanate threat and danger; his blood ran cold just to stand at the entrance to them, and he felt that if he were to take but a few more steps forward, his heart would burst within his ribs. The torch he thrust into the first such passage they reached guttered and nearly failed before he withdrew it, as if some invisible presence were hungry for its light and heat.

He remembered strange glyphs and symbols carved upon the walls, though he could not recall any details of them. The impression they left upon him was one of *wrongness*, of things carved by inhuman hands for purposes dark and unknowable.

One of his clearer memories was of Marchus rubbing his temple and muttering, "There's something trying to get into my head."

"What are you talking about?" asked Draen.

"Whispers . . . something talking to me . . . " Marchus sounded almost drunk, and he was unsteady on his feet.

"Shut up," said Kargin, the iron smith from Konfatine. "I don't hear nothin'."

Tyne worried that in this haunted place something unsavory was indeed happening to Marchus. "Can you understand what the whispers are saying?"

"Shut *up*!" shouted Kargin. "There ain't no bloody whispers!"

Marchus shook his head and mumbled something Tyne did not understand. Tyne was about to ask him to repeat himself when they turned a corner and came across massive double doors fashioned from black stone, each at least a foot thick. The doors had been thrown open from within, but Tyne could see nothing of whatever lay beyond them.

He drew a breath and crossed the threshold.

Inside he found a round room whose walls were covered with more of the strange symbols. He sensed a kind of energy radiating from them, that the alien words or ideas they conveyed were drenched with power.

His torchlight fell upon a massive slab in the center of the room. A stone table a dozen feet long and half that in width, with the impression of a massive body on it, an area darkened relative to the rest of the stone.

He trembled with fury as he stared at the resting place of the demon that had killed his brother. Why had it awakened? Why now?

"This is not a place made by men," whispered Draen. "It's cursed, damned. We should leave before—"

Marchus let out a wordless howl of pain and doubled over, clutching his head. His scream was almost painfully loud in the closed space. "Make them stop, make them *stop*!"

He shrieked and raised his head. Tyne gasped. Marchus's eyes were bleeding. No mere trickles of blood, but thick runnels, as if his eyes had been skewered.

Marchus began to thrash, and Tyne saw that his ears were bleeding as well. In the flickering torchlight it was a ghastly, nightmarish scene.

Marchus shifted his knife in his hand. Tyne had a sudden premonition of what was about to happen. "Hold him down!" he shouted.

But it was too late. Marchus drove the knife into his ear with incredible force. It penetrated his skull nearly to the hilt; the tip punched out the other side of his face in a hot spray of blood.

Draen and several others screamed in horror. Tyne rushed forward and caught Marchus's convulsing body before he struck the floor. Tyne heard himself calling Marchus's name over and over, but his voice sounded distant, dreamlike, the flimsy wail of a ghost.

He remembered nothing of their journey out of the tunnels beneath the hills. His next recollection was climbing from the pit, covered in Marchus's blood, burning with a desire to kill the thing that had murdered his brother and now his friend. The desire was so strong, so deep, he wondered if he would ever feel anything else again.

And now he was burying his youngest brother next to Rukee, not far from Marchus's grave. He wondered how the gods could be so cruel. Tremmel had survived his encounter with the demon, only to be struck down by blood fever. He lingered for two unbearable weeks, his small body wracked with convulsions that grew so violent he broke his arms and several ribs with his thrashings. The membranes along his gums, fingernails, and rectum had all turned black, thinned, then bled. Toward the end, the amount of blood was so great they could not clean it away fast enough. They could only try to hold him down while he convulsed and screamed, lying in a stinking pool of his own dark blood and waste.

Losing yet another son, and in such a terrible way, was too much for even Loesta Fedron to bear. Something inside her broke when Tremmel drew his last breath. She'd hardly spoken since. She shuffled around their house like an undead creature of legend, as if the very things that made her human had been extinguished like a snuffed candle, leaving an empty husk that continued to act alive through inertia alone.

The small coffin reached the bottom of the grave and settled into its place of eternal rest. Tyne stood next to his mother with his arm around her shoulders. He held her tightly; without his support, he feared she would slump to the ground. She made soft whimpering noises as she stared at the coffin. Tyne did not think she was aware of what she was doing, or anyone around her.

"Tremmel, oh my Tremmel . . ." His mother barely moved her lips to speak, and it took Tyne a moment to understand what she was saying.

A week passed. It was strangely quiet without Tremmel's constant screams and shrieks. Tyne dreamed of the Bronze Demon Hills and the nightmare tunnels they had found beneath them. He woke often after dreaming of Marchus driving his knife into his ear, or seeing some vast dark shape lying upon the stone table in the darkness, about to stir to life.

"Mama, I'm leaving," he announced one morning. Loesta Fedron was standing outside their thatch-roofed house, staring blankly into the distance. He did not know how long she'd been there. He found her in odd places more and more, standing still as a scarecrow or slumped against a wall or post, her head down as if she'd fallen asleep on her feet.

She did not look at him. He moved so he was directly in front of her, but he could see that she was not aware of his presence. Her eyes stared through him at something he could not see. A part of his heart broke then as he thought about all he had lost; but another part hardened, driven by overwhelming anger and rage at what had happened to his family.

"I'm going to go find the thing that killed Rukee and I'm going to kill it," he said. "I know we went looking after he died, but it was long gone, and we didn't go far enough. That won't stop me now. I'll go as far as I have to." He took her hands. They were cold, rigid, as if carved from stone. She did not return his grip.

"You're going to be alone for a while, Mama. I don't know how long I'll be gone. Draen and Pennel will look in on you. But you need to start taking care of yourself again." He squeezed her hands more tightly. "I miss them, too. But we still have to live."

The only weapons he carried were his bow and hunting knife. He would have preferred a sword or crossbow, but the Fedron family had no such weapons and he didn't have the money to buy them, so that was that. The demon that killed Rukee was enormous, based on Tremmel's description and the slab they found in the tunnels. He would need a better weapon at some point, but for now these would do.

Draen and Pennel knew he was leaving and tried to talk him out of it, but once he made up his mind, there was no changing it. He did not say good-bye to anyone except his mother. He had no desire to have them try one last time to convince him to stay. This was something that needed to be done. The thing that killed his brother was going to pay.

Tremmel had looked back and watched the demon strike down Rukee. He said it had walked southward before disappearing. That was all Tyne had to go on. It was not much, but it would suffice.

He set off south.

He kept to well-traveled paths and roads. He needed information, and the only way to get it was to ask others what they knew. He could not find what he was seeking if he kept away from people.

He reached the Moriteri Pike when he was a day's walk from the capital. The road was crowded compared to what he'd traveled so far. He stopped at inns, when he found them, to ask if anyone had seen the demon. He spent nothing if he could get away with it; if the barkeep or a patron wanted coin for their answer, or if they pressed him to buy a drink or meal, he weighed heavily whether to pay from his meager sack of silver and bronze coins. Most of the time he did not.

One night he paid two copper pennies to a barkeep who whispered that he had seen an apparition himself some months ago; for his trouble, Tyne got an outlandish tale that so enraged him he walked out before he lost control and drove his knife through the fat bastard's eye.

He asked anyone he passed on the road if they had heard about the demon stalking the world. A few had heard rumors and tales of a gold-skinned monstrosity, but could offer no details of what had happened or where the encounters occurred. There were enough details, though, to convince him he was headed in the right direction.

A guard at the gates of Moriteri had no news of a demonic creature; instead, the man prattled on about the sorcerer who had recently joined the King's Court, a man who had come seemingly from nowhere and was now the king's most trusted advisor. "Strange goings on," said the guard with a shake of his head. "Strange enough without no demon causin' trouble."

Tyne cared nothing for the king or his sorcerer. Rullio was a weak ruler, as were all the kings and queens who had come before him since the time of the empire's collapse. Strong rulers would reclaim what the empire had lost. Rullio and his ilk had no pride, no love of their kingdom and its rich history. Helcarea needed a ruler with the strength of will to demand that his people become what they once were: the greatest in the world. And to winnow out those who would not follow.

But Tyne knew that would not happen while Rullio sat upon the throne. From what he had heard, the king cared for his concubines and horses more than ruling the kingdom and trying to rekindle its past glory. It shamed him to have such a worthless man as his king.

Tyne did not enter the city. He felt that if something so monstrous and deadly had entered Moriteri, word of the terror and death it caused would be everywhere.

He continued his journey south, asking his questions to anyone who would listen. Just across the border in Ellohar he spoke to a man who claimed his brother had been killed by a bronze-skinned monster whose mouth was filled with fire. "The bloody thing appeared out of nowhere while my brother was workin' to dig out a tree stump," said the man. He leaned against the rake he'd been using and mopped at his sweaty forehead with a worn, damp rag. "Then it touched him and Ullos just fell over dead."

"So you saw it yourself?" The hair on Tyne's arms stood on end.

The man nodded, oblivious to Tyne's excitement. "Damned thing was big as a tree."

"Where was this? Which way did it go after it . . . touched your brother?"

The man eyed Tyne suspiciously. "Why do you care? Are you lookin' to die?"

Tyne narrowed his gaze. "The demon you saw came out of the ground in the Bronze Demon Hills and killed my younger brother. When we went into its crypt, one of my friends was driven mad and killed himself. Now I'm going to kill it, but I have to find it first."

The man gave Tyne an appraising look. "Boy, turn around and go home. You don't look like you've seen your twentieth year. This thing can kill with a touch. Your flimsy bow won't even scratch it. If you find it, all you'll end up doin' is dyin'."

Tyne felt himself redden, but did not argue with the man. He needed only one thing. "Which way did it go?" he repeated. He tried to put iron in his voice, to make it impossible for the man to deny him. "Was it still heading south?"

At first he wasn't sure the man would reply. Then he shook his head, sighed, and said, "I don't really know. It started off toward the southeast, but after it went a few hundred feet it disappeared just like that." He snapped his fingers in front of

Tyne's face. "Like it was made of smoke, or had never really been there. Just somethin' I imagined. But my brother was still dead."

He kept his course to the southeast, following the Serel Road. No one he spoke to after the man whose brother had been killed had even heard rumors of such a creature. It seemed that when it vanished from the man's sight it vanished from the world itself. The trail had truly gone cold.

He was not discouraged. He'd known before he set out that the task would be hard. Too much time had passed. He should have gone after the creature with all the fury of the gods the moment Tremmel told them what had happened. But Tremmel had been alive then, and had needed his older brother more than ever. Tyne had been the glue holding his family together. He and others searched, but not far enough, and not long enough.

A dense forest came into view in the distance to his left. He did not know its name, but as it remained in his view day after day, he realized it was immense. It drew closer to the Serel Road until the road and forest were separated by only a few hundred yards of open ground.

It rained one afternoon, a light steady drizzle that soon soaked him to his skin. He made camp that night just inside the edge of the forest, beneath the dense canopy high above him. He managed to light a fire and keep it lit through most of the evening.

He dozed off after a meager meal. He heard something in his sleep and awoke to find a man rummaging through his pack. The rain had stopped. A half-moon hung low in the sky, shining in his face like an omen.

He'd fallen asleep with his back against a tree, and now jumped to his feet and pulled out his knife. But the other man was too fast, and before Tyne could take a step, the stranger had raised his sword.

"Ah, steady there, lad. I'd not want to skewer you 'cause you did something rash." The man spoke with a thick accent he did not recognize.

Tyne shook with rage and indignation. He'd never been robbed before, and felt violated in a way he never could have imagined.

"Toss the knife to me," said the man as he stuffed Tyne's sack of coins into a pocket in his tattered cloak.

Tyne did not move. He studied the man before him. Older, perhaps thirty, with long blond hair plastered to his head by the rain. Bulkier than himself, with broad shoulders and a thick middle. A scraggly beard covered his cheeks and jaw like patches of moss on a tree.

"I said toss the knife to me. You don't want to disobey me, lad. The One God guides my hand. Do as I say and you'll find yourself richly rewarded."

"So you'll give back what you've stolen?" Tyne put as much contempt into his voice as he could. He made no move to hand over the knife.

The man's face pinched in anger. "What I'm taking are contributions toward the work of the One God. You'll acknowledge him, boy, or I'll put you to the sword. There is a darkness coming, and the only way to defeat it is to convert all of Osseria to belief in the One God. You serve us, or you serve the Adversary. There is no middle ground."

"There are no gods but those of Helcarea. This is what I think of you and your god of thieves." Tyne spat on the ground, then tightened his grip on the knife.

The man snarled. "You'll regret that, boy. I won't kill you; that would be too easy. But you'll scream for your mother before I'm done, and you'll beg to worship the god of gods."

Tyne remained still and did not speak. He knew the man was trying to provoke a reaction, which he was determined to deny him.

The man grasped the hilt of his sword with his other hand and charged.

For his greater size and bluster, the man was clumsy and obvious in his attack. With his lithe frame, Tyne was easily able to sidestep his thrust. Tyne chopped back with his knife as the thief slid past and opened a deep gash along the man's hand and forearm.

The thief screamed in rage. "Now I *am* going to kill you, you fucking whoreson!"

Despite the hatred roiling inside him, Tyne remained silent. He waited deftly on the balls of his feet, ready to shift left or right depending on how the man attacked him next.

The man tried to shake some of the blood from his hand but only succeeded in getting more of it on his palm and fingers. His grip on the sword grew unsure because of the slick blood on the hilt.

"I'll cut out your heart and feed it to my dogs," said the thief. "Oh, yes. I have friends close by. They'll be here soon, and when we're done with you the biggest piece left will be the size of your shriveled little prick."

Tyne felt a thread of fear seep through the anger and hate. He'd never fought for his life like this. If the man were telling the truth about others, he needed to finish this fight and be gone.

The man lunged at him again. Tyne took a step back as if retreating, but then planted his right foot hard and sprang forward, deflecting the sword with the edge of his knife. Steel screamed as the two weapons scraped along one another.

Tyne shifted his knife to his left hand and wrapped his right arm around the man's hands, holding them in the crook of his elbow and forcing the sword to remain behind him where it could do no harm. The man thrashed about madly, screaming. Tyne knew he would lose his hold in a moment, but that was all the time he needed.

With his left hand, he drove his knife into the side of the man's neck.

Tyne stared hard into the man's eyes as the life drained from them. The sword fell from his slackened fingers. When he was sure the man was dead, Tyne yanked out his knife and dropped the corpse to the ground.

"That'll teach you to steal from me." He spat on the dead man's face.

He had never killed a man before. The anger and sense of violation he'd felt at being robbed did not retreat. If anything, they grew stronger.

"No one steals from me and gets away with it," he muttered as he retrieved his food and coins. He wiped the bloody hilt of the sword on the dead man's cloak, then unbuckled the battered sheath's belt and slid it from under the body. "No one."

He hefted the sword and liked how it felt in his hand. He put on the belt and slid the sword into the sheath. It was a satisfying weight on his hip.

"Garrel!"

Tyne crouched when he heard the faint shout in the distance. The man was just over the low rise that lay beyond the edge of the forest.

"Garrel, where are you?"

Tyne saw a figure appear on the rise, coming in his direction, led by his moon-cast shadow. He stomped on the dwindling fire, hoping he had not yet been seen.

"You!" shouted the man. He started running toward the trees. "Wait there!"

Tyne swore under his breath. The man running toward him shouted, "Borio, Faltrus! Get the others! I've found someone!"

Tyne made sure he had all of his belongings, then dashed off into the trees. There was no other way he could go. He had no idea how many men were out there. If he tried to get out in the open, he would almost certainly be caught.

"Garrel's been murdered!" the man shouted. "Get over here you bloody fools!" He cupped his hands around his mouth and shouted toward Tyne. "I see you, you damned killer! You won't get away from us! When I catch you, you'll wish you'd never been born!"

Tyne turned away then and moved as steathily as he could through the dense forest. It was very slow going. It was hard to see in the darkness; only a fraction of moonlight penetrated the intertwined canopy of branches and leaves. The ground was uneven and covered with deadfall, so he had to be careful with each step to avoid tripping over a rock or fallen branch. He tried his best to move quickly and quietly, but it was nearly impossible to avoid making noise.

He heard a number of men in the forest behind him. They had spread out in order to prevent him from doubling back and trying to escape past them. They had no need to be quiet and were moving alarmingly fast. He had no choice but to increase his own pace or risk being caught from behind.

"This way!" shouted one of the men. "I hear him! He's not far!"

"I see him!" shouted another.

Tyne was far more panicked by this pursuit than he had been when confronting the thief, Garrel. He'd broken out in a sweat, his breath came in stuttering gasps, and his heart hammered almost painfully in his chest. He could not fight so many men and hope to win. His only choice was to flee.

The gods damn these thieves! he thought as he raced through the trees. *That bastard got no more than he deserved for stealing! This is not right! They're the criminals, them and their damned thieving god, not me!*

A low branch whipped across his face, cutting a gash across his cheek and nearly blinding his right eye. He cried out in pain, then stumbled and fell when he tried to wipe away the blood. He landed hard on a thick root that drove the air from his lungs. It felt like he'd been kicked by a horse. As he staggered painfully to his feet, he wondered if he'd broken a rib.

He held his side as he continued through the trees. A heavy branch caught him across the neck, leaving a wide, painful burn.

A clearing opened before him. The ground was relatively clear, so he ran across it as fast as he could, then slowed a bit when he reached the trees on the far side. The air felt suddenly colder, as if he'd somehow crossed a threshold separating summer from late fall. He shivered, and the gooseflesh made the raw scrape on his neck hurt even worse.

The men were still close behind him. He had to figure out a way to lose them before they could cut him off, or before he stumbled across a deadfall or other obstacle that would leave him trapped.

The forest was growing even colder. He hugged his arms

close for warmth, and was startled when he saw his breath puffing from his mouth in small clouds.

The men chasing him sounded more distant now. He risked stopping to look back, stepping behind a tree for cover. He did not see anyone in the moon-spackled dark and could not pinpoint where they were from the sounds they made moving through the forest.

He kept moving in the direction he'd been going. A dozen steps farther and the air grew warmer again.

He did not know how long he kept going. He grew faint with fatigue, and felt half asleep on his feet. At some point during the night, he realized he no longer heard the sounds of pursuit. He stopped again and leaned against a tree, listening. The forest was strangely quiet.

They were gone. They had either given up or lost his trail.

He slid down the trunk and was asleep almost at once.

Dusty shafts of sunlight slanted down from the treetops when Tyne opened his eyes. He felt a moment of panic as he wondered where he was, then recalled the men who had chased him, but a quick look around showed him to be quite alone.

He wandered until he found a stream, then drank and refilled his water skin. He washed the crust of dried blood off his face, though doing so started the wound bleeding again. He was famished but rationed himself to three bites of dried beef.

He sat down on a rock by the stream and wondered what he should do next. He feared that if he attempted to backtrack in order to get out of the forest, the men would be waiting for him. He had no idea how long their patience would last. The death of their companion might compel them to remain quite some time if they thought they could catch him.

But he had no idea how big the forest was, or how close he was to another way out. He could keep going in the direction he had been and reach another border in hours or weeks—he simply did not know.

Even if he continued traveling in the same direction and was able to quickly leave the forest, he would be far from the

Serel Road. Having no real idea where the demon had gone, the road at least provided him with the ability to question the greatest number of people. Who knew what might lie on the far side of the forest? The lands might be empty, or full of wolves or bears.

He decided he would go back the way he came. He would be careful when he neared the forest's edge and veer southward before leaving it, hoping to remain hidden from view. With luck, he would avoid any of the thieves who might be waiting for him.

Tyne was not one to hesitate once he'd made a decision. He rose from the rock, stretched his back, and set off at once.

He quickly realized he had a problem. The forest looked distinctly different in daylight than it had last night, and he had not paid attention to the path he'd taken. He'd hoped he would find signs of his passage, but there was nothing apparent that he could see. He hadn't followed a trail through the forest nor marked his way—his only thought was to flee his pursuers.

Tyne soon realized he was lost. He tried to remember any distinctive landmarks he had passed, but could not recall anything. The wounds on his face and neck throbbed painfully, as did the rib he'd struck when he fell.

He wandered for several hours, growing angrier and angrier. Finally he sagged wearily to the ground, frustrated and frightened at his predicament. It was ridiculous, being lost in a forest. He was tracking a demon, by the gods!

Tyne tried to reason out what he should do. He was pretty certain he was headed westward, but the dense canopy overhead played tricks with the light, and he could not be sure of the sun's position in the sky.

He looked around and paid closer attention to the landscape around him. Now, for the first time, he noticed that the trees looked . . . strange. He recognized oak, maple, birch, and others, but the branches were bent in unusual shapes, the color of the bark was odd, and he saw dark splotches that looked like patches of disease on many trees, while others had what he could only think of as open wounds that leaked a brownish liquid he thought at first was tree sap. When he stepped closer, however, he realized it was not sap at all. The foul odor—a repulsive mingling of spoiled meat and bile—told him as much.

Even the leaves, now that he was paying attention to them, looked somehow wrong, with exaggerated serrations along their edges, almost like teeth.

What is this place? he wondered. The strange trees reminded him eerily of the twisted trunks that grew upon the Bronze Demon Hills. Could the demon's mere passage cause this kind of damage?

No, upon reflection, he did not think so. He'd seen no other sign of ruined trees during his long journey from his home. He was sure he would have seen something, or heard stories of dark and mysterious transformations, if such things had happened.

He decided the trees were unimportant. A curiosity, certainly, but they had no bearing on what he was doing. He needed to focus. It was time to get out of this place and resume his search.

He set off in what he hoped was a westward direction.

Tyne had walked for perhaps an hour when he began to hear what he thought was a voice whispering nearby. He pressed himself against a tree, suddenly afraid that the men had set an ambush for him. He strained his ears, but all he could hear was a faint voice that came and went upon the light breeze. He could not make out any words or determine where the sound was coming from.

He set off once more, keeping a watchful eye for any movement that would reveal where the mysterious whisperer was hiding. His nerves were on edge; he just wanted out of this damned place.

He caught momentary fragments of the voice, but never enough to hear distinct words or determine a location. He grew more and more angry. It seemed someone was mocking him, and if there was one thing he despised, it was being mocked.

Let him have his fun for now. He no longer bothered to be

careful in his movements. He walked at a brisk pace, wanting nothing more than to leave this cursed place behind. *But if he shows himself, he'll be in for a nasty surprise.* Tyne grasped the hilt of the sword hanging at his hip. It was reassuringly solid, a dangerous and deadly weight he was not afraid to use should the need arise.

His pace faltered when darkness seemed to fall in a matter of moments. The sun appeared relatively high in the sky from what he could tell; night, he thought, was still hours away. But it had fallen during the time it took him to walk twenty or thirty paces. He wondered if some dense cloud had merely blocked the sun momentarily. Tyne looked up and thought he could see a few stars twinkling through the small gaps in the canopy overhead.

Abruptly, the whispering voice grew louder, though he still could not make out any words. He wheeled about, knife in hand, afraid that the whisperer had somehow snuck up on him in the dark.

He saw no one, though the whispering continued. "Who are you?" he shouted. "Show yourself, you coward!"

No one appeared. The whispering continued. Now it seemed to him that the voice was speaking in a language other than Kelarin. He realized that in fact he could make out words, though not understand them. It might have been gibberish, the inane ranting of a madman like crazy old Taeven from Hevil's Well, but he didn't think so. It sounded like a language, with a definite structure—just one he could not understand.

He wondered again how night could have fallen so fast. It simply was not possible. There had been no dusk, no twilight. Just what passed for daylight in this forest, and then night.

He remembered the barrier of cold he'd passed through the night before and wondered if that could have something to do with it. He'd heard stories of enchanted mists and magical rivers that when crossed by hapless and unsuspecting travelers transported them to the lands of the Little Folk or the parched deserts where demons dwelt. Could the river of cold air have been such a barrier?

If it was, where was he now? And how would he get home?

Tyne stopped, almost paralyzed with fear. He had to push these wild conjectures aside. They only served to frighten him. His imagination was getting the better of him. Enchanted mists existed only in stories, not here in the real world.

He decided to walk a little farther in the direction he'd been going before stopping for the night. He hoped that when morning arrived, he would have a better understanding of exactly where he was and what he needed to do to escape this wretched place.

Tyne had terrible dreams that night. In them, he caught glimpses of a dark shape in the trees, watching him with ravenous eyes, whispering to him in its seductive, foreign tongue. It was not human, he was sure of that, though he could not say exactly why—he could discern no details of the nebulous silhouette. The figure was trapped in a glass or crystal sphere of some kind, whose surface glinted in the moonlight.

He tried to approach the thing, but as soon as he took a step, it vanished and reappeared some distance away, so that no matter how much he moved toward it, the shape remained the same distance from him. He felt it wanted him to follow, though to where, he could not say. *Maybe it's trying to lead me out of here,* he thought. Holding onto that slender hope, he followed the thing through the black forest.

He could see a brighter area up ahead. The figure seemed to be moving toward it.

The brighter area was a large clearing. The illumination came from unobstructed moonlight washing across the low hill in the clearing's center.

As soon as Tyne's gaze fell on the hill, he began to shiver uncontrollably. There was nothing unusual about it, nothing out of the ordinary—but he felt with absolute certainty that something was buried beneath it. Something of great danger, but also of great importance.

The figure and its crystal prison had now vanished, but he scarcely noticed. He could sense power here, as if the energy of ten thousand thunderstorms was coiled beneath the grassy mound, waiting to be unleashed.

He knew that this was what the figure wanted him to find.

He saw a pulsing light inside the hill, as if his sight somehow allowed him to see through grass and dirt and rock to the hidden heart within. He sensed that the figure he had seen was also within the light, that whatever lay buried beneath the hill was its true prison. He heard the whispering voice again, only this time it was louder, and he heard it not with his ears but directly in his mind, as if a second being shared his thoughts. He still did not understand its words, but he grasped its meaning well enough: *Come here. Unearth me. Free me.*

He awoke the next day with a renewed sense of purpose. His dream had been true, he concluded, a vision sent to him by the great gods of Helcarea to help him on his quest. His faith in his country and his gods was about to be rewarded.

The hill was real, and there was a weapon in it. A thing that would grant him the power he needed to destroy the demon. He was going to find it, and learn to use it, and at last have his revenge.

Unlike his attempt to backtrack through the forest, he could vividly recall the path he'd taken in the dream, even though the vision had taken place in darkness, and he now walked in daylight. He felt that he could have closed his eyes and found his way, as if guided by a power other than himself. It invigorated him. He was meant to come into this forest, to become lost and pass through the barrier of cold, all so he could be brought to this moment.

Tyne paused, and his breath caught in his throat when he saw the clearing ahead, the gentle rise of the hill visible between the trees. It *was* real! The gods truly were setting his feet upon the path to his vengeance!

He ran to the hill, a wide round hump like a boil rising from the center of the clearing. He took note that the trees around the rim of the clearing bent away from the hill—even the branches curled back like the arms of men trying to avoid the heat of a raging fire. *The trees don't like the power buried here,* he realized. *They'd run from it if they could.* He found this thought comforting rather than frightening—after all, this potent and deadly power would soon be his.

Tyne surveyed the hill for a time, trying to recall exactly where the vision had shown it to be buried. When he was sure he was at the right spot, he dropped his pack, then went back to the forest with his knife to fashion a makeshift shovel.

When he was ready, he began to dig. The whispering voice spoke once more, three words he did not understand.

But it sounded pleased.

Tyne dug for three days. He broke seven of his makeshift shovels gouging out the clay that lay a few feet below the topsoil, and cursed his lack of proper tools repeatedly.

At the end of the first day his fingers were caked with dirt and scraped bloody; they were so cramped he could hardly move them. When he woke the next morning, his hands hurt so much he was not certain he would be able to continue. He found a nearby stream and submerged them in the cold water for a while, then gently flexed them until he felt he could grasp the shovel tightly enough to continue.

The second night he dreamed that the bronze demon was laughing at him for his fool's errand, that there was no secret power buried beneath the hill. The spirits of Rukee and Tremmel stood behind the demon, watching him with sad and disappointed eyes.

But he would not be deterred. He had dreamed of the hill, and found it exactly where his dream had shown him it would be. The power within it was here as well. He would not let himself be swayed by doubts simply because the way was hard.

The whispering voice spoke little. When it sounded displeased, Tyne took that to mean that his digging was off course, so he corrected it until the voice spoke again in an encouraging manner. He did not question what it was or its intentions. It was helping him, and that was all he needed to know.

Late in the afternoon of the third day, the sharpened point of the thick branch he was using to scrape out the soil around some rocks at the bottom of his deep hole broke into an open space. His blood ran cold as he remembered the demon's crypt and the suicidal madness that had taken Marchus. Was there madness here, as well as power?

He drew the branch back and kicked out the stones. He would not be deterred by fear. His task had been appointed by the gods, and he would see it done.

The stones fell into a small cavity. He crouched down and reached in with his hand.

The whispering voice was euphoric as Tyne searched the cavity, jabbering to such a degree that he finally shouted, "For the love of the gods, shut up!" The voice fell mercifully silent.

His battered fingers touched the stones that had fallen in, then felt around the hard clay that formed the small pocket deep within the hill. The stones were in his way, so he removed them. *Where is the damned bloody thing?* he thought in frustration. He did not know what he would find, but reasoned it would be self-evident when he located it.

Other rocks were stuck in the clay. He decided to pry them out. If he did not find it after that, he would widen the cavity. Perhaps there was another opening behind it, or maybe the power was sunken beneath the clay.

He yanked three rocks from the cavity wall, then groped until he touched a fourth. This one was smooth, and it was hard for him to get a proper grip. He had to wiggle it back and forth to loosen it before he could pull it out.

This was no rock, he realized when he extricated it. It was a sphere the size of a large goose egg, with a milky pearlescent sheen visible through the caked layer of dirt.

This was the source of the power. It had to be.

As if in answer, the voice shouted a wordless, triumphant cry.

Using the rope he'd anchored to the hill, Tyne climbed

out of the hole, then took the stone to the stream, where he washed it. The pearlescence swirled across its surface.

He held it close, wondering what power the stone contained and how he could make it his own. Was there an incantation he needed to recite? A spell to make it work?

His knees buckled when a vision appeared to him with the force of a thunderclap. He saw sheer-sided mountains whose feet stretched to the very edge of a sea. Verdant forests lay in the mountain valleys, untouched by civilization.

But it was what he saw in the sky . . .

Dragons flew about the peaks on great leathery wings. He had never seen a real dragon, but he'd heard the old stories and seen drawings of them once in a book his uncle Lawren had. These were different in some ways, but not enough to make him doubt what he saw.

One dragon alighted upon an outcropping of rock shaped like the prow of a ship. Behind the outcropping was a cave in the mountainside. The beast folded its wings, reared its head, and let out a gout of orange flame before turning and vanishing into the cave.

He knew without question he was witnessing something real. These creatures of legend existed somewhere in the present world. But why was he being shown them? What did they have to do with the stone?

As if in answer, he felt a connection like an invisible thread appear between the stone and the dragons. Some of the creatures swung their sinuous necks back and forth as though searching for the tether they now felt but could not see. A few roared in anger and confusion, and a few others sprayed fire all around them, as if hoping to burn it away.

The stone was somehow linked to the dragons. They were the key to its power.

What have I found?

PART ONE

1

In the garret room study that had once been his father's, Gerin Atreyano studied the ebony length of the Staff of Naragenth. The staff rested upon a long table, the silver ferrules shining in the light of the magefire lamps. The shaft was so black it was difficult to see, reflecting no light and blending into the very shadows it cast. In some ways the shaft was more of an absence of a thing than a thing unto itself. Though Gerin could undeniably hold it, the length of the staff was not formed from a physical material—it was made of magic itself, somehow forced through the genius of Naragenth to take and hold a physical shape.

He peered at the staff intently, and did not like what he saw.

There were secrets hidden within it, tucked carefully away by Naragenth. The secret of how it was created, and how the long dead wizard, against all understanding, imbued the staff with a *mind*, a presence that served as a facilitator to control the energy flowing through it, fashioning raw magic into spells.

But the mind was crippled somehow, unable to truly communicate, to reveal what it was or how it had come to be. It spoke to Gerin in images that caused him great physical pain and which were often difficult or impossible to decipher. In some manner the Presence, as Gerin had come to call the staff's consciousness, was able to read his thoughts, to glean his intentions and create the corresponding spells to carry out his will. But it could not speak to him, at least with a voice.

Gerin and Hollin had studied it obsessively after the defeat of the Havalqa. The wizard Abaru Mezza had assisted them after his arrival from Hethnost, but so far they had learned little else. Neither of the older wizards knew of any means of imbuing a physical object with life. It was simply not thought possible, though now they had irrefutable proof that it could be done.

How did you do this, Naragenth? thought Gerin as he regarded the hazy edge of the staff. Up close, it was difficult to resolve, as if it had no clear boundary delineating where it ended and the air around it began. It made his eyes hurt to look for too long. *Why didn't you leave any writings about how you made your staff? You were the only one, apparently, who could enter the Varsae Estrikavis. Where are your records?*

Is what you did so unspeakable that you dared not keep an account, even in the safest place in Osseria, and possibly the world?

It was Gerin's growing fear that Naragenth had used dark magic to create the staff. Something so vile that even the greatest wizard of his day dared not write down what he'd done.

It was always possible that the reason for the lack of records was paranoia that other wizards would discover and replicate what he had done, and so by keeping the knowledge within his head, he could prevent the dilution of his incredible achievement. But for whatever reason, Gerin doubted this. He could not say why. They had not found any records of how the Varsae Estrikavis had been hidden away in another world, either. Abaru argued this implied that the first amber wizard merely had been overly cautious, rather than shamed by what he had done.

Gerin disagreed. He felt that hiding the library also involved dark magic, perhaps similar to the magic that created the staff. He knew he had no proof, and some of what little they did know did not support his point of view.

When he'd called Naragenth from the grave to discover the location of the Varsae Estrikavis, the first amber wizard had claimed proudly that the "Chamber of the Moon was a great secret, and one of my greatest creations." It was not exactly the pronouncement of a guilty man, yet neither was it conclusive proof that Naragenth had not employed dark or forbidden magic to accomplish his task. Naragenth could be proud of what he had done, while at the same time feeling ashamed of *how* he had done it. After all, Gerin reflected, he himself felt much the same regarding his summoning of Naragenth. His calling of the spirit of the dead wizard-king had led to the discovery of the Chamber of the Moon, though it took some time for all of the pieces to fall into place.

Yet Gerin also felt shame and embarrassment that he had stolen forbidden magic from the wizards who trusted him. That he was under a powerful Compulsion from a Neddari *kamichi* did little to ameliorate his humiliation. He should have been stronger.

And though he had discovered the Varsae Estrikavis, hundreds died because of the imbalance he'd created between the worlds of the living and the dead. He could not help but feel responsible for that, and there were times the guilt was a crushing, paralyzing weight.

Reshel died to close that door. She sacrificed herself to give me the power I needed to force Asankaru back through the door of death. He'd often wondered if he would have had the courage, the selflessness, to do the same. And when he was brutally honest with himself, he realized he did not know. He *hoped* he would have done as she had, but he could not say so with absolute certainty. That realization haunted him, made him feel even more guilty, and somehow a lesser man.

Hollin was reluctant to take sides. He, too, was troubled by the staff, though he could not explain exactly what it was. "Just a feeling that there is something wrong about it," he said one evening when pressed by Abaru. "I'm troubled whenever I look at it."

Gerin called out to the staff with his thoughts. Not to invoke a spell, but to see if it would respond when asked a question. Could it show him anything? It's only form of communication was visual, images it somehow planted in his mind. Maybe if he could formulate his questions in a way that would not require words to respond, he would have better luck.

Where were you created? Can you show me?

The staff was silent. He repeated his questions. He knew from prior experience that the Presence could take time to respond.

Nothing happened. He rubbed his eyes and slumped in his chair. So far the Presence had only responded when he wanted to use the staff to wield magic.

He stood and looked out one of the dormer windows to clear his mind. Yurente Praithas, the manservant who had served three Atreyano kings, entered and asked if there was anything he needed. Gerin shook his head.

"Your Majesty, if I may be so bold, do you have plans to make this room your own?" asked Yurente. "It is unchanged from when it was your father's. The former king, may Telros bless his spirit, moved quickly to leave his mark here after King Bessel's death."

"I know, Yurente. But for now I'll leave it as it is. I don't object to anything here, and find my father's things . . . comforting."

"Ah, yes," said the servant, though it was clear from the puzzled look on his face that he did not understand at all.

After Yurente left, Gerin glanced around the room at his father's rugs, paintings, furniture, and books. Keeping them as his father left them made it seem that Abran were somehow close by, drawn by the familiarity of the surroundings he'd known in life. To change these surroundings would be to lose that sense of connection with his father. He knew he was being superstitious and perhaps a little ridiculous, but he could not help it. He did not know why he wanted to keep a connection with his father, who had all but disowned him during the last few months of his life. Their relationship had strained to the breaking point, and Gerin had seen no way for them to reconcile.

Toward the end, he had hated his father.

And that, in part, was probably why he felt a need, now that his father was gone, to keep *some* kind of connection with him, with his memory. To salvage in death what could not be done in life.

He thought about his family. His mother and father both dead, well before their time. Old age had not taken them in their gray years. Both had been struck down far too soon.

And Reshel. *Gods above me, I miss her as much as ever.* He wondered if the ache of her death would ever go away. Would the pain of her loss be as keen a century from now?

Maybe that's my punishment for allowing her to die. That the pain will never dull, never lessen. Perhaps it's true that some wounds never heal.

He realized with a shiver that half of his family was dead. He, Therain, and Claressa were all that remained. Therain had come close to death, after his left hand was severed in an attack by quatans, vile creatures brought to Osseria by the Havalqa. The attack had been an attempt to capture Gerin so the Havalqa could take the Words of Making from him. So in that respect, he was also responsible for his brother's crippling, albeit indirectly.

I'm thinking the way my father did before he died, he chided himself. *Blaming me for everything, and holding no one else accountable for their decisions. I didn't bring the Havalqa here. I didn't start a war with them. I didn't ask the Neddari to invade us. They made those decisions. It wasn't right for my father to blame me, and it's not right that I blame myself. Not for everything, at least. The gods know there's enough I am responsible for.*

Still, it was one thing to tell himself he was not to blame, and something quite different to believe it.

He wondered about his mother, father, and Reshel. What hopes and dreams did they have for their futures that never came to pass? What had his mother wanted for herself and her children? Gerin knew of Reshel's secret hope that she might wed Balandrick, the captain of Gerin's personal guard and his closest friend, but what else had she wanted for herself?

All of those dreams were now lost forever. It saddened him immensely to think of what would never be. That Reshel, especially, had died so young, with so much of her life unlived.

He shook his head. He needed to break this melancholy mood. It had come over him far too often lately. He did not want it to become a familiar occurrence. *They'll make names for me like the Brooding King, or the King with the Furrowed Brow.*

He took the staff and set out to find the wizards. They would help him break his gloomy disposition. Abaru, especially, could usually make him laugh. At the very least he would watch the two wizards trade barbs and good-natured insults like an old married couple.

Gerin found them in the dining room next to the work chamber where he studied with Hollin. Since Abaru's arrival, he had attended Gerin's lessons with surprising infrequency, and when he was present, mostly observed or sat off in a corner reading some book or scroll recovered from the Varsae Estrikavis. Hollin, for the most part, acted as if he were not present. After one such session, Gerin had asked Abaru about his reluctance to participate.

"There's an unwritten rule about wizards and their apprentices," the big man said in an unusually serious tone. "One wizard does not meddle with the teachings of another. There were times before the founding of Hethnost when wizards would duel, sometimes to the death, over the right to teach the brightest or most powerful apprentices. Some would try to lure apprentices from their masters with gold or silver, or the promise of beautiful women for their pleasure.

"Venegreh wanted nothing to do with such practices. The positions of Wardens were created by him so teaching could be done without interference, while still drawing on the combined knowledge of everyone living at Hethnost, as well as what was contained in the Varsae Sandrova. I come sometimes to listen to Hollin teach you—he's one of the best, which is why he was elevated to Warden of Apprentices in the first place—but I'll never offer advice or make comments unless asked."

The old wizards were laughing when he entered. Two empty bottles of wine were on the table, and they were well on their way toward finishing a third.

"Shhh, your young apprentice-king is here," said Abaru, whispering loudly in Hollin's ear. "Or is he a king-apprentice? Is there a proper order for that kind of thing?"

"I have no idea," said Hollin. "But there's no need to be quiet. Gerin already knows all about you."

Abaru looked indignant. "You've been telling him lies about me!"

"I've told him nothing, but he does have two eyes and functioning ears," said Hollin, carrying on as if Gerin was not in the room. Hollin looked at the young king. "Your ears are working, right?"

"The last I checked." Gerin joined them at the table and poured himself a large glass of wine.

"See? There you have it," Hollin said to Abaru. "Gerin's a smart man. Very observant. You can't hide the fact that you're a troublemaker. A layabout. A bit of a glutton and heavy drinker as well. Someone who tells unfunny jokes—"

"My jokes are *always* funny! And the stories I could tell about you would—would—"

"Would bore most anyone half to death." Hollin shook his head sadly. "I have lived a long but rather dull life. Whereas *you*, my friend, have had all sorts of adventures. Or, well, misadventures. Accidents, perhaps, might be the best description."

"My adventures were always exciting, full of derring-do and death-defying escapes! Someone should write a book about me."

Gerin felt himself relaxing as he watched the two old friends have at one another. He took another sip of wine. This was exactly what he needed.

"There was that time you got so lost in Moriteri you couldn't find your inn and ended up sleeping in a stable," said Hollin. "Though I don't recall much derring-do."

"I didn't get 'lost,' you slanderous old goat. I was far from my inn, so it seemed more prudent to sleep in the hay with a few horses than to walk halfway across the city in the dead of night." He tapped his temple and winked at Gerin.

"That's not the story I heard," Hollin said. "I was told you were wandering around pounding on doors, shouting for directions back to your inn, and that you made so much noise you had to hide in the stables to keep from being arrested. *Then* you passed out from being drunk."

"That's outrageous!" Abaru said to Gerin. "Don't believe a word of it." He turned to Hollin and said, "Who told you that malicious lie?"

"You did. We were drinking and you decided to tell me the *real* story about what happened, not the version you told everyone else. You swore me to silence because if Delarra ever found out she'd make you wish you *had* been arrested."

"Then I *was* being prudent."

"Do you two ever have normal conversations with each other?" asked Gerin.

"We've known each other for close to two hundred years," said Abaru. "We've had our fill of normal conversations—these are much more entertaining."

After the two wizards left, Gerin wandered to the balcony overlooking one of the palace's courtyards and sat down on the cushioned chair.

He wanted to be alone with his thoughts. He'd had little of that since becoming king after the death of his father. It was so much harder than he'd thought it would be. Some of that was due to the circumstances of his father's death. The mysterious Vanil had appeared from nowhere, killed Abran, and then knelt before Gerin. They had not known what the creature was until Abaru Mezza arrived from Hethnost with news that an amulet thousands of years old had recently begun to shine. After an exhaustive search, the wizards discovered that the amulet was a warning device designed to awaken when a Vanil walked Osseria once more.

The Vanil were creatures that disappeared from the world

well over fourteen thousand years ago, before the Atalari had migrated to northern Osseria from their homelands in the West. Little was known about them, though the Atalari were able to deduce that the Vanil had the power to consume souls.

Gerin had no trouble believing that. When the Vanil had touched and killed his father, Gerin felt the king's spirit being ripped from his body. It did not go to the Mansions of Velyol, where his ancestors dwelled with Khedesh and the mighty Raimen—his father had been denied the afterlife by that monstrous thing.

Then it disappeared, and had not been seen since.

Arilek Levkorail, the Lord Commander and Governor General of the Taeratens of the Naege, had been grievously wounded by the creature. He had since made almost a complete recovery, though he walked with a limp and could not raise his left arm above his shoulder. Hollin had tended to him quickly; without the wizard's healing powers, the Lord Commander would almost certainly have died.

Unfortunately, his father's Minister of the Realm, Jaros Waklan, had been so horrified by the sight of the creature kneeling before Gerin that he all but accused Gerin of controlling it and commanding the murder of his father. He resigned his position before Gerin's coronation and retired to his home in Arghest. Gerin had done his best to convince Waklan that he had no hand in his father's death, but the old man could not shake the image of the kneeling Vanil from his mind. Gerin, accompanied by Hollin, visited him one final time after they learned the Vanil was a creature that had been gone from the world for tens of thousands of years. Gerin hoped that this knowledge would thaw the old man's animosity toward him.

"If that is true, the question remains, why did it acknowledge you by kneeling?" Waklan had asked, without addressing Gerin as "Your Majesty," and regarding him with a mingled expression of suspicion and hostility.

"We don't know, " Hollin had replied. "We're still trying to understand that."

"Then I pray you will let me know what you discover."
Waklan's tone made it clear there was nothing more to say.

Gerin learned that the former minister had been in contact with his aunt Omara, wife of Abran's younger brother Nellemar. Omara had no love for Gerin or his magic. She considered wizards to be almost a subspecies of human, and was mortally offended that a wizard now sat upon the Sapphire Throne of Khedesh. That Jaros Waklin, the highly regarded former minister, was speaking with her behind closed doors did not sit well with Gerin, yet there was nothing he could do.

His coronation had been a contentious affair. On top of the usual supplications by the nobles airing the many injustices they had to endure that only the crown—and its coin—could remedy, there had been whispered accusations of patricide and regicide, that he'd come to the throne through the spilled blood of his father.

The evening before his coronation, Baron Eolain Gremheld had the audacity to say, quite loudly when Gerin was within earshot, "It's been nigh on three hundred years since a king has risen to the crown in such a fashion. It will be interesting to see if history repeats itself."

The baron could only have been referring to Jollen Olmethrel, the last of his line, who had murdered his father, mother, twin brother, and two younger sisters during the infamous "Night of Blood." His two year reign of terror was called the Long Night—thousands had been put to death by Jollen's sadistic Wolf Guards before Mad Marya, Jollen's mother, plunged a knife into his eye. After killing her son, Marya had thrown herself from a balcony into the frigid, winter waters of the Cleave. There had been rumors for some time that spoke of mother and son as lovers, but nothing had been proved until her written confession was discovered after her death.

The comment by Baron Gremheld was shocking; even more shocking was the laughter his atrocious accusation had caused. He glanced at Gerin and stared at him unflinchingly while he sipped his wine, as if daring the young king-to-be to challenge him.

Gerin wanted to bellow in the baron's face that he had nothing to do with his father's murder, but he could never do such a thing. It would only make him seem weak, even guiltier than he already appeared. So he smiled at the baron, took a sip of his own wine, and turned away. He hoped he looked calmer than he felt.

There was nothing he could do to stop the rumors and whispers. Confronting the baron, or even arresting him for treasonous words, would do no good. Others would say he was acting out of guilt. He had to let these egregious remarks pass without comment or rejoinder.

Even if they discovered exactly why the Vanil had appeared and knelt to him, there would forever be a group who would not believe. To them, Gerin would always be a father-killer and king-slayer.

He tried not to let such things weigh upon him, but at times it was a terrible thing to bear.

But bear it he would. He was doing all he could to discover what had happened with the Vanil and why, but in the meantime he would not cower or hide. He was king now, and he needed to act like one. He would not let petty comments and whispered insults affect him, and he certainly would not acknowledge them.

Lonely is the head that wears the crown. It was an old saying, older than the kingdom itself, but it was more true than he would ever have guessed. He'd felt lonely and isolated at times as the crown prince, but his father had always been there, above him in both station and power, the ultimate authority to whom he could turn when he needed, at least before their relationship had broken after Reshel's death.

But now *he* was that ultimate authority. He had his ministers and counselors, judges and nobles to whom he could turn, but all they could give him was advice—only he could make the decisions a king needed to make. And he had to be careful to whom he turned for advice, and how often, because if he leaned on any one person or group too much, he would be seen as a weak boy-king, or worse, a puppet of others.

His training with Hollin only complicated matters. He would not give up learning more about magic, but his lessons had become even more discreet. He and Hollin labored in secret to defuse any accusations that he was being unduly influenced by the foreign sovereign power of Hethnost.

He sighed as he watched the sun set. *Lonely is the head indeed,* he thought.

"The Lady Elaysen to see you, Your Majesty," said the guard at the door.

Gerin had dozed off on the balcony. He stirred awake and rubbed his eyes. Twilight was settling over the city, the shadows stretching long and thin.

He stood and shook his head to clear the drowsiness away. "Give me a few moments, then show her in. And have some food brought. I'm famished."

Gerin gathered his thoughts as he splashed water on his face from a ceramic bowl perched on a pedestal sunken into a wall niche. He wiped his face on a cloth, took a breath, and faced the door.

"Hello, Your Majesty," said Elaysen as she crossed the room. She stopped a few paces from him, her hands folded in front of her. She wore a simple emerald dress trimmed in gold.

"Hello, Elaysen. I wasn't expecting you. I hope you and your father are well. Please, sit."

"We are, Your Majesty. Though he wonders at your silence. As do I."

Gerin was quiet for a moment as he considered how best to respond. His relationship with the Prophet of the One God was even more delicate than his training with Hollin. He had not seen Aunphar in weeks. Most of the nobles considered the religion of the One God to be little more than a ploy for power from an apostate priest of the Temple of Telros. They tolerated it because of its wild popularity with the common folk, and because the Prophet and his followers had so far offered no challenge to the king, nobility, or priests. Aunphar's teachings did not repudiate the gods of Khedesh.

Dalar-aelom, as the nascent religion was called, taught

that there was One God above all others, the true Maker
of the world and the gods and men who dwelled within it.
Those who followed it were taught, among other things, to
be vigilant for signs of the Adversary, the eternal opponent
of the One God who was entering the confines of the mortal
realm. Telros and the rest of the Khedeshian pantheon could
be worshipped by followers of *dalar-aelom,* as had always
been done—the two were not mutually exclusive.

Gerin and Aunphar had both been visited by the divine
messenger Zaephos, a servant of the One God, who had set the
Prophet on his path of creating a new religion. Zaephos had
warned Gerin that a Prophet may not understand everything
he is shown, and later appeared to remind him to visit the
Prophet when Gerin was in Almaris for his sister Claressa's
wedding.

"My time is not what it was, Elaysen," he said. "My duties
as king consume nearly every waking moment."

"Yet you still study with Hollin, do you not?" She spoke
evenly, but he could hear the hint of reproach in her voice
nonetheless.

"Of course I do. I need to learn much more as a wizard if
I am to reach my potential. Yet even that has suffered since
I became king."

"I'm sorry, Your Majesty. I do not mean to scold you. But
you have a great destiny with the One God."

He bristled at the idea that he had a destiny proclaimed by
a god—any god. "Zaephos gave me no commands like those
he gave to your father. He did not ask me to create a religion,
or help your father with his. I have learned much of *dalar-
aelom,* and practice it in my own way."

"Yet you keep your involvement secret, Your Majesty. Were
you to declare openly that you follow my father's faith—"

He held up his hand. "I would more than likely spark an
open revolt among the nobles and priests already uneasy
with the ill-omened start to my reign. They've known of my
wizardry for some time. Even those who despise me for it
can do nothing since I routed the Havalqa army and broke
their sea blockade with my powers.

"But if I said I am also a follower of this new religion they see as little more than a passing fancy to amuse and distract commoners—and I mean no insult by that, but it is what many of the nobles believe—they would think me mad. My rule is tenuous and tumultuous enough as it is, Elaysen. I cannot jeopardize it further."

"I do understand, Your Majesty. The nobles would not approve. But you would have the support of the commoners, who already adore you for driving off the Havalqa. Do you think the nobles would dare to move against you?"

"Perhaps not openly, but there are many things they could do to thwart my will and make my rule more difficult than it already is."

They lapsed into an awkward silence. Elaysen herself complicated his life in innumerable ways. He had feelings for her, strong ones, and he knew she had them for him. But they both knew that his abrupt ascension to the throne destroyed any chance they had of being together. There had never been much of a chance to begin with; Gerin's father certainly would have never sanctioned it. But before King Abran's death, and his own life was cemented into such an inflexible role, there had been at least a glimmer of hope.

That hope was now gone. He needed to solidify his position with the nobility any way he could, and that meant a marriage to the daughter of a strategically helpful house. Therain had already married Laysa Oldann, an arrangement their father had been working on before his death, and which Gerin was quick to finalize soon after his own coronation.

Which posed the question of when he would be married, and to whom. He did not yet know; all he knew for certain is that it would not be Elaysen.

"Aidrel Entraly has been cast out from my father's Inner Circle," she announced. "He believes my father is weak and has lost his way, and that we should convert followers forcefully rather than persuading them of the rightness of our ways."

"I'm sorry to hear that. I know your father feared the day

when his religion would splinter. It seems it's come even sooner than he thought."

"It was my father's hope that if you declared you are a follower of *dalar-aelom,* it would do much to defuse Aidrel's influence with the people. His violent teachings have unfortunately taken hold with many—he already has a substantial following of his own, as well as warriors he calls Helion Spears."

"Why doesn't your father denounce him as a heretic?"

"He has already done so, and excommunicated him from the practice of *dalar-aelom.* But Aidrel's bodyguards keep him well protected, and my father fears if he were to execute him for his heresies, he would make a martyr of him, a symbol for his misguided followers to rally around. He would prefer to discredit Aidrel and lure his followers back to the fold. My father had hoped you would help with this."

"I'm sorry, Elaysen, but I cannot. At least not in the way you mean. If Aidrel or his followers break any of the kingdom's laws, the repercussions will be swift and severe. That I can promise you. But no more."

She nodded, a look of deep sadness on her face. She stood, but would not look at him. "I will not trouble you further, Your Majesty. Should you decide to resume your teachings, you know where to find me."

"Elaysen, please. Regardless of what you believe, I am still a follower of *dalar-aelom.* I have long disliked the idea of being a tool of a god, but I am certain enough of the rise of the Adversary that I will do what I must to fight him. My ways may not please you or your father, but for now it is all I can do."

2

Vethiq aril Tolsadri, the Voice of the Exalted, surveyed the city of Turen with growing impatience. It
was a feeling he had experienced far too often over the past
several months. Plans gone horribly wrong, his own death
at the hands of the accursed Gerin Atreyano, his stature
dangerously reduced in the eyes of those who either despised
him or longed for his position as the Exalted's Voice, the
opening of the Path of Ashes delayed three times so far—
though if Bariq was merciful, that would be ending today.
There seemed no end to the calamities occurring upon this
continent.

The Harridan holds sway here, he thought, his hands gripping the stone rails with such force his fingers ached. *She
must. She thwarts the will of the other Powers and laughs at
the chaos she creates.*

*But in the end we will prevail. We always do. It is only a
matter of time.*

Still, this particular campaign was proving exceptionally
trying, all the more frustrating for him because of its importance to the Havalqa. Indeed, their very survival depended
on it. They needed the Words of Making to fight the coming
Great Enemy—of this the Dreamers were certain. Their visions of possible futures all contained that common thread.
Tolsadri had imprisoned the man that the Dreamers said held
the Words of Making, or was the key to finding them: Gerin

Atreyano, a troublesome prince with extraordinary powers of his own. His escape and subsequent destruction of the Havalqa naval blockade, as well as the routing of the army marching to take the capital city of his kingdom, were grievous blows from which they had not yet fully recovered.

But they would soon. When the Path of Ashes was finally opened, they would overrun these lands with their armies until every man, woman, and child had been converted. He hungered for that day with an almost physical desire.

Far below him a portion of the Havalqa fleet choked the calm waters of the partially walled harbor, a forest of masts draped with canvas sails and slack rigging that dangled from the spars like bits of moss. He watched men move along the waterfront like ants. Some strolled aimlessly. Others loaded and unloaded cargo, while prisoners disembarked from captured ships under the watchful gaze of armed guards. Insignificant men with insignificant lives, worshipping their false and filthy gods until they accepted the light of the Powers.

And this city! It was filled with shrines and temples to all manner of infidel deities. He'd learned that Turen was a holy city in this kingdom of Threndellen, a pilgrimage site visited by tens of thousands of ignorant peasants who beseeched their gods to bring them fortune and good luck. Fools, all of them. Gods who did not exist could bring them nothing. They lived in darkness but somehow believed it was day.

He turned away from the balcony, filled with impatience. Where was that infernal Enbrahel? He should have arrived by now with an update on their progress. They needed to open the Path of Ashes. The delays had been maddening, all the more so because he could do nothing about them. It was all in the hands of the Dreamer.

After they'd sailed from Kalmanyikul, the Dreamers in the Pahjuleh Palace had begun fashioning an arch of their own, an end point to the Path, to be ready if the Dreamer who accompanied the fleet determined there was a need to open the way between worlds. Such power was dangerous, to be used only if circumstances warranted it. That was why the Dreamers had kept knowledge of the Path from all except the

Exalted herself. They did not want the commanders of the fleet to feel complacent, that a connection to the homeland could be easily established should they need it.

But the sheer size of this continent, coupled with the displays of power they had witnessed from Gerin Atreyano and his companion wizard, demonstrated quite clearly the need for even more resources than they had brought with them. The Dreamer decided the Path should indeed be opened.

His patience at an end, Tolsadri had decided to go in search of the wretched Enbrahel when there was an urgent pounding on the door. "Enter!" he called out.

Enbrahel's pudgy frame burst into the room. His red, puffing face matched the scarlet panels on his flowing silk robes. He was half a head shorter than Tolsadri, his hair thinning at the crown, as if trying to escape down toward his ears.

"Honored Voice, the Dreamer commands your presence. It says the arch is ready to be opened onto the Path."

"At last," Tolsadri muttered. "I thought this day would never come."

He swept past Enbrahel, out of the room, and down the wide stone stairs that waited at the end of the hall.

The Magister's Palace where he'd set up his residence rose from the center of a wide, flat hill that fell toward the sea in a series of staggered, walled terraces. The hill itself was broad but not exceptionally tall; its slope, however, was quite long, and was truncated near its western edge by a deep river rushing through a gorge.

Tolsadri left the palace and crossed the plaza, whose sides were bordered by massive temples. Enbrahel kept close to his side, remaining mercifully—and uncharacteristically—silent while Tolsadri pondered his words to the Exalted should they finally succeed in reaching the Path.

The arch had been placed within an empty warehouse just outside the walls enclosing the Magister's Palace and temples. Prior to its construction a great deal of discussion took place among the Havalqa leaders and the Dreamer about where to locate it. The purpose of the arch, after all, was to effect the transfer of armies from Aleith'aqtar to conquer these heathen lands. Some of the military commanders argued for placing the arch outside the city in a fortified position that would allow for the quick bivouacking and subsequent deployment of the arriving troops. Others, including Tolsadri, wanted a more secure location within the confines of the city.

He, of course, had won the day. He disliked the idea of having to journey so far to reach the arch each time he needed to travel the Path of Ashes, though he did not state this reason aloud. *Let the soldiers walk from the arch to their staging ground outside the city*, he thought. He would not be inconvenienced more than necessary.

The warehouse was closely guarded by both Herolen soldiers and Sai'fen—the latter a sure sign that the Dreamer was present within. Tolsadri straightened his shoulders a bit and did not even glance at the hated Sai'fen as he passed them and entered the warehouse.

He crossed two more cordons of soldiers before reaching the section where the arch was located. The Dreamer was safely ensconced within its wheeled carriage. Several Drufar stood close. Tolsadri hated the sight of them, Loremasters who had turned their backs to Bariq to become *servants*. It did not matter that they served a being as powerful as a Dreamer. The ridiculous hurils encasing their heads were a sign of emasculation to the Voice, a willingly worn mark of the depths to which they had fallen. He did not understand what drove men of power to volunteer to serve another, and above all else, Tolsadri hated what he did not understand.

He bowed before the Dreamer's carriage. Unlike their carriages in Aleith'aqtar, this one contained a small window covered with heavy fabric so the Dreamer could speak to others. "I have come, Great Dreamer. Is what I have heard true? Are we ready at last to open the way to the Path?"

"Yes, Voice of the Exalted." The deep voice rumbled from the carriage. "You need no longer attempt to hide your impatience and displeasure. The time has come."

Tolsadri clenched his jaw at the Dreamer's rebuke. Since Gerin Atreyano's escape, the Dreamer had made its displeasure with him known in ways both subtle and overt. What galled him most was that there was nothing he could do to stop it. The Dreamers were above the games of political intrigue that he so dearly loved to play. He could not engage it or move against it in any way. They were as inviolate as the Exalted herself.

"I am only impatient to return to Aleith'aqtar and beseech the Exalted for the troops we need to carry out our mission, Great Dreamer." The words wanted to stick in his throat, but he managed to force them out and sound appropriately obsequious.

"The opening of the way to the Path has been fraught with peril," said the Dreamer. "It has proven to be even more difficult than I thought, but at last my brethren in Aleith'aqtar and I have succeeded in joining our arches. We need only open them now, a trifling compared to what came before."

Tolsadri's breath caught for a moment. It was finally about to happen. For a short time, at least, he would leave these accursed lands and return to the home of his fathers.

He had heard rumors of the Path but never believed it anything other than a fanciful story until the Dreamer told him otherwise. He had been shocked at the idea of a doorway that pierced the fabric of reality, leading to another world where distances were far different than they were here. A walk of a few hundred yards there would cover hundreds or thousands of miles in this world. He still did not fully comprehend it.

"Will you need our assistance?" asked Tolsadri.

"No. My powers alone can open the arch."

Tolsadri was not certain he believed that. He thought it more likely the Dreamer did not want to share its secrets with him and his fellow Loremasters. He, certainly, would never share such a power were it his to command.

He walked around the arch, looked closely at the massive frame. The Dreamer had dictated a detailed design for it, which their metalsmiths had then set about making. The Loremasters, at the Dreamer's direction, had imbued the metals with various types of power; the Dreamer itself had also poured much of its own strange but potent energies into it.

Energies it brought with it from another world, Tolsadri thought. When interrogating Gerin Atreyano, they learned that the Dreamers had fled to this world after their own was destroyed in a catastrophe of some kind. The Dreamer refused to describe what had reduced its homeworld to a "boneyard of ash and dust," despite several attempts by Tolsadri to learn more. Tolsadri feared the Great Enemy had been the cause of the destruction, which made him more anxious than ever to acquire the means to conquer these lands and find the Words of Making.

The arch was wide enough for at least ten well-armored men to walk through side by side. Its frame was inscribed with arcane symbols in gold and silver. Tolsadri did not recognize any of them. When he asked the Dreamer about them, he was told only that they were designed to pierce the barrier that separated one world from another. He was given no other details, and the Dreamer's tone made it plain that none would be forthcoming.

"Great Dreamer, how will you know if the arch on the other side has been opened?" asked Enbrahel.

"It is already open, and has been for some time. Even from this distance I can sense such power." The Dreamer sighed. "Step away from the arch and prepare yourselves. You will find the power I must use disturbing."

Tolsadri moved to stand with Enbrahel, who kept his wide-eyed gaze locked onto the arch.

The Dreamer exhaled its power. This was far longer—and far stronger—than any previous example of it that Tolsadri had experienced.

Reality within the warehouse trembled in its usual nausea-inducing manner whenever a Dreamer invoked its power. But this time, instead of ending in moments, it continued, growing, deepening. The world around Tolsadri seemed to flex and twist. He could feel the world thinning like rotted silk. Gripped with a sudden sense of vertigo, he feared the stone floor beneath his feet would vanish like a popped soap bubble and plunge him into a void from which there was no return.

Beside him, Enbrahel clutched his hands to his stomach and squeezed his eyes shut in a grimace of pain. Everyone in the warehouse, even the Sai'fen and Drufar, were affected. Some had fallen to their knees. To Tolsadri's left a Herolen vomited violently.

The space within the arch grew dark. Within moments the area had become solid black. It reflected nothing, Tolsadri noticed through his distress. It looked like the mouth to a cave, or a pit into which no light could reach.

The Dreamer's sonorous exhalation continued. Tolsadri marveled that reality could withstand such manipulation without shattering.

One final sound came from the Dreamer, so low in tone that the Voice felt more than heard it. The arcane symbols etched onto the arch glowed with a dim yellow light.

The note ended. As it faded, so did the absolute blackness within the arch and the light of the symbols.

When the blackness was completely gone, Tolsadri could see the warehouse through the arch once more. There was no sign of Aleith'aqtar, or that anything had changed.

"I beseech you, Honored Voice, to never let me feel something like that again," muttered Enbrahel, who was still bent over, his hands on his stomach as he took deep breaths.

Tolsadri stared at the empty arch with a growing sense of trepidation. "What happened?" he said to the Dreamer. "Is it open?"

"The door is opened, Voice," said the Dreamer. Tolsadri could hear no sound of fatigue in its voice despite the enormity of the energy it had just used. He'd felt some of it flowing past him into the arch. More power than a dozen Loremasters could summon.

"But I see nothing, Great Dreamer."

"Your eyes cannot ken the nature of this opening, but I assure you it is there. The arch now exists in two worlds at once. You have but to step through it and you will be on the Path of Ashes. From there it is a short distance to the arch leading to Aleith'aqtar."

There was a hint of a challenge in the Dreamer's words. If

he hesitated, Tolsadri would lose face before all those gathered here.

"I will step through first, Honored Voice," said Enbrahel. "To ensure the way is safe."

"You will do no such thing," snapped Tolsadri. "Remain here, Enbrahel. I will not need you in the Pahjuleh Palace."

The younger man was clearly disappointed, but knew better than to argue. "I hear and obey you, Honored Voice."

Without breaking stride, Tolsadri walked through the arch—

And found himself in a barren, twilight landscape. He looked behind him and saw the arch, though the view through it was not of the warehouse in Turen but a line of distant mountains beneath a low ceiling of heavy gray clouds.

He began to cough. His eyes filled with tears. The cool air was dry and filled with dust carried on a swirling wind. Through his watery gaze he could see dirt devils twisting across the dry land.

He wiped his eyes. There were no trees here, no water that he could see. No animals, no birds in the air. The ground was dead, but it was no desert—this was not a place of sand or hard-packed earth. Beneath his feet was a sooty mixture of dust and ash several inches deep, as if the land as far as he could see had been burned in a great fire. *Path of Ashes indeed,* he thought.

Then, off to his left, he saw what he was looking for: another arch, perhaps a thousand strides distant.

Behind him a number of Sai'fen stepped through, their weapons ready. They spread out in a protective formation, scanning the dead world for any sign of a threat. The Drufar came next, followed by the Dreamer's enormous wheeled carriage. Tolsadri did not deign to wait. *It challenged me to go first, and so first I shall be.*

He reached the second arch and strode through without pausing.

Sunlight erupted in his vision. He raised his hands and squinted against the brightness. The hot, humid air was a shock after the cool winds that blew upon the Path of Ashes, but he did not mind. He found them welcoming. *I am home,* he thought. He felt at peace for the first time in a very long while.

The arch in Aleith'aqtar had been constructed in a training field on the Herolen encampment of Rujha situated several miles beyond the walls of mighty Kalmanyikul. While Tolsadri waited for a sedan chair to be brought for him, the Dreamer and his coterie of protectors and servants appeared.

Tolsadri was fascinated by the sight of their arrival. He opened his senses and watched closely as their emerging bodies broke the plane of the second arch. There was no sound, no light, no discharge of power of any kind that he could detect. They seemed to be stepping through a curtain, as if the image seen through the arch was a mere illusion. He marveled once again that in a few minutes he had covered a distance it had taken the Havalqa fleet many months to traverse.

He paused before settling into his sedan chair to drink in the view of Kalmanyikul, the greatest city that had ever existed. Its mammoth limestone walls projected an air of invincibility to all who saw them. In all the long years of its existence it had never been besieged, either by land or sea.

It stood upon a wide headland that jutted like a balled fist into the Strait of Xormae, which separated the Sea of Henisia from the Mujaarai Sea. The walls enclosed eleven hills, one for each of the ten Powers, the last for Holvareh the All Father. The Pahjuleh Palace was built upon Holvareh's Mount, the highest of the hills. Its spires, which he could just make out in the hazy distance, grasped toward the heavens, a physical manifestation of the lofty and holy purpose entrusted to the Exalted and her people.

Rujha sprawled across a grassy plain to the southwest of the city, beyond the wide currents of the Vareh River. The military encampment was a small city unto itself. Tolsadri did not know—and did not care—about many details of the Herolen, but he was vaguely aware that Rujha contained several fighting schools, each devoted to different combat techniques. These schools were adjuncts to the Cataar itself, housed within Kalmanyikul upon the Hill of Herol, where the best of the best were taught the art of war.

He stretched out on the chair, allowing the gauzy curtains to fall closed. Within a few minutes he had dozed off, lulled to sleep by the heat and rhythmic swaying of the chair.

He awoke in the Grand Courtyard of the Pahjuleh Palace. Staggered levels of colonnades rose above him for hundreds of feet. The immense Fountain of Lepri splashed into its marble pool behind his chair, surrounded by a wide band of grass and ring of olive trees.

Loremaster Jurje Dremjou awaited him, his skeletal, silk-encased frame lurking in the shadows. Dremjou held the title of Wahtar, leader of the Jade Temple, where the followers of Bariq the Wise were trained to become Adepts and Loremasters. He was second in authority only to Tolsadri himself, and in some respects exercised more day-to-day power since Tolsadri's role as Voice of the Exalted often kept him far from the halls of the temple where such games were played.

Tolsadri would ordinarily have despised anyone with so much authority, but he did not despise Dremjou. The Wahtar was his creature through and through, and had been for many years. Tolsadri had played a key role in helping him succeed Tuzad Lekreim as First Circinate of the Adepts, and continued to assist Dremjou as often as he could, eliminating rivals and discreetly encouraging those in positions to help the young Adept, all the while making sure that Dremjou knew who was responsible for his somewhat startling rise through the temple.

"Welcome home, Honored Voice," said Dremjou with a slight incline of his head. He spoke, as he always did, in a soft, raspy voice. Tolsadri sometimes imagined that the Wahtar's thin chest could not draw enough air into his lungs to allow him to speak any louder. "We are to meet with the Exalted in two hours. I have acquired a room where you may prepare and gather your thoughts."

"I'm famished, Jurje. See that food and drink are brought as well."

"Food is being set out for us as we speak. Come, I will take you." They set off for the doors leading into the palace proper. "You must tell me what transpired in these lands across the sea. Something extraordinary must have occurred for the Dreamers to have opened this Path of Ashes. And you must tell me what the Path itself is like. An extraordinary thing. I was not aware such power existed in the world."

Behind them the Dreamer's carriage moved toward the well-guarded wing of the palace reserved for its kind. Tolsadri wondered if the Dreamer would speak to the Exalted before he did. Would it spread word of his failures into the Great Court? The thought set his teeth on edge. The details of his humiliation would be known soon enough, one way or another. There was nothing he could do to stop it.

"You knew of my coming?" he asked.

"I was summoned here a short time ago," said Dremjou. "The Dreamers sensed the opening of the arch across the sea and knew someone would be arriving soon. They assumed the Dreamer, you, and the Sword of the Exalted would journey along the Path, and so I was called to meet you and told of the means of your coming."

"The Sword is not with us. He was killed during a failed siege."

"Indeed. Most unfortunate."

"Not at all. We are well to be rid of him. He was done in by his incompetence." One of Tolsadri's agents had murdered the Sword during the confused retreat of the army, but the Voice did not consider his words to be a lie—Drugal had indeed died because of his incompetence. If he had been better prepared to play the games of power, Drugal would have anticipated his move. That he did not only served to illustrate his unfitness for the lofty station he had held.

He would deflect some of the damage to himself by casting Drugal in an even worse light, which certainly would not be hard to do, considering the colossal failure of both the naval blockade and attempted siege.

While Tolsadri ate he gave Dremjou an abbreviated account of what had transpired on their voyage: the sinking of his ship the *Kaashal* in a storm and his subsequent capture in a heathen nation called Khedesh; the astounding fact that he was visited in his cell by the man shown in the Dreamer's visions to be the one who controlled the Words of Making—though the man, Gerin Atreyano, who commanded great power unlike anything in Aleith'aqtar, denied any knowledge of them—and the disastrous sinking of much of the fleet and routing of Drugal's army by Gerin's own hand. Tolsadri made no mention of Gerin's capture by the soul stealer, and his escape while being interrogated.

"An amazing tale," said Dremjou. "I can see why the Dreamer felt the need to open the way to the Path."

"The heathen lands will require even more resources to subdue than we first anticipated. And they have these accursed wizards with powers whose full nature I was not able to fathom. I fear they will cause us no end of trouble."

"What of the Words of Making themselves?" asked Dremjou. "Were you able to—"

"I wish for silence now," said Tolsadri. "We will speak later."

Tolsadri finished the meal of spiced fish, prawns, and seasoned rice, then paced the room's balcony, rehearsing his arguments to the Exalted and anticipating her objections to providing additional troops. In this, at least, he expected the Dreamer to be his ally, no matter the creature's personal feelings toward him.

A member of the palace guard—the Serpent Fangs—appeared and told him the Exalted was now ready to see him. Silver bands hammered into the shape of open-mouthed snakes twined about the soldier's massive upper arms. Crimson serpents were also worked into his breastplate and vambraces, and curled about the hilt guard of his sword.

Tolsadri did not speak to the man or acknowledge in any way that he heard him. After a long moment, the Voice turned from the balcony and followed the soldier through the palace's twisting corridors to the Celestial Hall.

The hall was one of the few places Tolsadri had visited where he was awed by something as mundane as architecture. Ordinarily he would never note such things; buildings and rooms were fashioned for utilitarian purposes, and he cared nothing at all about the decorations or furnishings heaped upon them in an attempt to set them apart from one another.

But the hall was so grand, so majestic, that even he felt a stirring in his heart, a sense of the magnificence of the Powers who ruled the world in Holvareh's Holy Name. He drew a deep breath as he entered through giant cedar doors.

The domed ceiling high above him was painted with an image of Metharog's appearance to Gleso in'Palurq in the desert wastes of Tumhaddi. Serpents coiled across the sand, servants of the demons who had ruled Aleith'aqtar until the arrival of the Powers. They spat and hissed at Metharog in their fury, knowing their reign was about to end. Paintings depicting Gleso in'Palurq's life adorned other panels in the ceilings and much of the walls.

Two columned galleries spread out to Tolsadri's left and right; a third lay directly ahead, and it was there that the Exalted awaited him. The great shuttered doors in the massive curved wall behind her dais were opened to grant a splendid view of the city's harbor—so much greater than the meager waterfront of Turen!—and the choppy waters of the strait. Gulls rode the winds above the city, wheeling and crying among the towers of the Kandurq District. Dusty rays of sunlight slanted through the openings behind the Exalted, creating a nimbus of light upon the golden arch that formed the back of the Eternal Throne. He of course did not look directly at the throne or the Exalted. To do so before being spoken to by her was a horrible breach of etiquette.

The Dreamer was already present, its carriage resting at the foot of the dais. He wondered what lies it had told about him and how much effort he would have to expend to counter them in the Great Court.

He dropped to one knee and bowed his head. "Greetings, Great One. Your humble servant has returned to ask for guidance."

Tashqinni lumal Neyis, the Exalted of the Havalqa, laughed. "You have never been humble, Vethiq. It is as impossible for me to imagine as some of the concepts and proofs the mathematicians are so fond of." She had a strong, clear voice. It contained a quiet authority even he could not deny. He had never heard her raise it in all the time he had known her, even after the disaster with her daughter. She had been hurt, angry, distraught; but even then she did not shout, despite the magnitude of the betrayal.

"But that is how I would have you," she continued. "It is one of the reasons I chose you to be my Voice in the lands of darkness. Rise, and attend."

He looked at the Exalted for the first time in many months. She was unchanged to his eyes. Dark hair fell about her shoulders in tight ringlets, framing her flawless brown face, devoid of blemishes or wrinkles. The makeup on her eyes and lips was, not surprisingly, impeccable. She wore a small, highly revealing sharfaya—the gold cloth wound loosely about her slender body, revealing most of her right breast and left hip and leg. Bracelets hung from her wrists, gold bands circled her upper arms; rings encrusted with diamonds, pearls, and sapphires adorned her long-nailed fingers. Other than a number of Serpent Fangs standing behind her on the dais, the Celestial Hall was clear of the usual courtiers.

She regarded him with a wry, amused expression, but he knew all too well that her mood could shift in an instant to one of annoyance or displeasure. If only he knew what the Dreamer had said to her about him!

"I have heard what transpired in the lands across the sea from the Dreamer, but I would hear the tale from you as well. You say you come for guidance, but it is more than words you seek from me." Her voice had hardened a little, as had her eyes.

He paused to collect his thoughts. Without knowing what the Dreamer had said, he did not dare downplay his own failures too drastically or shift too much of the blame to the thrice-cursed Drugal. This was the trap he feared the Dreamer would set for him. He was blind here, with no idea of what the Exalted had been told. He always desired to be the first to have her ear, and as her Voice, that was usually the case. Then he could craft the tale to suit his needs. Often she heard no report but his own.

But not this time. The Dreamer had inserted itself where it normally remained aloof, distant. He would have to be especially careful if she asked about the death of the Sword. Did the Dreamer suspect his involvement, and if it did, had it spoken its suspicions to the Exalted? He did not want a Truthsayer summoned to examine him.

Still, he could be truthful yet still minimize his role in Gerin's escape. The real fault lay with the Harridan spawn. He needed no lie or prevarication when speaking of those hateful events upon the island.

"I will tell you all I know, Great One."

He spoke for more than an hour, standing before the throne with no seat or refreshment offered, though servants brought the Exalted herself both fruit and wine. Her expression did not waver through his tale. She asked no question, gave no indication that any of what he said surprised her.

When he fell silent, she said, "And what is it you would have of me, Vethiq?"

"These heathen lands are vast, Great One, and they have powers to resist us that we were unprepared for. Despite the size of the armada that in your wisdom you commanded to be built, it is not enough for us to accomplish our task. That is why the Dreamers have opened the Path of Ashes. We need more warriors if we are to succeed."

"I marvel at the many failures of all of my servants," she said. Her face was touched by a scowl, and the chill sound of annoyance he so dreaded had crept into her voice. "You had the very man we sought in your grasp and allowed him to escape. The Sword's disaster with the military campaign is so colossal I can scarcely comprehend it. And even the Dreamers failed me." She swung her gaze toward the carriage and the unseen being within it. "I created the largest fleet in Havalqa history at your behest, and now you both come to me like beggars telling me it is not enough. This was something you were to have *seen,* Dreamer. Is that not what your visions tell you?"

A disconcerted rumble emerged from the carriage before the Dreamer spoke. "Our visions do not see all things, Great One, and we cannot convey what is hidden from us. We did not see that the man who has the Words of Making is also a wizard, a practitioner of what they call 'magic.' These wizards can manipulate unseen energies to devastating effect. We also did not grasp the sheer size of the continent we need to conquer. Our visions showed us but a small portion of it. Is that a failure on our part? Perhaps, and if that is how you choose to regard it, then I will not disagree. But the point remains: if we are to win, we must use the Path of Ashes to deliver more troops to these new lands."

"You would have me drain Aleith'aqtar of its Herolen to fight this distant war," said the Exalted. "I cannot leave the homelands defenseless when you've shown you cannot keep the most important prisoner you have ever held within your grasp."

Tolsadri did not know if that remark was directed solely at him or more generally at the two of them. He was not sure he wanted to know, and so remained motionless, silent, scarcely daring to blink, waiting to speak until the Exalted asked him a direct question.

"Great One, if we do not recover the Words of Making and defeat the Great Enemy who will arise in those lands, Aleith'aqtar will be lost," said the Dreamer. "The Great Enemy will not stop until all the world has submitted to his will. If we do not win now, nothing else will matter. This is the most decisive battle the Havalqa will ever face. The need for more soldiers was always a possibility. That is why we made preparations to use the Path of Ashes in the first place."

"Do not be disingenuous with me," she said sharply. "The Path of Ashes was to provide a quick means to convey intelligence back and forth, as well as the Words of Making, once they were recovered. It was never intended for troop movements."

There was a long silence while the Exalted weighed her options. Finally she said, "I shall provide you with more Herolen. I will also send several companies of mursaaba eunuchs, and command the Loh'shree to accompany you. Their powers may help you combat the magic of these wizards." She turned to Tolsadri. "You look displeased by my decree, Vethiq."

"Great One, it is just that the Loh'shree are . . . unreliable in certain aspects. They are Havalqa, yes, but they are not true followers of our ways, and the light of the Powers does not shine fully in their hearts."

"They have served me well when I have commanded it," she said coolly. "I do not presume to know what is in their hearts, and unless unbeknownst to me the abilities of Loremasters have undergone a drastic change, neither should you. They have no love for followers of Bariq and will not obey you, which is the true source of your displeasure. Do not bother to deny it. But I will send along commanders they *will* obey, along with instructions directly from me. You may feel diminished by this, Vethiq, but that is not my concern. You have told me that you need men to conquer this new continent, and that we also face strange powers arrayed against us. I give you what you ask, and more. Are you not grateful for my generosity?"

There was nothing to be done. The eunuchs would help. Most of them were mad, but also pliant, and their demons would be a boon to their efforts. He would have to contend with the vile Loh'shree and their dark, mongrel powers. But perhaps there was a way he could yet turn this to his advantage. He would have to think on it.

Tolsadri bowed his head. "Yes, Great One. As I am your Voice, you are the Voice of the Powers in this world. As you say, so it shall be."

3

Tyne Fedron carefully descended a deadfall where, more than five thousand years earlier, Atalari priests had knelt in prayer with the commanders of the Army of Ending, the final few thousand soldiers who had pledged their lives to the destruction of the dragons that had eradicated their Shining Nation from the face of the world. The morning after those prayers had been uttered, the army marched to meet its doom. Old men walked alongside boys of nine and ten wearing oversized bits of armor scavenged from the battlefield corpses of their fathers. They marched in grim silence, knowing there would be no return from this campaign. Success, if it came, would be measured by the deaths of every last one of them.

They challenged the dragons and their master in the valley of Tonn Suérta, and there, with the flames of two hundred circling dragons washing across them like a cyclone, their bodies bursting within their rainbow armor from the heat, they unleashed the terrible power of the Unmaking. In a blinding flash their world ended, an event to mark the end of an age.

The ragged survivors of the Atalari knew their soldiers had kept their vows to deliver them from the madness of the dragonlord. From their miserable camps far off in the central plains of Osseria they had seen the cloud of the Last Battle, a pillar of fire and ash reaching into the sky like a fist of vengeance, a moniker of doom.

Tyne knew none of this, however. He stepped carefully

across the fallen trees, worried that the deadfall might suddenly shift and trap or break one of his legs. From the top it had looked like an easy descent. He regretted his decision to climb it rather than go around, but there was nothing to be done now except go on. Trying to reverse course and go back up seemed even more dangerous to him.

He hoped he reached the edge of this damned bloody forest soon. He was sick of walking in the gloom beneath the trees. He wanted to breathe air that didn't stink of mold and rot, and longed to feel unfiltered sunlight upon his face. In places, the forest smelled as musty as the tomb beneath the Bronze Demon Hills, a recollection he did not like in the least.

There had been no great forest here those many thousands of years ago when the Doomwar had come to an end. Just small copses sprinkled across the prairies that ran to the foothills of the Graymantle Mountains. The stone altar the Atalari priests erected for their final invocations had been blasted to ash by the power of the Unmaking. The ground around Tonn Suérta had been scorched black and heaved and convulsed like a living thing trying to rid itself of deadly poison, breaking and changing the very face of the land. Every living thing within twenty miles of the valley had perished in that instant. A decade passed before the first blade of grass found root in the once sterile ground.

In the ages since the Last Battle, the world had healed, and no scars of that conflict remained to be seen. But some memories lingered, tattered remnants of the Atalari who had died to save their kin, their spirits bitter and hateful. The power of the Unmaking was so virulent that it seared some of the spirits into the burned stones and scorched earth. They found themselves trapped, too weak to break free from their material prisons. They raged in their impotence, jealous of the living and their own inability to join their brethren in the afterlife.

At times Tyne heard the malignant whisperings of these dread spirits in the deep of night. Like the voice in the stone, he did not understand the words. They spoke in his mind like a breath of cold. He tried to shut them out, willed them to be gone. Sometimes they went away, but sometimes they did not, and he could only grit his teeth and shout back at them with his thoughts to be silent. He did not want to die like Marchus, slaying himself because of voices in his head.

He continued to have visions of dragons. They came when he touched the stone he guarded jealously, fearing its loss or theft. He slept with his hand curled around it, his dreams haunted by the sight of those distant aeries and the majestic creatures circling the snowcapped peaks. He felt the tether between him and the dragons grow stronger, though at the same time he grew weaker, lethargic, as if the bond was sapping his strength. *It's this damn forest,* he told himself. *It's unhealthy. Too dark, too musty, too old. I need to get out of here. Then I'll be better.*

He thought of his dead brothers and the demon that had killed them. Where had it gone? He had not forgotten his vengeance. It would die at his hands. Now he had *power.* The stone was magic from the old stories, like Maergo's Cup or Prince Dirlek's sword Saeletyn. He did not yet know how to use the power he had given, but he would. And the thing that had destroyed his family would pay dearly for what it had done.

And then . . .

What? Once the demon was dead, what else would he do with such power? *First, I'll find those thieves and kill the rest of them. Them and their lies about a god above the gods of Helcarea. Blasphemy. I'll teach them all a lesson about what happens to anyone who tries to rob me. Dead is what they'll be.*

He would have to think about what else he would do once he figured out how to work the magic stone. Once he got out of this Urlos-damned forest.

Two days after descending the deadfall the trees began to thin out, and not long after that he finally reached the forest's edge. He laughed and bent over, bracing his hands on his thighs. "Thank the gods I'm out of that wretched place," he muttered to himself. He took a deep breath of air, then stretched out on the grass and closed his eyes, the warm sun upon his face.

He did not know how long he'd been asleep when he started awake, his heart thumping.

There was a man standing nearby, watching him.

Tyne scrabbled away from the man. "Get away from me, thief!" He wrenched himself to his feet, then yanked the sword from its scabbard. "Take another step and I'll run you through, I swear!"

The man tilted his head, as if puzzled. "I am no thief, Tyne Fedron, and mean you no harm. Put your weapon away."

"Why should I believe you? You're a damned thief like that other one! Talking about his One God while he tried to steal from me."

"I am no thief."

"You're a thief and a liar. Get away from me or you'll feel the bite of my steel."

The man took a step closer and . . . changed. There was an instant of time far briefer than the pauses between the beats of his heart in which Tyne saw something wreathed in tendrils of shadow standing where the man had been. Tyne thought he saw dark leathery hide in place of flesh, a sinuous tail curling around clawed feet, enormous wings folded around massive shoulders, eyes the color of blood—

And then the man was there, his own dark eyes regarding Tyne the way a snake might size up the mouse it was about to devour.

Fear clutched at Tyne's bowels. The hands holding the sword trembled. "What are you?"

"I am not something you can harm. Neither am I a thief. Now put your weapon away."

"You're a demon like the one I'm hunting."

"I am nothing of the kind. *Sheath your sword.*"

There was such authority in the man's voice, such a palpable sense of command, that Tyne felt compelled to obey. Disobedience to that voice seemed unthinkable. The sword nearly tumbled to the grass as he fumbled to sheath it.

"If you're not a demon, what are you?"

"I come from the realm of the divine."

"You mean you're a . . . a god?" He could barely get the final words past the sudden tightening of his throat.

"No. I am but the servant of a god."

"Which god do you serve? Urlos? Fenen? Turgil?"

"You do not know the name of my master, and I will not reveal it. Do not ask again."

"What is your name?"

"That, too, I will not reveal."

The man stepped closer to Tyne. The stranger was richly dressed in fine silks. His skin was unblemished, as pure as the purest marble. Lustrous, straight black hair framed his chiseled face.

"Why are you here?" asked Tyne. "What do you want with me?"

"You carry something you found buried in the forest—"

"I knew it! You're a thief!" Tyne reached for his knife.

"Stop!"

The man's voice was like a thunderclap. Tyne cried out and slapped his hands over his ears. His knife fell to the ground, momentarily forgotten.

When he lowered his hands there were drops of blood on his palms.

The stranger's mouth moved, but Tyne could not hear him. "I'm deaf!" he yelled in horror. He could not hear his own words.

A look of irritation flashed across the stranger's face. He stepped forward and cupped his hands over Tyne's ears. Tyne heard a whooshing sound, like a sudden gust of air.

"You are healed. It was not my intention to deafen you. But do not draw your weapons again or you will incur my wrath. I am losing patience with you. I am here to help you, Tyne Fedron, if you will only listen."

Tyne recovered his knife and put it away. "All right."

"The power you found is not . . . *compatible* with my being. I am here to help you use it. Do not speak!" The stranger held up his hand as Tyne opened his mouth to ask why he wanted to help him. "I will answer your infuriating questions in time. For now you will be silent."

Tyne knew better than to argue. He sat down on the grass and waited for the man—although he really *wasn't* a man, judging by what he had seen and the stranger's own admission to being divine—to continue.

"I know what is in your heart. You wish to kill the creature—the demon, as you call it—who killed your brother. But what if I told you that the demon was not the ultimate cause of your brother's death? That there was someone else, a man, who could just as easily be said to have brought about the horrors that have stricken your family?"

Tyne thought the stranger was asking him a question, and so he felt relatively secure in replying. "Who is this man?"

"His name is Gerin Atreyano. *He* awoke the being beneath the hills, ending a sleep that had endured for thousands upon thousands of years."

"How did—" Tyne quickly clamped his mouth shut, but the stranger did not take umbrage at the interruption.

"Gerin Atreyano is a wizard, and used his power to call the being beneath the hills. It is not a demon, Tyne Fedron. It is a Vanil, a creature of great majesty and power, and it and its brethren ruled this part of the world ages before the coming of men to these lands. It did not intend to kill your brother. The Vanil did not realize how weak humans are. How fragile."

"I don't care if it meant to or not. Rukee is still dead, and I'm going to kill it. If you really want to help me you can tell me where to find it, since you seem to know so much about it."

"I cannot tell you where it is because it has veiled itself. It walks unseen through this world. But I can tell you where you can find Gerin Atreyano."

Tyne didn't care much about the man who awakened the demon. Why should he? Did he know what it would do? But the more he thought about it, the more he felt he should be interested in this man. *If he did call the thing, maybe he can tell me how to find it. If he won't help me willingly, I'll make him tell me. Once I understand the stone, he won't be able to keep from me what I want. And when I have what I need, I'll kill him. If he called the demon, he'll feel my wrath. And anyone who helped him.*

"Who is this Gerin Atreyano, and where can I find him?"

"He is the King of Khedesh," said the stranger. "He is also a wizard, a devious and manipulative creature who is said to have killed his own father to take the throne. He used his magic to awaken the Vanil. You would do all of Osseria a service by eliminating his pernicious influence."

"A king! How do you expect me to kill a king! You must be mad!"

"You have the power to kill a king, or make him bend his knee to you," the stranger said. "I told you, I know what it is you found, and I also know that you have no idea what it is or how to use it. That is how I can help you."

Tyne's hand reflexively fell to the stone to protect it. "I won't give it to you if that's what you're thinking. Not even for a second."

A thin, cold smile touched the stranger's mouth. "I have no need to touch it. I've already explained that its power is of no value to me. But it is of *great* value to a creature such as yourself."

Tyne didn't much like being called a creature, but he also didn't think now was the time to argue the point. "What it is then?"

"It is called the Commanding Stone. It is ancient beyond measure, older even than the hills the Vanil raised over their sacred chambers. I will not bore you with a lengthy recounting of its history. None of it matters now. What does matter is that you can use the Stone to summon and control the dragons of which you dream."

Tyne was startled to realize this being could peer into his sleeping mind. *Who knows what a divine being can do?* he thought.

"How do I control them? I've dreamed of them, and I can feel a . . . *connection* between me and them, something binding us together. But I don't know how to make them do what I want."

"Are you asking for my help? Do you want me to teach you how to use the Stone?"

"Yes."

"And in return, will you kill Gerin Atreyano?"

Tyne answered without hesitation. "He deserves to die for calling the thing that killed my brother. But I'm going to kill the demon, too. Let's just get that out of the way right now."

"If you feel you must, then I will not interfere."

Tyne did not like the look on the stranger's face when he spoke. It was what his mama called a *knowing* look—that the stranger knew something he didn't and was absolutely not going to tell him what it was.

To the Pit with him and his smugness. I don't care. Just so he tells me how to use the Stone. That's all I care about. That's all I need.

"It will be hard to use it, especially at first," said the stranger. "It will weaken you, and if you are not cautious, it will kill you."

"I'll be careful. Just tell me what to do."

"The connection is not yet strong enough for you to attempt to control the dragons. Keep the Stone with you at all times. Touch it with your flesh as much as you can. That will strengthen the bond. When you are ready to take the next step, I will return."

"Can't you tell me how to—"

The stranger was gone. One moment he simply . . . was not.

"To the Pit with him, then," he murmured. "I'll keep the Stone close, and if he doesn't come back I'll figure out how to use it without him."

Images of the Vanil writhing in its death throes filled his thoughts as he started walking. *Kill the demon, kill the king who called it, and then . . . raise an empire from the ashes. One to match—no, to better!—Helca's Empire. I'll be someone to be reckoned with. I already am. That fool who tried to rob me already found that out.* His hand dropped to the sword at his side.

No one would ever take from him again. He would make sure of that.

4

The origins of the Seawall of Istameth were wreathed in myth and legend. The first inhabitants of Istameth, the Persa, who arrived long before the coming of the Pashti, believed the massive cliffs facing the Gulf of Gedsuel and the Maurelian Sea had been formed during a titanic battle between their chief god and his son, who was attempting to usurp his father's throne. The god had cursed his son to the everlasting darkness and slain him with a thrust of his spear. The son fell back, and in doing so dragged his sword across the land, cutting away the original coastline and forming the face of the cliffs.

The Pashti held that a land bridge had once connected Istameth to the Pelkland Islands. Because of the constant raids from the Pelklanders, the shamans of the Pashti fashioned a great spell that caused the waters to rise and swallow the land bridge in a terrible tumult, leaving the seawall as an eternal sign of warning to the Pelklanders to leave the shores unmolested.

The Raimen who later conquered the Pashti believed that a promontory had thrust into the sea from where the cliffs now stood. The promontory was the home to a wicked people who worshipped demons to whom they sacrificed outsiders. They raided villages and towns, clad in black and wearing fearsome masks. They kidnapped men for their altars and to serve as slaves, and virgins to be wed to their leaders. Some of the Raimen villages sent armed parties onto the promontory to retrieve their lost kin and punish their kidnappers, but none ever returned.

One of the wicked people's raiding parties took a priest of Paérendras and made him a slave on their shores, tending to the fishing nets placed along the rocky shoals of the promontory. After witnessing the rape of a young Raimen girl by a gang of men who tossed her screaming onto a raging bonfire when they were finished with her, the priest bent all his will toward the sea god and beseeched him to punish these people for their wicked deeds, even if it meant his own death.

Paérendras heard the priest and answered his prayer. He raised a mighty wave above the promontory, which drowned the wicked people and sank the promontory into the sea. No trace of the people or their civilization remained. Even their name was forgotten, erased by the sea god's curse.

"And your sister Reshel told you all these tales?" asked Laysa.

"She did indeed," said Therain Atreyano. "She loved to read about things like that—she practically lived in the castle library, her nose buried in some old book or another. And she was gifted in telling them. Far more so than I am."

"I like those stories, the way they try to explain the world around us. But they can't all be true. Which one are we to believe?" she asked with a sly grin.

Therain knew she was teasing him. It was one of the things he loved most about his new bride—how playful she was.

"Since we are the proud descendants of the Raimen, I believe it's our *duty* to believe that particular tale," he said with mock solemnity.

"Yes, but if everyone died, how do we know what the priest did?"

He rolled his eyes. "My wife the heretic and doubter. Best be careful what you say, else you'll find the ghost of Khedesh himself haunting you, sending you foul dreams of drowned lands, wicked masked riders, and a painful nighttime indigestion."

"Ah, but how would I tell the haunting of Khedesh from the meals concocted by our stalwart company of soldiers?"

"You can't, which means the haunting may have already started."

She laughed, which made him smile. He wanted to reach out and take her hand, but could not. He needed to grip the reins of his horse with the only hand he had. He glanced down at the stump of his left arm, concealed beneath a decorative steel and leather cap. There were times he almost forgot about his maimed arm. Then there were times, like this, when he was acutely, painfully, aware of it.

"We're near the Seawall now?" she asked.

Self-conscious about the stump of his arm, Therain gestured to the left with a tilt of his head rather than pointing. "To the northeast, maybe five miles or so. You can't see it from here because of the woods, but the ground starts to rise the closer it gets to the coast, until suddenly it all just drops straight down into the sea."

She gave him an earnest look from beneath the hood of her riding cloak. "I hope we'll be able to see it. Please?"

Therain craned his neck to look at Captain Rundgar, riding a few paces behind him. "Captain, I do believe we'll take a minor detour to the coast."

His broad face as expressionless as stone, the captain said, "As you wish, my lord."

Therain, Laysa, and the soldiers with them adjusted their course. They rode in silence for a while, Laysa by his side. He was enjoying himself immensely. He had never expected to find married life so . . . *comfortable.* So easy, as if he'd been missing a part of his life and only recognized its absence after he'd found it. *Of course Laysa has everything to do with that. Father picked well when he made these arrangements, though the gods know why he never did anything about it.* Before Abran's death, he'd made overtures to the Oldanns of Rentioch, but a formal engagement had never been made. Of course, there'd been an invasion to deal with.

After Gerin had been crowned king, he spoke to Therain about the prudence of trying to cement support for him by having Therain wed Laysa sooner rather than later. The commoners were still mostly in awe of Gerin after witnessing the incredible display of power he had used to drive back the invasion force of Havalqa, both on land and at sea. But many among the nobility regarded him with open suspicion because of his magic and the rumors surrounding the manner of his father's death.

Therain had obliged, knowing full well that his marriage was for political gain. It was a fact of his existence he'd accepted since he was old enough to understand it. *And I apparently understand it better than my thick-headed older brother, who seems determined to die a bachelor.*

"I wonder how your sister is doing," said Laysa after they had passed through the woods and were once more on open ground. The rise of the land ahead of them was now clearly visible. "I only met her briefly when she was married to Baris Toresh. It will be interesting to see if being wed and moving so far from the only home she'd ever known has changed her."

Therain barked a laugh. "Kindled some compassion in her icy heart? Blunted a bit of her haughty arrogance? Softened her hard-as-stone demeanor?"

Laysa gave him an annoyed look. "That's not what I meant."

"Of course it is. You forget that dear Claressa is not only my sister but my twin. I know her moods, both good and bad. I know she feels she is almost a goddess cast alone to earth who must suffer unduly and quite unfairly by having to endure the presence of us mere mortals, as if we were all a particularly odious form of grime she'd managed to step in with her delicate, slipper-clad foot."

Despite herself, Laysa laughed. "I can hardly imagine how magnificent Reshel's storytelling ability must have been if you feel so inferior in comparison."

"Oh, I have my moments. But they're usually when I'm talking about Claressa."

That night, sleeping beneath a crescent moon knifed through with frosted slivers of clouds, Therain dreamed.

He stood in a clearing in the woods. He knew he was waiting for something, but did not know what. The sense that he was supposed to remember something was very strong, but the more he tried to grasp at the elusive memory, the more it receded.

He heard movement in the trees, the soft sound of animal paws stepping through dry underbrush. The sounds came from all sides, circling him slowly.

Wolves stepped into the clearing, their eyes shining in the darkness. He counted seven, equally spaced around him, cutting off any chance he had of fleeing.

Yet he felt no desire to flee. He was not afraid of the wolves. He sensed, somehow, that they meant him no harm. There was a connection of some kind between him and the animals. He could *feel* them in his mind, their own sense of curiosity as to what was happening here. They had come here for a reason they did not understand, following a strange yet alluring scent they had never before encountered.

More movement in the trees, followed by more animals entering the clearing. Deer, rabbits, foxes, wild dogs. None of them paid the least attention to each other. Therain watched, fascinated, as a hare settled back on its haunches between the forelegs of one of the wolves, the tips of its ears nearly brushing the wolf's lolling tongue.

They were all watching him. He felt all of them in his mind now, a jumble of noise that threatened to crowd out his own thoughts. The animals were confused, some were afraid, but despite their fear something stronger kept them rooted to the clearing.

They want something from me, he realized.

As one, the wolves threw back their heads and yowled, shattering the still quiet of the night. The other animals flinched but did not run.

"Stop that," said Therain. The wolves halted their yowling. "Go away." The noise in his mind was making his head hurt. "I don't have anything for you. Go away and leave me alone."

Some of the animals cocked their heads at him quizzically. But somehow they understood him. He felt his command reach out to them through the connection in his mind, and it was *that* connection, the silent one he did not understand, that they obeyed.

In a few moments the clearing was empty. He heard them moving away through the dark trees, leaving him alone and confused, with a throbbing in his temples.

"You were talking in your sleep," said Laysa after Therain stirred awake and propped himself up on his elbows.

"Oh? Did I say anything incriminating I need to apologize for?"

"Not that I could hear. Most of that will wait, of course, until Claressa and I can sit down for a private chat and discuss, in excruciating detail, your history with the ladies."

"I expect you think a comment like that should make the blood drain from my face and my balls shrivel into my belly, but the sad truth of the matter is that my 'history with the ladies,' as you so quaintly put it, contains very little other than an occasional dalliance with the daughters of some local vassals and, on a few very drunken occasions, visits to one of the brothels in Padesh. And I was so drunk I honestly don't think I can remember which one. The front door was red. But then again, I think most of them are."

Laysa slapped his shoulder. "Therain! How dare you tell me such things!"

Captain Rundgar tried to cover a burst of laughter with a sudden cough.

Therain could not help smiling. "Sorry. I thought that's what you were asking about."

He recalled nothing of the strange dream. After breakfast they broke camp and rode toward the sea. They passed a number of crumbled buildings that may have once been outposts along a road, the ruts of which were just barely visible beneath the tall gasses. Wherever the road once went, it had not been traveled in many years.

Within sight of the Seawall, they came across the long abandoned ruins of a small village. Little remained; most of it had been swept away in the ravages of time. A few foundation stones poked from the soil here and there, their edges worn and blunted by the elements, their surfaces dark and stained. Occasionally enough remained to suggest the shape of the building that had once stood there. On the seaward side of the ruins they found a ring of stones that had once been a tower. It had toppled toward the south, depositing a jumbled line of stones to mark where it fell like a makeshift cairn.

"I wonder if this was a village of the wicked people in the Raimen story?" said Laysa as she stepped into the broken ring of the tower.

Therain entered behind her. "Well, for one thing, I really don't think these ruins are old enough. The story of the priest and Paérendras was supposed to have happened—"

She wheeled on him, hands on her hips, a sharp look in her eye. "Don't be so literal! I know the story isn't real, but it's fun to believe that this was a part of it, that we're standing in a piece of the story you told me yesterday." She shook her head in dismay. "I swear, if your sister Reshel was here she'd thump you on the head for ruining such a poetic moment."

He stopped short, surprised by his wife's outburst. "Sorry. I'll try not to be so literal from now on. I'll speak only in similes and metaphors. My speech will become wholly incomprehensible to everyone, which will lead priests, scholars, and the unwashed commoner to believe I am a prophet—no, an oracle!—and that if they could only decipher the profound meaning buried within my inscrutable mutterings they would gain heretofore unimaginable power, wisdom, and wealth. But mostly they will gain a headache from thinking about it too much."

Laysa was holding her stomach, doubled over with laughter. She straightened, wiped tears from her eyes, and kissed him. "I'm so glad you can make me laugh. I don't know what I would have done if my father had married me off to some dour, humorless—"

"And smelly. Don't forget smelly."

"And smelly old man. Gods above us, I'm lucky to have you." She twined her fingers in his.

No, I'm the lucky one. Hand in hand they walked to the edge of the Seawall and stared down the five hundred foot drop into the churning, frothy waves.

He had never been happier. Which made part of him wonder, as he was wont to do, what disaster would happen next to bring it all crashing down.

Over the next few days, Therain grew increasingly aware of the wildlife around him. He could sense birds in the sky, and would turn to look behind him at the circling hawks he knew, somehow, were there. He felt the presence of rabbit warrens and squirrel nests as if they were glowing with some secret light only he could see. He pointed toward a ridgeline late one afternoon and said, "Here come some deer." A few moments later a doe and three fawns crested the ridge, their sleek bodies silhouetted by the bronzed twilight sky.

"How did you know that?" asked Laysa.

He shrugged, having no idea how to answer. He hadn't even intended to point them out. It just happened, a reflex more than anything. "I don't know. I just had a sense they were there."

She gave him a long, penetrating stare, then turned to look at the deer. After pausing for a few seconds, the deer disappeared once more behind the ridge.

As if a wall had fallen away in his mind, he suddenly remembered the dreams he'd been having. The animals in the clearing, the connection he felt to them. All of it. Until now he'd awakened each morning with a groggy sense that he'd had a strange dream, but the details eluded him, and Therain was not one to waste time pondering dreams. He'd shrugged it off and gotten on with his day.

But now he remembered. Reflecting on them, he felt that somehow they were more than dreams. That they represented a kind of truth, even as a part of him considered it absurd. *I don't have any connection with animals,* he told himself. *It's just a coincidence. Nothing more, nothing less.*

The awareness of animals, however, continued to grow stronger, until he had to admit that something strange was going on. He made a conscious attempt to see if he could accurately tell where animals were located. He was uncanny in his ability to sense them.

He was not wrong once.

One night around their fire he confided to Laysa and Captain Rundgar what was happening. The other soldiers were around their own fire and out of earshot. He did not want everyone to think he had gone crazy.

"I know how it sounds, but I'm telling you, I can sense where everything is around us."

"I don't doubt you, my lord," said the captain.

Laysa was far more concerned. "Do you feel well? Do you have a fever?" She held the back of her hand against his forehead. "Are you sure these dreams haven't made you jumpy? That you're seeing things you want to see?"

"Yes, I'm sure. Something's happening to me. I don't know what it is, but it's real. I wish Gerin or Hollin were here. They might be able to explain it."

She took his hand and held it between her own. "I don't know what to tell you."

"I know you doubt this, and that's fine. I would doubt it, too. But tomorrow I'll show you."

"And if what you hope to show us doesn't work?" she asked.

"Don't worry. It will."

Rundgar was shoveling dirt onto their fire while Therain stared off into a line of trees to their left. "There's a wild dog in there that's been following us for a few days," he said. "It's hungry, and it's been hoping to find scraps in our camps."

"And you know this how?" Laysa asked.

"I told you. I can feel it. The way I sensed the deer. I'm going to call it to us."

She regarded him with a look of worry tinged with more than a little fear. *She's concerned her new husband is insane. It's time to show her I'm not.*

At least he hoped that's what would happen. Maybe he truly was crazy. Did crazy people ever understand that about themselves? Wasn't that lack of critical insight one of the signs of being crazy to begin with?

Enough of this. He could sense the dog keenly, hunched down just inside the tree line, waiting for them to leave.

Come here, he called out with his mind. Willing his thoughts toward the hidden presence in the trees. *Come to me. You won't be hurt. Remain calm. Do not attack.*

An undernourished, scraggly dog burst from the trees and raced toward him. He heard Laysa gasp. Rundgar watched its approach impassively, though Therain noticed the captain kept his hand on his sword hilt. *Gods above me, the man doesn't even trust a dog.*

The mangy dog stopped in front of Therain and prostrated itself, its tail thumping in the grass. Therain bent down slowly and scratched it behind the ears.

Laysa was wide-eyed. "You called to it?"

"Yes, with my mind."

"My lord, perhaps the wizard blood in your family is causing this," said the captain.

"Maybe, though I'm no wizard, at least according to Hollin's crystal."

Laysa stepped forward and carefully extended her hand toward the dog. Therain cautioned the animal that she meant no harm and that it was not to bite or growl. It obeyed him, and he sensed contentment and happiness from it as she, too, scratched its ears.

"I'm amazed," she said. "It's like a story come to life."

Therain got some food from his pack and fed the dog, which devoured it greedily. "I'm going to keep him," he said. "I'll call you Kelpa."

"Why that name?" asked Laysa.

"When I was a five, I got a dog and named him Kelpa. He was one of the few things in our house that did not favor Gerin or Claressa. They both hated him, and he hated them. Which was why he was my favorite."

5

The walled city of Urkein on Hreldol, the largest of the Pelkland Islands, still bore the scars of the siege it had endured at the hands of King Bessel Atreyano and his eldest son Abran more than two decades past. The massive stones flung from the Khedeshian trebuchets had crushed the battlements in a score of places and gouged enormous pits in the face of the wall. A section of the northern expanse had completely collapsed after Khedeshian sappers dug their way beneath the foundations and lit a massive fire beneath them. After King Qadir's surrender, the Pelklander stone-masons did their best to shore up the sagging section, but in the end they decided to demolish it and rebuild. The new section, and the repairs to the pits and gouges in the wall's face, were easily spotted, even from ships out in Heldekar Bay, like the mottled flesh on an old man's hands.

King Daqoros had been a child when the siege occurred and his father shamefully surrendered to the bastard king of the mainlanders; he himself had been taken as a hostage for five years to ensure Qadir's compliance with the treaty. When Daqoros first returned to Hreldol the repairs in the walls galled him, visible monuments to his people's everlasting shame. The sight of them never failed to make his breath catch in his throat, his heart thud almost painfully in his chest. He begged his father to tear down the entire northern face of the wall and rebuild it so it was complete and whole, the scars of the siege erased completely, obliterated from the physical world if not from his memory. But Qadir refused. The walls were strong, he said. That was all they needed. And the cost to do what Daqoros asked, on top of the tribute they were forced to pay to the Khedeshian throne, would bankrupt them.

If the walls were so strong, Father, why did you surrender? Daqoros thought as his carriage rolled along the cobbles of the Tureld Road toward the city's main gate. *If the walls were strong enough, why was I taken away into bondage for five years to be humiliated in the house of a foreign king?*

He kept the curtains of his carriage closed. He had no desire to see the walls that had failed them, though even without seeing them, the shame still burned hotly within him.

In one respect his father had been right. To level and rebuild the walls was too costly. The treasury could not support such an undertaking. Not with his other plans already in place and moving quickly to fruition.

Daqoros's well-guarded carriage reached the Tuothon, the palace built upon the very spot where their legends said the god Murakos had fashioned Father Hrona, the first Pelklander, from the mud and stone of the island. Murakos had cut open his wrist and let the blood drip on the lifeless statue, infusing it with life and will. Daqoros knew the tale. "You will be the father of a mighty people," the god said to Hrona. "I grant these islands to you and your descendants. Remain true to my faith and they will be yours until the end of time."

When settled in the palace, Daqoros summoned three of his wives to his bed, where he relieved himself of the sexual urges that had been building in him so he could clear his mind. After spilling his seed into Jyunel, he sent them away, bathed, then retreated to his council chamber and sent for the Darom.

The four men who comprised the king's advisors arrived shortly and seated themselves after bowing low to Daqoros. He knew they had been gathered with their spies, who recently returned from the mainland, and he was eager to hear what they learned.

"Tell me, Kadahm, what is happening in the land of our enemies?" he asked.

The senior advisor of the Darom, an old man with a wind-burned face and a beard the color of rusty steel, inclined his head toward his ruler. "Your Grace, our most recent intelligence indicates the Khedeshians are vulnerable. Despite breaking the blockade of the Havalqa invaders and repelling the land invasion, they are fearful of incursions. The bulk of their fleet now patrols the waters north of Gedsengard, and the king's eyes are on the Threndish border."

"Are the rumors that these Havalqa invaders have taken Turen to be believed?"

"Yes, Your Grace," said Kadahm. "But I believe Ormo has more information in that regard."

"Your Grace," Ormo began, "these foreigners have indeed taken Turen, and much of Threndellen as well." He absently tapped his fat, bejeweled fingers on the table as he spoke. "They have not yet taken Trothmar, though it appears only a matter of time before it falls or King Kua'tani surrenders. These Havalqa are fearsome soldiers, and have not lost a battle since their defeat at Almaris. They have pushed all the way to the Bedan Plains in Armenos."

Daqoros clenched his jaw at the mention of a king surrendering to an enemy, even if the king was a despised fool. "Where are these Havalqa getting their men? They cannot have brought so many with them, even if their fleet is as big as reported. Are they using conscripts?"

Ormo leaned his round face over the table, as if about to impart a great secret. "No one knows for sure, Your Grace, but my spies have heard rumors of a magical door that opens into the heartland of these Havalqa far across the sea. Through it, they bring a nearly endless number of soldiers."

"Bah," said Kadahm with a dismissive wave of his hand. "Your spies are drunkards or liars, or both."

Ormo bristled. "I tell you, I heard from more than one of my men that soldiers march out of the royal compound of Turen day and night, but none go in! There is some black conjuring happening with these invaders, I am certain of it."

Kadahm rolled his eyes but made no further comment.

"What else do we know of these invaders?" asked the king. "Why are they here? Will they turn their eyes toward us?" The thought chilled him. If the Pelkland Islands were to face an invasion of their own, all of his plans would be for nothing.

"Unfortunately, we know little, Your Grace," said Kadahm. "They do indeed seem to have come from lands across the Maurelian Sea. They appear particularly interested in the Khedeshians, especially their new king, Gerin Atreyano."

"A sorcerer of some kind, is he not?"

"Yes, Your Grace. It was he who almost single-handedly broke the blockade and routed the Havalqa army about to lay siege to Almaris. The power he unleashed was said to have been formidable. Almost incomprehensible."

"And we have no counter for it, do we?"

"No, Your Grace. Yet his gaze is turned to the north, toward these Havalqa. We do not know exactly what they want with the young Khedeshian king, but our informers do not feel the Havalqa have given up trying to obtain it."

"Do you think they will come after us?"

Kadahm shrugged. "It is impossible to say for sure, Your Grace. But since fleeing Gedsengard, the invaders have kept their fleet at Turen and along the mainland coast. It does not seem they are aware of our existence. If they *are* aware, they seem disinterested."

Daqoros was conflicted. On one hand, he was relieved that the attention of the invaders was turned elsewhere. On the other hand, he was annoyed that if they were aware of the existence of the Pelklanders, they did not consider them a threat, or a people worth the attempt to conquer.

No matter. They are a distraction. All that matters is that they have drawn the might of our enemy away from us and left them vulnerable to my plans.

"We will launch our attack as soon as possible," he announced. There. It was said. There would be no turning back. A king did not change his mind about such matters.

Nolmaar cleared his throat and regarded Daqoros evenly

through his spectacles. "Your Grace, would it not be prudent to wait until we have more ships?"

"I will wait no longer," said the king. "I have spoken, and you will see that my desires are carried out. The longer we wait, the more chance that Khedeshian spies will discover what we are doing, and then the element of surprise will be lost. I want only the coastlands that are rightfully ours. Not one acre more, but also not one acre less. I have no desire to steal from the Khedeshians the way their ancestors the Raimen stole from us."

"Your Grace, I must in good conscience point out that to hold as much land as you intend to recapture will leave our islands almost defenseless should either the Khedeshians or the Havalqa assail us."

"Once we have a firm foothold on the mainland, the Khedeshians will do nothing," said the king. "They cannot afford to leave their own waters defenseless against their enemy. And the Havalqa, as you have just pointed out, have taken no notice of us."

"That is true, Your Grace. They have taken no notice of us *yet*, but they might, especially if they learn that the bulk of our forces are on the coast."

"That is a risk we must take. Prepare our captains for war. I have dreamed of this day since I was a boy. We will return our people to the glory we once knew."

The men of the Darom rose as one, bowed to their king, and left to ensure that his will was done.

6

The gods take me, Hollin. Look at this."

Abaru held up a shallow porcelain bowl decorated with an intricate spiral pattern. He had lifted it from a velvet-lined wooden cask partially hidden by vellum manuscripts he'd been removing from a wide, cluttered shelf in the Varsae Estrikavis, where he and Hollin were working. His hands trembled with excitement.

Hollin craned his neck to look at the bowl. He was seated at a nearby table carefully sorting parchments and scrolls. "What is it?" he asked. "I mean, other than a bowl."

"This belonged to Demos Thelar! The wizard who created the *awaenjir* and *methlenel*!"

Hollin smiled. "Yes, I know who he is." He joined Abaru at his table and studied the bowl. "What does it do?"

Abaru gave him a withering look. "It doesn't *do* anything! It's just a bowl. But according to this inscription"—he tapped his finger on the tarnished bronze plate inset on the lid of the box—"Demos Thelar used it in some of his early experiments when he was trying to create the first *methlenel*."

"Ah. His soup bowl. I think I can still see some porridge in the bottom."

"You're utterly hopeless."

"I do my best."

Abaru looked around the gallery. "I still can't grasp the fact that we're not in Osseria. What would happen if we knocked a hole in the wall? What's out there? A void? A landscape? A sea?" The Varsae Estrikavis had no windows and no doors leading out of it save the one opened by the Scepter of the King.

"Gerin and I discussed that once, but decided there were no doors and windows for a reason and left well enough alone. Which surprised me."

"A case of prudence. Perhaps the lad is growing wise."

"We can only hope. Though his rashness and his intuitions have proved invaluable, I must admit."

"Do you think Naragenth ever added to the library himself?"

"I can't believe he wouldn't put his own contributions here. It's the safest place he could have kept them, since only he seems to have had access. And his staff was found here, arguably the most precious item in this entire place."

"Maybe they're hidden. Without the design of the library or a way to look around outside to see if there are missing spaces, there could be an entire other wing devoted to the first amber wizard himself. We'll have to look for secret doors."

Hollin snorted. "You'd think Naragenth would have been satisfied with hiding the entire library in another world, Harel. But maybe you're right. Maybe he had some kind of secrecy fetish."

Abaru's heart skipped a beat when Hollin called him Harel by mistake. It was the third time since Abaru's arrival in Almaris that Hollin had called him by the wrong name. He'd thought nothing of it the first time and jokingly corrected Hollin, but the other wizard seemed not to hear. When he teased Hollin about it later, he was startled when Hollin quite sincerely claimed to have no recollection of it. The second time it happened, Hollin had been looking right at him and called him Versan. Abaru asked who Versan was, and added, "Come now, you can only have one friend as large and handsome as me!"

Hollin shook his head and asked Abaru to repeat himself. When he did, Hollin once again said he didn't remember calling him by the wrong name.

And now it had happened a third time. Hollin's eyes had an

unfocused, faraway look in them that made Abaru's breath catch. *The gods preserve me, what is happening to him?* He was no longer willing to dismiss this as inconsequential. Something was wrong.

He feared his friend might be suffering from tevosa, a rare disease that sometimes afflicted wizards later in life. They began to lose their memories of the present, unable to recall who they were speaking to just moments before. They also confused the present with the past as distant memories became more and more real to them.

He knew that sometimes the effects never became worse than what Hollin suffered from now—the confusion of names, and the kind of faulty memory that also afflicted nonwizards of an advanced age. But the disease could also ravage, stripping away so much of a wizard's mind that his personality was destroyed, leaving little but a demented shell that could linger for years before finally, mercifully, dying.

Abaru had known only one wizard who suffered from it. Old Hop, as he'd been known, had lingered for almost five years after the disease made its undeniable appearance. The final year of his life he'd been confined to his bed, unable to care for himself, entirely unaware of those around him while he held conversations—and sometimes violent arguments— with the long dead ghosts of his past.

He was unsure if he should say anything to Hollin. There were no spells that could determine the presence of tevosa, and no magic to cure it. Telling his friend might only alarm him needlessly, make him wonder if normal forgetfulness for a wizard his age was a sign of something sinister. Was he certain enough to speak his fears aloud? Once said, such a thing could never be unspoken or forgotten.

He decided he would watch Hollin carefully for more signs of the disease, and have a candid conversation with Gerin. The more people keeping an eye on Hollin, the better.

Abaru returned the bowl to its box and continued to search for records pertaining to the Vanil. What little they had found was piled on the center of a table.

After a few more hours of fruitless searching, the two wizards took a break and went for a walk along one of the palace terraces to clear their heads before resuming the task at hand.

Returning, they read through the new writings they'd found about the Vanil, but the parchments held no information they hadn't already found elsewhere. Hollin finished reading the faded ink on a brittle scroll, then settled back into his chair and crossed his arms.

"Let's discuss what we *do* know," he said, and started to count off on his fingers. "First, the Vanil lived in these lands before the coming of the Atalari, and were long gone when the Atalari got here, which means there hasn't been a living Vanil in Osseria for well over fourteen thousand years. What's next?"

"We don't know what happened to them," Abaru said. "Whether they died out, migrated somewhere else, or . . . something. I don't know. Were killed off by something else."

"Considering how powerful they were rumored to be, I'd hate to think about what kinds of creatures might have been able to eradicate them. And don't forget I've *seen* one. It was a damn impressive being.

"But, regardless of what may have happened, their disappearance is unexplained. Also, until one showed up here in the Tirthaig, no one was sure if they were real beings or part of some mythic folklore to scare Atalari children. The stories said that the Vanil could consume souls and therefore prevent them from reaching the afterlife."

"My mother used to tell me stories like that to make me eat my dinner," said Abaru.

"I can't imagine that you *ever* needed a threat in order to eat a meal."

"You never tasted my mother's cooking. That's why I eat so much now. To make up for all that time I spent as a starving child."

"Anyway, we know now they're real. And that this soul-devouring power they have appears to be real, too, considering what happened to the king. I could sense his soul being torn from his body. Gerin felt it too."

"The amulet Rahmdil found came to life, signaling that a

Vanil was walking Osseria," said Abaru. "Sometime later, one appears in the Tirthaig, kills the king, *kneels* to Gerin, and then vanishes."

"It was drawn to Gerin. That much is obvious."

"But why? Why him and not someone else?"

"He is the only amber wizard in the world," said Hollin.

"Yes, but then why didn't a Vanil appear when Naragenth was alive?"

The two men were quiet as they pondered the question of what had drawn the Vanil to Gerin.

"Maybe it was the Staff of Naragenth," said Abaru. Then he shook his head. "No, because we're back to wondering why it didn't draw the Vanil when Naragenth created it."

"Gerin didn't have the staff with him when the Vanil appeared," said Hollin. His eyes widened and he sat up straighter. "But he did have that bloody sword of his! In fact, the Vanil pointed to it before it vanished."

"Yes, yes. I think we're on to something. But how do we test it? I don't think we should have your young apprentice try to call the damn thing."

"Absolutely not. But I do think this is close to the answer." Hollin stood. "Come on. There's not much more we can do at the moment. I need a drink."

Gerin was in his study when the two wizards arrived to tell him their theory that the Vanil might have been drawn to the power of his sword.

"And why do you think this?" he asked.

They explained that the weapon was the only thing unique to Gerin that Naragenth didn't share.

"But you're assuming it never appeared to Naragenth," said Gerin. "Maybe it did. It's not as if we're overflowing with accounts of his life. Maybe it appeared to him in secret. Maybe it showed him how to construct the Varsae Estrikavis and his staff."

"Hmmm. We didn't think of that," said Hollin.

Gerin was about to ask another question when he heard a faint musical sound, like bells or chimes. They had a strange sound to them, a kind of echo, as if they were sounding in some vast chamber. He wondered what was making the sound since there were no chimes or bells in his rooms or anywhere else in this part of the Tirthaig. It also was not time for the city's bells to be ringing.

"Do you hear that?" he asked the other two.

Abaru made a dismissive gesture. "Just some bells." He took a large swallow of wine.

But Hollin was frowning, sitting up straighter in his chair. "No, not just bells. There's power in it."

Something moved at the edge of Gerin's vision. He turned toward the corner of the room, where he saw the apparition of a man.

He stood so quickly that his chair flew out from behind him and toppled over, cracking loudly against the floor. The other wizards turned, saw the apparition, and assumed defensive postures. Gerin noted that Abaru moved amazingly fast for a man of his size. He drew magic into himself and felt the others do the same.

"How did you get in here?" Gerin asked.

The apparition was very tall, and far thinner than a living man could be. The edges of its form were blurred and wavering, as if seen through a depth of water. Its long hair floated about its head in defiance of gravity—again, giving Gerin the strong impression that the apparition was in some way submerged.

Its face was narrow and unremarkable, devoid of any kind of readable expression. Only its eyes were alive, deep green with yellow vertical slits for pupils. Those eyes darted about the room as if cataloging its contents. When its penetrating gaze fell upon Gerin, he could almost feel the weight of it pressing against him, as if it were trying to lay bare the deepest secrets of his heart.

It seemed to be wearing a dark robe, but this was so indistinct that Gerin could not be sure. The apparition was translucent, insubstantial, and kept to the side of the room farthest from the sunlight.

"I ask again, how did you get into the palace? I won't ask a third time."

Hollin fashioned a Warding between them and the apparition. The being looked directly at it, obviously aware of its creation, even though the spell should not have been visible to nonwizards.

"Your spells are not necessary," it said. When it spoke, the sounds of the bells grew louder. Its voice had a musical quality to it that Gerin found beautiful and soothing, though it also sounded distant, as if coming from far beyond the walls of the room.

"What *are* you?" asked Hollin.

"I am an *akesh*, sent by the Telchan of the Watchtowers." It faced Gerin and grew larger, expanding like a sponge dropped into water. "I have come to give you a message."

"The Watchtowers!" said Abaru.

"What is your message?" said Gerin. "I'll listen to what you have to say, but only if you agree to answer my questions."

"I cannot," it said. "The power of the Telchan is not in words. It is difficult for me to be here. You must listen.

"If you wish to learn the secret of the Words of Making, you must come to the Watchtowers, to the *en pulyan ar-anglota*, so that we may tell you what we know. Our knowledge is not in words as you understand them and cannot be sent such distances. Even now I grow dim."

It was true. As Gerin watched, the apparition grew more transparent, its edges fading into the air like ink bleeding off a wet page. "You must come to us. This time we will permit your passage."

Then it was gone.

Gerin realized how tense he was and made an effort to relax. "What in the name of all that's holy was that about?" He released the magic he'd drawn into himself. "I didn't understand a thing it said. What's an *akesh*? Or a Telchan? And what in Shayphim's name are the Watchtowers, for that matter?"

Abaru gave his empty cup a quizzical stare. "I don't think I had *that* much to drink."

Gerin had to resist a very strong urge to punch Abaru in the side of the head. "Do either of you have any idea what just happened here?"

Hollin was clearly troubled. "We'll tell you what we can, but I fear that may not make this any clearer."

Gerin recovered his chair and sat back down at the table. "Abaru, since you have heard of the Watchtowers, why don't you start there. What are they? *Where* are they?"

Abaru gestured for Hollin to speak. "They're located in a range of mountains," said Hollin, "whose name now escapes me —"

"The Ozul," said Abaru.

"The Ozul Mountains. The Watchtowers are somewhere along the southern end of the range, on the western side."

"Isn't that Threndish territory?" asked Gerin.

"Whether the Threndish lay claim to those lands or not is irrelevant," said Hollin. "They have no authority or control over the Towers. No one does."

"Have you ever been there?"

Hollin shook his head. "No. No wizard has ever set foot in them. Wizards, in fact, are forbidden from going there. It's been a proscribed place for centuries."

This intrigued Gerin. "Why? What happened?"

Hollin looked at Abaru. "Do you remember the details? I know it happened seven or eight hundred years ago. The wizard who started all of the trouble, Parcla-something . . . "

"Paraclade." Abaru straightened a little. "His name was Paraclade. From what I recall, he found an old manuscript that mentioned the incredible wealth and power to be gained by anyone who could enter the Watchtowers. It said the inhabitants watch and record all things that occur in Osseria. Many wizards at the time dismissed the manuscript—apparently it was riddled with inaccuracies and all kinds of fanciful nonsense—but Paraclade became obsessed with the place and decided to lead an expedition to take the Towers by force if they couldn't get in peacefully."

"I'm surprised an Archmage would go along with something like that," said Gerin.

"The Archmage at the time didn't go along with it. He forbid the expedition, but Paraclade had gained so much influence and so many followers—he was apparently a rather talented demagogue—that there was a very real threat of a rebellion. In the end the Archmage allowed Paraclade and a few hundred of his followers to march on the Watchtowers."

"So what happened?" asked Gerin. "What did they find? You said no wizard has ever entered them, so I'm guessing they didn't get in."

"When they reached the Towers, a wall of flame sprang from the ground to block their path. The wizards spent days trying to break it down, but they couldn't even make a dent in it."

"Think about that," added Hollin. "Hundreds of wizards working in concert to break down a single barrier, and they failed."

"The *akesh* knew about Paraclade," said Gerin. "That must be what it was referring to when it said, 'This time we will permit your passage.'" He pondered the image of a wall of flame standing in defiance of wizardly power. "The fact that they couldn't gain entry somewhat validates Paraclade's belief that there's something of importance in those Towers."

"And he made that exact same argument when he finally gave up and returned to Hethnost," said Abaru. "But his failure effectively broke his power, and he never regained it. The Archmage officially declared the Towers a proscribed place. Any wizard who ventured there would be banished from Hethnost."

"Is that proscription still in effect?" asked Gerin.

"As far as I know," said Abaru. "I don't think anyone's given it much thought, but it would take a declaration from another Archmage to repeal it."

"So if I go, I'm breaking more rules."

"I think it's premature to decide whether or not anyone's going there," said Hollin.

Gerin was not going to argue with Hollin, but he already knew he was going there whether the old wizard consented or not.

"Who's in them?" he asked. "You mean to say that these Towers are millennia old, but no one ever comes out? Who made them?"

"We don't know," said Hollin. "Whoever's in them has tremendous power at their command, as Paraclade's expedition discovered. But that's all we know."

"What was that other phrase it said?" asked Gerin. "It said I had to go to a specific place." He snapped his fingers as he recalled it. "The *en pulyan ar-anglota*. It sounds Osirin but I don't recognize the words."

"It's Osirin all right," said Abaru. "A very old form, one that has long gone out of use. It means 'place of learning.'"

"If they've kept hidden in their Towers for so long, why would they contact me now?" asked Gerin. "And how did they know about the Words of Making to begin with?"

"It's impossible to know," said Hollin. "Perhaps they truly can see events that occur all across the continent."

"Can you imagine the knowledge they must have accumulated if that's true?" asked Gerin. "It might put the Varsae Estrikavis to shame."

"Or they could be interested in tax payments, tariffs, crop yields, and other bureaucratic drudgery," said Abaru. "And the minutiae of rug weaving and cow defecation. Never overestimate someone's ability to be boring. It helps lessen the sting of disappointment."

"I'm going to the Watchtowers," Gerin announced. "You both are welcome to come along, but please don't waste your breath trying to talk me out of it. I don't care if it's proscribed or not. If this displeases the Archmage, so be it, but I've been *invited*, and I plan on accepting."

He waited for the older wizards to object, to tell him he was being rash, that they needed to discuss this further before making any decisions. It didn't matter. The *akesh* claimed it could tell him the secret of the Words of Making. That alone was worth the journey.

The other wizards both nodded. "I agree," said Hollin. "I think you should go. This invitation, as you call it, is far too unique to ignore. Of course, I'll accompany you."

"So will I," said Abaru. "I wouldn't want to miss the chance to peek inside the Towers."

"Good," said Gerin. He let go of the counterarguments he'd been ready to make. "It's settled then. We'll leave as soon as I can make arrangements."

7

The garden on the grounds of Castle Tolthean had been built by Guthwen Toresh for his sickly bride Morweil a century ago. A waist-high stone wall enclosed the grounds on seven sides; one side of a square five-story tower delineated the eighth. Flowers were in bloom everywhere, clusters of them interspersed at regular intervals among tall shade trees. At the center of the garden, all of the paths converged on a sacred grove dedicated to the sea god Paérendras and his wife Niélas.

A salty wind blew from the sea, whose choppy surface was visible over the garden's eastern wall. At the wall's midpoint was a monument to the Twins, the gods Volraneth and Merel, charged with lighting the stars each night and keeping the sun and moon on their courses. The Twins had been the favorite gods of Morweil, who died during the birth of her first child.

A shame they didn't tear down these miserable gardens after her death, thought Claressa as she stared out over the sea. The assault of fragrances from the flowers caused her no end of sneezing fits and watery eyes. At the moment, the stiff wind from the sea was helping to keep her head clear, but she knew that as she made her way back through the gardens, her sinuses would swell and her temples begin to throb.

The sea, though . . . that, she loved more than she would have thought possible. She'd enjoyed it on her visits to Almaris before her marriage, but her sea journey to Tolthean had stirred something new within her. The sound of it, the smell of it, how it constantly changed yet remained the same, the mysteries hidden in its boundless depths. It called to her heart in a way she found impossible to describe yet equally impossible to ignore.

Right now the sight of the ocean far below her was the only thing keeping her sane. The inane chattering of her ladies-in-waiting was enough to make her want to toss the lot of them from the parapet. They sat on a stone bench a few feet behind her, gossiping like a gaggle of hens. She tried to ignore them, but they were speaking too loudly for her to completely shut them out.

"He's *so* handsome!" cooed Trené. "I make sure to pass by the stables as much as I can, even if it's out of my way."

"Does he even know you exist?" said Elezan.

"He waved and smiled at me yesterday!"

"How much of your tits did you flash him to make that happen?" said Elezan.

"You're just jealous because I've *got* some to show."

"He's not part of the castle household," said Verdel. "He goes back to Ordéas at night."

Trené made a disappointed noise. Claressa did not turn around to look, but easily imagined the young girl crossing her arms and pouting. "No chance of me sneaking into his bed at night then. But maybe the next time we're in town, I'll slip away for a bit of fun—"

"Don't even think of it," warned Verdel, the oldest of the group.

"I'm just talking. I wouldn't break the rules like that. But Olassa take me, I'd give anything to ride him for a night. The *shoulders* on that man!"

"You watch your mouth," said Verdel. "I swear, the filth that comes out of it . . . "

"Nothing filthy at all. I'm just saying what I want," said Trené. "There's nothing wrong with that."

No, there's not. Claressa admired the young girl's forwardness. She found it refreshing. Trené was going to have a difficult time in the castle, however, if she didn't learn to fit in a little better. The other women would make her life miserable. They'd find all manner of petty ways to punish her for daring to speak her mind. The fact that she was of Pelklander descent didn't help matters. While Claressa found her flawless bronzed skin—the girl never had the slightest blemish! It was infuriating!—and dark, curly hair alluring and attractive in an exotic way, they also clearly marked her as different, a descendant of a race of enemies.

But she was also irritated by their conversation, their lighthearted talk of men and sex. She rubbed her belly and thought of the baby now growing inside her, and the one she had lost. She'd missed Gerin's coronation because of her first pregnancy. It had left her sick and bedridden, unable to travel. The physicians warned her that a trip to Almaris would almost certainly cause her to miscarry, and that if it happened at sea there was a high probability she would die as well. Baris had forbidden her to go, and so she had remained behind while her new family went off to see her brother crowned king.

While they were gone, she had lost the baby anyway.

She squeezed her eyes shut as she remembered the pain in her abdomen like a knife thrust. She'd been curled up on her bed in the dead of night, alone, in so much pain she could barely draw enough breath to call for help.

Verdel had heard her and rushed into the room. "My lady, what's wrong?"

Claressa had not been able to speak. The pain was too intense. Something inside her broke, and she felt a hot gush between her legs. She screamed, and distantly heard Verdel gasp and yell for Torlmek Arghan, the castle's Tanu physician.

Telling Baris about the loss upon his return had almost been worse than the event itself. She dreaded his arrival, worried about what he would think. Would he blame her for her failure to produce an heir? And in her heart she felt she *had* failed, that some flaw within her had caused her child to die. It was a new and unsettling feeling for her.

When his ship was sighted sailing toward the harbor, her

anxiety grew so bad that she threw up in the privy. Ashamed, she told no one.

Baris had comforted her when, in tears, she told him what happened. She studied his face for signs of disappointment, of blame. She saw none, but that might only mean he kept his feelings buried down deep to prevent them from appearing in the lines of his face. She *hated* that she did not know how he felt, and that she felt too unsure to ask him, afraid of what his answer might be. Even if he denied it, would she believe him?

Now she was with child again, sick each morning and irritable and tired the rest of the time. She fervently hoped she did not lose this baby. Living with fear was a new and unpleasant experience for her.

Such things had been so much easier with Reshel. Her younger sister had not been able to hide her feelings at all. Whether happy, sad, angry, annoyed, Reshel's emotional state was readily apparent to anyone with eyes. Claressa had always thought her weak for her lack of control. Displaying one's feelings so openly left one exposed, with no ability to use the hiding of those feelings to advantage.

Yet she did hide her infatuation with Balandrick well, I'll grant her that. And Reshel's unimaginable bravery atop the Sundering was something Claressa still could not reconcile with the bookish sister she had known. A few times she secretly wondered if Gerin had sacrificed Reshel against her will and only told the story he had to protect himself and Reshel's memory. But that was even more unlikely, she had to admit. Gerin was strong, but he'd adored Reshel, and might very well have let all of Osseria perish rather than draw a knife across her throat.

The Daughters of Reshel were another irritant to her. There were none in the castle itself, but in the town of Ordéas at the foot of the bluff upon which the castle sat—the sight from the harbor of Castle Hurien perched above the town created the unshakable image in her mind of a vulture hovering over some dying animal—the strange cult had multiplied alarmingly when it became known that the saint's sister—and she simply could *not* grasp that the Temple priests had declared Reshel a *saint!*—was to be the bride of the baron's son.

Claressa shunned the members of the order as if they were plague carriers, refused to see them despite numerous requests for an audience, but in the town, it was impossible *not* to see them. They had even managed to acquire a small chapter house. She disliked being reminded of her sister's glory and fame, no matter that she had died to achieve them. Claressa now dwelt in Reshel's shadow, a rather startling reversal of how things had been in life, and she did not enjoy it one bit.

Especially since I can see no way of changing it. What she did is not something I can ever do or surpass. The gods take her, she was having trouble producing an heir!

"I'd love to marry him and have his babies," she heard Trené say. "Gods, wouldn't that be wonderful?"

"Do you even know his name?" asked Verdel.

"Not yet, but what does that matter?"

Claressa turned about. She could not take any more of their nonsense. "Stay here. I'm going for a walk."

Verdel rose from the bench. "But my lady, we should—"

"I said stay! I'm not going to leave the gardens, but I *am* going to have a few minutes of peace and quiet."

She really could not wait for Therain to arrive. The idea of him married was still sinking in. She'd also missed his wedding and her father's funeral because of her pregnancy. The thought that her father was no longer in the world struck her at times with such force that it quite literally took her breath away. There were times when she hid in her rooms to weep quietly for him. *It's not fair that I couldn't be there when they buried him,* she thought. She did not like that he was interred in Almaris, far from their mother at Ailethon. She might ask Gerin to have their mother's body moved so they could be together. It seemed the right thing to do.

She could not imagine Therain without his left hand. It was simply too strange an image for her to conjure. She missed him a great deal. More than she would have thought when she'd left Almaris to begin her new life here. Gods above, she even missed Gerin!

But she was an Atreyano, the strong daughter of a proud
and strong family. She would adapt and endure.

*Still, it will be wonderful to see Therain. I hope he gets
here soon.*

Claressa was having trouble sleeping. Midnight had come and
gone, Baris was snoring softly beside her, but she could not get
comfortable, nor could she stop thinking about their father and
the strange manner of his death. Gerin and Therain had both
written her detailed accounts of what transpired, but it seemed
so . . . preposterous. An ancient monster appeared from
nowhere, killed her father, kneeled to Gerin, and disappeared
again? What in Shayphim's bloody name was going on?

Claressa rolled onto her side in a futile effort to relax. Her
husband's profile was just barely visible in the darkness. She
sighed as she realized another fundamental underpinning of
her world had changed since her marriage. She had always
been the object of men's desires, a woman they yearned and
lusted for but could neither approach nor have. She could dally
with them if it struck her fancy to do so, but she was always in
complete control. Their wishes did not count in any way.

But now things had changed. Before their wedding Baris
had seemed a rather timid man. Handsome enough, true—
she thanked her father for that small favor—but still, a man
who would fall all over himself attempting to please her.
She assumed that she would be able to do as she pleased. It
seemed to her that very little would change after her marriage, other than the landscape.

How wrong she'd been. It did not take long for Baris to
show an inner strength she had not suspected existed in him.
He told her *no*, by the gods! A month after their arrival in
Tolthean, she asked him to remain with her one evening after
he'd expressed a desire to visit a friend of his, some son of
a vassal. She hadn't actually cared whether he went or not;
she simply wanted to see how deep her influence over him
extended.

"Not tonight," he said. Then he left without another word.

At first she was furious. How *dare* he do such a thing! The
next few days she was distant and aloof, frosting the air with

her mood, waiting for him to grovel and apologize. But he did neither.

"I'm growing weary of your games, Claressa," he said a few nights later. "I won't play them." He gave her a hard stare. "I suggest you soften your disposition or you'll find life here lonely and unpleasant."

She was so shocked she did not know what to say. A helpless rage built inside her, and she considered shouting a hundred hateful things at him. But in the end she did not.

Baris treated her with tenderness and respect, but he did not worship her. She hated it at first, despised that she could not wiggle her finger and have him come begging to please her. But slowly she softened to it. She found that if she were respectful to him, he treated her as something of an equal, discussing the governance of Tolthean or other subjects of interest to him. She had not the slightest interest in what he said, but the very fact that he talked about such matters with him made her, in some strange way, feel needed.

She did not love him. Not yet, and perhaps never. But she cared about him, oddly enough. And cared about what he thought about her, which created the unique situation of having *her* wanting to keep *him* pleased. Imagine such a thing!

Therain would be amazed if he knew. Of course she had absolutely no intention of telling him any of this. That would be—

She heard bells sounding in the distance. From the harbor town, Ordéas.

Baris propped himself up on his elbows. It was too dark for her to see the expression on his face.

"The bells just started," she said.

The castle's bells joined the others. Baris jumped out of bed and went to the window. He threw back the curtains and swore.

Claressa joined him. "What is it? What do the bells mean?"

The night was black, moonless. But from their tower window in the castle they could see down to the harbor and the town that circled its rim.

Fires were awakening in it.

8

"Stay here," said Baris. "I'll send guards, but for now I don't want you to leave these rooms."

"But what if I—"

"I'll send word about what's happening as soon as I know." He stopped in the doorway. Flickering torchlight in the corridor cast harsh shadows across his face. "Please don't do anything foolish. I'll be back as soon as I can."

Then he was gone.

What was that supposed to mean? Don't do anything foolish? She fumed that he was placing her in the same category as her handmaidens, women prone to panic and hysteria at the first sign of trouble.

I'll show him who's foolish and who's not.

She peered down at Ordéas, trying to discern what was happening. She thought she could hear distant shouts carried on the wind. More fires blossomed, and it was plain to see now that they were not bonfires or torches. Buildings were burning, and in the light of the growing fires she could see people running up and down the streets.

There was a frantic knock on her door, then Verdel entered, followed by Elezan and Trené. They were all in nightclothes. Verdel and Elezan had thrown shawls over their shoulders. Claressa could not help but once more admire Trené's lustrous hair, unbound and falling to the small of her back.

"My lady, what's happening?" asked Verdel. The castle

bells rang again. The very walls seemed to reverberate with the sound.

"A disturbance in the town," she said, gesturing to the window. It was hard to tell, but it seemed that she could make out columns of men marching from the waterfront, with people fleeing frantically before them.

There was a momentary flare of light at the harbor as a cask of oil exploded. Claressa gasped. Not from the explosion, but rather what it illuminated.

Ships in the harbor. Dozens of them.

The fire dwindled and the view of the ships receded into darkness.

"The gods take us all, did you see those ships?" said Trené. "Is it the Havalqa? Have they come to take us away?"

"It's not the Havalqa," said Elezan. "Those are Pelklander ships."

Verdel made the sign of Telros. "What are we to do?"

Claressa straightened. "We wait, and pray that our men kill these invaders swiftly for daring to set foot on Khedeshian soil. It doesn't matter if they're Havalqa or Pelklanders. They're invaders, and their souls should be sent screaming to Shayphim."

The women huddled by the window and watched the skirmishes unfold in the town. Every so often soldiers of the castle would cross the wall-walk or courtyard below them, whispering among themselves, their armor and weapons clanking.

"What news of the battle?" Claressa called out to a group of four soldiers hurrying along the wall. "Who are they?"

The soldiers stopped. She sensed they were about to ignore her and move on, so she quickly added, "I'm Claressa Toresh, wife of Baris! A quick answer, then go about your duties."

"We've word it's the Pelklanders, my lady," called one of the men.

"Just as I said," said Elezan. She tucked some loose strands of her honey-colored hair behind her ear.

"But not why, or how the battle is going," said Verdel.

"The why is obvious," said Claressa without taking her eyes from the fires in the town far below. "Daqoros chafed under the treaty imposed on his father, and now that the little whelp's become king, he's having a tantrum and throwing off his chains."

"These were once Pelklander lands," said Trené. "Maybe he wants to take them back."

"And you would know all about that, wouldn't you?" said Elezan. "You little spying bitch. I'll bet you're feeding information to them! That's why you've been flashing your tits everywhere! So you can get—"

Trené slapped her hard across the face. "I am *not* a spy, you fat stupid cow!"

Elezan's mouth hung open in shock. "You . . . you . . . !"

Claressa stepped between them. "Enough! I'll have no more talk of spies, Elezan! You deserved that slap, and if you say something like that again, I'll be the one to deliver the next one.

"As for you," she said to Trené, "try to control your temper."

Trené bowed her head contritely. "Yes, my lady."

Elezan rubbed her cheek and glared daggers at Trené. "Yes, m'lady. It's just—"

Claressa turned back to the window. "Don't try to explain. You'll only make it worse." She decided when this incident with the Pelklanders was over, she would send Elezan away. The woman would cause no end of trouble now for Trené, and she had no stomach to deal with it. She would send her to some vassal's household and be done with her.

The battle was going badly for the Khedeshians, it seemed to her. The fighting was coming closer to the castle, the sounds of it growing louder, while the town itself had quieted somewhat, the resistance there quashed. *Perhaps our men are making a strategic retreat toward the castle where they can better defend against the Pelklanders,* she told herself.

The soldiers in the corridor pounded on her door. "My lady, I must have a word with you."

A soldier who seemed even more massive than the solid

oak door she'd just opened loomed in the corridor. She took note of his insignia. "What is it, Lieutenant?"

"Your husband has sent word that I am to take you from the castle at once."

Her heart fluttered, but she remained outwardly calm. She heard Verdel moan at the soldier's words and wanted to throttle the fool.

"Why? Is it no longer safe here?"

"My lady, I have my orders."

"And I'm telling you I'm not going anywhere without understanding exactly what is happening. I am not one to blindly obey. I require reasons, Lieutenant."

The big man paused to consider. He bent down a little and lowered his voice. "We fear the castle is going to fall, my lady. The Pelklanders have too many men. They captured Ordéas quickly, which was bad enough, but they also landed additional troops up and down the coast who are moving to surround the castle. It's one thing if we only had to defend an assault from the town, but with the enemy in the countryside—"

"Thank you, Lieutenant. I understand. Wait while we dress. Then we will accompany you out of the castle."

Her heart was pounding as she closed the door. Gods above and below, the castle was going to fall to the Pelklanders!

Verdel was close to hysterics. Her eyes were huge, the whites showing all around her pupils, and her breathing came in ragged gasps. "My lady, what are we going to do? Oh, Olassa preserve us all, what is going to happen to us?"

The woman's panic helped to calm Claressa. "Hysterics will accomplish nothing. Go and get dressed. Don't dawdle! Your lives may depend on it. I'll dress myself so you can hurry. Do not question me, do not argue with me! We're leaving with the soldiers, and that is the end of it." As the women rushed off, she added, "And make sure you put on something sensible!"

The keep of Castle Hurien was nicknamed the Kettle because of its rounded shape and the dark stone with which it had been built, giving it something of the appearance of a large black pot. Claressa had thought the name ridiculous when Baris told her of it on their voyage here from Almaris, but her first sight of the keep convinced her of its appropriateness.

They were making their way down a circular tower stair in the Kettle when an arrow shot through the window and splintered on the inner wall. The hulking lieutenant ducked and swore. Claressa screamed and was instantly angry at herself for doing so.

"We need to hurry," said the lieutenant. He ordered the other men of his company to raise their shields whenever they passed an open window.

They reached the ground floor and raced across the Grand Hall. Claressa could hear sounds of fighting outside. Shouts, screams, the ringing of steel on steel, the dull *thwack* of bowstrings. She was trembling with fear. *Is this how it was for Therain when Agdenor was overrun by the Neddari?* she wondered. *How could he lead his men if his insides were shaking the way mine are? For that matter, how can men fight if they feel this way?* Were men and women really so different? Was it possible for her to be trained in such a way that she could fight and not feel such overwhelming fear? Or did soldiers learn to ignore their fear? She would have to ask Therain about it when she saw him.

"Where is my husband" she asked the lieutenant.

"I don't know, my lady. He did not tell me where he was going when he gave me my orders. But be assured, he's well protected."

They were halfway across the courtyard when a postern door in the castle wall burst open and a number of fierce warriors plunged through, shrieking and brandishing their weapons. Their hair was long and wild, braided with fish bones and seagull feathers; slashes of war paint streaked their faces and arms.

Verdel screamed in terror. The guards closest to the women brought their shields around to protect them while their companions released a volley of crossbow quarrels at the invaders. Five of them fell dead.

"Protect them at all costs!" shouted the lieutenant as he surged forward to meet the Pelklanders, shield and sword ready.

Claressa heard more than saw the skirmish. Her view was blocked by the shields and the need to keep her eyes focused on where they were going so she did not trip or stumble. The wall of shields was like a moving prison enveloping them and moving them away from the fighting. Two of the soldiers broke ranks momentarily to dispatch an approaching Pelklander, but quickly returned to their positions. *Thank the gods these men are well trained.*

Verdel and Elezan whimpered and clutched each other as they made their way toward another postern. The sounds of fighting were coming from all around them.

They reached the door, but before they could escape through it, the soldiers in the rear spun madly around and engaged a sudden surge of Pelklanders. The Toltheani soldiers used their shields to drive the invaders back, but to Claressa it looked as if their defenders would be overwhelmed in moments. There were just too many of the fearsome, painted Pelklanders.

I'm going to die. Without my husband, my family. She would not allow herself to be raped. One of the Toltheani soldiers would have to kill her first. And if none of them would, she'd fling herself on a sword. She would not be defiled in that way. Not ever.

She wondered what Therain would see when he arrived. Would every Khedeshian in this part of Tolthean be dead? Would her body ever be found? *At least I'll see Reshel again. I wonder if she'll annoy as much as she did when she was alive?*

A rough hand grabbed her shoulder and shoved her through the postern. "Forgive me, my lady, but you need to run!" said one of the soldiers.

Sudden darkness as she passed through the wall, and then another hand grabbed her on the other side. "We must be quick," said a voice. Another soldier, but it was too dark to see him clearly.

Verdel and Elezan appeared, followed by Trené, and then the postern was slammed shut, muffling the sounds of fighting. Verdel and Elezan were sobbing hysterically despite the soldier's command to be quiet. Claressa wondered if the lieutenant was still alive.

"Come quickly," said one of the men. Claressa counted seven soldiers in the darkness. He led them off across an open field of tall grasses.

"Where are we going?" she whispered.

"Bathrel," he said, naming a coastal fortress to the north. "Now, my lady, please, be *quiet*."

A line of men suddenly appeared ahead of them. They'd been hiding in the grasses. Claressa heard arrows pass close by and ducked reflexively. One passed close enough to blow her hair.

The Toltheani soldiers were shouting to one another, but Claressa had no idea what they were saying. A part of her was surprised that someone could experience such an overwhelming amount of terror and not die.

Three arrows shot past her from the opposite direction. Still crouched down, she looked up just in time to see an arrow strike Elezan in her mouth, shattering her teeth. The barbed arrow point burst through the back of her head and sprayed Claressa with blood and bits of bone.

She heard screaming and realized it was her. She wanted to stop, she truly did, the soldiers had told her to be quiet, but Elezan was lying on the ground in front of her, and even though it was dark, so terribly dark, she could still see the ruin of her mouth, the broken, bloody teeth, her dead eyes wide, staring at nothing, the arrow shaft rising from between her lips like a freakish wooden tongue or impossibly straight sapling.

The Toltheani soldiers were falling all around her, feathered with arrows. She continued screaming, powerless to stop, until a Pelklander cracked her on the back of her head with the pommel of his sword.

9

Tyne Fedron had been walking for what seemed an eternity. After the divine stranger dressed in fine silks had left him near the border of Nirovai Deep—which he learned was the name of the forest where he'd found the Commanding Stone—he continued southward until he reached a town on the outskirts of the city of Serel. He continued to ask anyone he met about the Vanil, though he did not use that name; he called it the bronze demon, as he had since leaving home.

He did as the stranger asked and kept the Stone touching his skin at all times. Truth be told, he probably would have done so even without encouragement. He liked how it felt in his hand. He felt safer touching it than the hilt of his sword. When he was walking, he either held it in his hand or kept a grip on it in his pocket. He felt the bond between him and the dragons strengthening.

It seemed there was something almost alive within the Stone, an awareness of him and his actions. He had the sense of being silently observed by whatever dwelled inside of it. He remembered the dreams of the figure trapped in crystal and the sense of an entity urging him on when he was digging it up. He hadn't thought about it much after recovering the Stone, and later assumed his dreams had been the work of the divine being.

Now he wasn't so sure. Perhaps there really was something alive within the Stone.

He talked to it, but it did not respond. He felt foolish doing so, but he was alone most of the time and there was nothing else to do, so he spoke to the Stone about his brothers, his mother, what the Vanil had done to them, and how he wanted to kill it in revenge.

By the bloody Pit, when is he going to show up and tell me how to use this thing? The dreams of the dragons were coming more frequently. They were so vivid that he felt almost a dragon himself, his strong heart beating in a chest protected by iron-hard scales, powerful wings propelling him down through cool mountain air into the humid jungles below, hunting large animals that reminded him vaguely of elks. He watched them through the connection. The dragons sensed it and were frightened by it. Their movements and behavior became erratic, nervous, as they realized some unseen entity was observing them. Did the connection feel like a leash around their long necks? Maybe that was why they were frightened—they recognized that he would bend them to his will, to do his bidding.

He decided he did not much like these southern Elloharans. They were gruff, unfriendly, unwilling to speak to him when he asked for news of the demon. A few said they didn't like the way he talked and that he'd best go back to wherever it was he came from if he knew what was good for him. "Don't much like foreigners in these parts," one toothless old man had told him at a market located at the juncture of two dirt roads. "Mostly causin' trouble. Seems to me a man huntin' a demon don't have long to live in this world, and he might be bringin' a heap o' trouble with him before he dies. So you best move along, y'hear? That's your advice o' the day, and you'd best take it and be grateful." The man had laughed then, a sound so dry and raspy that Tyne half expected a cloud of dust to fly out of his mouth.

For a moment he was so angry at the old bastard that he considered whipping out his sword and chopping the fool's head off. That would wipe that smug, stupid look off his face and stop his insipid laugh. Tyne imagined himself staring down at the man's severed head, the eyes open in surprise, his gaping, toothless mouth forming a silent O. Then he'd kick it across the market for good measure, and as a warning for others not to mock or belittle him.

But he did not murder the old man. He turned and stalked off, weary to the bone, and did his best to ignore the raspy laughter that followed him down the road.

The trail of the Vanil in southern Ellohar was cold. The few who deigned to speak to him had no stories to share, no sightings of it or deaths at its hand to relay.

He passed through the Gap of Ellohar, the immense divide that separated the Graymantle Mountains from the Mendan Mountains in the south. He had a much better idea of where he was now because of a map he'd stolen from a sleeping shopkeeper in a small town whose name he never learned. *Serves these fools right for laughing at me.* He would show them, though. One day all of them would bow to him as emperor. They would all know his name, and whisper it in fear.

He smiled at the thought.

The Stone drained more and more energy from him, and his pace slowed accordingly. He simply could not stave off the fatigue it caused. The stranger had warned him of this, but Tyne had not expected his weariness to become incapacitating. Twice after passing through the Gap of Ellohar, his exhaustion became so severe that he was unable to move for an entire day.

"Tyne Fedron, it's time for you to take the next step," said the voice of the stranger.

Stretched out on his back beneath a huge old oak tree, Tyne forced his eyes open, though his body was so weary he did not think he could move. "I'm not sure I can stand up, let alone take a step," he said.

"Get up." The stranger sounded annoyed. "It is difficult and dangerous for me to be here, Tyne Fedron. Do not trifle with me."

Tyne managed to sit up and open his eyes. "I'm not trifling. I'm worn out from the Stone. I feel like an old man sometimes."

"I warned you of this."

"There's a difference between hearing a thing and experiencing a thing. Though maybe the servant of a god wouldn't know that."

The stranger ignored Tyne's mocking tone. "Despite your weariness, the bond between you and the dragons is now strong enough for you to call them."

Tyne sat up a little straighter. Finally, he was going to get some answers. "How?"

"The bond has reached a point where the Stone's power will now nourish and strengthen you. You will tire after using it, but the power of the Stone will help to sustain you. Do not fight your desire to sleep! Each time you awaken you will be stronger, and using the Stone will become easier. But you must find a secure place to rest and recover. A place where you will not be disturbed for some time."

"How long? I don't have a lot of money to pay for inns."

"Days. Perhaps a week or more, depending on how deeply you use the Stone."

"A week! I'll starve to death!"

The expression on the stranger's flawless face darkened. "As I said, the Stone will nourish you. It will not let you die while you recover. You have passed that danger. But you will be defenseless while your body is being strengthened and replenished. You and the Stone must be safe when that happens."

Tyne didn't like the idea of sleeping for weeks. It seemed impossible. But then his resolve hardened. *I'm being tested, as all great men are tested. To see if I'm afraid, a coward who'll turn tail and run away when things get difficult. I won't. I'm not afraid.*

"Tell me what I need to know. But first, tell me your name. I have no idea what to call you."

"I told you before, it is not for you to know."

"I remember. But you need me since you can't use the Stone for yourself. You've made that much plain. I want a name. I don't care if you make something up, but I'm tired of not knowing."

The stranger pondered this for a moment. "You may call me Drexos. But do not think to try my patience too often, Tyne Fedron. If you do, you will regret it."

"Fair enough. Now, how do I call the dragons?"

"There is a word you must speak," Drexos said. "It will

align the power of the Stone with your mind so that your will, your desires, will be transferred through the connection."

"And what is this word?"

"Prepare yourself before you speak it. Its power is derived from the Stone. It will be painful."

"Just tell me."

"The word is *alharohm*."

Tyne steeled himself as best he could, then said, "*Alharom*."

Pearlescent light filled his vision as numbing energy surged through his arm from the Stone. He had the vague sense that he was falling down, but his senses were so overwhelmed he could not be sure. He thought he might be convulsing, and felt a sudden cool wetness around his mouth.

He was going to die. Speaking a word was going to kill him.

The power reached his skull, where it somehow mingled and blended with the pearlescent light in his eyes. He heard a deep hum, like a distant rumble of thunder that did not end. He could not think on his own—the light and power overwhelmed his mind.

He felt the connection grow stronger. If it had been a thread before, now it was a rope as thick as his arm. Power and images poured through the connection like floodwaters through a broken dam.

He sighed, then blacked out.

"Tyne Fedron, awaken."

The stranger's voice—*Drexos, he told me his name is Drexos,* Tyne thought—reached him distantly through a haze of fog and pain. He felt as if he'd been beaten around his head. He was sure his skull had been shattered into pieces, that if he tried to move, his head would simply collapse into a lump of structureless flesh.

"Get up," commanded Drexos.

Tyne opened his eyes. "I thought I was dead."

"You are not. Now your true work begins."

It was as if a phantom muscle had appeared in his mind, one he could flex in ways he could never describe to anyone else. The connection to the dragons was vastly different than it had been. Stronger, to be sure, but also drastically altered in kind. It was no longer a mere conduit for visions and impressions—now it was an instrument of *will*, a thing through which he could exert influence and desire.

But this muscle was new, and weak, and exercising it left him exhausted and ill after a few minutes.

He continued to practice over the next few days. The exertions drained him, but he also grew stronger and more able. He could sense the dragons much more keenly. He intensified the bond to a number of the beasts, which would allow him to more easily command them.

Drexos remained by his side. He was a maddening creature. He did not eat or drink; the bastard didn't even sit down. Drexos stood and watched him and from time to time uttered cryptic comments or haughty pronouncements about the need to destroy Gerin Atreyano.

Finally, Tyne was ready to issue his first command. He sent part of his mind through the connection, felt his consciousness merge with the primitive, brutish thoughts of the dragons. He felt them recoil when they sensed his presence, an intruder lurking unseen in their minds, able to assume some measure of control over them and their actions. His presence, his will, caused them pain, but he didn't care. They were weapons, nothing more.

Come to me. Follow the connection to my mind. Obey me!

With a roar that echoed from the mountainsides, the dragons turned about in the sky and began their long journey northward.

It worked! They listened to me! He could barely believe what he'd accomplished. Such a feat! If only Tremmel and Rukee were there to see it.

He would avenge them with dragonfire.

"I've done it," he said. He was filled with excitement. "They're coming."

Though a smile did not touch his lips, Drexos seemed pleased. "Good."

His success made him bold. "Why don't you kill Gerin Atreyano yourself? Why do you need me?"

"There are rules that govern how I may interact with mortals."

"Then why should I listen to you? If you can't hurt him, you can't hurt me. Now that I can control the dragons, I don't need you anymore."

Drexos's body grew larger and darker, as if a cloud had passed before the sun whose shadow fell only on him. Tyne once again caught the briefest glimpse of tendrils of shadow wrapped about a great dark *thing* with leathery flesh, batlike wings, and burning, crimson eyes. Inhuman eyes. He shrank back in horror—

And then the human form of Drexos was before him, his expression grim, murderous. "Do not fool yourself into believing you may do whatever you wish, that the power of the dragons will keep you safe from harm."

Drexos clenched his fist. Tyne shrieked in agony and thrashed about on the grass. It felt as if he'd fallen into a raging fire, that his flesh was burning from his bones.

Then it was gone. He lay still, gasping for air, his body drenched in sweat.

"That is but a taste of the pain I can provide. If you defy me, I will find another to wield the Stone, but my displeasure at your disobedience will be *quite* severe. I will cause you no end of pain, but you will not die. I will not allow it. I will torment you until your mind is gone. You will become a drooling husk, but still I will not let you die. I will torment you for my amusement, keep you alive for years, until—"

"I understand," panted Tyne.

A cold smile touched Drexos's lips.

"If you can do that to me, I don't understand why you don't kill the Khedeshian king yourself. I still want to know why you need me." He tensed, wondering if his insistence would anger Drexos again and bring agony upon him once more.

"I already told you. There are rules that govern the mortal realm, rules I do not have the power to defy. They prevent me from touching Gerin Atreyano directly."

"Then why can you hurt me?"

"Because you asked for my help." Drexos's smile sent a chill down Tyne's back. "Such a request can be a dangerous thing, Tyne Fedron. Remember that."

10

Gods, look at all the smoke!" said Laysa.

"Bloody Pelklanders," said Therain. He spoke softly, but there was an edge of rage in his voice. *That imbecile Daqoros! His father's body is barely cold in its grave and he decides to toss the treaty to the winds.*

"Therain, your sister . . . "

"She's fine," he said tightly. "I'd know if something happened to her."

He felt a coldness inside him as he watched smoke rising from the countryside ahead of him. They were hidden behind a line of trees on the blind side of a slope that occluded their view, but Therain had caught a glimpse of the castle and countryside around it before they pulled back.

It's Agdenor all over again, and I'll be damned to Shayphim's darkest pits if I'm going to stand by and let it happen.

He was deeply worried for Claressa. Despite his words to Laysa, he feared the worst. He could only hope Baris had the foresight and ability to get her out of the castle before it fell. They'd passed refugees on the road who told them of the invasion, but no one had any news of his sister or the Toresh family.

A soldier Rundgar had sent to reconnoiter the situation returned. "My lord, the Pelklanders have landed many ships in the harbor and along the coast. They've taken the town and castle."

"How many men?"

"Difficult to say, my lord. Several thousand at least. More ships are arriving. They're obviously planning to entrench themselves against a counterattack."

"My lord, we should leave at once," said Rundgar. "I don't have the men to protect you if we're discovered. As the king's brother, you must be kept safe."

"Duly noted, Captain, but I'm not going anywhere until I find out what's happened to Claressa."

The large captain made a very uncharacteristic sigh of exasperation. "My lord, please be reasonable. We have no way of getting closer."

"Oh, but I do. You're forgetting what I've been practicing."

Rundgar looked momentarily confused. "My lord, you don't mean your . . . *thing* . . . with the animals?"

"I mean exactly that."

"Are you sure that's wise?" asked Laysa. "You don't really understand how your power works."

"I've been practicing over the past few days. I'll be fine." He turned to the captain. "I'll find out what I can, and then we'll retreat to a more secure location."

Rundgar did not look happy about Therain's decision but did not argue further.

Therain got off his horse and folded his legs beneath him. Kelpa sat beside him, his haunches against Therain's thigh. He found the dog's presence comforting.

"Is there anything I can do to help?" asked Laysa.

"No, but thank you. I'm on my own with this one."

Therain had been experimenting with his ability to sense the location of animals and his apparent ability to call to them with his thoughts. He'd had several more vivid dreams in which he was able to see through the eyes of animals. It was strange to experience the world in such a radically different way. Soaring through the air, scurrying along the ground, or scampering up a tree. The dreams were too real for him to ignore. He felt that, like his earlier dreams of animals, which seemed to presage his power, there was some truth in them.

He decided to test it.

While riding, he closed his eyes and reached out with his mind toward Kelpa, who was padding along beside him. *Let me see through your eyes,* he thought, trying to project his will, his vision, to the animal. *Let me see as you see.*

Nothing happened for several days, though he could feel something stirring within him, growing stronger each time he reached out to a different animal.

One morning he was sitting with Kelpa and almost offhandedly tried to see through the dog's eyes. He closed his own eyes and willed his vision toward the animal.

He jumped as he felt something break inside of him, as if some inner wall or barrier had collapsed.

And suddenly he was looking at himself through Kelpa's eyes. His view was slightly distorted, like looking through one of Master Aslon's lenses, and all of the color seemed to have been leeched from the world. He had never seen himself from this vantage point—it was not at all like looking in a mirror—and found the view disorienting.

He snapped back into his own body with a gasp. Laysa noticed and asked if he was all right.

"Yes. At least I think I am." He explained to her and Rundgar what had just happened, then tried it again.

It worked a second time. Now that the barrier within him had fallen, he could readily enter an animal's point of view. *Perhaps the barrier is something to protect my soul, to keep it from leaving my body while I'm alive.* He decided against telling Laysa about that particular line of reasoning.

He saw a hawk and entered it easily. How far he could see! And despite his own strong fear of heights, he felt no fear at all at being so high above the ground when looking through the bird's eyes.

He continued to test his power and found he could jump from animal to animal. His sight leaped from bird to squirrel to fox to chicken. He tried to leap from the chicken to a spider lurking in the center of a nearby web, but found he could not. When he tried to make the leap, it was as if a new wall sprang up to thwart him. After some more experimentation he seemed certain that, for whatever reason, he could not enter the minds of insects. *Maybe they're too small, or too different from me.* Another question for the wizards, but for now he would put it aside and hone his technique with animals.

He tried commanding the animals when he was looking through their eyes and found that they obeyed him, at least to a certain degree. They were easily distracted in their never-ending quests for food or avoidance of predators, so it took all of his concentration to bend them to his will.

So this is why Gerin is so enamored of magic. It really is an incredible thing. He wondered if even his mighty brother could do what he was doing. He did not remember any discussion or examples of Gerin exerting control over animals, let alone seeing through their eyes. *Ha! I would love to be able to work magic that he can't! Won't that just stick in his craw!*

Sitting on the grass with Kelpa at his side, he concentrated on sensing nearby animals. He found a raven flying toward Castle Hurien and entered it.

He was a hundred feet in the air, wings outstretched to catch the wind and warm updrafts, searching for something to eat. Therain instantly felt hungry and was drawn into the hunt for food with the bird, something that often happened when he first leaped—the mind of the animal overpowered him for an instant until he could reassert his humanness. This was another thing he had not shared with Laysa. He did not want her worrying that he would become lost in the animal minds he entered.

He wondered suddenly what would happen if an animal died while he was seeing through its eyes. Would he return to his own body, shoved unceremoniously from something no longer capable of hosting him? Could he die with it, or would his consciousness become lost, cut off from his own mortal flesh?

Best to make sure that doesn't happen. It was not an experiment he was eager to undertake.

He exerted his will and tried to turn the raven's course

toward the castle, but it did not like the smell of smoke, and Therain was using all of his strength to fight it. He would rapidly weaken at this rate and soon have to return to his own body. He had a wide view of the castle and town below it, and took note of the many Pelklander soldiers stationed at the castle entrances, on the walls, and throughout the town; but he was too far away to discern any detail, and knew he would never be able to see Claressa from there.

Just before he was about to leap out of the raven, he saw a group of prisoners being led from the main castle gate. He knew they were prisoners because they were bound together with a length of rope and surrounded by Pelklander soldiers. He made one last effort to force the raven closer, but it stubbornly refused to obey.

He leaped into a robin perched on a branch near the castle gate. The quick darting movements of the bird's head disoriented him, and again he had to exert his will to keep it as still as possible. He hopped along the branch to gain a better view of the passing prisoners.

Claressa was in the middle of the line, shoulders hunched, her head bowed. She was dirty and disheveled, and that alone was a shock. He had never seen his sister in such a state.

Where were they taking them? There were about a dozen prisoners in the line, but she was the only one he recognized. He did not see Baris or any of the other Toreshes.

He could only think of two possibilities, neither of which he liked.

He returned to his body and opened his eyes.

"I found her," he said.

"Is she all right?" asked Laysa.

"So far. But they're marching her and some other prisoners out of the castle. I'm worried they're going to take them back to the islands as hostages, or execute them as examples. I don't know if they're aware of who she is."

"What is your command, my lord?" asked Rundgar.

"Get your men ready. We have to get her now." Rundgar vehemently protested, but Therain would have none of it. "She's my sister and I'm going to rescue her. This is our best chance, and we're going to take it. I've noted your objections, Captain. Now you can either obey me, or I'll find someone to take your place who will." They were the harshest words he'd ever said to his fiercely loyal captain of the guard, but he was in a foul mood after seeing Claressa in such a state, and filled with dread that, even moving as quickly as they were, they would not be able to rescue her in time.

It was growing dark, which Therain hoped to use in their favor. He sent Laysa away with an escort of five soldiers. She wanted to stay with him, but he explained that it would be more dangerous for them all if he had to worry about keeping her safe while trying to rescue his sister. "Please, trust me in this," he said to her. "Go back to Mileon. Once we have Claressa, we'll meet you there."

"You'd better take care of yourself," she said before leaving. "You've never seen me angry yet, and if you get hurt I'm going to be *very* angry."

Despite the heaviness in his heart, he smiled. "I'll do my best."

"You'd better." She kissed him, and then left with her escort.

Therain had used his power to track Claressa as best he could. The Pelklanders had taken her and the other prisoners to the harbor town and locked them in a small warehouse near the waterfront.

Fortunately, the town was not surrounded by a wall or other defensive fortification. A road wound down from the castle and entered the town from the northwest; another road coming from the farming fields farther inland joined the castle road just outside the town.

Therain and his men were in a long, narrow forest that looked out onto the crossroads. His bowmen had killed five Pelklanders who were watching the edge of the woods, and so far their disappearance had not been noted. But Therain did not count on their luck holding. They had to move quickly.

"Captain, are your men ready?"

"Yes, my lord. They await your command."

"Move as soon as I create the diversion. I don't think you'll have much time, so move fast."

Rundgar signaled his men. Therain sat down and leaned his back against a tree. He cleared his mind, then reached out in a way he never had before. Not to find one animal, or to leap from one to the next, but rather to reach as many as he could find at one time, and issue a single command.

Go to the town! Now! Food there! All the food you will ever need! Go now! Go now!

He tried to include an impression of satiated hunger, of contentedness, to coerce them into going. He needed as many of them to obey as possible, and this seemed the best way to achieve that. By now he well knew that animals were constantly hungry, continually searching for food. He hoped this would overcome their natural aversion to going near humans.

He'd leashed Kelpa to the tree he was propped against. As soon as his command went out, the dog yelped and tried to dash for the town. Therain did not want to lose him, and had not known of any way to exclude the dog from his command, so he'd bound him to the tree. Kelpa yelped again when the rope went taut and struggled against it fiercely but could not get away.

Rundgar and the men around him gasped. Therain opened his eyes.

Hundreds of animals were rushing out of the trees toward the town. Deer, rabbits, squirrels, gophers, even a few bears. And many smaller animals whose trails could be seen in the deepening darkness.

A moment later the air was filled with the screeching of thousands of birds, all swooping toward the town like a cloud. The sound of their screeching and the flutter of their wings was amazingly loud, and sent an instinctive wave of panic through Therain. He saw his men hesitate, overcome by the same fear, and shouted, "Go, damn you, go!"

His soldiers dashed out of the trees and across the open ground toward the town. They were surrounded by the charging animals racing past them in a mad frenzy. Therain had never seen anything like it.

He issued the command again, reinforced it so the animals would not themselves panic and try to flee. Not just yet. Not until Claressa was free.

The Pelklanders on guard had no idea what was happening. The streets were suddenly overrun with animals darting every which way, scrambling up walls and across roofs and into open doors and windows.

They never saw the Khedeshians race into town. Therain had told his men exactly where to find the warehouse. They carried crossbows and killed a dozen Pelklanders before the invaders had even registered that an attack was under way. Several Khedeshians lit torches and hurled them onto thatched roofs that had not burned in the initial assault. Fires blossomed in the growing darkness.

Therain tried to see through some of the animals to determine how well his men who were now out of his direct line of sight were doing. But he was too weakened from the exertion of the command and could not remain in any animal for more than a second or two. He finally gave up trying. He would just have to trust his men.

He issued one last command, this one directed at the birds, who seemed to be causing the most confusion. *Fly low. Into the streets. The men with painted faces are your enemy! Peck out their eyes! Claw their faces!*

Columns of birds darted through the streets, screeching and cawing. People in the town were screaming and shouting, but their cries were almost completely lost in the clamor created by the birds.

A few minutes later the animals began to retreat. He tried to hold them in place, but his efforts had taken so much of his energy that he could not overcome their natural fears. Exhaustion dragged at his limbs; he could barely keep his eyes open. The birds still covered the town like a swirling black cloud, but even they were beginning to disperse.

"My lord, the men are returning," said Rundgar. He

pointed toward a section of town where flames blazed across several roofs.

Therain saw a number of his men, silhouetted by the fires, running out of the town. With an effort, he got to his feet. Kelpa still strained at his leash, but not as madly as before, and more now from annoyance at being bound than from Therain's command.

"Have the archers provide cover if any Pelklanders appear," said Therain to one of his men.

"Already done, my lord. They are positioned at the edge of the forest."

The soldiers and women fleeing the town crossed the open stretch of ground and entered the trees. Though it had grown quite dark, Therain was able to see that one of the women was indeed Claressa. He shrugged off his fatigue and ran to her. When she saw him, she threw her arms around his neck.

He hugged her back. "You got yourself into quite a mess," he said.

She squeezed even harder, as if afraid to let him go. He felt tears against his neck.

"Thank you for coming for me," she said. She pulled away and wiped at her eyes.

"Always."

"Do you know—have you had any word of Baris?"

"None. I'm sorry. We need to leave now. It won't take them long to realize you're gone. We need to be as far from here as we can."

"How did you get the animals to go into the town? I've never seen anything like it. And the birds—"

"I'll tell you when we're away from here. It's a long story."

11

They managed to avoid the Pelklanders and reach Mileon without another fight. The invaders were tightly concentrated in and around the castle and town. They'd heard that two or three smaller sea fortresses had fallen or were besieged, but even those were relatively close to Castle Hurien. Once Therain and the others slipped past the thinly spread outer picket of the Pelklanders, they had no more fears of encountering the enemy ahead of them. So far they had seen no sign of pursuit.

Therain's tale of his newfound magical abilities stunned Claressa. Was everyone in her family a creature of magic except her? She'd once told Balandrick that she had no desire for magic, that the jealousy she felt when Gerin learned he could become an amber wizard was a fleeting thing, a fancy she rejected after learning that a wizard's very long life could not be shared. But that was not true. Deep in her heart she still yearned for both the ability of wielding such might and the long life it granted.

Gerin, then Reshel, and now Therain. "How did this happen?" she asked when he told her about his abilities. "What caused it?"

"Haven't the foggiest," he said. "I just started having dreams about it, then it happened for real."

She'd managed to get Trené and Verdel out with her, along with most of the other prisoners. Verdel was still a wreck, sobbing almost every waking moment, but Trené possessed a resilience and resolve that seemed to grow with each passing day.

They encountered a number of refugees on the road, but no one had any word of Baris or the rest of the Toreshes. Several nights Claressa cried herself to sleep worrying about him. She hated herself for being so weak, but she could not help it. Her emotions had overwhelmed her. She felt powerless and useless. She did not know whether to grieve for her husband or hold out hope that he was still alive.

"What are we going to do about them?" she asked Therain one night around the campfire. "How are we going to drive them out?"

"I don't know. Our resources are stretched dangerously thin. Daqoros knows this. He knows he can't take and hold onto a large piece of land. He doesn't have the men for it even if he emptied the isles. He's taken a small area and is working feverishly to make it his own before we can even consider mounting a counterstrike. I admit, it's clever, using our own weaknesses to his advantage."

"Then we have to move faster. He can't be allowed to keep what he's taken."

Therain sighed. She did not like the sound if it. "There are pressing problems to the north, Claressa. I don't know that we *can* get rid of them."

"Don't even think such a thing. What about Baris and his mother and father?"

"Until we know what's happened to them, it's hard to say what we can do. But let's change the subject. I don't want to upset you, and it will be up to Gerin to decide how the kingdom responds."

How could he talk of defeat, of surrendering to the bloody Pelklander savages? Tears of frustration sprang to her eyes. Day and night she was filled with a consuming hatred toward the invaders so intense that at times she felt that's all there was to her: hate, and a desire for revenge. To do to them what they had done to her.

"Does it hurt?" she said, gesturing to his stump. She was still not used to seeing it.

"Sometimes. I still reach for things with it before I realize my hand's not there anymore. It's like the memory of it keeps it real in my mind."

Laysa shouted with joy when she saw Therain, and ran to meet him. She hugged him and wept, then kissed him hard on the mouth.

"I'm happy to see you, too," he said.

They remained in the town for a day before setting off for the port city of Edonia. From there, Therain planned to catch a ship back to Almaris. It would be faster than traveling overland, and he felt the need for haste.

One drizzling morning two days after leaving Mileon, Therain sensed something he hadn't experienced before. As his powers grew stronger and more refined, he found he could tell one type of animal from another. If he closed his eyes, they appeared in his mind as different points of light of various sizes, shapes, and colors. He could now easily identify a large number of animals with great accuracy.

But this latest sensation was unlike any other. He closed his eyes and saw a deep bluish light that swirled chaotically. He was having trouble sensing exactly where it was, but sensed that it was close.

Then he realized there was more than one.

"Captain, have your men set a perimeter. Something's out there. I don't know what they are, but I don't like them much."

"Yes, my lord."

"Therain?" said Laysa. "What is it?"

"I don't know. I'm going to see what I can find." He held out his hand; she knotted her fingers through his.

He tried to see through the eyes of one of the creatures, and was shocked when he was rebuffed. It felt like he'd slammed his head into a stone wall. Pain shot through his temples. He drew a hissing breath of air through clenched teeth. If he hadn't been sitting, he would have fallen to the ground.

"By the gods, are you all right?"

He opened his eyes and found himself on his back. Laysa was leaning over him, her face drawn with worry.

He sat up. "I'm fine. Whatever's out there doesn't want me to see what it is."

"But Therain, it's an animal. How could it do that?"

"I'm not sure it is just an animal."

"I didn't think your power worked on people."

"It doesn't. I don't think this is a person, either."

The Khedeshians had formed a circle around their camp. "My lord, what are we looking for?" asked Rundgar.

"I don't know." He tried to sense where they were, but the damned things were somehow masking their presence. He could still sense them out there somewhere, but could not discern in what direction. It was maddening.

Then they disappeared.

"Captain, I've lost them. I want to get moving. Keep your men on alert. I can't tell if they've gone beyond my range or are somehow hiding themselves from me."

He did not sense them the rest of that day. He slept fitfully that night, worried that the things would try to enter the camp when he was asleep. But the night passed without incident. He kept his men on alert the next day as well, but the things, whatever they were, did not reappear.

Therain was almost asleep the next night when he sensed them. They were very close; it was as if their dark light had erupted from nowhere.

He jumped to his feet. "Be ready! Something's out there in the dark!"

It's like they can mask their presence until they get too close to hide any longer, he thought. *But what in Shayphim's bloody name* are *they?*

One of the soldiers on the perimeter screamed. Therain instinctively stepped in front of Laysa and Claressa.

Three quatans—the same bloody things that had bitten off his hand—were charging the camp from different directions.

Two of his men held firm as a quatan lunged at them with its four arms, the halo of tentacles darting forward from the back of its head, the tiny mouths at the end of each open and hungry. The creature was blindingly fast and avoided the first sword-thrust aimed at one of its claws. Its lower set of arms were long enough to catch the ankles of both soldiers. Before the men could react, the quatan heaved up and knocked them on their backs. It slashed open the throat of one man, then fell upon the other, its tentacles latching onto his face, where they began to feed.

Laysa and Claressa were both screaming. Kelpa stood by Therain, legs splayed, hackles on end, ears flat against his head, growling fiercely. The other quatans were darting about the perimeter, trying to find an opening, but Therain's archers were keeping them at bay. One of the creatures let out a howl of rage as an arrow sank deep into its shoulder.

"Enough of this bloody nonsense," said Therain.

He reached out toward the creatures with his powers. Now that he knew what they were, he had no hesitation. He battered against their defenses with such brutal force that they immediately opened to him.

The next instant, he was inside their minds.

He lost his balance and fell into Claressa, knocking them both over. The view through the quatan's eyes was disorienting. Everything was tinted red, and fractured as if he were looking through a piece of shattered glass.

But he didn't care what he was seeing. He didn't need to see anything at all. He needed to send a command.

Pain! Deep, burning pain!

The quatans howled and began to flail.

Shayphim take you all, I want you to die!

But he did not have the strength. Sending pain was far too difficult for him. He knew he had to stop. He was already so weak that he would have to vacate them in moments and return to his own sweat-drenched body.

Go away! Go away and never come back or I'll send even more pain! Enough to kill you!

Therain sent the command with all the strength he had left. He did not think the creatures could know he was bluffing. If they understood him, it was not because they grasped his words; they did not, after all, understand Kelarin. But

like other animals, he hoped that they could understand the
intent of his words, divining the meaning the same way he
could tell the difference between a dog growling in anger
and barking in happiness.

He was about to return to his body, his strength almost
gone. But just before he left the creatures, he sensed a power
similar to his own, a power of *command*, that connected the
creatures to something else.

A man.

Therain tried to follow the connection, to see if he could
learn anything about the master of these monsters, Kursil
Rulhámad. Gerin had learned the man's name during his
captivity at the hands of the Soul Stealer. If only he could—

His strength abruptly failed. His eyes snapped open—his
own eyes—but he was so exhausted it was all he could do to
keep them from closing once more.

"Captain . . . "

"They're retreating, my lord," said Rundgar.

"What *were* those things?" shrieked Claressa. Therain had
never seen his sister in such a hysterical state before. It was
shocking, almost unseemly. He looked away, oddly embarrassed, as if he had caught her half dressed.

Laysa knelt down and stroked his face.

"The same gods-damned things that bit off my bloody
hand, that's what."

Kursil Rulhámad, wretch of Tulqan the Harridan, white-
haired and red-skinned maegosi of the Kelanim tribe, who
possessed the power to control quatans with his thoughts,
reeled at what had just happened. It should not have been,
could not have been. Yet it was.

Someone else had controlled his quatans. Sent them commands, sent them *pain*.

Kursil had sensed the man who had done this just before
his quatans were forced to retreat, driven off by the stranger's power. The same power that had drawn Kursil to this
place to begin with.

He remained hidden in the ruins of an abandoned building, his back against the inner corner of a fieldstone wall, and waited for his quatans, wounded and in pain, to return.

He did not understand what had happened. Days ago he had faintly sensed another being with powers similar to his own. Not another true maegosi, but something similar. He was both curious and afraid. Had the Steadfast brought another maegosi to these foreign shores without his knowledge? Had this being been sent to kill him and steal his quatans?

But the power was strange, different in many ways. He felt he could block the stranger from commanding his quatans, and so had drawn closer, wondering what he would find. He had expected to find another of his own kind, or at least one of the Steadfast. Not a native of these lands, which had no maegosi or quatans, if one believed that bastard Gerin Atreyano.

The quatans limped miserably into the ruins, the protrusions on their spines glinting in the moonlight like silvered knives. One had an arrow in his shoulder. Enraged, Kursil rose and removed it, then tended to the creature.

While he worked he pondered this mystery. After a time he gave up. He could not explain it, and was not one to devote much thought to abstractions. He would shadow this man, and if the opportunity arose, he would take him. It was the only way he could understand what had happened.

12

The land of Curitaen near the northern border of Khedesh had been disputed and fought over since before the coming of the Raimen. Curitaen was a fertile stretch of ground straddling the Candago River, whose deep, swift waters formed a natural border between Khedesh and Threndellen. When the Targee and Huliquana had first migrated to these lands from the far south during the height of the Atalari's Shining Nation, the two tribes warred bitterly for control of the forested hills and fertile pastures, until they nearly annihilated one another. Weakened by generations of battle, they were no match for the more advanced Tlot'ka, whose bronze-clad warhorses finished off the remnants of the Targee and Huliquana forever.

The Tlot'ka enjoyed several centuries of relative calm before the Doomwar scorched large swaths of Osseria, Curitaen among them. After the war, the Tlot'ka migrated northward for several generations while the burned lands healed, then returned to their abandoned settlements and rebuilt and refortified them. Nine hundred years later they were eradicated by the Great Plague that killed half of the surviving Atalari and a third of the Gendalos races.

Gerin crouched behind a horn of rock sticking out of an exposed hillside. The horn had once been the foundation stone of a Tlot'ka shrine, and was now all that remained visible of what had been their largest settlement.

"Looks to be upward of fifteen thousand people down there, Your Majesty," said Balandrick from over Gerin's shoulder. They were perched above a long, narrow valley in which hundreds of campfires burned. "Can you tell if they're Threndish? It's too dark for me to make out any standards."

Gerin created a Farseeing and directed it at the encampment. The men they saw were not regular soldiers. Only a few wore armor, scrounged bits of plate and mail and an occasional helm. He could see no uniforms, no insignia of rank, though it was apparent from the way certain men were treated that some sort of command structure existed.

"I don't think they're Threndish," said Gerin.

"What's a small army doing camped on Khedeshian soil?" asked Balan.

"I have no idea. If we'd kept to the roads, I'm sure we would have come across someone who could answer that for us."

"Come now, Your Majesty. You know very well why I insisted we stay off the roads. It would be insanity for the king of Khedesh to be seen heading into Threndellen. Sometimes *I* still can't believe we're going to do it."

Gerin slowly moved the Farseeing across the army until he found what looked like the command area. The tents were larger and watched by well-armed guards. There was also a raised platform where someone could address the assembled men.

Behind Gerin, Elaysen let out a gasp. "It's Aidrel!"

Gerin jumped at her cry. "Where? I don't see —" Then he spotted the excommunicated member of Aunphar's Inner Circle. Aidrel Entraly had appeared from within the large tent in the center of the command area. Three other men were with him.

"So this priest of the One God has gone and raised himself an army?" asked Balandrick. "What for?"

"He's not a priest," said Elaysen. "He never was."

Balandrick shrugged. "Still, what's he planning to do?"

"If he's going to carry out the plans he told my father, then this army of his is for waging a holy war against those who refuse to accept the teachings of the One God," said Elaysen. "They're his Helion Spears." Her voice was tight with rage.

"Someone in Ezren has to know what he's planning," said Gerin. "I can see the damn city walls over that ridge."

"I'll send some of my men to find out," said Balandrick.

Gerin used the Farseeing for a few more minutes, then returned to the camp on the other side of the hill. The two companies of Taeratens accompanying them were well hidden from the ragtag army in the valley below them.

"You can't allow him to do this," said Elaysen. "This is an abomination of my father's ideas. You have to stop him."

"First I need to learn what he intends," said Gerin. "But if all he's going to do is march his fanatics into Threndellen so they can get ground up between the Threndish army and the Havalqa, I'm going to let them go, and good riddance to the lot."

After the visit by the *akesh*, he had quickly made arrangements to leave the city. He told his Minister of the Realm, Terl Enkelares, that he was going to visit Ailethon, and gave as few details as possible. Balandrick had arranged the Taeraten escort. Only after they were on their way had the Taeratens been told their true destination, and why. Gerin knew that if he'd revealed it to Enkelares before leaving, the minister would have done everything in his power to prevent the journey, so his only option was secrecy.

Impulsively, he sent word to Elaysen that he was leaving the city for a time and that if she wanted to accompany him, he would be pleased to have her teach him more of *dalaraelom,* away from the watchful eyes of the court.

She had complained to him that he neglected his studies of her father's religion because of political considerations, which was quite true. He thought this was a way of remedying that.

It was nearing midnight when Balandrick's men returned from Ezren. They'd learned that Aidrel had been building his army there for months. "Hundreds more keep coming every day. Seems this Aidrel sent messengers out all across this part of Khedesh, whipping people into a frenzy about this One God of his, and that if they wanted to fight a holy war against evil they should come to Ezren."

"Where is he planning to fight this holy war?" asked Gerin.

"Everyone in Ezren said his eyes are turned toward Threndellen, Your Majesty. They say he constantly talks about the infidels to the north and how they'll cleanse the land with their holy spears until only true believers remain."

Elaysen made a sound of utter disgust, then wheeled about and stormed off to her tent.

"Balan, I want you to leave a few men here to observe these Helion Spears. If they give *any* indication that they're going to wage their little war within our borders, I want Aidrel arrested immediately and this army dispersed. I'll write a letter for the men to send to Lord Commander Levkorail with instructions for carrying out my will. If Aidrel resists, kill him. If they don't disperse, kill as many as it takes to drive the point home that I will *not* tolerate a religious war on Khedeshian soil."

They crossed the Candago River on an old stone bridge on lands claimed and controlled by Khedesh, though it had not always been so. In fact, the region of Pelmae changed hands about once a century, alternating between Khedeshian and Threndish control. Those who lived there were a mix of peoples from the two countries, so intermarried by this point that they felt no strong allegiance to either kingdom. Whenever skirmishes broke out for control of the fertile stretch of countryside, the natives simply kept out of the way until the fighting was done, then began paying their taxes and tributes to whatever side emerged victorious.

For the past sixty years Pelmae had been controlled by the Khedeshians, since the Battle of Tarloe's Mill, when the Threndish general Melaisa'odon was soundly defeated in a three day battle that ended with the near total destruction of the Threndish forces in the fields surrounding the eponymous mill. The bridge that Gerin and his company crossed stood within easy sight of the mill, which had survived the battle virtually untouched.

Balandrick did not want them to keep to any roads. As

soon as they crossed the bridge, they set out toward the northwest, passing farming fields and homesteads. They did not light fires and kept careful watches at night. The wizards set up tocsin spells beyond the perimeter set by the Taeratens to alert them should any people approach.

One evening at dusk, the sky ahead of them lit up with flash after flash of lightning. It was an odd sight since the sky above was clear except for a few thin wisps of clouds. The lightning struck a small area, as if drawn by something on the ground.

"Something seems wrong with that storm," said Gerin to the other two wizards. "Look at that lightning." He invoked a Seeing, but the spell revealed no magical power or anything unnatural about it.

"Looks fine to me," said Abaru. "It's just a small storm."

"It does seem a little strange, but nothing to worry about," said Hollin. "It's not coming this way."

They witnessed one final crack of lightning, then the sky was silent and still.

"There, it's already passed," said Abaru.

Gerin said nothing, but he could not shake the strong feeling that something about the lightning had been unnatural, wrong.

The following evening, Gerin was almost asleep when he heard a commotion outside his tent.

Someone was approaching their camp.

He found the two wizards already conferring with Balandrick. "Someone tripped our tocsin spells," said Hollin.

"Where?" asked Gerin.

Balandrick pointed westward. They all started in that direction when a soldier ahead of them called out, "I have him!"

Three Khedeshians escorted a lone man to the center of the encampment. Gerin was startled by the sight of him.

He was naked, but seemed neither concerned nor embarrassed by his lack of clothing. But almost more startling than his nakedness was the absolute perfection of his body. Lean, well-muscled, his skin pale and unblemished, with no scars of any kind that Gerin could see.

He did not look deranged, and was obviously well fed and in peak physical health. *Then why is he wandering the countryside without any clothes?*

"What brings you here?" said Balandrick. "Were you robbed? Are you injured?"

"No. I am quite well." His voice was deep, strong. He did not speak with a Threndish accent; indeed, he spoke with no discernable accent at all. He sounded almost amused. Several times he glanced at his own hands as if marveling at them.

"Someone get him clothes," said Balandrick. He gestured for the soldiers to keep him at some distance from Gerin. "What's your name?"

"My perceptions here are quite amazing," he said. "Much different from what I had expected."

Maybe he is mad, thought Gerin. *A lunatic escaped from a prison.*

"Greetings, Gerin Atreyano."

The sound of steel rang out as soldiers drew their swords and pointed them at the stranger.

"How do you know my name?"

A soldier arrived with a robe that he tossed to the stranger, who regarded it as if unsure of what it was. Then he pulled it on over his head.

"The servants of the Adversary have begun to meddle in the affairs of the world," he said. "Your sword, the one that pierces the heart of this mortal realm, and the opening of the Path of Ashes, have altered the world in such a way that the Adversary's powers are growing much faster than they had been."

The hair on Gerin's arms and the back of his neck stood on end. "How do you know these things? Who are you?"

The stranger smiled, revealing perfect white teeth. "I am Zaephos," he said, "messenger of the One God."

13

Drexos had been right about one thing. Using the Stone made him sleep.

The connection was constantly with Tyne now. When he blinked he could sometimes see flashes of the dragons as they winged across the sky on their way to him. At first the images were so disorienting that he stumbled and at times fell. He tried to stop them, but could not. Apparently, the connection could not be constricted, at least that he could find.

He did grow used to the images so that they no longer impaired him and marveled at how a body could acclimate itself to the most extreme circumstances.

When he concentrated, he could close his eyes and spend long minutes among the dragons. The sense of vertigo he'd experienced from having a vantage point so high in the air and moving so swiftly also lessened over time.

But the price for such time spent using the connection was sleep.

When the fatigue washed over him, he staggered to the closest place that offered concealment—usually a stand of trees, as these lands were flat and open—and collapsed. He had no way of knowing how long he slept, but it often felt like days. He had strange dreams, not only of the dragons, but of Drexos and his shadow-wreathed form, which inspired only terror and dread in him. He dreamed sometimes of the figure within the Stone, a thing that raged against its prison.

Tyne was ravenous when he woke. He needed more food, and spent some time hunting and dressing his kills so he could replenish his provisions.

He passed a handful of villages and towns on his journey eastward and continued to make discreet inquiries about the bronze demon, but the trail was still cold. He did not tarry in most places, preferring to sleep alone in some secluded spot away from people. He feared that others would somehow sense the Stone and try to steal it from him.

He did, however, stop at taverns from time to time to listen to the locals and spend some of his precious coin on an occasional beer. He wondered if he might overhear a snippet of conversation about the bronze demon that the taverngoers would be reluctant to share with an obvious foreigner when he inquired directly. He was always given suspicious looks when he asked about the demon—whether because of his accent, the subject of his inquiry, or both, he could not say. But he worried that even if they knew something, they would not tell him out of spite.

In one tavern in a town whose name he did not know, he overheard a conversation that made his heart skip a beat and a chill run down his spine.

"I hear things are quite a mess along the coast," said the barkeep to a well-dressed fat man seated at the largest table in the room. From the cut of his clothes and the many jeweled rings on his thick fingers, Tyne took him for a merchant.

"Rumors of invaders from across the sea and kingdoms falling to them left and right," continued the barkeep. "Just so they stay to the coast and don't turn their eyes toward us."

"You have no idea, Jarmayne," said the merchant. "Eastern Khedesh is in chaos. Yes, their new king drove the invaders off their shores, but they haven't fully recovered from the blockade. Trade is erratic at best. Threndellen is so awash with the invaders that I can't get so much as a bolt of wool or a single ruby out of the country. It's been a disaster for business. I did what I could in Khedesh and got out. Not sure when I'll be going back. I've heard the invaders kidnap anyone they come across for slave labor. That's too much of a risk, even for me."

"That'll be the day, you doing labor." The barkeep snorted a laugh. "And what about the Khedeshian king? A magician of some kind, is what I heard."

"Yes, and that's not the most scandalous thing about him." The merchant's voice dropped a little, but he was a big man and even a whisper for him carried through part of the room, so Tyne had no trouble hearing him. "There are rumors in the city he had his father murdered so he could claim the throne."

"You don't say!" Jarmayne slapped his hand on the scarred wooden surface of the bar. "And he's still king? The nobles didn't rise up against him?"

"Oh, some of them are grumbling, but they can't prove he did it. It's such a strange story . . . "

"So let's hear it!"

"What I heard is that a demon of some kind appeared and killed the king—the *old* king—and then knelt before the new one, like it was his servant. They said this thing was ten feet tall! Ten feet!"

"So what happened to it?"

"Just vanished. Disappeared like it had never existed. The new king swears he had nothing to do with it, but I don't believe it."

"Me, too. To think, a son killing his father." He shook his head.

Tyne could not believe his good fortune. For months he'd been searching for word of the demon, with little success. And now he not only learned it was somewhere in Khedesh, but that it had apparently done the bidding of the new king— Gerin Atreyano.

Drexos was right, he thought. *Gerin is someone I need to kill. Such an evil man does not deserve to live.*

Several days later Tyne could feel the dragons getting close. The connection was stronger than it had ever been. Images of the dragons flashed in his vision every few seconds, but he'd learned to ignore them as easily as he ignored the blinking of his own eyes.

His heart raced when he saw a smudge on the horizon and realized he was actually seeing them for the first time. In the distance, they looked like a large flock of birds, but he knew with absolute certainty that it was the dragons he had called.

He waited on the hard-packed dirt road for them to arrive. Around him, waist-high grass swept unbroken toward the horizon like a vast green sea.

It did not take long for the dragons to close the distance. Though he'd seen them in his visions for weeks and weeks, the sight of them took his breath away.

They were majestic, powerful—and *beautiful*.

They reached him and began to circle overhead, creating a cyclone of wind that swirled the grasses and blew across him like a gale. He could smell them in the wind; a scent of leather mingled with a metallic odor and the faint whiff of sulfur. They cast enormous shadows on the earth as they wheeled over his head.

He felt reborn in the wind, becoming something greater than what he had been.

Come to me, he commanded through the Stone.

The largest of the dragons veered off from the rest, and with an ear-shattering roar, dived toward the ground. Tyne felt no fear at the approach of such a gargantuan beast. He knew he controlled them completely, that they could cause him no harm while he carried the Stone.

The dragon's massive wings extended to their full span to break its dive; it alighted almost gently in front of him. Its thick back legs touched first, then its long body dropped slowly until its forelegs reached the ground, the long claws flexing on the grass. The wings folded above its back as its neck arched high, the triangular head bent down toward him.

"You're the leader of the flock," Tyne said aloud. "Or whatever they call groups of dragons. Bow your head. Recognize me as *your* leader."

He sent the command through the Stone into the dragon. He sensed the pain it caused the beast, bending it to his will. The Stone's touch was not gentle.

The dragon's head lowered until it almost touched the ground.

"Very good. Get up now. We have work to do."

The dragon raised its head and released a gout of fire high into the air. The others circling overhead roared and belched fire of their own. The swirling wind grew hot and carried a stench of sulfur.

Tyne could not stop grinning. The world was about to change.

14

Gerin stared at the stranger in shock. "You can't be Zaephos," he said at last. "Zaephos is not a man."

"I assure you I am who I say I am. Do you remember when I appeared to you on the road to Hethnost? And again in the palace of the king?"

"Come with me," Gerin said, turning toward his tent. This was not a conversation he wanted to have in public. He told Balandrick and the other wizards to join him.

In Gerin's tent, Zaephos looked around with an expression of amusement. "Interesting, this mortal form." He ran his fingertips along the canvas of the tent, then down one of the wooden support poles.

Hollin was already working a Seeing. "He's human as far as I can tell."

"Of course I am," said Zaephos. "I've created this body in the mortal realm. I wished to experience this existence directly. It is quite different from my earlier visitations to you and Aunphar."

"Then you *were* the one who appeared to him," said Gerin.

"Yes. It was my task to set both of you on your paths."

Gerin fought down his sudden anger at the idea of being manipulated, of his fate determined by another. "What did you mean when you said my sword, Nimnahal, was helping the Adversary grow stronger more quickly?"

"And what is the Path of Ashes?" asked Balan.

Zaephos cocked his head. "I thought I was clear. The power of your weapon pierces this mortal realm. It has allowed the power of the Adversary to grow more quickly than it would have otherwise. Already he has assumed a physical incarnation."

"The gods save us, Gerin," said Hollin. "You must destroy Nimnahal at once."

Zaephos shrugged. "You may if you wish, but it will have no effect on the Adversary, for good or ill. He has made use of what he can. And it may be that your sword will have some part yet to play in the battle against him. I would counsel you against rash actions.

"As for the Path of Ashes, that is a gateway those you know as the Havalqa have built that connects this continent to their homeland across the sea. It, too, pierces this mortal realm to create a bridge that allows them to pass easily from this land to Aleith'aqtar."

"That's how they're getting so many soldiers!" said Balandrick.

"Yes," said Zaephos. "A brief march takes them from the far side of the sea to this continent."

"Are you here to help us fight the Adversary?" asked Gerin.

"Not directly. There are laws that govern what I may and may not do. But I will give you what guidance and counsel I may."

Later, alone in his tent, Gerin thought about what Zaephos had said. The news that Gerin's creation of Nimnahal was partly responsible for the Adversary gaining power faster than he would have otherwise was devastating. *What have I done?* he wondered, unable to sleep. *Every choice I make, no matter how well-intentioned, goes awry.* The guilt and self-doubt that had gripped him after his failure with the Baryashin spell and Reshel's death returned with renewed fury. He felt paralyzed, unsure of every decision. Was this journey to the Watchtowers also destined to end in disaster? Was he sending them all headlong to their doom?

Once more he missed Reshel keenly, with a palpable, physical ache. She would know what to say to help him recover his courage, his determination, his certainty in the rightness of his choices. Something that now, in the dead silence of night, he could not find for himself.

Elaysen was stunned upon meeting Zaephos the next morning. When she was told who and what he was, she began interrogating him with the ferocity of a high inquisitor, asking him questions about the One God, the strictures of *dalar-aelom,* the role of emissaries, the heresies of Aidrel, and more.

Zaephos listened to her questions with a decided lack of urgency or interest.

Gerin watched as Elaysen grew agitated with the lack of answers from the One God's messenger. He either ignored her questions outright or offered unhelpful comments, such as, "It is not for me to reveal such knowledge."

At one point, after receiving that answer for the fourth or fifth time, she threw up her hands and groaned in frustration. "Then why are you here?"

"As I told the others last night, I have come to experience this existence as mortals do."

"But why won't you answer my questions?"

"Because they are questions you need to answer for yourself."

She faced him squarely. "Will you answer this for me? You said to King Gerin once that even a prophet may not fully understand what he is shown. What is it my father does not understand? What has he done wrong?"

"That is something I cannot answer. That message was for Gerin."

"Cannot or will not?"

"That is all I will say."

They kept their course close to the southern border of Threndellen. The lands were less populated, and should they find themselves confronting overwhelming military odds, they could flee back into Khedesh relatively quickly. It was Balandrick's intent to continue on this path until they reached the Redhorn Hills before angling their path more to the northwest, toward the Ozul Mountains and the Hollow, where the Watchtowers stood in their millennial silence.

"We've been lucky," Balandrick said to Gerin one night. "I must say I'm surprised we've come so far without running into anyone."

"It's a big country," said Abaru. "Even with all of these soldiers, we're still just a speck in the wilderness."

"Don't forget that the Havalqa are farther to the east," said Hollin. "Their presence may have drawn off some of the fighting men from all across the country. Most of the castles and fortresses we've seen looked relatively empty."

The company was riding across an open field hemmed to the south with a low line of tree-capped hills, when arrows began to rain down upon them. One Taeraten caught a shaft in his neck, just above his mail shirt, and tumbled from his horse.

Instantly the other soldiers angled their shields and formed a protective cordon around Gerin. Arrows clanged against steel and caromed off armor. Gerin and the wizards formed Wardings to protect the company, overlapping their spells to achieve a wide area of coverage.

The attackers were among the trees atop the line of hills. Balandrick shouted orders for the Taeratens to charge up the slopes and kill whomever they found. Elaysen hurried to the wounded soldier and implored him to be still so she could tend to him.

A third of the men broke away and galloped toward the hills, hunched low behind shields and their horses' armored necks and heads. The wizards raised their Wardings to allow them to pass.

Gerin saw movement in the trees. He created a Farseeing but could not discern much. He could not make out if the men who'd attacked them were regular soldiers or a band of locals who'd foolishly decided to attempt to drive off a company of well-armed and well-trained men riding through their lands.

"Your Majesty, I think we should retreat to a more secure location," said Balandrick. "We're in the open here, exposed on all sides."

The Taeratens disappeared into the trees. "Not just yet, Balan. We've erected some protections of our own, though you can't see them. We're quite safe."

Balandrick looked displeased, but resigned himself to Gerin's wishes. "As you say, Your Majesty."

The distance and the trees muffled any sounds of battle. Gerin strained his hearing, but even his sensitive ears could not make out anything.

A single rider emerged from the trees a short while later. He kept his horse to a quick trot as he crossed the field.

"Your Majesty, Captain Balandrick, the enemy has been routed," the man announced after a quick salute. "They look to be a band of outlaws. Poorly trained, though a few fought well. We killed most of them, but a handful managed to reach their horses and made off. Commander Gertheles decided not to give pursuit. If you decide otherwise, Your Majesty, I'll relay the message to him and we'll give chase."

"No. There's no need for us to spend time hunting down outlaws in Threndellen."

Zaephos had watched the exchange with a stoic expression. It seemed to annoy Balandrick.

"If we'd been attacked by trained soldiers, would you have helped us?" he asked the messenger of the One God.

"No." Zaephos did not bother to look at Balandrick when he replied, but it did not seem to Gerin to be a slight or a sign of contempt. Zaephos was watching four deer running in the distance and did not want to shift his attention away from them.

Balandrick looked shocked by the answer. "No? You would do *nothing*?"

His eyes still on the deer, Zaephos said, "There is nothing I could do."

"Doesn't a god's messenger have magic or power of some kind?"

"I do not use magic. That is a mortal power, consigned to this realm and those who dwell within it. My power springs from beyond, in the realm of the divine." The deer had vanished from sight, and finally Zaephos turned to faced Balandrick. "Divine power is not for use in the mortal world. When I assumed this mortal form, I severed myself from much of my divine nature. This body could not endure the might of my native power. Even if I were to destroy this form and grasp my divine energy, you would be destroyed along with your enemies. It is too potent. As I told you, there are laws that bind even such as me. Laws the Adversary seeks to overthrow."

"Do you enjoy this mortal form?" asked Abaru.

"I am intrigued by this experience," he replied. "It was difficult and costly for me to assume it, and if this body were destroyed, it would be a long time before I could enter the mortal realm again."

The Taeratens appeared atop the hills. It did not look as if they had lost a single soldier.

Gerin saw that they'd taken a captive. A lone figure, hands bound together at the wrists, which were in turn connected to one of the Taeraten saddles with a length of rope, ran along behind them, barely managing to keep from falling and being dragged.

Gods above, it's a woman! Gerin realized when they got a little closer.

Commander Gertheles saluted Gerin and bowed his head. "Your Majesty, my men dispatched the enemy. All are dead but seven or eight who fled on horseback."

"Who is your prisoner?"

Gertheles grinned. "Ah, Your Majesty, she's a feisty one. Handy with knives. Almost took poor Karhl's head off throwing one from thirty feet away. If he'd got his shield up a second slower . . . " He drew his finger across his throat. "Mengol managed to swing around behind her and kick her in the back to knock her down, then jumped off his horse and pinned her. I guess I should say *tried* to pin her, since she flipped him on his back and broke his nose with her elbow before he knew what hit him." The commander barked a laugh.

"Wasn't funny, sir," said Mengol, whose mashed nose was still leaking blood. "I was trying not to hurt her. She just got away from me, is all. Slippery, like she was greased up."

"You were lucky Pelli was there to save your sorry hide," said the commander. "Corporal Pelli threw himself on her as she was getting to her feet. He just laid on top of her until some of the others could come over and get her tied up all nice and tight. We took the rest of her knives, too. Decent weapons. She had thirteen on her, if you can believe it."

"Bring her here, Commander," said Gerin. He needed to decide what to do with her.

She was brought to him, hands still bound, flanked by two Taeratens, with a third behind her.

She started at Gerin proudly, defiantly. Her thick red hair was bound with a strip of cloth across her forehead and tied again at the base of her neck, though in the attack much of it had pulled loose and hung down wildly across her face.

She wore tight-fitting pants tucked into knee-high leather boots. Thin strips of leather wound about her thighs; tucked into the strips of leather were knife sheaths. The gentle curve of her hips narrowed to a slender waist, cinched with a belt from which dangled more sheaths. She wore an open-collared tunic beneath a leather vest.

"Answer my questions truthfully and you may yet live," said Gerin. "I have no use for you if you lie or defy me. A simple question first. Who are you?"

Her eyes narrowed a little with suspicion. "You are not the king's men. You speak like a Khedeshian."

"Do not try my patience. Answer me, or this conversation—and you life—will come to a swift end."

She spat blood onto the ground. "My name is Nyene Isadoura." She stared at him coldly, still full of defiance. He saw no fear in her.

"And who were your companions? Outlaws?"

Her expression darkened with fury. "They're *fools*. I told him that attacking you was absurd. I told him to wait at least until night, but that idiot Loár never listens to a word I say, and the other fools follow his inane advice without question. I hope the whoreson is dead. He is a disaster."

"You did not answer my second question."

"We are the Hael Kouref. We fight the king's dogs who stole our lands and drove our families from our homes."

"As you noted, we do not serve King Kua'tani," said Gerin.

She spat more blood. "You are Khedeshians. You have no right to be in our lands."

"We are only passing through, Nyene Isadoura. If you had not attacked us, we would have left you alone."

"Now who is the one telling lies?"

One of the soldiers cuffed the side of her face. "Watch your tongue," he growled.

She glared murderously at the soldier, then returned her gaze to Gerin. "And who are you that I should believe what you say?"

"Who I am and what we are doing is of no concern to you. But I believe you have been truthful, and for that I grant you your life. You'll accompany us. I'll release you when we reach the northern border of Threndellen, provided you attempt no treachery before then. And do not try to escape. If you do, your punishment will be swift, and final. I guarantee you cannot get away from us before we wish it. There are wizards among us."

"I'm not such a fool as to believe your lies."

"Fortunately, your lack of belief does not change the facts. You'll find out for yourself soon enough."

"You'll never make it through our country."

"Then you'll suffer whatever fate befalls us."

15

They buried the soldier who'd been struck with an arrow in the neck. Elaysen was joined by Hollin soon after the Taeratens charged the hills, but the man's injury was too severe. Nyene was given his horse, though her hands remained tied and leashed to a Taeraten who rode close beside her.

That night, Abaru worked a Binding spell on the Threndish woman to prevent her from moving while she slept. "What has happened to me?" she cried out in alarm as she lay on the ground.

"A precaution to ensure you don't sneak off," said Gerin.

"How did you do this?" She seemed close to panic.

"I told you, there are wizards among us. One of them has put a spell upon you. Struggling against it is pointless."

Gerin watched her ignore his advice and strain against the invisible bonds.

"You're just going to grow exhausted, but if that's how you want to spend the night, enjoy yourself. I'm going to get some sleep."

She swore at him as he walked away.

For a few days Nyene was mostly silent, answering only the most basic questions put to her by Gerin or one of the wizards. The soldiers did not speak to her except to issue orders; even Balan had no interest in her other than ensuring that she did not escape or interfere with their plans.

"So why must Khedeshians come to the great land of Threndellen?" she asked one evening. It was the first question she'd posed since they set out after the battle. "What is it we have that you feel you must steal?"

"We're not going to steal anything," said Gerin. "And our destination is not in Threndellen."

"Then you are either lying or very lost," she said. "There is nothing to the north except the Landwall Mountains, and our border runs to their foothills."

"The Hollow is not claimed by the Threndish," said Gerin.

"There is nothing in the Hollow but dark spirits and shadows," she said.

"Then you don't have to worry about us stealing anything from it."

"Why did you say 'the great land of Threndellen'?" asked Elaysen. "I thought you hated your country."

Nyene looked at Gerin. "Is she your whore?"

Elaysen let out a gasp of shock as her face reddened. "I am no such thing! I'm a healer!"

"You are as stupid as some of the whores I have met. I do not hate my country. I love my country. Threndellen is the greatest nation in the world. What I hate is our *king*, an inbred monstrosity who should have been strangled with his umbilical cord the moment his neck emerged from his mother's diseased womb. I will fight him until he is overthrown and his foul carcass fed to the dogs, or until I am dead. Until one of those things happens, there will be no peace."

"You said before he was stealing your land," said Gerin. "What for?"

"Because these regions are some of the richest in our country. The whoreson Kua'tani was not content with making himself rich from the jewels and gold we sent him. No, that was not enough. He wanted the mines for himself, and so he sent his men to drive us off so he could claim them as his own. He murdered hundreds of my people." Her voice had gone flat, cold. "Others he forced to work the mines and build him a palace atop the Surbal Heights with a view of the valley below.

"That is what brought the Hael Kouref into existence. We fight against the injustices of our mad king. That is what your men destroyed." She could not keep the bitterness from her last words.

"Then you shouldn't have attacked us," said Gerin. "We're not your enemies."

For the first time since her capture, Gerin saw tears in Nyene's eyes. "That fool Loár has ruined everything," she muttered, more to herself than anyone else.

"I'll tell you this," said Gerin. "Our mission will benefit every nation in Osseria, not just Khedesh. If you truly love Threndellen, then you won't try to thwart us."

"I still do not believe you," she said. The tears were gone, her expression hard. "The truth will come out."

"Yes, it will. And if you are present to witness it, you'll be quite surprised." .

The One God's messenger was staring at the sunset and the pink-splashed sky surrounding it. "It is beautiful, is it not?"

"Yes, very," said Gerin.

"That will change if the Adversary achieves his goals."

"That's why we're going to the Watchtowers. So we can find the Words of Making." A sudden thought occurred to Gerin. "Wait! Do *you* know where they are?"

"I do not. There are many things hidden from me, and many others I am forbidden to speak of."

Gerin's excitement drained away. He doubted now that Zaephos would prove to be much help at all.

"I have another question for you." Gerin described the attack by the Vanil that killed his father. "We know little about them. How could one appear now, after so many thousands of years? And why did it kneel to me?"

Zaephos scowled, and that alone sent a shiver down Gerin's back. He'd never seen the messenger show displeasure before.

"Many of the Vanil were servants of the Adversary," he said. "They warred violently with one another, until those who followed the Adversary were victorious. The defeated Vanil left this world through doors now long shut. The victors worked to help their master enter the world, but when they realized that he would not emerge for tens of thousands of years, many of them followed their brethren and left this world for others.

"But a few remained behind, unwilling to forsake their goals. They fashioned barrows where they could sleep until the Adversary finally arose."

"So that's what awoke it?" asked Gerin. "The Adversary achieving physical form in this world?"

"Perhaps. But I also said your sword's creation helped the Adversary. It may be that the Vanil who appeared to you was drawn by the power of your sword and believed that you, too, were a servant of its master. Or it may have wished to acknowledge you for awakening it."

Gerin felt light-headed. "So *I'm* the one who awoke it?"

"I cannot say for sure, but I think it likely."

He turned away from Zaephos, his chest tight. Hollin and Abaru had proposed this very idea to him, but he had not been convinced by their argument, and the interruption of the *akesh* drove it from his thoughts.

But now Zaephos confirmed that his sword had drawn the Vanil.

He felt cursed, that every choice he made was doomed to turn against him. First Reshel, now his father. *I'm responsible for his death. Gods above, what other tragedies will I inflict upon my family?* He wondered if those who believed he called the demon to kill the king were so wrong after all.

"What is it?" asked Elaysen, who saw him walking past. "You don't look well, my lord." Gerin had commanded everyone not to refer to him as "Your Majesty" or make other references to his station because of Nyene. Regardless of her feelings toward her Threndish rulers, he did not want her to know that she traveled with the King of Khedesh.

Gerin opened his mouth but could not speak. How could he make her understand the magnitude of what he had done? It was unimaginable. It was too much; words failed him. He shook his head and walked on, his heart drumming in his chest like something broken, the image of his father's dead body seared into his mind like an accusation.

* * *

Gerin was quiet and withdrawn as they crossed the wide plains of central Threndellen, heading north toward the Hollow. Elaysen repeatedly tried to get him to talk about whatever was bothering him, but he refused. Finally, in frustration, she asked Zaephos to tell her what he had said to the king, but the messenger would not say. "If he will not speak of it, neither will I."

The plains gave way to more rugged lands in the north, the steeply sloped hills capped with copses of dark-needled pine. They wound their way through the gullies that twisted through the hills, hemmed in on both sides by walls of exposed rock.

Gerin and Elaysen managed to spend a few evenings together talking, but they did not speak of *dalar-aelom*. It was too strange to talk about religious practices when a divine being of the god being worshipped was a few feet away. Zaephos remained steadfast in his refusal to discuss or sanction the practices of *dalar-aelom*. It left Elaysen feeling frustrated and unsettled, doubting her beliefs.

"Why not assume since he hasn't criticized any of your father's teachings that they're right?" said Gerin.

"Because he hasn't criticized Aidrel, either!" she snapped. "I'm sorry, my lord. I know it's not your fault. But my father and Aidrel both can't be right. If he's silent about both, what am I supposed to think?"

"You have to remember that he's a different order of being. He's not like us. He may seem human, and his body may be human, but his mind certainly is not. His point of view is vastly different from our own. He *is* frustrating, I readily admit that. But I don't think it's purposeful on his part. It's simply part of his divine nature."

"You people are mad," said Nyene. "You travel to an empty land for no reason and claim that the servant of a god walks among you." She pointed at Zaephos. "That is no god, or creature of a god. I've spoken to him. He's suffered too many blows to his skull. He speaks nonsense."

"We have a very good reason for going where we are," said Gerin.

"Which you will not tell me."

"I've told you what I can. What would you do if our situations were reversed?"

She laughed. "I would have killed you rather than take you with me, so in that regard I'm glad you are not me. Perhaps you are a fool, but at least it is to my benefit."

"I'll release you when we come within sight of our destination," said Gerin. "I hope you return to your lands and make no attempt to thwart our return."

"What will you do?" asked Elaysen. "Where is your family?"

Nyene's face twisted with anger. "They are not your concern. You will not speak of them again."

The hills ended at a tree-speckled plain that stretched to the southern tip of the Ozul Mountains. "Is that where we're going, my lord?" asked Balandrick, pointing toward the peaks on the far side of the plain.

"Yes," said Gerin. He'd been studying maps the night before and was certain it was the Ozuls across the plain. "We'll be there soon."

When they reached the foothills of the mountains that afternoon, Gerin said, "Nyene, you may go. Keep the horse as a reward for honoring your word."

"I would go with you a bit farther," she said. "I would see where this mad quest of yours is to end. Do you really intend to go into the Hollow?" She gestured toward the flatlands on the western side of the range.

"Yes. Our destination lies within it." He considered her request. "If you still wish to accompany us, I won't forbid it."

"Why do you hide your powers from me?" Nyene asked.

"What do you mean?"

"The two who bind me with spells each night have bleached skin and green eyes. It is a mark of their magic, obviously. You look the same, yet you perform no spells. Why? Who are you that you do not wish to reveal such things to me?"

Before Gerin could reply, a Taeraten outrider galloped toward them from the east. "My lords, an army is coming this way!"

16

"How far off are they?" asked Gerin.

"Not far enough," said the soldier. "Their vanguard is made up of cavalry and is just beyond that low rise. About five hundred horsemen. The rest are well-armed infantry. My lords, we must hurry. We're exposed on this plain."

Gerin glanced around. There was nowhere to hide, and the Ozul Mountains were still several miles away.

"Who are they?" asked Balandrick.

"I did not get a good look, Captain. I was trying to avoid being seen. But I don't think they're Threndish. I believe they might be Havalqa."

"Gods, I thought we wouldn't have to worry about those bastards this far west," said Balandrick.

"Who are these Havalqa dogs?" asked Nyene. "I've heard rumors that they've conquered parts of eastern Threndellen—"

"My lords, we need to move *now*." The soldier's expression was urgent.

They heard a piercing cry from the east. Armored horsemen had crested the rise, spotted them, and now were coming at a full charge.

"Shayphim take me," muttered Balandrick. "Ride!"

The company took off at a gallop. "Is there anything you can do to slow them down?" Balan asked the wizards.

"Not yet," said Hollin. "They'll have to get closer."

"Let's hope it doesn't come to that," said the captain.

They reached the mouth of the Hollow. The soil was thin, hard, covered with sparse pale grass that barely concealed the rocks and stones beneath. Few trees grew there, and most that did hugged the lower slopes of the mountains.

The Havalqa cavalry entered the Hollow behind them, riding fast and hard.

The pursuit continued for several miles, with the followers unable to close the gap appreciably. Gerin wondered how far it was to the Watchtowers. The maps were maddeningly imprecise, their location varying from one to another by tens of miles. It might be just beyond the next spur of the Ozul, or it might be a score of miles distant.

He sensed a strange emanation of power behind them. Not wizards' magic, but definitely power of some kind. "Hollin, Abaru!"

"Yes, we felt it!" shouted Hollin. "I don't know what it was!"

A tickling between Gerin's shoulder blades made him look up.

Creatures of some kind were flying in the air behind them. Spiderlike limbs protruded from slender bodies, the arms thrust forward, claws grasping, the shorter legs held out straight behind them. Leathery wings propelled the creatures through the air at an incredible pace. They emitted a piercing shriek that made the Khedeshians flinch.

This answered the question of who was following them. It had to be the Havalqa. The Threndish had no means of summoning demonic beings.

Above them, the demons shrieked once more, then folded back their wings and dived for the Khedeshians.

The three wizards frantically fashioned Wardings between themselves and the demons. A second later the foremost creature struck a Warding with enough force to shatter bones, but it did little more than stun the thing. Gerin felt the spell's power waver as the demon thrashed about, trying to claw its way through the invisible barrier.

To his horror, the demon was able to work its way through the Warding, shredding the power with its claws as if the spell were no more substantial than a canvas sail. Once through, it resumed its dive toward their party.

The demons that struck the other wizards' barriers had either gone through or around them. They created another set of Wardings to slow the creatures down, but at this rate the demons would be upon them in minutes.

After his second Warding failed, Gerin fashioned a death spell and managed to strike the creature dead center in its slender chest. The spell hurt it—the thing shrieked again and thrashed in momentary pain—but it did not die.

"Gods above, what can we do to kill these things?" he called out to the other wizards.

Abaru tried to Bind one of the things and succeeded for several seconds. The demon's wings crumpled against its body and it fell from the sky like a stone. But it exerted all of its strength and managed to break the spell. The shock of the breaking caused Abaru to cry out in pain and nearly tumble from his saddle.

Though it had broken the Binding, the demon was too close to the ground to avert a collision. Its wings unfolded to their full width just as it slammed hard into the ground.

Gerin hoped the fall had killed it, but he watched in horror as the demon slowly straightened, flexed its wings, then took to the air once more.

Hollin spoke a Word of Reflection, a powerful convergence of dangerous magic that if not carefully controlled could easily kill them all. It began as a point of golden light in the air above them that rapidly expanded into a translucent disk of energy a hundred feet across. Its edges curled upward to form a shallow bowl. The power then inverted itself, releasing a concussive force of magic directed up at the demons. A funnel of energy the color of burnished bronze erupted through the air and engulfed all but one of the creatures.

The shockwave that hit the ground nearly tumbled them from their saddles and flattened the grasses around them. Gerin had heard of such spells but had yet to work one, and was startled by its potency. He glanced at Hollin and saw that the wizard was slumped against his horse's neck, barely conscious.

The demons writhed within the vortex of energy, unable to escape it. He saw one of them vanish in a flash of dark light, and his heart leapt with hope.

The power of the Reflection began to fade. Within seconds it was gone. The remaining demons shrieked and renewed their pursuit.

"Do you know how to do what Hollin just did?" Gerin shouted to Abaru. "It's the only thing that's worked so far!"

"Yes! But if I use it I won't be able to do anything else. It's too draining."

"If we can't get rid of them it won't matter. Do it!"

Abaru nodded, then began the incantation.

Gerin drew Nimnahal from its scabbard and pointed the weapon at the closest demon. The damned things were almost upon them. He released a searing stream of unshaped magic through the sword, adding his own power to the magic contained within the blade itself. The magic struck the demon's wing and splashed off it. Gerin swore in frustration. It should have incinerated the whole wing. The force of the magic spun the demon about, causing it to tumble from the sky until it could regain its balance, but otherwise it seemed unharmed.

Abaru's Word of Reflection erupted, catching seven of the demons within its vortex. This time two of them winked out of existence with dark flashes of light before the power of the Reflection faded.

Then the rest of the demons were upon them.

The things swooped down low from behind, slashing at the Khedeshians with their outstretched claws. They terrified the horses; Gerin had to fight hard to keep his mount from throwing him.

One of the demons latched on to a Taeraten and lifted him from his horse. The frantic soldier tried to slash at the demon with his sword, but the thing had him from behind and he had no leverage with his weapon. The demon carried him straight up with several powerful beats of its wings. It shrieked, then ripped the man's arms from his sockets. He fell screaming, blood spurting from the ghastly wounds in his shoulders. He struck the ground with a bone-shattering crash and lay still. The demon flung the severed arms away, then dived toward them again.

"It looks as if your quest is about to end badly," said Nyene.

Gerin had no time to reply. The demons were back for a second pass. Three more Taeratens had fallen to the creatures. The horses were frantic, barely controllable. He risked a glance behind him and saw that the Havalqa cavalry had closed the gap between them considerably.

One of the demons swooped in behind Elaysen. She saw it coming and threw herself from her horse an instant before its claws would have sunk into her back. The creature raked its claws across the horse's neck, nearly taking off the poor beast's head in a gout of dark blood.

Gerin wheeled about and charged back for her. Balandrick shouted at him, but he did not hear what his captain said, nor would he have listened. He would not leave Elaysen behind.

She sat up in the grass, cradling her right arm as Gerin reined to a halt beside her and thrust out his left hand. "Quick!"

She grasped his hand in her own. With a single fluid motion he swung her up on the saddle behind him and spurred his horse into motion. "Hold on tight!" he shouted.

"We have to get my medicines!"

He shook his head. "We can't!" He was already past her horse's corpse, and the demons were swinging about to come in low once more. He would have to charge right at them to get her pack.

"No! We have to! I need them! We can't leave them behind!"

He ignored her. There would be time later—at least he fervently hoped so—to replace her medicines. To try to retrieve them now would be suicide.

"Zaephos!" shouted Gerin. "Help us!"

The divine messenger shook his head. "I cannot. Even if I threw off this mortal form and unleashed my power, it would destroy all of you as well, and level part of these mountains."

"Will you die?" asked Nyene, hunched low over the neck of her horse.

"This mortal body can be slain, but I will not die. I will return to the divine realm."

"So you need not fear death," said the Threndish woman.

"You need not fear it, either. The Maker is altering his covenant with mankind. He returns now for a reason. What lies beyond death is not what it once was."

"You are truly mad," said Nyene.

"My lord!" shouted Balandrick. "Look!"

In the distance, rising from behind a long root of the mountain that stretched far into the valley, they could see the tops of several black towers.

Gerin redoubled his efforts, this time releasing powerful Forbiddings from Nimnahal in an attempt to hold the demons back. The enemy cavalry was close enough now to rain arrows down upon them, though none had yet hit their mark.

He placed as much of his power as he dared into the Forbiddings, making them as large as possible. They held the demons back a little better than the Wardings had, but the creatures battered his spells relentlessly, and he knew the barriers would shatter in moments.

With a coordinated effort, the demons clawed at his Forbiddings. There was more than sheer physical strength in their attack—their bodies contained energy of a kind that warred with wizards' magic, trying to cancel it out.

The Forbiddings shattered beneath the weight of the assault. Even the Khedeshians could see a sudden amber glow in the air above them that grew bright for an instant before winking out.

The backflow of magic from the shattered spells stunned Gerin. Nimnahal slipped from his fingers as he slumped forward over the pommel. Elaysen frantically tried to hold onto him, but he was too heavy, and a second later he fell from the horse.

He heard Elaysen scream for Balandrick, who swore loudly and swung about. The Taeratens followed him as Elaysen tried to grasp the reins of the terrified animal.

Gerin had broken his arm in two places and cracked a rib when he'd fallen. He sat up slowly, his body wracked with pain. The Taeratens formed a line behind him while Balandrick leaped down from his saddle.

"My lord, are you hurt?"

Gerin took a breath and winced as pain stabbed through his chest. "We have to keep moving."

Balan helped him to his feet. His broken right arm was on fire, and each breath felt like a roundhouse punch. Balandrick picked up Nimnahal and flipped himself up onto his mount, then held out his hand to help Gerin. With a great deal of effort, Gerin managed to get onto the saddle behind his captain.

"Elaysen . . . ?" he asked.

"Up ahead, my lord."

The Taeratens had raised their shields against an incoming volley of arrows. Four thudded into the ground within a few feet of Gerin and Balandrick. The king turned his head and saw that the Havalqa cavalry were frighteningly close. And the demons were again descending upon them.

Balandrick and the Taeratens raced off, but there was now no chance they would reach the Towers before both the demons and the Havalqa caught them. He was spent. He could release more of the spells contained within Nimnahal, but they were not enough to hold off their pursuers. The most he could hope to do was kill some before they swarmed over them.

The Staff of Naragenth was still bound to his horse. Since its vast reservoir of accrued magic had been depleted driving back the Havalqa army marching on Almaris and breaking their naval blockade of the city, he had found it a less useful weapon than Nimnahal. Still, he would wield it now if he could get his hands on it.

He looked ahead for Elaysen and saw her coming back toward them, her face frantic. Time seemed to slow down;

his perceptions grew almost painfully sharp. He saw Hollin and Abaru, both exhausted, their eyes upon him as if hoping for a miracle. Far ahead, Nyene had paused to see what was transpiring with her captors. Zaephos was a short distance behind her, his face calm. *I wonder if he's curious what it will be like to die,* thought Gerin. *Or maybe he's interested to witness the deaths of mortals from a mortal point of view.* He wished bitterly that the One God's messenger would do something, *anything,* to help them.

The demons were almost upon them. There was nothing to be done. They would have to make a stand. Gerin raised Nimnahal to release everything left within the weapon. He pointed the tip at the nearest demon—

—and nearly dropped Nimnahal when a curtain of blue fire erupted from the ground behind them. It rose with blinding speed, a sheet of translucent flame that stretched from the foothills into the valley as far as he could see. He felt no heat from the fire, and the grasses at its base did not burn. It was not wizards' magic, but it was similar, a kind of distant relative to his own power.

The demons could not halt their trajectories or veer off in time. They smashed into the barrier and stuck fast to it, like flies in amber. Their bodies ignited moments later, bright spots visible through the cool blue flame. The wall continued to rise, carrying them quickly out of Gerin's sight.

On the far side of the wall the Havalqa cavalry came to a sudden halt. They fired arrow after arrow at the barrier, but the missiles turned to ash the moment they touched it.

Gerin looked up. The top of the wall of fire was at least a thousand feet high. He could not imagine the kind of energy necessary to create such a thing.

"My lord, is this your doing?" asked Balandrick.

He shook his head. "No. This is beyond anything I can do."

"Who, then?" He craned his neck to look at Zaephos.

The messenger and Nyene were trotting toward them. There was a look of awe on the Threndish woman's face.

"Did you find a way to help us?" Gerin asked Zaephos.

"This barrier is not my creation. It comes from the Towers."

The wizards approached, staring at the barrier with open wonder. "This is the barrier that kept Paraclade from reaching the Watchtowers," said Hollin.

They were all startled when the barrier began to move.

The section closest to them remained stationary, but the distant ends of the wall curled away from them, bending back toward one another, closing to form a cylinder. The Havalqa on the other side realized they would be trapped were it to close completely and turned quickly about. The barrier closed faster, and its ends came together before the Havalqa could escape. Through the translucent flame, Gerin could dimly see them darting about, trying to force their way through. Some of the soldiers tried to push through the barrier when they realized it emitted no heat, but the moment they touched it, their bodies flared and turned to ash.

When the barrier closed, it was a massive cylinder reaching far into the sky. Where the power moved across the ground, the grasses and trees it had touched were gone. The ground was cut to an absolute smoothness, fused somehow, leaving what looked like polished stone.

"This was certainly provident for us," said Hollin. "I wonder if they'll hold these soldiers here until our business at the Towers is concluded and we're safely away."

"I hope not," said Balandrick. "Just kill them and be done with it. And take care of the infantry that's coming for good measure."

As if in response to Balandrick's wish, the cylinder began to contract.

The blue fire moved across the earth with a steady rumble, leaving smooth, dead ground in its wake. Every contour of the land disappeared beneath its touch. When the fire contracted over a small hillock, it left only a flat expanse of stone and the smell of burned earth.

Within the shrinking cylinder they could see the Havalqa cavalry racing about frantically, trying to find a way out. More and more of the horsemen collided with the barrier and vanished in a cloud of ash.

The contraction became more rapid as the cylinder shrank, until, in the final few moments, it raced across the earth with the speed of a war horse at full charge. It shrank all the way down until it was nothing more than a line of blue light no thicker than a finger.

Then it winked out, leaving no trace of any living thing in its wake.

"Shayphim take me," muttered Balandrick. "I'm glad they're on our side."

"I'd hesitate to say they're on any side," said Hollin wearily. "They have a message to deliver to Gerin. The Havalqa interfered with that, but I doubt we can count on their help outside of this valley. We must be careful not to anger them."

"Who *are* they?" asked Nyene. "What manner of being commands such might?"

"No one knows," said Hollin. "These Towers have existed for thousands of years, but the inhabitants do not venture from them. Or if they do, they leave no trace of their passing."

"Or no witnesses," said Abaru.

Hollin and Abaru together managed enough strength to work a spell that healed the bones in Gerin's arm. He relieved some of the pain of his cracked rib himself, but did not want to do too much for fear of losing consciousness. As it was, he felt ready to drop.

Elaysen was frantically searching for her pack of medicines, but it quickly became apparent that it had been destroyed by the blue fire.

"You don't understand," she said when Gerin said they needed to go. "I can't lose it. There are medicines in there I can't replace here. Things I can only find in Khedesh."

"Then you'll have to wait until we get back to get more," he said as gently as he could. "It's gone, Elaysen."

She set her jaw and blinked away tears, but said no more.

"Come on," said Gerin. "Let's get to the Towers and hear what they have to tell us."

17

The long root of the mountains that thrust into the Hollow was too rocky and steep for them to cross, forcing them to swing their path to the west to go around it. The tops of the Towers loomed above the root like glowering giants, black and brooding. Gerin could not take his eyes from them, and wondered what answers awaited them there.

About a mile from the Towers, they encountered the ruins of an ancient road elevated above the ground of the valley, a ribbon of broken stone with tall grasses sprouting from the cracks and fractures in its surface. The road extended all the way to the Towers and ended in a slender bridge that spanned a wide chasm.

Beyond the chasm the massive bulk of the Watchtowers rose into the sky.

Closer to the Towers the road was in much better repair. A stone curb now bordered its length, its mortar strong and unbroken. Gerin sensed powerful preservation spells at work, similar to the magic of wizards yet different in a number of fundamental ways.

The chasm's walls plunged straight down, its bottom lost from sight. He wondered if the chasm were a natural formation or something created by the Telchan. After the display of power they'd just witnessed, he did not doubt them capable of it.

Gerin felt strangely reluctant to speak, as if there were a spell of silence around the Towers. It was not that he thought this was a sacred or holy place; but it was a place of power, ancient and unknowable, and in that regard was worthy of reverence and respect.

There were nine Watchtowers in all. The tallest was in the center of a circle formed by the other eight. Their windowless, obsidian sides tapered gradually as they rose hundreds of feet into the air. The summits were capped with peaked turrets, also windowless.

"There's magic flowing all around the Towers," said Abaru. He spoke in a hushed tone, as if he, too, sensed something of the reverence for this place Gerin had felt.

"They look untouched by time," said Hollin.

As they neared the Towers, Gerin studied them more closely. Hollin was right—the Towers were flawless. No cracks, chips, or blemishes marred the perfection of their black exteriors. They had an odd, unnatural appearance. It took him a moment to realize that there were no seams or masonry visible; the Towers were as smooth as glass.

The stony earth within the circle of the Towers was inscribed with geometric symbols the wizards did not recognize. Paved paths stretched from Tower to Tower, but always in a curve or arc—never in a straight line. Gerin wondered if the paths and symbols were part of a spell of some kind.

Gaps like dry moats surrounded each Tower, as if they sat in great pits hollowed out of the bedrock. The pits themselves plunged into an impenetrable blackness, shrouded in a fog that crawled up the Towers in slow, writhing movements, like the hands of ghosts.

"It's darker here," said Nyene.

Gerin realized she was right. There was a gloom around the Watchtowers that was more than the deep shadows cast by their massive bulk. When they crossed the bridge, the sun had been shining brightly; but now, though no cloud had passed before the sun, twilight seemed to have fallen in this small valley.

They dismounted at the central Tower. Gerin told the commander of the Taeratens to watch the horses and for signs of the rest of the Havalqa army. "If they appear, we need to know at once."

"I will remain here," said Zaephos. "The inhabitants do not welcome me, and will not allow me to enter."

"How do you know that?" asked Gerin.

"They have spoken to me, but not in a way you would understand. I will not press them on the matter."

This news made Gerin uneasy, but there was nothing to be done. He was not about to argue with Zaephos or force some kind of confrontation with the Telchan over his admittance. If the messenger was fine with remaining here, so be it.

A single arching walkway was the only means of reaching the deeply recessed door. They kept to the middle of the walkway, which had no curb or railing. Gerin stole a glance over the side, down into the pit in which the Tower sat, but could see nothing through the fog.

In the center of the metal door was a heavy iron ring, which Gerin grasped and pulled. To his and everyone else's surprise, it opened.

"That was easy enough," said Abaru.

"A little too easy if you ask me," muttered Balandrick, whose fingers were firmly wrapped around the hilt of his sword. "I don't like this place at all."

Beyond the door was an empty antechamber. Once they were all inside, the door closed of its own accord. Balandrick swore and lunged at it when he realized what was happening, but was too late.

"It seems we are at their mercy," said Nyene in the sudden darkness.

"We have been for some time now," said Hollin.

Gerin created a spark of magefire, but just as it flared to life, some other power snuffed it out. "What the . . . ?"

"What happened?" asked Hollin.

"Something stopped me from making it."

Hollin and Abaru tried to make magefire. Both failed.

The sound of bells filled the room. Then a voice spoke from the darkness. "You will not be harmed, but do not work your power here. It is forbidden."

"You're the *akesh* that appeared to me," said Gerin, recognizing the voice.

"Yes." It did not sound strained, as it had during their

first brief encounter. Now its voice was full of strength and vitality.

The form of the *akesh* materialized in front of them, glowing faintly of its own accord. The room grew brighter, illuminated by four glass hemispheres set into the walls.

"Why did you forbid our companion entry?" asked Gerin.

"That being has power we cannot control," said the *akesh*. "Our laws forbid such a creature from entering our domain."

"Why have you locked us in?" asked Balandrick.

"The door will open in time. There are things we would have you know. Come. I will take you to the *en pulyan ar-anglota*."

The *akesh* turned away from them, and as it did, the bright outline of a door appeared in the wall. The outlined faded in a moment, and the door opened silently onto a stairway landing. They followed the *akesh*, with Gerin in the lead.

The stairway spiraled down toward a bottom lost in gloomy darkness. The curved walls were lit by the same glowing hemispheres they had seen in the antechamber, though they were not very bright—apparently the Telchan did not care for or need much light. They were filled with magefire, Gerin realized, but operated on a different principle than the lamps wizards produced. *Who created this place?* he wondered. *Why is wizard-like magic in use here?*

There were no doors or other landings visible as they descended. Even after they had gone a considerable distance, Gerin could not see the bottom.

Far off sounds like the tearing of metal drifted up the shaft from somewhere below. "What is that noise?" Gerin asked.

"That is the power of the Telchan at work," said the *akesh*.

"When will we meet the Telchan? Are you taking us to them now? Are they in the *en pulyan ar-anglota*?"

"You will not meet them. It is forbidden for them to have direct contact with anyone who is not Maitalari. Only through me can they hold communion with you."

The statement confused Gerin. "Maitalari" was an Osirin word of very archaic form that he thought meant "people of knowledge," or perhaps "servants of lore." He had never heard the word before.

He was about to ask the *akesh* another question when

it stopped and faced the wall. Another luminous door appeared, identical to the one in the antechamber, the white light slicing a knife-edged trail through the stone.

"This is the *en pulyan ar-anglota*," announced the *akesh*. "Where your questions will be heard and answered."

Gerin drew a breath to calm himself and passed through the doorway.

He entered a huge domed room, the walls of which were ribbed with curved beams that shone with a wan bluish light. The light brightened and dimmed in rhythm with a deep pulsing noise, a low thrumming that Gerin felt more than heard. The ribs converged on a hemisphere of some dark metal at the apex of the dome.

There was power in this chamber, a great deal of it. Forces ebbed and flowed like the tides, washing over him with energies so potent they made his head swim. His exhaustion dragged at him, and the pain from his wounds made it difficult for him to concentrate. But he had arrived at his destination. He fought to clear his mind and learn what the Telchan wanted him to know. They had promised to reveal the secret of the Words of Making. He needed that knowledge if they were to have a hope of defeating the Adversary.

The *akesh* grew even more distinct and luminous than before, as if the power in the *en pulyan ar-anglota* were saturating its being. Gerin thought it had grown larger, but without an easy reference point it was difficult to be certain.

"The air in here feels heavy," said Nyene.

Balandrick nodded. "There's a kind of pressure on my skin. It's uncomfortable."

"What will happen now?" Gerin asked the *akesh*.

"I must leave you. I cannot remain while the *pulyaril* is awake. Do not fear. I will return when it is done."

"When *what* is done?" asked Gerin. But the *akesh* was already fading. In a moment it was gone from the chamber.

"I don't like this place," said Elaysen.

Gerin did not reply. There was nothing they could do now except wait for whatever was going to happen to occur.

The low thrumming sound increased in intensity. The

ebbs and flows of power in the chamber grew stronger, more chaotic, as if a storm were building.

The hemisphere at the top of the dome pulsed with a blood-red light that seemed to take command of the energies in the room. The chaotic swirl of magic began to order itself; Gerin could almost imagine the flows of power suddenly aligning themselves along the ribs within the dome, encasing them in thickening sheaths of magic.

Pressure began to build behind his eyes. He squeezed them shut, but the pressure quickly grew painful.

"Gods, it hurts . . . " said Nyene. "What's happening?"

There was a crisp smell in the room that reminded Gerin of a biting winter wind. He heard a ringing in his ears as well, but it was not the melodious sound of the *akesh*—this was a discordant, strident sound, dark and ominous.

He pressed his hands to his temples as he sensed a living presence moving through his thoughts, exploring like a shadowy stranger wandering through an unfamiliar house in an attempt to understand the placement and purposes of each room. It echoed the feeling of the Presence in Naragenth's staff, only this was even more painful, the power having little regard for the damage it might cause.

Elaysen cried out and sank to her knees, her eyes squeezed shut. "Make it stop! Please!"

The pain intensified, building toward some impossible crescendo.

There was a flash of light that he saw in his mind rather than with his eyes. Then the pain and the thrumming vanished. The immense energies receded. The hemisphere above them once more grew dark.

They all gasped for breath, many of them doubled over. The air in the chamber was stale and close. Gerin felt light-headed and nauseous. His ribs hurt immensely.

The *akesh* appeared before them, as luminous as before, and regarded them with a piercing light in its eyes. Behind them the door swung open to the stairs.

"You have been given what you came for," it said. "Now you must leave. There is nothing more for you here."

18

Gerin and the wizards protested as the *akesh* led them back toward the surface, but it would not respond or acknowledge them in any way. At one point Abaru said defiantly, "It's not right that we should be herded out of here like cattle. We came here for answers, and the gods take me, we're going to get them!" He turned and started back down the stairs, but had gone only three paces when a curtain of blue fire erupted below him, blocking his path. Abaru reeled and fell back against the stairs.

"Do not unleash your power here," warned the *akesh*. "Even your combined might could not break the barrier. If the Telchan were forced to extinguish your magic, it is possible you would be harmed, perhaps irreparably."

"We didn't get to ask a single question!" said Abaru. "Some of our companions died coming here!"

"The Telchan knew your questions before you entered the Tower. They have answered what they could. Be patient. All will be revealed."

"What about the rest of the Havalqa army?" asked Balandrick. "Are they waiting for us in the valley?"

"We were forced to destroy them," said the *akesh*. "It was unfortunate, but the Telchan had no choice."

"If you have such power, will you help us against the Havalqa?" asked Gerin. "You could drive them back across the sea."

"The magic of the Telchan is bound to this place," said the *akesh*. "It is rooted here, and cannot be moved. By the laws of their creation, they may only defend themselves. They cannot help you."

Then it turned its back to them and spoke no more.

It was fully dark when they finally exited the Tower. A half-moon was rising from behind the Ozul Mountains like the luminous sail of a ship.

They did not speak as they journeyed along the causeway. They traveled only until they were beyond the causeway's end before making camp. Gerin was too weary to travel farther.

Disappointment weighed heavily on all of them. The wizards made a feeble attempt to discuss the unique powers they'd witnessed within the Tower, but none of them had much enthusiasm for conversation and in a little while fell silent.

"You came far on a fool's errand," said Nyene. "Those within the Towers play games with you. To see if you will come when they call, like good dogs." She whistled as if calling a dog to dinner.

"Unless you want to spend the night gagged, I suggest you say nothing else," said Balandrick.

Gerin was bone weary and still in a great deal of pain from his wounds. Hollin recovered enough of his strength to work several more healing spells on the king. Gerin curled up in his blankets and stared at the looming bulk of the Towers with the moon behind them. He saw flashes of lightning to the north, followed by the distant rumble of thunder.

He could no longer fight off his fatigue. He closed his eyes and was asleep within a few breaths.

A cool autumn twilight settled over Hethnost as the sun sank behind the Redhorn Hills. The leaves had begun to change. The gardens of the immense fortress were set afire with colors—red, gold, orange, bronze—intermingled with leaves still stubbornly clinging to green. But it was only a matter of time before they, too, would change, and then fall. Time could not be stayed for anyone, or anything.

Gerin wandered through the fortress, strangely at ease. Hethnost was empty; he saw no one, saw no lights in any windows, no lanterns in the gardens. Even the massive Varsae Sandrova, where lights burned day and night, was dark.

But none of this troubled him. A light breeze ruffled his hair and brought him the scent of roses. He knew where he was to go, though he could not have said why.

When he reached the walled garden where the statue *Death of a Son* stood, he saw a woman sitting on a bench with a magefire lamp beside her. The warm yellow light bathed her with a luminous, almost unearthly glow.

His breath caught when he saw who it was.

Reshel looked up from the book she was reading and beamed at him. The sight of her, and her radiant smile, almost broke his heart. Tears stung his eyes.

"Hello, big brother. It's good to see you."

He could not speak. He knew this was a dream or vision of some kind, but it was so real, so tangible, that he felt he might never wake from it, that he would continue on here, living this life instead of the one he left behind. *And maybe that would be better,* he thought. *Reshel is alive in this place.*

He stood looking down at her and finally found his voice. "Hello, little sister."

She rose from the bench and hugged him. "I've missed you." She sat back down and patted the bench beside her.

"I've missed you, too," he said as he sat down. "This is more than a dream, isn't it?"

She smiled again. "Yes." The light from the magefire lamp sparkled in her eyes, as if they were filled with stars. "What would you have of me?"

This seemed perfectly natural to him. Of course she would have the answers he needed. She always had answers.

"Are you alive? Truly alive?"

"I'm alive in your heart and mind, which is why I'm here to show you what you need to know."

"Have you seen . . . how are Father and Mother?"

A glint of sadness touched her eyes. "Gerin, I'm not her spirit. I'm your memory of her. I can't know what's beyond this life."

"I suppose I knew that, but I needed to ask."

"You wouldn't be you if you didn't. Now, what is it you would have of me?"

He paused to consider what he needed to know. "Tell me of the Telchan and Maitalari. Who are they?"

She crossed her legs beneath her skirts and folded her hands across her knees. It was something Reshel often did when pondering how to explain something complicated. He remembered the gesture well, and it stirred a deep sadness in his heart.

"That answer is bound up with the reason you were summoned," she said. "With the Words of Making." She absently drummed her fingers, then began.

"The Maitalari were a group of Atalari who devoted themselves to the preservation of knowledge. When their order was founded three thousand years before the Doomwar, much of the history of the Atalari had already been forgotten, and this alarmed and saddened them. They could not bear the thought of important and sacred knowledge passing into oblivion, and so they took a vow that they would watch the Shining Nation from afar and record what they saw for future generations. They came to this secluded valley and built a haven where they worked to create a means of seeing across the length and breadth of Osseria, and ways to record it.

"At first their labors were not entirely successful. They petitioned the Matriarch of the Atalari for help. They asked her to create beings who could better perform the tasks of watching and recording. The Matriarch granted their request. She wanted her deeds and those of her descendants to be remembered for all time.

"And so she created the Telchan, the Watchers of the Maitalari who still dwell in their ancient Towers."

"How did the Matriarch *create* living beings?" asked Gerin. "How is that possible?"

Reshel reached out and took his hand. "That's a long story, but I'll be brief. Ages ago the Atalari discovered ways to open doors to other worlds. In one of these worlds were a people called the Mirgard, a godlike race who bestowed upon the Matriarch the power to create life itself from wood and stone and earth. This power was called the *kalaya mithran*, and for thousands of years the Matriarchs used it wisely—and sparingly—to create new beings.

"The first peoples created by this power were the Kholtaros and Lheltaros, shapers of stone and wood, who fashioned cities of unsurpassed beauty. Vacarandi was the greatest of these, the Royal Seat where for millennia the Matriarchs made their home. Nothing remains of it or the Ten Cities except perhaps some scattered stones lost among the grasses of the Kaldas Highlands or the Igrin Hills. All were destroyed by the twisted malevolence of the dragonlord."

"This power, the *kalaya mithran*. Is that what the Havalqa call the Words of Making?"

"Yes. The visions of their Dreamers were not wholly accurate. It is not the power of creation itself that fashioned the world and all things in it. But it and its sister power are potent, and may be of use to you in your struggle against the Adversary."

"Where is this power now?" he asked. "Please tell me you didn't bring me here to tell me this if you don't know where I can find it."

"Don't worry, big brother. We'll show you where it's been sleeping these long ages."

There were so many questions he wanted to ask, but he felt that his time with Reshel—or this dream world representation of her—was growing short. "Why don't the Maitalari share the knowledge they've gathered with the rest of the world? What is the point in keeping it locked up inside those Towers?"

Reshel shook her head. "It's not possible to share it. The Telchan are permitted to release their knowledge only to the Maitalari. This prohibition was made so the Maitalari high priests could control their knowledge and power. But the

Maitalari are gone. They were wiped out in the Great Plague that devastated Osseria in the tenth century of the Dark Age. The Telchan were left to carry on their duties, and will do so as long as they exist, but they are bound by the laws of their creation. There was much debate about whether this knowledge could be released to you, and many still do not agree with the decision, or the admission of your companions who are not wizards. It comes dangerously close to violating the laws under which they were made. If you did not have the blood of the Atalari in your veins, their doors would have remained shut."

"Will you tell me where to find the *kalaya mithran*?" he asked.

"Yes. But it will be best if they show you."

"How will they do that?"

She stood and regarded him with a wistful sadness. "Close your eyes."

He did. He felt her hands touch his face.

"One final thing," she said. "The Telchan at times can glimpse the future. Their augury is not infallible, and much of what they see does not come to pass. But some visions are stronger than others. Some of what you will experience will assist you with matters that have not yet happened."

"I'm not sure I understand."

"That is all I can say. Good-bye, big brother." She kissed him gently on his forehead. "It was good to see you again, if only for a little while."

A pearly whiteness expanded across his vision. He no longer felt the stone bench or Reshel's hands upon his face. Other images stirred to life within him, taking form in his mind . . .

. . . the distant ceiling of a hall, far bigger than anything he has ever seen. He is lying on his back, staring up at great beams of red wood. He has just awakened, but can recall nothing from before. His life had only now begun. The Matriarch Hená-Ishendis has stirred his inert form to life, creating flesh and muscle and bone where before there had only been a shape made of earth and stone, a form waiting for the Matriarch to fill it with the essence that is him. He knows this and other things, the knowledge placed within him by the power of the Matriarch. He knows his name: Hakirien. That is the name he has been given. And he knows that the name of his people is Telchan. That is what he is, and it is different from those who created him, the Atalari.

His mind is whirling with myriad thoughts, all clamoring in his consciousness. He knows how to speak, though he has not yet done so. He sits up and looks about. The hall—which he knows is called the House of Life—is a sea of other beings like himself, all of them rising from the tables where life has been breathed into them.

At the head of the hall is a dais, and upon it stands the Matriarch and other members of the Royal House. They are all very tall—much taller than he and the other Telchan. Their limbs are hidden beneath voluminous robes bursting like the sunrise with bright colors. To Hakirien, they are the most beautiful creatures in the world, and his heart is filled with a sudden love for them.

The Matriarch raises her arms. The Circlet of Emunial is a brilliant star on her forehead, held by a band of braided gold. When she speaks, her voice has no difficulty filling the vast space. Hakirien senses power of some kind at work, subtle yet potent.

"I greet you, First Brood of the Telchan, and welcome you into our Shining Nation." There is a faint shimmer about her head and shoulders, the pulsing glow of the power that has brought him and his brethren to life. He knows its name—*kalaya mithran*—granted to the Matriarchs by powers not of this world. It dwells within the Circlet of Emunial.

On the table next to him lies the still-warm body of a lamb, slain by a priest with a sacrificial knife, the hot blood poured onto him. It is the same for all of the Telchan; a lamb sacrificed for each one. He understands that this is the nature of the *kalaya mithran's* power, a life for a life so the Balance of Creation is maintained. He touches the body of the lamb and silently thanks it for the life it has given him.

Hakirien can now hear the thoughts of other Telchan leaking into his mind. He understands that this kind of communication is possible, but is unsure how to use it. He will have to learn, as he will have to learn so many other things. He desires to see the world that lies outside these high walls, to explore it and learn all that he can of it and the creatures that inhabit it, but what burns brightest in his heart is the desire to watch and record, to remember history as it unfolds and never forget it . . .

. . . He is no longer Hakirien. Now he is Telkorel. A message has recently come to him from a Telchan in the Citadel. The Matriarch is dead. The Shining Nation has fallen into mourning. The lamps of Vacarandi and all other cities have been dimmed.

Telkorel is in the High Tower upon which the Light Eternal burns, the oldest object in the Shining Nation, the lamp that Emunial herself carried to guide her way when she led the first wanderers from the Old Lands. Of all the lamps in the Shining Nation, only it burns with its full intensity, a sign that the nation she fashioned yet endures. It is said that the light became a receptacle of her spirit when she died, so she could watch over and guide her descendants until time itself comes to an end. There is no tomb for Emunial. She lived to a great age, and then vanished one night, never to be seen again. Some said that as a reward for her great life she was taken bodily to the Gardens of Ulkëormethë, where the gods live. Others argued she was so strong that when she died the power of her spirit utterly consumed her body.

It is also said that because of the manner of their making, the Telchan have no spirits. He does not know, and cares little either way. Because of what he is, he is not subject to the laws that govern all mortal things. It means he will never die. He does not understand death, although he has tried many times to penetrate its secret. No Telchan has ever died, though nearly a thousand years has passed since the First Brood was made.

An Atalari approaches and asks, "Will the rest of the

Telchan come from your home for the Changing?" He is wearing a black robe as a sign of his mourning for the dead Matriarch. His face is painted an ashen gray. The few people visible on the streets are also wearing black and have painted their faces for mourning, their bright colors put away for one cycle of the moon.

Sadness does not suit them, he thinks. They are usually such a glad people. It disturbs him to see them with darkness on their hearts.

"No," he answers. "It is too far. There is not enough time to make the journey. Only those of us now here will attend."

Only once before has he seen a Changing. A woman must always rule the Shining Nation, but Hená-Rhiondal had borne only sons. Her eldest will undergo the Changing so he can assume his mother's station as Matriarch. It is to take place tomorrow in the House of Life. He remembers the last Changing, six hundred years ago. Nelien had been the Chosen. He had fasted and prayed to Emunial for days, knowing the rigors of the ordeal to come.

The Changing was held at midnight, so the Chosen might greet the new day as Matriarch. The floor and balconies of the House of Life were filled to overflowing with those eager to watch the creation of their new ruler.

Nelien emerged from behind the dais, led by two acolytes of the Keepers of the Rites, marked by their tattooed faces and tall headdresses. Nelien held out his arms; the acolytes stripped away his robes, leaving him naked. The air was smoky with incense rising from copper pots held aloft on ornate stands.

Ahead of Nelien, standing in a circle around the railed platform where his Changing would occur, waited the Elders of the Keepers of the Rites, those Atalari to whom the ancient mysteries had been entrusted. Those taken into the order could never again speak with an Atalari who was not also a member; only the Matriarch herself was exempt from this restriction. To all others, they were forever silent.

Nelien stepped onto the platform. Though his hands trembled, his voice was steady and strong when he spoke.

"I am Nelien, the Chosen of Emunial the Great Mother. I am ready to undergo the Change so the Shining Nation might endure."

That was all. The Keepers said nothing to him in return. Instead they bowed their heads and began to summon the power that would work the Change. They surrounded themselves with barriers of power so that those in the hall would not hear the chanting of the sacred words.

The Keepers raised their staffs. As they did, the Changing Fire engulfed the platform. Even over the roar of the flame, Telkorel could hear Nelien scream as the metamorphosis began. The ends of the Keepers' staffs shone with a cold blue brilliance as they directed the Change. The fire around Nelien was first scarlet, then green, yellow, and finally the same cold blue as it Changed him until there was nothing left of what he once was.

There was a shout from the Keepers. They raised their arms and wheeled their staffs in a single circle, then dropped to one knee, lowered their heads and thumped their staffs on the floor.

The Changing Fire went out as suddenly as it had begun.

Nelien was gone. In his place stood a beautiful nameless woman, the new Matriarch of the Shining Nation, created by a power older than the nation itself, a power that reached back into a time before recorded history, ages before the Telchan began their watching and recording.

She would have to choose her own name, one fitting for a Matriarch.

The High Priest of Knossren stepped forward and placed the Circlet of Emunial on the new Matriarch's brow. A moment later a faint aura appeared above her head. Telkorel knew it for the *kalaya mithran*, which bound itself to each Matriarch in turn. The glowing power descended until it touched the woman's dark hair, then coalesced until it vanished into the diamond, as if the jewel had somehow inhaled it. Then it dimmed, though a luminous halo remained around her head.

He knew the power was communing with the new Matriarch, speaking directly to her thoughts, telling her of itself and what was expected of her. The *kalaya mithran* was unlike the Atalari's other powers. With those powers there was simply action—an Atalari had a thought, expressed a desire to have it made manifest, and if the Atalari had sufficient strength, it was done. But the *kalaya mithran* was different. It chose how it would be used, and if it did not approve, there was no power within the confines of the world that could compel it otherwise. It was a living thing with a will of its own. All these things he had learned in his youth, taught by the priests and scholars of the House of Life, and later his masters, the Maitalari.

Each time he sees the *kalaya mithran* he feels drawn to it, connected by some unknown means to the power that gave him life so long ago, almost as if it is calling out to him, one of its many children. Even the memory of it, as he stands in the High Tower, brings out the same feeling, the tugging at his heart of a power that, in its own strange way, loves him and all his kind. How could it not?

He remembers again the Changing of Nelien and the joining of the *kalaya mithran* to the new Matriarch. He had watched in amazement and wondered that the Atalari themselves could not see it. They had told him many times that the power so bright to him, and his kind was invisible to them. He did not know why this was so, but had no reason to doubt it.

And now that process would repeat itself, so many centuries later. Again he, Telkorel, would be there to witness it, a mystery he would never understand despite his own immortality . . .

. . . "Teshuan, you stand accused of high treason against the Shining Nation, of plotting to murder the Matriarch and her daughters, your own mother and sisters. Your guilt is not in dispute, nor is your punishment. Your conspirators have been captured and confessed their crimes and your complicity. Your doom is upon you. Prepare yourself. Your life has come to its end."

The man speaking is an Atalari dressed in ornate silk robes of scarlet and blue. His white hair is cropped short, though several long braids fall to the middle of his back. He is old, even by Atalari standards. His strong face is creased and weathered like a craggy map of the years of his life.

The man is standing in a grass-covered courtyard bordered by the high walls of an imposing stone building. A slender woman with straight black hair stands before him, her body bound with bands of steel across her chest, waist, and legs. Her arms are pinned tightly to her sides. She wears a simple white shift; her feet are bare. A score of people are gathered around the two, and armored Atalari soldiers ring them all, their spears held upright like silent sentinels.

Gerin has seen those spears before, in the vision of the slaughter of the Eletheros atop the Sundering. The sight of them troubles him. He remembers the young boy who died upon one of those blades, skewered like a fish and then hurled against a wall.

Gerin has no physical body here. He is not experiencing the memories of an individual Telchan in this vision. Instead, he watches unnoticed, his view flitting through the air like a hummingbird. He knows he is experiencing the power of the Telchan, the ability to watch and record events from afar. He is as fascinated by the power as by what he is seeing.

He knows that this courtyard is within the Kulyur, the dreaded prison of Vacarandi. None who are remanded here ever leave alive. He knows that the man speaking is Gurë, the Arktos of Kulyur, who rules the prison with a will of iron. The woman before him is Teshuan, youngest daughter of the Matriarch Hená-Durilethen. And, oddly, he knows *how* he knows all of this. There is knowledge embedded in the recordings of the Telchan, passed along to observers so they might better understand what they are seeing. He thinks it is an ingenious power; if he had a body, he would smile.

Teshuan looks at Gurë with defiance and hatred. She does not speak. Gerin knows there is power in the metal bands that prevents her from using magic and silences her voice.

"Judgment has been rendered," says Gurë. "Your doom is

sealed. You will be destroyed by the Arsailen. No trace of you shall remain upon this earth or beyond it. Your spirit will not journey to the Gardens of Ulkëormethë and will not know the succor of the gods. Your name will be stricken from the Annals, and will never be spoken even at the End Days and the final Call of Knossren. You will be erased from the world, as if you had never been."

Teshuan's hatred gives way to fear as her mother the Matriarch steps forward. The vision of the Telchan allows Gerin to see the power of the *kalaya mithran*, a halo of numinous light around her head and shoulders. The Matriarch is a beautiful woman, but this day her face is drawn, grim with both sadness and anger. She must render an unspeakable doom upon her daughter, and it weighs heavily upon her.

The Matriarch touches the fingertips of her right hand to the diamond on the Circlet of Emunial. As she does, everyone around her draws back, leaving her standing alone with her daughter.

Teshuan struggles to speak; Gerin can almost feel her straining against her bonds. But she cannot speak, can only plead with her eyes. Her mother gives her one final glance before her daughter is to die by her command. There is regret in that look, but no love.

Then she looks away, casts her eyes to the sky. The Matriarch stretches out her right hand, then clenches her long fingers into a fist. She pulls that fist toward her forehead, lowers her eyes, and backs away from her doomed daughter.

There is a pause, a silence broken only by the soft whisper of wind. Then a crack of thunder, loud enough to make many of the Atalari flinch.

The sky above the courtyard darkens as heavy black clouds appear in the sky. The wind intensifies, blasting down into the courtyard. The halo around the Matriarch's head and shoulders glows more brightly, pulsing in rhythm with a faint glow shining within the heart of the diamond upon her brow. She stands still, silent, ignoring the wind swirling around them, her gaze fixed upon the maelstrom above them, waiting.

The wind in the courtyard darkens to the color of smoke and coalesces into a whirlwind thirty feet high. There is power holding it together; or rather, the smoke *is* the power, a potent energy that spins faster and faster without losing cohesion.

A figure appears within the whirling column of smoke.

All of the Atalari except the Matriarch and Gurë take another step back. Gerin can see Teshuan trying to recoil from the figure within the smoke, but she cannot.

The figure is at least fifteen feet tall, a giant whose features are obscured even from the penetrating sight of the Telchan. From the knowledge contained in this recording, Gerin knows that he is seeing the Arsailen, a creature fashioned with the power of the *kalaya mithran* for a single purpose: to execute those who commit treason against the Shining Nation. Its power is more than death. As stated by Gurë, it destroys not only the mortal body, but the spirit as well. It is the bringer of oblivion; indeed, that is the meaning of its name.

The column of smoke moves closer to Teshuan. Gerin catches glimpses of the Arsailen itself through momentary gaps in the swirling smoke—a hairless skull, eyes like black pits, with no mouth, nose, or ears; an unnaturally slender frame that seems unsuited for supporting a being so fantastically tall; dark skin mottled with spots the color of bleached bone.

The smoke reaches Teshuan and engulfs her.

Gerin again catches fleeting glimpses of the Arsailen placing its massive hands upon the woman's shoulders. Her white dress darkens, as if light itself is having trouble reaching it. Teshuan fades, as if she is little more than a wisp of fog burned away by the sun, or a dream vanishing upon waking. Gerin can see her bones through her fading flesh in the instant before she disappears completely.

The column of smoke contracts to half its width. Already the Arsailen is gone. Then the column erupts violently outward with another thunderclap. The dark clouds above the courtyard begin to disperse and are gone within moments, leaving a clear sky.

Nothing remains of Teshuan. She has been utterly destroyed.

With a single graceful move, the Matriarch turns and leaves the courtyard. Atalari flow out of her way like waves parting before the prow of a ship. Gerin wonders how she could have done such a thing to her own daughter, no matter what crime she may have committed. Death is one thing, but to destroy her very spirit seems unfathomably cruel . . .

. . . An army of three thousand weary Atalari is camped upon grassy plains, their tents arranged in near perfect columns like rows of wheat. Colorful banners flutter in the wind. Outriders patrol well beyond the camp's pickets, stirring up clouds of dust in the dry, parched earth. But they are not seeking an enemy upon the ground. Their eyes scan the vast stretch of sky above them, looking for signs of the approach of dragons.

Gerin again watches from the flitting vantage point of the Telchan, their strange watching power darting through the air at incredible speeds, unseen and undetected by the Atalari or any other living thing. His initial view is from several hundred feet above the army, granting him an impression of its size and formation, and of the lands in which they are camped.

The Telchan's power reveals to him that this is the Army of Ending. He marvels again at this ability of the Telchan. The knowledge is in his memory as if it has always been there, something learned long ago, something familiar even though he has never heard the name before this moment. This is the army that would end the Doomwar, he realizes.

And it would happen this day.

His view suddenly shifts, falling toward the earth and then zooming through the encampment at great speed, passing through men and tents and horses as if they did not exist. The view is both exhilarating and dizzying.

He comes to rest inside one of the larger tents, hovering near the center pole, looking down at six Atalari standing around a battered table. There is a strange creature with them,

the likes of which Gerin has never seen. It is shorter than the
Atalari, its head reaching only to the height of their shoulders.
It reminds him of a weáru, a creature of legend formed of clay
and animated by evil spirits trapped within it.

This creature is hairless and wears a simple sleeveless
shift that falls to mid-thigh. Its features have few details. Its
eyes look like black gems pressed deeply into the flat flesh of
its face. Instead of a nose, the creature has two narrow slits
like the openings in a skull. Above a narrow, pointed chin is
a lipless mouth filled with two solid arcs of bone rather than
individual rows of teeth.

Its legs are thick and powerful, as are its broad shoulders
and long arms. Its hands, though, seem almost out of place.
Long, delicate fingers that seem to have an extra joint, they
remind Gerin of a sculptor's hands.

A moment later he knows what it is: a Kholtaros, made
with the power of the *kalaya mithran* to shape stone.

"We must be certain we destroy them all," says another of
the men. His silver hair is tied in a topknot that falls to his
shoulders like a horse's tail. "Not a single one can escape, or
all this will be for naught."

"The dragonlord and the Stone must perish as well," says a
younger man with prominent cheekbones and piercing gray
eyes. "They are the true cause of this disastrous war. The
dragons are merely his weapons."

The man with the horse-tail topknot faces the creature.
"Hukari, will you and your brethren take and guard the
second *kalaya na'ethrem*? Only if we fail here will you
take the diamond to the survivors in the heartlands. It is too
potent and too dangerous a power to be used other than for
the destruction of these cursed dragons."

The Kholtaros nodded. "We will do as you ask, Elesuremé.
The secret will be safe with us."

"Thank you. I would ask that you and your companions
leave at once. I would not have you caught in the cataclysm
we will soon unleash."

"I will pray that your spirits find peace in the Gardens of
Ulkëormethë." Húkari turns and leaves the tent.

Gerin's view leaves the tent and shifts forward in time a number of hours. The army is marching. The day is growing late. Their shadows stretch long before them. They are quiet as they march, their eyes downcast. The bright rainbow armor he remembers from the vision atop the Sundering is not here; their plate and mail are colorless, the power drained from it as if already in mourning for what is to come.

They reach a long forested valley that Gerin knows is called Tonn Suérta. The van of the army halts at the valley's rim. Behind them the rest of the army and their train come to a stop.

Gerin's high view drops once again into the midst of the Army of Ending's leaders. The priests and most powerful of the Atalari gather in a circle. The priests utter a prayer to their gods, and then without further fanfare or ceremony, begin the great incantation that will call forth the Unmaking.

Elesuremé produces a diamond like the one that contains the *kalaya mithran*, but this diamond has a distinctly bluish cast to it and is not bound in a circlet. In a moment the knowledge comes to him: this is the *kalaya na'ethrem*.

The source of the power of the Unmaking.

Elesuremé and the others face the east. They know it will not be long. They can feel it in the air. The entire Army of Ending waits, transfixed.

What appears to be a flock of birds appears over the far end of the valley, but Gerin knows these are no birds. These are the fabled dragons, hundreds of them, winging their way toward this final confrontation that will alter the very face of the world. He sees young boys clutch the hands of older brothers or fathers or uncles, and men clasp the hands of other men as they watch their deaths approach in a twilight sky. They all bend their strength to the creation of the Unmaking, sacrificing themselves to ensure that the dragons who destroyed their nation will die here, today.

Elesuremé, his generals, and the priests begin the incantation that will call forth the Unmaking. The blue diamond that houses the *kalaya na'ethrem* shines like a star within Elesuremé's fist. Though Gerin can sense nothing of the power itself, he sees the very air shimmer with the growing might of the Unmaking.

The dragons are closing with incredible speed. Gerin sees a single man sitting in a strange saddle on the lead dragon's neck. A mad light burns in his eyes as his black hair whips about in the wind.

The dragonlord shouts a command. The dragons open their slavering jaws, and the sky is suddenly filled with flame—

Gerin moaned in his sleep. A single tear slid from the corner of his eye. He mouthed a word: *Reshel*.

In the east, the first glimmers of dawn began to bleed into the sky. The storm had remained to the north and passed without touching them; the day would be clear and bright.

The power of the Telchan dispersed. The night of magic had ended.

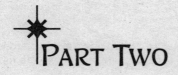

PART TWO

19

I think we can all agree that the dreams we had were true," said Hollin the next morning.

"I don't understand everything I was shown," said Elaysen.

"Neither do I," said Balandrick. "And it seems we weren't all shown the same things."

Gerin was lost in the memories of the night before, of what the dreams meant and what they now had to do. He did not fully understand the reasons he was shown all of the different visions, but he knew enough to decide on their next step.

"We need to get to Hethnost," he said.

"Yes," said Hollin.

"I still can't believe it's true," said Abaru with a shake of his head.

"That what's true?" asked Balandrick.

Abaru stared at the captain as if he were the worst kind of simpleton. "You've been to Hethnost, Balan. You've seen the Archmage, haven't you?"

"Yes, but—" His eyes suddenly grew wide. "Are you trying to tell me that *that's* the . . . thing . . . "

'Yes," said Gerin as he got to his feet. "The Ammon Ekril of the Archmage contains the *kalaya mithran*. It's what the Havalqa have been searching for. The Words of Making."

"I always knew there was a hidden power in the circlet," said Hollin.

"All of the knowledge we could ask for is right there!"

Abaru pointed to the Watchtowers. "It's absurd that they won't tell us more."

"Can you imagine what they know?" said Hollin. "But they're bound by the laws of their making. A tragedy for us."

"Rules were made to be broken," said Abaru. "One day I'm coming back here and I'm not leaving until they open their damn doors."

"Paraclade said the same thing," said Hollin.

Abaru glowered at him. "Shut up."

Gerin was quiet as they broke camp. The others shared their dreams with one another, with the nonwizards asking Hollin and Abaru question after question about the history they'd been shown. They knew nothing of the Atalari and found much of it confusing.

Gerin was shocked when Balandrick said Reshel had appeared to him in his dream. "It was wonderful to see her again. But by the gods, it hurt too."

Gerin was surprised to find himself upset and angry with Balandrick. He did not like the idea of sharing Reshel, no matter that it was with the man with whom she had fallen in love. It seemed to cheapen his own dreams in a way, robbing them of their uniqueness. No matter how much he told himself it made sense that Balan would see her as well, he could not dispel his displeasure.

When Balan asked Elaysen who had come to her in her dreams, she replied, "My mother," and would say no more. Gerin could tell she found the experience unsettling, but he was too wrapped in his own thoughts to reach out to her.

Hollin's mortal wife Katara had appeared to him. He was deeply moved by the experience. He beamed when he spoke of seeing her so vividly. "I think of her often, even now, but there was a *tangibility* to the dream that I can't deny."

Abaru's eldest daughter, Lemsha, long dead, was the form the Telchan plucked from his thoughts. Tears sparkled in his eyes as he described seeing his daughter as a young woman, and at one point had to stop speaking for fear of weeping, his jaw trembling as he tried to maintain control of himself.

Gerin continued to ponder what they had been told. That the Words of Making and the *kalaya mithran* were the same thing was inarguable. He also had no doubt that the Circlet of Emunial and the Ammon Ekril were the same. All this time, the power had been before them. They simply had not known it was there.

But that knowledge created a host of additional questions. From what he'd seen in the visions, the *kalaya mithran* truly was a power of creation—he did not understand how it could be used as a weapon against the Adversary. He'd been shown the Army of Ending using the *kalaya na'ethrem*—known to history as the Unmaking—but the blue diamond and the power it contained must have been destroyed in the Last Battle of the Doomwar. Nothing had survived that cataclysm. That power was destroyed. The Kholtaros was given a second diamond containing the power of the Unmaking in case it was needed later, but the first attempt to use it by the Atalari had succeeded, and the Kholtaros themselves were lost to history. That route was a dead end.

The Arsailen might be part of the answer to defeating the Adversary, but he did not see how even that power, if it could be replicated somehow with the *kalaya mithran*, could destroy a god manifesting himself in the mortal realm.

And how exactly did one use the *kalaya mithran*? None of the dreams had shown how the power was called upon or used. And if it were indeed still residing within the Ammon Ekril, why had no wizard ever discovered any trace of it?

When he asked the wizards that question, neither of them had answers. "I think we can surmise two things," said Hollin. "One, that the power is of such a unique nature that wizards cannot detect it, similar to divine power." He cast a sidelong look at Zaephos. "The other is that it may no longer be within the Ammon Ekril. We saw in the vision of the Changing that the power was separate from the circlet until the *kalaya mithran* joined with the new Matriarch. Perhaps the *kalaya mithran* is not in the Ammon Ekril, having fled after the destruction of the Shining Nation. We don't know the full history of the Ammon Ekril, so there is no way to know when the power might have left it."

"But if that's what happened, we're no better off than we were before," said Balandrick. "We still won't know where it *is*, only where it *was*."

"Not really," said Abaru. "Even if the *kalaya mithran* is not in the Ammon Ekril, we know that the circlet is its 'home.' We'll just have to figure out how to call it back from . . . well, wherever it might have gone."

"Did any of your dreams show you how to do that?" asked Balan. "Because mine didn't."

Gerin's thoughts whirled with questions, but he realized most of them would not be answered until they could examine the Ammon Ekril in person. How could it be used as a weapon? Why was he shown the Arsailen and the Army of Ending? He did not understand how they fit into this puzzle, but he would. He had to. This was the key to defeating the Adversary. He felt closer than ever to grasping the complex tapestry he'd been woven into several years ago with the manifestation of a divine presence in his rooms at Hethnost. A tapestry he'd only glimpsed in bits and pieces, something almost unknowably vast that encompassed everything from his magic to the arrival of the Havalqa. He'd fought against his inclusion in this plan, believing it robbed him of his self-determination, made him nothing more than a pawn in someone else's game; that it made him *common*, a mere tool to be used and discarded when his task was complete.

"Zaephos, was it you who came to me in my rooms at Ailethon?" asked Gerin. "I felt a divine presence several years ago. It spoke my name and told me my time was coming."

"No," said the messenger. "My first contact with you was on the road to Hethnost."

That surprised him. He'd always thought the manifestations were by the same being. "Then who was it?"

"I don't know. It's possible the Maker spoke to you directly, but I cannot say."

He wondered what that meant, if anything, then decided he would not concern himself with it. He'd come to the conclusion some time ago that he would no longer worry about things he could not control. He could only live his life and do what he thought was right. It had lifted a great weight from his shoulders. He had not realized how oppressive this burden was until he'd been relieved of it. He'd decided that fighting the Adversary was a worthy endeavor—no, it was *vital* that the Adversary be defeated, if Osseria itself was to be preserved.

And what an accomplishment that would be! A deed unheard of since history itself began, far surpassing the great accomplishments of his ancestors. It aligned with his own secret dreams and fears—his desire to become the greatest Atreyano who ever lived, and his worry that he would not live up to his promise or the lofty goals his father had always wanted for him.

Defeating the Adversary won't bring back Reshel or Father, but in some small way it may atone for my mistakes that led to their deaths, he thought. *I can't ever forgive myself, not completely, but perhaps those who come after me will realize that I always tried to do what was right, even if I sometimes fell short.*

Once out of the Hollow, they swung back toward the southeast in order to reach Hethnost, which lay on the far side of the Redhorn Hills. The hills themselves were too rugged, too heavily forested, for them to cross. They would have to go around their eastern end and approach Hethnost from that direction.

Two nights after leaving the Hollow, Balandrick approached Nyene. She was sitting away from the others, her back against a sturdy oak as the stars awakened above them. She regarded him with an amused smile as he sat cross-legged in the grass a few feet in front of her.

"Have you come to gag me?" she asked. "Has my mouth gotten me into trouble yet again?"

"Not today, though you came close earlier when you kept arguing the route we should take."

She shrugged. "I was only pointing out that your plan will take longer than a more direct path."

"Yes, but as I said, we're trying to avoid the more populated areas of your country. Better a longer route than to fight our way along a more direct one. But that's not why I'm here."

She folded her arms. "Very well. Why are you here?"

"I want to know why you dislike Elaysen so much. I would have thought the only two women on this journey might find a way to be friendly."

Nyene rolled her eyes. "How can you not see? She's insufferable with all of her talk of her father and the One God. She acts humble but believes she's better than everyone else. Her feelings for your leader are plain for anyone to see even though she denies it, or he denies her."

"That's more complicated than you know." Nyene still had not been told that Gerin was King of Khedesh.

"But you will tell me nothing more of this 'complicated' relationship with your lord."

"Sorry, no." He stood and stretched his back. "Good night, Nyene."

It was a beautiful evening, and Balan decided to walk the camp perimeter. They were near a small lake nestled in the crook of three wooded hills. He ambled around the lakeshore in no particular hurry. He saw a big-antlered deer on the slope ahead of him and wished he had his bow. They could use some fresh meat. The buck saw him a moment later and darted up and over the hill.

He climbed up the slope after it for lack of something better to do. He had not gone far when he saw a woman lying on the ground ahead of him. She was crumpled in a way that made him certain she'd been attacked and wounded. He could not tell if she was alive or dead.

He ran to her and knelt. She lay curled on her side, as if she'd been warding off kicks to her body. Her face was hidden, covered by her hair.

Then he saw the dark skin of her hands.

He started to jump back just as she whipped her hand out and grasped his own as he was reaching for his sword.

The instant she touched him, he went cold. All of his volition left his body. His conscious mind seemed to retreat within him, replaced by something that controlled him utterly from outside.

"You are mine," said Katel yalez Algariq. "Follow me, and remain silent."

Screaming in his own mind but powerless to resist her, Balandrick followed her over the hill and away from the camp.

20

"W̲here the bloody hell has he gone?" Gerin's feelings were a jumble of fury toward and anxiety about
his missing captain. When they first noted that Balan was not
in the camp, Gerin was annoyed, and sent a handful of Taeratens to find him and bring him back. Now, after searching
for three hours, the soldiers had returned without the captain
or any clues about what might have happened.

A round of questioning determined that Nyene was the last
to see him, but she said only that he'd wandered off around
the western side of the lake as night was falling.

"Did he say where he was going?" Gerin snapped.

The Threndish woman kept her composure in the face of
his outburst. "No. He said good-night and left. That's all."

"If you've hurt him . . . " said Elaysen.

That angered Nyene. "Are you a fool? A simpleton? Why
would I harm him? What would I gain? I like the captain."

Elaysen's face darkened. "He means a great deal to us,"
she said. "We're concerned. I apologize for accusing you."

Elaysen's apology caught Nyene off guard. She appeared
not to know what to say.

Night had come on and it was too dark to search any-
more. The wizards tried to locate him with Farseeings and
Seeking spells, but could not find a trail or any other sign of
Balandrick.

They searched the next day, spreading out methodically

from their camp by the lake. Gerin's anxiety turned to dread. The wizards used their power to search the lake in case he'd somehow fallen in and drowned, but they found no body in the water.

Shayphim take me, where has he gone? thought Gerin. *He wouldn't have run off. That's absurd. We've seen no sign of the enemy in these lands, either Threndish or Havalqa. We didn't find a body. There's been no sign of magic. Zaephos can't tell us what happened.*

Balan, the gods save me, where are you?

He hadn't felt this frantic since Reshel had died. Even his father's death had not sent him into such a dark spiral of doubt, fear, and anguish. Balan was his only remaining friend. He and Therain had grown closer over the past few years, but they saw each other seldom since Therain had gone to Agdenor, and less since he became king. Claressa . . . well, Claressa was Claressa, and nothing else needed to be said. Balandrick was the only constant in his life.

A coldness clutched his lungs, and he had difficulty drawing breath. He could not conceive of losing Balandrick. It was unthinkable. Yet it had happened. Two days of searching, and no sign of him. They could not stay here much longer. They needed to get to Hethnost. Every day they remained was another day their enemies might find them, and this time there would be no miraculous fire from the Watchtowers to save them.

Gerin allowed them to stay and search one more day, but by then all of them knew Balandrick would not be found. No one voiced their fears aloud, but it was plain enough on their faces, their dejected glances at one another. They spoke little, and what they did say was dispirited and gloomy.

On the evening of the third day, Gerin told them they would be leaving in the morning. They had to continue on to Hethnost. They could not keep waiting and hoping for something it was now obvious would not happen. Balandrick was lost.

"Let's hope he can find our trail and follow us. But waiting is no longer an option. He's a soldier. He'll understand." He disappeared into his tent, where the little sleep that came to him was dark and troubled.

They made their way past a few farms and homesteads on their journey toward the Redhorn Hills, though they skirted by a wide margin any towns spotted by their outriders.

They endured a fierce rainstorm that lasted for three days, soaking them to the bone and turning the earth to deep, sucking mud. The stream they'd been following rose quickly and overflowed its banks. It led them to a river they might have been able to ford before the rain but which was now a swiftly flowing current they dared not enter. They followed its course for more than a day until they reached a covered bridge that allowed them to cross to the southern bank.

Gerin found some time every night, if only a few minutes, to study *dalar-aelom* with Elaysen. It reminded him of better days, and took some of the sting out of Balandrick's absence.

Elaysen had been scouring their route for medicinal plants and herbs so she could replenish the supplies she'd lost at the Watchtowers, but nothing she found, even the plants she kept, seemed to please her.

"Is there something in particular you're looking for?" Gerin asked her.

"I want everything I lost, my lord, but there's little in this country I can use."

"Perhaps you don't know where to look," said Nyene.

"I know perfectly well how to gather what I need," Elaysen shot back. "But Threndellen is so wanting for proper medicines, it's a wonder any of you survive your first year, or have any teeth in your head past the age of five."

The plains gradually gave way to rougher, forested land as they neared the Redhorn Hills, whose pine-covered slopes were barely visible on the horizon.

"You're free to go, Nyene," said Gerin a day later, with the hills looming ahead of them like a great natural wall. "You've been true to your word, and I thank you for that. But I think it's time for you to return to your people."

"I will continue with you," said the Threndish woman. "I saw many things in the dreams of the Telchan, and I believe now what you said when you told me that all of Osseria may depend on what you do. How can I best serve my people if I win a small skirmish, only to lose everything because I turned away from you? No, Lord Gerin, I will see this to the end."

Gerin's initial reaction was to refuse her, but then he pondered the thought a little more. She had been granted dreams by the Telchan. They all had, and some of the dreams were different than others. Hollin had seen bits of the building of the Watchtowers themselves, Balandrick shown more of the gathering of the Army of Ending and its final march, Elaysen some of the Atalari healers at work, and Abaru had described the construction of a new quarter of Vacarandi by the unique stone-melding power of the Kholtaros. Nyene had seen some of that construction also, and the Last Battle of the Doomwar.

That made him wonder if she had a part to play in the coming battle against the Adversary. Perhaps the Telchan had given them all dreams for a reason, to provide them not only with knowledge of the *kalaya mithran* and *kalaya na'ethrem*, but to give hints and clues that they would discover as time went on.

Hints and clues that might be vital in the coming days.

Why take the chance? She had proven herself so far, and now they were about to leave her native lands. If she wanted to accompany them, who was he to deny her?

"You may join us," he said. "You're not bound or obligated to me or this company in any way, and may turn back at any time. That decision is yours."

Nyene was clearly surprised by his decision. "You've chosen wisely."

"See that it's a decision I don't come to regret."

21

Balandrick could not believe how effectively the Soul Stealer had overpowered him. He'd heard both Hollin and Gerin speak about the absoluteness of her power, that the very will to resist was removed from any interaction with one's body, so he could not even attempt to challenge her magical bonds.

He'd privately thought their descriptions were exaggerated so as to make their inability to escape seem more understandable in the eyes of others. Now he knew they had not exaggerated at all.

He wondered if this was the same Soul Stealer who had captured Gerin. She looked like the woman he'd described—small, thinly boned, with delicate features and dark skin and hair—but for all he knew, the Havalqa could have brought dozens of these Soul Stealers with them. Maybe they all had to be women, or they all came from the same region. He had no idea. She'd not yet told him her name, and he had no way to ask it, so for now he would have to be content with conjecture and uncertainty.

As soon as she captured him, she led him away from their encampment. She had a horse waiting beyond the hill, and soon they were galloping eastward across the plains. She commanded him to get on the saddle behind her and place his arms around her small waist. His body obeyed instantly even as he screamed against her within his mind.

They rode fast and hard until they had to rest the horse. When they dismounted, she gave him a small amount of water. He watched her intently, trying to determine a weakness. She was efficient and calm. She did not waste words. She told him what she wanted him to do, then fell silent. There was no idle talk, no questions. Just commands, then silence.

He spent much of the time thinking of Reshel. He still missed her keenly; more than he would have thought possible. When he'd seen her body lying in a pool of blood atop the Sundering, he felt something break in his chest. In a way, his future ended in that moment, and even now he had not regained it. All of his dreams for the two of them together, no matter how unlikely, were still a *possibility* while she lived and felt the same way about him. There was always a chance they could have convinced the king to allow them to wed, and if no decision had been made before King Abran's death, he felt certain—well, relatively so—that Gerin would have sanctioned it.

But that future was gone. The future where they were together, happy and comfortable with each other, perhaps even with children. Sometimes that lost future was so vivid in his mind it was like a memory of something actually lived. And he still did not know what path his life would take. He was like a man wandering lost in a fog.

He thought of their time together and held it close to his heart, though the memories had edges and cut him as well. Memories of holding her hand and speaking quietly with her, their faces so close their noses sometimes touched, which made them both laugh. Of the excitement of stolen kisses, the scent of her fresh skin, her fingers twining through his hair, his hands cupping her face.

Tears would have sprung to his eyes from his pain if the Soul Stealer's power had allowed it. But it did not, and so he bore his pain in anguished, utter silence.

The wound of Reshel's loss was as fresh as ever, and he despaired of it ever healing.

When they stopped for the night at the edge of a small woods, she gave him some food and commanded him to eat. "Some of those I've captured tried to starve themselves as a way to escape me," she said in her strangely accented voice. "There is no escape unless I grant it. The sooner you realize it, the better you will be."

They did not make a fire. Sitting in the growing darkness, she said to him, "What did you discover in those black Towers? I saw the destruction of the Steadfast army. Was it Gerin Atreyano who called the wall of blue fire? You may speak."

He felt control of his voice return to him. It was a small, subtle change, and he was surprised at how relieved he felt.

"Who are you? Are you the same—"

"Silence."

As quickly as it returned, the control of his voice vanished.

"You will only answer questions I ask. If I am pleased, I may allow you to speak more. If I am not pleased, you will remain silent until I deliver you to the Herolen, and I promise you that they will make you tell them whatever they want to hear. Tell me what you found in the Towers. Do not lie. Speak."

Balandrick felt a deep compulsion to tell her everything he knew about the Watchtowers. He tried to resist, to say something, *anything,* else.

But her power was too great. He could not fight it, and the words spilled out of him.

Her eyes grew wide when he spoke of the Words of Making, the only emotion she had shown since capturing him.

"Do you know how to reach this fortress where the wizards live?" she asked.

"Yes." Inwardly, he cursed himself for betraying Gerin. *How can I be so weak?* he thought miserably.

A wild, animated light danced across her dark eyes. "You have told me more than I would have thought possible." She fixed her stare upon him once more. "You may ask me questions. Speak."

His volition moved forward in his own mind, as if he were rising to the surface of the sea from dark depths. There was no other way to describe the sensation. He was now free to speak.

He wanted to weep, but he steeled himself. He needed to be strong if he hoped to escape and prevent her from taking the knowledge he'd just given her back to her masters.

"Are you the one who captured Gerin before?"

"Yes. That is obvious. Do not waste the gift I give you or I will silence you again."

"Where will you take me? Are there—"

"Silence. I am no fool. I know you are trying to find a weakness in what I am doing, a way to escape." She turned away from him, pondering what he had told her, leaving him to rage against her in the quiet spaces of his mind.

For the first time, he realized she had never asked him his name.

Katel's mind raced with possibilities. The soldier had told her everything she had hoped to learn when she first set foot upon these shores with Rulhámad. That seemed so long ago now. A lifetime ago. So much had happened since then, but one thing remained constant—the fire in her heart that refused to be quenched despite her many setbacks.

Her hope for her son, Huma. Hope that she would one day see him again, and set him free from the bonds of the Harridan. That they could live normal lives without being shunned by all others of the Steadfast. She would rise above the life she had been given.

And now she had the means to do it. Knowledge of the Words of Making. What they were, and where they could be found.

With some satisfaction, she realized Gerin had not been lying to her when he said he knew nothing of the Words. She'd always known it had to be so—no one could defy her power— but had never been able to explain the discrepancy between what he'd said and what the Dreamers had seen in their visions. She was still not certain how the Dreamers could have seen him with the Words if he had yet to retrieve them from their hiding place within the circlet worn by this Archmage. Perhaps they saw a vision of the future but had not realized it as such. It was the only explanation she could think of.

Still, it was no matter if the Dreamers had seen the future or not. She knew the mystery of the Words. It was a secret she controlled, and this time she would accept nothing less than absolute freedom for herself and her son as the price of handing over this prize.

22

"What do you mean he's gone?" Therain asked the palace guard at the Tirthaig. "Where?"

The man stammered and dropped his gaze to his toes, as if hoping beyond hope that the answer was inscribed somewhere on his boots. "I—I don't know, my lord. All we've been told is that the king returned to his castle in the westlands. No one's sure when he'll return."

"Why would he go to Ailethon?" Therain said, more to himself than the guard. "There's no need for him to go there." The ancestral home of the Atreyanos was nominally in Therain's control since Gerin had ascended to the Sapphire Throne, though Matren Swendes was charged with the day-to-day administration of the castle and its holdings, which he did according to Therain's wishes. Therain had considered moving to Ailethon after his wedding, but having become comfortable in Agdenor, he decided to remain there, at least for the present.

"Again, I don't know, my lord. I wasn't told the reason, only that he was leaving."

"Why isn't Gerin here?" asked Claressa behind him. "His kingdom is under attack and he's taking a leisurely ride through the countryside?"

The guard looked up. "Under attack, my lord?"

Therain turned to his sister, grabbed her upper arm firmly and said, "Say nothing more, Claressa."

She glared at him and crossed her arms, but remained silent.

"Repeat nothing of what you've heard here," Therain said to the guard, but had no illusions that his command would be obeyed for longer than it took for him to leave the soldier's sight.

"Of course, my lord."

A servant took them to Terl Enkelares, who was in his salon, poring over the most recent report from the Minister of Coin regarding the state of the treasury. When Therain and Claressa entered, he rose from his table and inclined his head.

"My lord, my lady, it is good to see you, though I admit to some surprise," he said. "I had no word that you were coming."

"Then our messages did not reach you?" asked Therain. "Have you heard anything about the Pelklander invasion?"

"What?" The minister's alarm was genuine. "I have not. Please, my lord and lady, sit and tell me what's happened."

Therain described the invasion of Tolthean. Claressa continually interrupted, interjecting her own comments about needing to hurry up so they could rain "death, destruction, and despair" upon the vile islanders, until Therain barked at her to be quiet. "You can give your account when I'm through, but for the sake of the gods, Claressa, let me finish!"

When Therain concluded his account of the Pelklander troop movements and his belief that they were keeping to a relatively small area, Enkelares asked him a few pointed questions about armaments, supply routes, and total troop strength. Therain had deliberately not mentioned his new-found ability to control animals, and described Claressa's rescue in purely standard military terms, embellishing where he needed to. Enkelares nodded, impressed with the prince's ability to retrieve his sister, then gestured to Claressa. "My lady, please, I would hear your point of view. It must have been harrowing."

"More than you can know, Minister." She filled in more detail of the earlier parts of the invasion than Therain had been able to, then described her harrowing attempt to flee the castle as it fell. She tried to describe poor Elezan's death, but though her mouth worked, no sound came out. Tears filled her eyes and splashed down her cheeks.

Therain reached out and squeezed her hand. "It's all right," he said soothingly. "We understand. Just move on."

She, too, did not mention his newly discovered magical abilities. He had told her when they were still at sea that he did not want anyone to know about it until he could discuss the matter with the wizards. *And damn everything to Shayphim, when I get here I find they've all left the city!* He felt as if he would never have answers.

After Claressa finished, they ate and talked a bit longer with the minister about Gerin's absence, which Therain still found mysterious despite Enkelares's quite sincere protestations that he was telling them all he knew. "If there is something untoward about the king's departure, my lord, he did not deign to share it with me. I'm sorry I can't be more illuminating."

"Don't worry, Minister. I'm sure everything's fine."

"Just terribly inconvenient," said Claressa. "And *so* like him."

Therain was taken to rooms prepared for him. Laysa was already there, and asked him what happened.

"The seat of government apparently knows nothing about the invasion," he said. "The messages we sent never got here. We're meeting later tonight with the rest of the ministers to inform them."

"When will we be able to go home?" she asked.

"I don't know," he said. "I just don't know."

The news of the Pelklander invasion was met with a sense of urgency from the eastern lords, while the western nobles, if not quite indifferent, cautioned that they could not afford to rush headlong into another conflict without knowing more of what the Pelklanders wanted.

This incensed Claressa. "They've taken our lands! They've kidnapped and perhaps killed the rightful lord of

Tolthean and his family! It's *outrageous* that they want to do nothing."

"They don't want to do nothing," said Therain. "But they want to be cautious."

"I agree with Claressa," said Laysa, who had grown close to her sister-in-law during their journey to Almaris. "You men need to make up your minds and do something about this affront to Khedesh. Just because it happened far from here doesn't make it any less important."

Therain decided to refrain from arguing and went for a walk around the Tirthaig with Kelpa. He was leaning on a stone balustrade overlooking the Cleave, Kelpa resting by his side, when he saw a large ship making for the harbor. He went cold, though he could not say exactly why. It was too far away for him to make out the colors it flew, but there was something about it that disturbed him.

He sent his power into a gull and commanded it to fly toward the ship. The giddy exhilaration he would normally have felt was subdued by the unease that filled him.

It did not take the gull long to swoop close enough to the ship for him to make out the flags flapping from its masts. He cancelled his power, then turned from the balustrade. "Come on, boy," he said to the dog. He had to find Enkelares.

Pelklanders, he thought.

And below their colors, the flag of parley.

The Pelklander embassy was brought to the Tirthaig bearing flags of truce and parley. The City Watch closely surrounded the ten men—one ambassador and his guards—as they made their way through the city streets. People crowded the cobbles and leaned out of open windows to gape and catcall as the strangely garbed visitors from the islands marched past. A few dared the wrath of the City Watch by hurling rotten tomatoes and cabbage. Three watchmen veered off from the main group and chased after them, but they vanished down dark twisting alleys and escaped the beating they certainly would have endured had they been caught.

The ambassador was brought to the throne room, his guards

forced to remain in the rear of the hall while he was escorted to the dais where Therain and Terl Enkelares waited. Both were dressed in fine wool and silk bearing the colors of the realm and of House Atreyano.

The Pelklander ambassador looked to be in his fifties, with receding gray hair that swept straight back from his high forehead. Both ears and his left eyebrow were pierced multiple times with hoops of gold and silver. His skin was wind-burned and rough. He wore layers of leather dyed black and scarlet, and carried an ornate staff that he leaned upon for support. His right leg was lame, and he walked with a pronounced limp.

He stopped a few feet from the dais. "Greetings to King Gerin Atreyano of Khedesh, from His Grace the noble King Daqoros of the Pelklander Islands. I am Hurkun, sent to convey the king's wishes regarding the dispensation of the territory known to you as Tolthean, formerly the Pelklander province of Arduun."

Therain bristled at the man's words, but held his temper in check. He had agreed to let Enkelares speak to the Pelklanders, though he'd told the minister he reserved the right to interrupt if he felt the need.

"Greetings, Hurkun. I am Terl Enkelares, Minister of the Realm. This is Therain Atreyano, the younger brother of the king and Duke of Agdenor and Ailethon. King Gerin is presently outside the city and not available to meet with you."

Hurkun scowled. "My words are for the king."

"Then you should have sent advance word of your coming," said Terl dismissively. "You may either present King Daqoros's wishes to us, or you may leave and return home. You will not be permitted to wait for the king to return, unless you wish to do so in your ship on the open sea. We will not house you while our two countries are effectively at war."

"Minister Enkelares, that is precisely why I have come. To avert war that will result in pointless bloodshed on both sides. We merely seek a resolution over disputed land."

Therain decided it was time for him to speak. "Your king *has* waged war against our kingdom and occupied Khedeshian lands and property, and will be held accountable. Baron Toresh and his family are missing. You will return them at once and depart our lands, or we will once again destroy Urkein as my grandfather did, only this time we will raze it to the ground and drive your people into the sea so they'll trouble us no more."

He could see Enkelares wince from the corner of his eye, but he didn't care. He was not a diplomat, thank the gods. He didn't have the stomach for all the banter and pointless dancing around the crux of the problem with verbal niceties and stiff, insincere politeness. His mother and father had tried to make him understand the necessary nuances of politics, but their lessons had not taken hold. He spoke his mind, and Shayphim take anyone who didn't like it.

Hurkun forced himself to smile in an attempt to seem pleasant and friendly. In Therain's estimation, it failed miserably.

"Since you have broached the subject, I have news of Baron Toresh and his family," said Hurkun. His smile now looked like a wolf baring its teeth. "They are safe and well."

"So you have them as hostages?" said Therain.

Enkelares could not contain himself. "My lord, please."

"They are safe and in our custody," said Hurkun with the same wolfish grin. "Rest assured they will not be harmed."

"What terms is King Daqoros offering for their return?" asked Enkelares.

Hurkun first issued a statement. "The region now known as Tolthean was once the sovereign territory of the Pelkland Islands. The present reoccupation of those lands was carried out to right an ancient wrong. We want no more than what was once ours."

"Theft is theft, Ambassador, no matter how you try to dress it up," said Therain.

"You are correct, my lord. And theft done generations ago also remains theft, no matter how long the passage of time. We seek only what was once ours."

"What are your terms?" asked Enkelares with a trace of impatience. Therain wondered if that was aimed at him or the ambassador.

"We will release Baron Toresh and his family, and all other captured nobles and commoners, in return for control of the coastal region known as Tolthean. That territory shall become a sovereign part of the Pelklander kingdom and subject to all its laws and customs. Those now living there will be permitted to remain if they so wish, though they will pay tribute to Urkein. Those Pelklanders wishing to migrate from the islands to the mainland will be permitted to do so."

Therain had to resist a very strong urge to strangle the grin from the ambassador's face. *Having one hand makes strangling a bit harder, but I'd still like to give it a go,* he thought.

"You may return to your ship while we discuss your terms, Ambassador," said Enkelares.

Hurkun bowed. "I shall await your decision."

"You're not seriously thinking of giving him what he wants?" said Claressa.

"Please tell me you're going to sink his ship in the harbor and send these criminals to their graves," said Laysa.

Gods above me, when did she get so bloodthirsty? She's definitely spending too much time with Claressa.

"*I'm* not thinking of giving him anything," he said.

"Good," said Claressa.

"However, Enkelares and the Assembly of Lords—those who are here in the city—will probably agree to the terms, with stipulations. I would expect that Hurkun will accept our offer."

"*What?*" The two women spoke together, aghast.

"How could they agree to giving away part of the kingdom?" said Claressa.

"Because we do not have the strength to drive them out," he said. "Most of our fleet is in the north, guarding the gulf against the bloody Havalqa, who are moving seemingly at will through Threndellen and Armenos. We've several thousand men along our border and we can't risk withdrawing them for a campaign to the south."

"We can pay for mercenaries if it comes to that," said Claressa.

"There's no money to pay for them. The treasury has been sorely drained. One of our stipulations is that the amount of tribute to be paid to us according to the Treaty of Urkein will increase substantially to help refill our coffers."

"Gerin should make a decision of this magnitude," said his sister.

"I agree. But he's not here, and he left Enkelares in charge. I hate this, but we have very few options."

Claressa rose from her chair and stood before him, her face twisted with rage. Her entire body was tensed, her fists clenched.

"You're a bloody coward," she said. "Father would be ashamed."

She wheeled about and stormed from the room, leaving Therain stunned and speechless.

23

Tyne Fedron rode his horse down a road of hard-packed earth, the Commanding Stone held firmly in his hand. The dragons wheeled in the sky above him. Most flew high, but he kept a few low to the ground to protect him should the need arise. They could not fly slow enough to match his pace and so had to continually circle him, the beating of their wings making a constant wind. He could sense when they tired, and then he allowed them either to rest upon the ground or join their kin higher in the sky, where they could glide upon currents of air.

In those first days after their arrival, he'd attempted to ride upon the neck of one of the smaller dragons, but it was impossible to hold on. The scales could flex and bend where they were attached to its hide but were as hard as steel and too rough-edged for him to hold. Just raising its head almost dislodged him.

So he walked, and the dragons flew.

His dragons ate cattle and sheep wherever they found them. Their appetites were huge, and he had to allow them to hunt while they traveled, which meant that at times they flew well out of his sight in their search for food. But no matter where they were, he could sense them through the Stone, and when they ate, he could feel contentment through the connection.

He'd destroyed three villages so far. When he came across

the first one, the villagers ran screaming at the sight of the dragons.

"Kill them all!" he screamed.

The dragons swooped from the sky. They set the thatch-roofed houses on fire and devoured dozens of shrieking villagers. Others perished in the flames. The dragons killed all of the horses and mules before he could think to command them to allow at least one to live so he could ride instead of walk. He did find some food in the wreckage, which he stuffed into his pack.

He'd continued on, the smoke of the devastation churning into the sky behind him.

He pondered the devastation he had brought about as he rode across the plains on a horse he'd taken from the second village. He did not just want to destroy, he told himself. That should not be his goal. He needed to instill fear, to be sure, but if he destroyed everything, killed everyone, then there would be nothing for him to rule.

He reached a rutted path that eventually gave way to a better maintained road of hard-packed dirt. He spied a caravan of merchants on the road ahead of him, but they were already turning about, attempting to flee.

Tyne felt the dragons' desire to devour the caravan in their hunger, but he forbid it. He wanted the merchants to flee, to spread the word of his coming.

And with that, fear.

The merchants had apparently come from a small walled town with a lone hillock rising from the prairie on its southern face. The road he was riding upon led to a wooden gate that was now closed. Atop the hillock were several manor houses and a single, central tower surrounded by a stone wall that rested like a crown on the hillock's head. He spied some movement behind the wall atop the hill. Men with bows peeked through the crenellations, then quickly ducked down.

He would not destroy this town. He wanted, instead, to exert his power over the people here.

Feed on the sheep and cattle, he called out to the dragons. *But do not kill people unless they attack you.*

The dragons swooped from the sky and tore apart the terrified animals grazing in the pastures as Tyne continued on toward the gate, concerned that someone might try to kill him with an arrow. When he got to the edge of what he gauged was the range of a longbow, he paused. *Let the dragons eat their fill. Then I'll tame this place.*

If there were problems, he could always burn it down and try again at the next town.

He waited a few minutes for the dragons to eat, then commanded them to circle the town only fifty or sixty feet above the thatch roofs. He ordered two of them to land on either side of him to act as escorts as he closed the distance to the gate.

Tyne saw two eye slits slide open in the gate. "By the gods," shouted a man who remained hidden, "what manner of devils have you brought upon us?"

"The dragons are mine to control," said Tyne. He sent a command to the two beasts flanking him. They reared back their heads and sent gouts of flame into the air. Even over the roar, he could hear people screaming inside the walled town.

"Obey me, and you will live. Defy me, or attempt to harm me in any way, and the dragons will burn your town and devour each of you as hungrily as they did your cattle."

"What is it you want?" said the same man. His voice quavered with fear.

"I already told you: obedience," said Tyne. "And a harness."

It did not take long for him to claim the largest manor house as his own. He allowed the few household servants to remain, but turned out the family immediately. From the haste at which they ran from the house, he did not think they minded overmuch. The dragon sitting in the yard outside the manor was obviously not to their liking.

He told the servants he was not to be disturbed for any reason, then locked himself in a bedroom and slept for two days. When he awoke he was famished, though not as hungry as he should have been. Drexos had been right: when he slept after using the Stone, the power within it sustained him somehow, so that he did not die of starvation or thirst.

He commanded that a saddle or harness maker be brought to him. He enjoyed the way everyone leapt to obey him. They recognized his power, the authority he carried with him. *Soon everyone will obey me the way these people do.*

The servants led a balding, broad-shouldered man into the room. Despite the man's imposing size and obvious physical strength, he stared at Tyne with wide-eyed terror. The sight of his fear made Tyne grin. By the gods, he could almost *smell* the fear on him!

"I need a harness," said Tyne. "Can you make one for me?"

"I . . . of course, my lord."

"This is not for a horse or mule. I need a saddle and harness for one of my dragons."

The man's eyes widened even farther, and his knees buckled. "My lord, please. I—I can't."

"If you can't, then I'll allow my dragon to feast on your flesh and find another to make what I need."

The man swallowed thickly. "But, my lord, to make a harness I will have to measure it. The beast will gobble me up!" He looked ready to weep.

"I control them completely. Never forget that. I will not permit it to harm you while you work. Get whatever tools you need, then return here. You'll be fitting the dragon that waits outside. Tarry, and I will not be pleased."

Trembling, the man bowed low. "Yes, my lord." Then he ran from the room.

While the saddle maker labored over his task, one of the servants entered—a pretty dark-haired girl who reminded Tyne of Ula Joleshra back home—and said there was a young man outside who wanted to speak to him.

Curious, Tyne told her to show him in. People avoided him as if he were the physical incarnation of death. They did not seek him out. What could this person want?

The servant girl ushered in a thin boy who looked to be in his late teens. His clothing and long matted hair were filthy. He had a half-starved, ravenous look to him, but there was also a gleam of cunning in his eyes.

"What do you want?" asked Tyne.

"To help you."

Tyne laughed. "And what could you possibly do to help me?"

"Whatever you need me to." He stepped forward, a hungry look on his face. "I hate it here. I hate everyone in this place. I'll do anything to leave with you. Just say it. If you want someone dead, I'll kill them for you. Anything."

Tyne regarded him for a moment in silence. His first impulse was to tell the boy no and send him away, but he held back on that while he thought about it a little more. Would there be a benefit to having someone else along? While he was fine being alone, it would be nice to have someone to talk to from time to time. And to guard him while he slept after using his power. He still felt vulnerable when in the deep sleep caused by using the Stone.

And if the boy caused trouble, it would be simple enough to be rid of him.

"All right. You can come with me."

The boy looked shocked and confused, as if he had not heard Tyne correctly. "You saying you'll take me?"

"Are you an idiot? That's what I said. Though I may have to rethink my decision if you're a simpleton."

The boy shook his head. "I'm not a simpleton. My name's Marrek Drayke. I know how to listen and shoot a bow and set traps and fish so we can eat. I'll do whatever you tell me."

"Will you swear to it by whatever gods you worship here?"

The boy nodded.

"Then swear it. Swear that you will serve me without question, and that if you ever doubt me or betray me, you will suffer the wrath of your gods and die a traitor's death."

"I swear by Lord Nural that I'll serve you and never betray you."

Tyne nodded, pleased. *This is how it begins. With one boy swearing an oath to me. But it won't end here. Before I'm done, tens of thousands will swear their lives to me.*

"As my first command to you, find the saddle maker and tell him he needs to make an adjustment. He'll need to make two harnesses for the dragon."

A smile split Marrek's thin lips. Tyne had wondered if the boy would change his mind when he realized he would be flying on a dragon.

"Yes, my lord. At once."

24

Algariq allowed Balandrick to speak each night, though he quickly learned what questions to avoid. If he displeased her in any way, she simply commanded him to be silent. He could not ask about her son—Gerin had told him about her only child—or what her life had been like in Aleith'aqtar. Military questions were also off limits.

One night he asked her about Gerin's escape from Gedsengard. "He felt certain you would have been executed."

"As did I. And if I had not left the island before Tolsadri returned from death—"

"Wait a minute! You mean he's not dead? The Voice of the Exalted that Gerin killed?"

She frowned, annoyed that he'd interrupted her, and he felt certain she would not answer him. But after a brief pause, she replied.

"Loremasters have the power to return from death if the damage to their bodies is not too severe. As I was saying, if I had not fled the island before his return, he certainly would have had me killed."

"And you don't think he will have you killed now?"

"Oh, he will try." The hatred she felt for the Voice of the Exalted was evident when she spoke of him.

They were quiet for a time before she broke the silence. "Do you know why Prince Gerin spared my life in the prison cell? I was powerless. He should have killed me. I can make no sense of it."

"He hasn't spoken to me about it, but I would wager he felt pity for you despite what you had done to him. You'd told him about your son, and how you were treated by your people. I'm sure he felt you had no choice but to do what you did. He showed you mercy, and you should be grateful for it." He could not help adding that last point, though he was sure it would draw her ire.

Her brows knitted above her nose as she pondered this. She did not seem angered by his comment. "I still do not understand," she said. "If I had regained consciousness sooner, I could have prevented his escape. It was dangerous to him to leave me alive."

"And that was a risk he was willing to take to show you mercy. It sounds as if you've never been merciful. You should try it sometime. It may be the only way you'll ever understand."

One evening after a hard ride, she'd ordered him to disrobe. "I need to replenish my power, and you are the only source." She looked exhausted, drained, her eyes sunken and hollow.

He screamed in his head, but his body obeyed. She took off her clothes as well, then stretched out on the grass, spread her legs, and commanded him to have sex with her.

As his body obeyed, his horrified mind wondered if this had happened to Gerin as well. If so, he understood why the king had not spoken of it. Such a violation was obscene.

He felt energy drain from him, sucked out of his body by the power of the soul stealer. He thought he would die, that she would take all that he had to give. But then there was a crescendo to both her power and the climax of their sex. He collapsed, exhausted. She pushed him off her and ordered him to dress.

Filled with misery and self-loathing, he obeyed.

The gods take me, look at that army, thought Balandrick when he and his captor first spied the Havalqa encampment.

There must be fifty thousand solders, and half again as many to keep them supplied.

The Havalqa army was camped outside the walls of a small city that hugged the northern shore of the Candago River. Two stone bridges spanned the narrow, swift current, connecting the city to a smaller settlement on the far side.

The banks of the river were nearly vertical, like the rain gutters cut into some of the curbs in Almaris. Dense trees lined both banks, though they only extended a few hundred feet from the water before yielding to the plains.

The city walls had been thoroughly smashed in a recent battle. Balandrick saw gaping, scorched holes in the stone. In several places the entire wall had collapsed under the assault.

Whatever fighting had occurred here was over now. The city had fallen to the Havalqa. He could see Havalqa standards upon the battlements above the shattered gates.

"We must find the Voice of the Exalted," said Algariq as they made their way toward the camp perimeter. "I believe this is the army he was to be traveling with. If it is not, we'll find where he is and move on."

The Voice of the Exalted. Vethiq aril Tolsadri. Balandrick had heard a great deal about him from Algariq during their journey. He despised himself for having betrayed such an important secret, but part of him knew there was nothing he could have done to prevent it. *Fat lot of good it does to tell myself that,* he thought. *I should have found a way to fall on my sword, if nothing else.*

They were quickly confronted at the perimeter, where Algariq spoke to the soldiers in their native tongue. Balandrick eyed the soldiers carefully. He noted the strange armor Gerin had described, and the variety of races that comprised the Havalqa military. Skin color that ranged from olive to brown to nearly jet, as well as paler flesh like his own. Exotic eye shapes and intricately tattooed symbols.

The soldiers treated Algariq with contempt, though they grudgingly allowed her to pass after gesturing toward an area deeper in the encampment. "Follow," was all she said to him, though he could hear the shame and anger in her voice.

They reached the command area of the encampment. It was well-guarded, and contained the largest and most colorful tents, dyed with broad stripes of crimson, purple, and gold. Algariq was once more shamed and treated poorly by the soldiers before finally being ushered into one of the larger tents. Balandrick could almost see the tension growing in her as they stepped through the flap. *She doubts whether she'll leave here alive,* he thought.

She approached a dark-haired man whose back was turned toward them. He was bent over a table, studying a large stained map. A single manservant lurked in the shadows near the tent wall. Stopping several feet behind him, she bowed her head. "Honored Voice, I have brought an important captive to you."

The man spun about as if he'd heard the voice of Shayphim himself. "You!" he snarled. "How dare you sully my quarters with you filthy presence!" He struck her with the back of his hand, hard enough to stagger her. Balandrick saw a streamer of blood fly from her mouth.

The dark-haired man raised his hand once more, his expression contorted with murderous rage. Before he could swing, she said, "Honored Voice, if you touch me again, I will die before revealing the location of the Words of Making. I swear this on the name of Holvareh Himself, and upon the honor of Bariq the Wise."

Tolsadri paused. "You threaten me now, wretch?"

He moved with the speed of a striking snake. A small knife appeared in his hand—*the same one Gerin had used to kill him on Gedsengard?*—and flicked it toward her. Its blade hovered at the side of Algariq's neck. She did not so much as flinch. She stared at Tolsadri with cold defiance.

"I should kill you now," he said. "You deserve death for your failure on the island. I will have your naked corpse dance for my amusement."

"Kill me and you will learn nothing. I know where the Words can be found. If you want that knowledge, you will agree to my terms."

He laughed harshly. ' "Terms'? You do not set 'terms' with

the Voice of the Exalted, wretch. You will tell me what you know, or you will know the true meaning of suffering."

"I will die before I reveal anything to you if you do not agree to my wishes." She spoke in a matter-of-fact tone, as if discussing the weather. "You can sense the truth of some things, Honored Voice, if the stories about you are true. You should know I mean what I say."

"Why should I believe you have the secret of the Words?"

"If I had nothing to offer you, I would be worse than a fool to come here."

Balandrick saw Tolsadri tense the arm that held the knife, and felt certain he would slit Algariq's throat and be done with it.

But Tolsadri withdrew his hand and stepped back. "State your terms. I will decide whether they are to be honored."

"Before I reveal anything, you will elevate me to the caste of Yendis, as was promised to me in the decree from the Exalted herself before we set sail for these lands. That was to be my reward for accomplishing my task, which I have now done *twice*. Defy this again, and you will be an oath breaker in the eyes of Bariq, a dangerous thing for an Adept and Loremaster.

"Second, you will swear by the holy power of Bariq the Wise that you will attempt no retaliation against me for demanding what is rightfully mine to begin with. I will be permitted to leave here unmolested and unharmed."

Tolsadri cocked his head, as if trying to decide whether to laugh at her or drive his knife into her eye.

"I will agree to your terms, wretch," he said after a moment. "Let it never be said that I do not honor my word. But if you do not have the knowledge you claim to have, I promise you will not leave this tent alive, and that it will be a long time before you die."

"That is acceptable, Honored Voice."

Tolsadri spoke to the servant in their native tongue. The olive-skinned man bowed and left the tent. He returned shortly with a pudgy, red-faced man.

"Enbrahel," said Tolsadri, "you must witness the elevation

of this woman to the caste of the Mother. The requirements of *tel'fan* must be observed."

The shorter man's eyes widened in surprise. Then he remembered himself and bowed his head. "Yes, Honored Voice. I will do as you command."

Tolsadri issued another command to the servant, who once more departed the tent.

The Voice then began an invocation in his native tongue. It did not seem to Balandrick that any magic was involved. It appeared to be more of a religious ritual, with the shorter man interjecting ceremonial phrases at periodic intervals. Algariq stood with her head bowed, her hands clasped in front of her.

The servant returned and placed a new set of clothes, a flagon of water, and a few small objects on the map table. Without faltering in the invocation, Tolsadri turned and filled a hammered bronze bowl with a small amount of water. He said something directly to Algariq, and she raised her head and accepted the bowl from his hands. He issued what was obviously a command, and she took a sip from the bowl. Balandrick noticed that her hands were trembling.

Tolsadri spoke a clipped sentence, after which Algariq extended her arm. He picked up a small wooden statue of a woman and held it firmly in his hand. His voice changed, grew deeper and more powerful. He placed his palm over the back of Algariq's hand—Balandrick wondered how much revulsion Tolsadri had to overcome in order to touch her skin in a way that wasn't intended to harm her—and began to rub it in a small circle.

A few moments later he withdrew his hand. There was a white symbol on Algariq's flesh, a spiral radiating straight lines from its center with an eye-shaped oval above and below.

Tolsadri stepped back and spoke the concluding phrase of the ritual. From his tone and everyone's change in demeanor, it was obvious to Balandrick that the ceremony was over. Enbrahel clapped his hands once and bowed his head. Algariq shuddered and stared, transfixed, at the white mark on her arm.

The servant gathered the clothes from the table and positioned himself behind Algariq. To Balandrick's surprise, he helped her remove her garments until she was in only her underclothes. She did not seem ashamed or embarrassed. Indeed, there was a look of elation, almost religious fervor, on her face.

The servant then helped her dress in her new clothes. They were plain, unadorned, but from Algariq's expression, might have been the garments of a queen. She was trembling openly as the servant finished.

Tolsadri held out a large coin. She took it and held it in both hands.

"It is done," he said. "You and your line are now of the caste of Yendis."

Algariq drew a deep, ragged breath, like someone gasping for air after a near drowning. She muttered something too quietly for Balandrick to hear, but it had the cadence of a prayer.

Tolsadri loomed over her. The threat in his posture and expression could not be clearer.

"And now you will tell me everything there is to know about the Words of Making."

Algariq barely heard the Voice speak to her. She had done it. At last, after so many years, a lifetime of pain and regret and sorrow, she had achieved her goal of escaping the clutches of the Harridan. *I am free,* she thought. *And Huma is free as well.* The mark on her arm would have appeared on his as well, a sign that he, too, had been elevated.

But she knew she was not truly free yet. Indeed, she was still in mortal danger until she could get away from the Voice of the Exalted.

She commanded her captive to tell the Voice all he knew of the Words of Making. Her captive described where the fortress could be found and what he knew of its defenses. While he talked, the witness to her raising was called away; the servant, too, disappeared from the tent on some unknown errand. Algariq smiled inwardly. *The Mother's grace shines upon me this day,* she thought. *Truly, I have been blessed.*

Tolsadri asked her captive a number of questions, some of which he could answer and others that he could not.

"That is everything he knows?" Tolsadri asked her.

"Yes, Honored Voice."

Tolsadri folded his arms and tapped his fingers against his beard. "Very well. I am done with you. Go, but do not let me ever see you again."

She inclined her head to him as custom dictated, but every nerve in her body was ready to spring. He did exactly what she expected him to do. The moment she bowed, he lashed out with a long knife he kept tucked up one of his sleeves. Prepared for such an attack, she leapt backward, before the blade buried itself in her heart. As she did, she shot her hand out and brushed it across Tolsadri's wrist. The edge of the blade sliced into her forearm, but she ignored the pain and released her power.

She felt the Voice's will enter her. She had not known if her power would work on an Adept and Loremaster—it was possible that the Mysteries of Bariq would provide some element of protection—but she had no choice. It was either control him or perish.

"Put your weapon away and remain silent," she commanded.

Tolsadri tucked the knife back into his sleeve, his expression slack.

She longed to know how he raged inside the silence of his mind, lusting to kill her for what she had done to him. She rarely took pleasure in the use of her power, but this time was different. This time she felt a great deal of joy in controlling this evil man, even though she dared not harm him. There was only so much she could risk.

"I knew you would be false," she said to him quietly. "You're unworthy of your lofty station, 'Honored Voice.' I was once a wretch of the Harridan, yet I have more honor than you can comprehend.

"You will forget what I have just done to you. When you

think on it, you will recall only what you were told about the Words of Making and that my captive and I departed soon after. You will not think about us again.

"You will do one more thing for me. Write a letter granting me safe passage through the Path of Ashes so that I may return to our homeland and my son. Do it now, and be quick." She again took great joy in commanding Tolsadri, but her stomach fluttered with fear that she would be caught and her freedom would end before it truly began.

Tolsadri turned to the table, retrieved a pen and parchment, and quickly wrote out her grant of safe passage, which he then sealed with his Ring of Bariq. She took it from him and hid it within her new clothes. *New clothes for my new life.*

"Go to sleep, Tolsadri. If your servant returns, tell him you do not feel well and order him not to disturb you until morning. Again, you will forget what I have done to you. Keep the knowledge of the Words of Making, but all else will vanish from you mind, including any desire to harm me."

To her captive, she said, "Come. We are leaving."

As they made their way through the encampment, Balandrick wondered how long she would keep him alive. She no longer had any need for him. Killing him in the camp might draw attention that she did not want and delay her escape, but he did not hold out any illusions that he would live long once they cleared the perimeter.

Reshel, it seems I'll see you soon. I hope you'll be waiting for me inside the gates of Velyol. I've missed you dearly. He did not attempt to fight Algariq's control of him. He knew it was futile. It was time to resign himself to his fate. The idea of seeing Reshel again was a small comfort to him, one he held close to his heart, like a candle in a darkened room.

Algariq did not speak to him as they hurried through the rows of tents, but he could sense a change in her nonetheless. On their journey here, she had hunched her shoulders and lowered her head, trying to make herself as small and inconspicuous as possible, fearing to draw notice to herself and her station and the scorn and loathing accompanying that recognition.

Now she walked almost proudly, a new woman reborn in the ritual performed by the Exalted's loathsome Voice.

They retrieved her horse without difficulty. The soldiers scarcely looked at her when she spoke to them.

"Get onto the saddle behind me," she commanded. "Put your arms around my waist. We need to be far away from here come the dawn."

She rode to the east, following the course of the river. By now full night had fallen. She did not speak to him, concentrating instead on their path along the edge of the trees. A few times he nodded off in the saddle. Strange, that he could sleep so close to his own death.

He felt remorse over his inability to keep his secrets from the soul stealer, but also knew there was no way to resist her. Her power over him was absolute. There was nothing he could have done.

What he experienced more strongly was a resignation toward his own death. He was a soldier. His country was at war, and he was in the hands of the enemy. It was simple: his time had come. He needed to accept it for what it was—the inevitable end of his life.

He also felt oddly elated at the thought of seeing Reshel again. He knew he should not be *happy* about his death; that was an unworthy thought, akin to suicide, an act frowned upon by the priests of Telros. There had been some debate about Reshel's death among the priesthood. Did her own suicide preclude her from sainthood? Was she condemned to the darkest halls of Velyol for that sin, or was the selflessness that compelled her actions upon the Sundering sufficient to redeem her?

In the end they decided that sacrificing herself so that others might live was reason enough to declare her a saint. There were historical precedents: the last, hopeless stand of Noren at the Battle of Kuldain's Crossing sprang to mind, and also Elg's leap from the Tower of Sumlar. The priests had not debated the point long. They knew of the people's love for the royal daughter and what she had done for them. To sully her memory was to flirt with open rebellion.

So he could not be happy about his own death, but he could accept it peacefully, and with grace. There was no point in anguishing over what he could not change.

Algariq reined the horse to a stop. He could just barely make out the shape of a barn perhaps a quarter of a mile ahead of them, its thatch roof frosted with starlight.

"Get down," she commanded.

As always, he obeyed.

"Lie on the ground."

Now it comes, he thought. He hated that he feared the manner of his death. Would she slit his throat, or plunge a knife into his heart? He did not want to be slaughtered like an animal. If only he could fight back! He wanted to die like a soldier. *Please, not like this.*

She crouched beside his supine form. "I have no desire to harm you," she said. "Such a thing would not be worthy of me now, of who I have become. You have done no harm to me, and in truth, you have helped me achieve my life's desire. If there is any debt owed, it is I who owe you."

Her eyes glistened. Was she actually near to weeping?

"You said I did not understand mercy, and perhaps that was so. But I think I do understand it now. And even if I do not, I will at least follow the example that was shown to me.

"I give you your life back. Sleep now. I will hold you in my power until I am far from here, and then I will release my hold on you."

Balandrick could scarcely believe what he had heard. She was going to spare his life. He was going to live.

Just before he slipped into unconsciousness, he heard her say, "If I have brought harm or shame to you, I am sorry." Then he remembered no more.

25

The Telır Osarán, the Valley of Wızards, looked the
same to Gerin as it had when he'd left Hethnost several
years earlier. The great wall of the Hammdras enclosing the
mouth of the wide oval valley; the Tower of the Clouds and
the Tower of Wind rising from the summits of the hills into
which the Hammdras was anchored; the high, sheer cliff on
the valley's far end, from which the Partition Rock protruded,
a long ramplike spur that bisected about a third of the valley;
the Kalabrendis Dhosa, the seldom used gathering hall, built
upon the flattened summit of the Partition Rock; the towers
of the Varsae Sandrova. All of it was unchanged.

But the familiarity was not particularly comforting. To his
surprise, he found himself unnerved by the sight of Hethnost.
His mood darkened as they drew closer to the Hammdras,
and his heart quickened its pace. This was the place where
he had stolen dark magic in order to learn the location of the
Varsae Estrikavis. He'd been under a powerful compulsion
placed upon him by a Neddari *kamichi*, but over the years,
as he'd pondered his actions, he wondered if he would have
behaved the same had the spell never existed.

He'd broken into the vaults below the Varsae Sandrova
and stolen the book of spells and devices of magic of the
Baryashin Order, a now extinct group of renegade wizards
devoted to discovering a path to achieve eternal life by any
means necessary.

Gerin had blown the Horn of Tireon to summon Naragenth's spirit from the grave. It was during this encounter with the spirit that he first heard of the Chamber of the Moon, but the spell had collapsed before Naragenth could tell him anything else.

The collapse of the spell had caused an imbalance between the worlds of the living and the dead. Not only did people in Osseria begin to die at random as the power of the world of the dead moved through this world like a black wind, but a spirit named Asankaru had come through the doorway as well. Asankaru was the Storm King of a long dead race of beings called the Eletheros, who were annihilated in a brutal act of genocide perpetrated by the Atalari, an act lost to history until Gerin and Reshel had seen a vision of the murder of the Eletheros atop the Sundering.

He sighed, and a pain gripped his heart. Reshel had died to give him the power he needed to return Asankaru to the realm of the dead and seal the doorway between the worlds.

It had all begun here.

"You look troubled," said Nyene.

"My memories of this place are not all good ones," he said. Would he have acted the same without the Neddari compulsion? He'd been so driven then. He ached to achieve some lasting greatness, and finding the first amber wizard's lost library seemed the perfect means to achieve that goal.

If I would have acted no differently, then Reshel's death is truly my fault. I can't blame it on the Neddari spell. Perhaps his father had been right to blame him as he had. The king might have had more insight than he'd given him credit for.

A gloom settled over Gerin that was not dispelled by the appearance of Seddon Rethazi, the steward of Hethnost. The old man's moustache was as thick as ever, though Gerin thought he detected a bit more stoop to his shoulders.

"Hello, hello!" he said as he and a number of the Sunrise Guard approached them. "It's wonderful to see you, but I've had no word of your coming."

"We did not send word, Seddon," said Hollin. "We were not expecting to come here."

"I sense an interesting story behind this visit."

"Do you know where we can find the Archmage?" asked Abaru.

"I believe she is in her manor house." He took a quick count of everyone, then hurried off, barking orders about preparing rooms to a number of nearby servants.

The Khedeshian soldiers departed with the Sunrise Guard. Gerin and the others followed Hollin and Abaru. Elaysen and Nyene were awed by the splendor of Hethnost, and both women asked questions about the purposes of the many buildings and towers. Abaru took great delight in answering them. Zaephos took in everything but said nothing.

The Archmage's manor house was near the base of the Partition Rock. A servant ushered them in and took them to a council chamber with a large round table filling most of the space. The servant returned with water, wine, bread, and cheese. "The Archmage will be with you shortly," said the young woman.

It was not long before Marandra strode into the room. As regal as a queen, tall and beautiful in a stern, cold way, she swept into the room with two other wizards close behind. Gerin's eyes were immediately drawn to the Ammon Ekril upon her brow. His pulse quickened with excitement. *There it is, a few feet away from me. The receptacle for the* kalaya mithran. *The Words of Making.*

Gerin recognized Sevaisan Barlaechi, the First Siege, and Kirin Zaeset, the Warden of Healing.

"I am surprised and pleased by your visit, unannounced as it is," said Marandra. She gave Hollin a pointed stare. "Please, introduce your new companions, and tell us why you are here."

Hollin gave her a warm greeting, then introduced her to Elaysen, Nyene, and finally Zaephos. He gave his name only. "I will leave it to you to tell them who and what you are," Hollin said to the messenger.

Marandra cocked an eyebrow. "Indeed. An interesting statement." She fixed her gaze on Zaephos. "Please, sir, explain Hollin's curious introduction."

Zaephos inclined his head slightly. The expression on his face was unreadable to Gerin. What went on in that mind of his? Were his thoughts completely foreign to those of mortals? What did the world look like through his eyes?

"Greetings, Archmage of Hethnost. I am a messenger of the Maker, known in the mortal sphere as the One God as taught by the Prophet Aunphar, Elaysen's father."

Sevaisan scratched his dark beard, then folded his arms. "Preposterous. Hollin, I hardly find this appropriate. You may have thought it would be amusing, but I assure you it is not."

Gerin had never liked the First Siege. A dour, humorless man, all hard edges and filled with judgment and condescension. He'd wondered during his first stay here how such a man could have risen to such a position of power, and still had no idea what the other wizards saw in him.

"This is no joke, First Siege," said Hollin, more than a trace of irritation in his voice. "This is the divine messenger who appeared to Gerin when he first came here, and later appeared to him again in Almaris."

"He appeared to my father as well," said Elaysen. "He is indeed who he claims to be."

Sevaisan made a scoffing noise and settled back into his chair.

"What do you say, amber wizard?" the Archmage asked Gerin.

"Zaephos is exactly who he says he is. But whether you believe that or not, it's almost incidental to the reason we're here."

"You've not been able to take your eyes from the Ammon Ekril since I entered the room," she said to him.

"And with good reason."

The wizards of Hethnost already knew of the Havalqa search for the Words of Making from letters Hollin had sent to them. Now, Gerin, Hollin, and Abaru told the other wizards the story of the appearance of the *akesh*, their journey to the Watchtowers, and the dreams imparted to them by the Telchan.

"Incredible," said Kirin when they were done. "You actually entered the Watchtowers! Your abilities never cease to amaze me, Gerin."

Most of the food on the table was gone by then, and Marandra commanded a servant to bring them more.

"So you see why I cannot take my eyes from the Ammon Ekril, Archmage," said Gerin.

Carefully, she removed the circlet from her forehead and placed it on the table. "Hollin long believed there was some power hidden within its depths, much to my own annoyance. It has been studied for thousands of years, and no trace of power was ever discovered. I myself have worked countless spells on it but found nothing."

"The *kalaya mithran* may not be in the Ammon Ekril right now," said Gerin. He described the dream in which he saw the power enter the circlet from outside of it after the Changing of Nelien, waiting for the proper summons or incantation—it was unclear from the vision what catalyst had caused the power to join with the circlet. The dream indicated that the power was alive in some way, so perhaps it simply chose when and under what conditions to return to its receptacle.

"But you don't know how to determine if it's in the Ammon Ekril, or to summon it if it's not?" asked Kirin.

"Unfortunately," said Gerin.

The Archmage granted them permission to take and study the Ammon Ekril. "See what Rahmdil might know of this," she said. "Who knows what knowledge he has locked away in that private library of his?"

Elaysen made her way through the massive Varsae Sandrova toward the office of the Warden of Healing. She'd had to ask a number of servants for directions, and got lost three times before finally reaching the solitary door at the end of a darkened hallway.

"Hello, Warden," she said when he opened the door.

He looked surprised to see her. "Elaysen, come in. What can I do for you?"

"I came to ask you some questions, if I may. Aside from

being the daughter of the Prophet, I am a healer in Almaris, what the common folk call a witching woman."

"I know of them well. Some of your remedies are quite potent. What questions would you ask?"

"First, if you would direct me to the section of the library where you keep books about nonmagical healing, I would love to read what you've gathered here. I can scarcely believe the size of this place."

"There are days when it still astounds me, I assure you."

"My pack was lost during the fight on our way to the Watchtowers. All of my medicines were lost with it. I'd like to replace them. Here is a list of the herbs and medicines I had." She held out a single sheet of parchment. "Is it possible you have these here? They're not magical in any way—at least that I'm aware of—so you may not bother with such things."

He took the parchment, put on a pair of reading spectacles, and examined the list. "We may have some of these, Elaysen; perhaps half. We keep some medicines here—magic is not always the best remedy—but our stores are limited because no one makes a study of these kinds of cures the way I'm sure you do."

"Do you know if you have any gypsa weed? It's also known as tallow weed or tallow root."

"I don't know. We'll have to check. I'm not familiar with any of those names. What is it used for?"

She paused, unsure how much she should say. "It's used to calm the mind," she said. "You may not have it here. It's native to the lands around Almaris. I've never heard of it growing elsewhere."

"Then you're right, we may not have it. Most of what's here has been grown at Hethnost or found relatively close by."

"Thank you for whatever help you can offer, Warden."

"You're most welcome. Come, I need a break. I'll take you to where you can read to your heart's content about healing in all its forms."

*   *   *

Gerin and the other wizards spent a week studying the Ammon Ekril in Rahmdil Khazuzili's private library. They probed it with every possible spell but could not determine whether the *kalaya mithran* was even in the circlet.

"Do you think our mysterious divine guest might have any insight?" asked Rahmdil. "I've tried to talk to him about the nature of the divine realm, but he declined to speak of it." He looked to Gerin. "Perhaps he would better respond to a request from you about this?"

"I've already asked him," said Gerin. "He said there's nothing he can do to help us." Gerin had not completely believed Zaephos, but he also knew there was nothing he could do to coerce him. The messenger followed his own path.

He was growing increasingly frustrated with their lack of progress, but tried to temper his impatience with the fact that the Ammon Ekril had been in the possession of wizards for thousands of years, with no one able to penetrate its secrets. They were farther along than anyone else had ever been. A week of failures was to be expected. *Look how long it took to discover the location of the Chamber of the Moon after Naragenth gave me that name.* Still, it was hard, with the receptacle of the power lying on the table in front of him. They'd had no idea where the Chamber of the Moon was located—all they had was the name. But this was something he could pick up and hold in his hand. They simply needed to understand how it worked.

"I'm at a loss as to what to suggest," said Kirin.

"We've found nothing in the library that can help us," said Rahmdil. "All knowledge of the *kalaya mithran* seems to have been lost."

Gerin closed his eyes and recalled the dreams sent by the Telchan. There had to be some clue in them, some critical piece of information he was overlooking. He replayed the vivid images in his mind, tried to hear the words exactly as they were spoken. There had been something about the origin of the *kalaya mithran*, that it had been a gift to the Matriarchs—

A gift from another world.

That was it. The *kalaya mithran* had come from outside Osseria, outside their very world. *Like the Dreamers, or the place where the Varsae Estrikavis resides.*

But how did that help him? He pondered the question and could come up with no satisfying answers. He finally voiced his thoughts to the others.

"I don't see how knowing that the power came from another world helps us," said Abaru.

"Are there any spells that connect in some way to other worlds?" asked Gerin.

Kirin gave him a pointed stare. "Other than the Baryashin spells you've had some experience with, there are none. And even that was a connection to the world of the dead, not another inhabitable realm, which is what I think is implied here."

Sudden guilt welled in Gerin at the memory of his theft of the spells. He felt his face redden. "Point taken, Warden."

He took their leave for a time and went to the dining hall. Nyene was there, seated alone. She'd been training with the soldiers, who reported that she was exceptionally skilled with weapons.

She saw him and waved for him to join her.

"So you are the King of Khedesh!" she said. "I thought they were mocking me, but others have convinced me that it's true."

Well, it had to come out sometime, he thought. "Yes, that's true."

"You are a man of many layers and many mysteries, Gerin Atreyano. A wizard and king who desires to save the world. I would think you were mad had I not witnessed these things for myself."

"People will think I'm mad anyway. That's why I try to keep things quiet."

"Do you have a queen chosen? I will offer myself if you do not. We Threndish women are strong. I will bear you mighty children. And we are exceptional lovers, unlike your cold Khedeshian women. Like the healer, who has eyes only for her plants and herbs. If we were to marry, the kingdom might fall to ruin because you would never want to leave our bed!" She laughed and stared hard into his eyes.

"I'm flattered by your offer, Nyene, but my plans for a queen are still a closely kept secret."

"Ah, you flirt with me. Would you not enjoy loving this body?" She wriggled in her chair in an entertaining way. "We could fill a bath and—"

"Nyene, enough, please."

She laughed. "You find me impossible to resist, so you must silence me instead. I understand, King Gerin Atreyano." She stood. "Enjoy your meal. But you know you will be thinking about me. Men cannot resist."

He could not take his eyes from her as she left the dining hall. When he found himself wondering what she looked like undressed, he laughed quietly. *Damn, she was right!*

"I knew when you left here you were never going to return," said Marandra.

"I'm here now," said Hollin.

"You know what I mean. That you would never return here to live. To be with me." She tried not to sound petulant, wounded, but was unsure how well she succeeded.

He sighed. They were in her rooms, wrapped in towels. They'd just finished bathing, and the lavender scent of soap filled the air.

"Things had not been well between us for some time, Marandra. We both knew that."

"Yes, and sending you away from here to train Gerin was something we both needed."

"Why are you so sure I'm never going to return?"

"I can sense it in your demeanor. I knew it then but said nothing. Now I'm even more sure."

"There's no point in talking about something that has not yet come to pass. Should I leave?"

She went to him and put her arms around his shoulders. "No." She remembered quite well how poor their relationship had been when he'd left for Ailethon. She had been glad to see him go. But her strong sense that he was here almost out of obligation, out of duty, made her feel unwanted, and hurt her deeply. She felt a need to reassert herself into his life, to make him *want* her again. She knew it was a childish desire, but could not help herself.

And what Abaru had confided in her! That he feared Hollin was afflicted with tevosa. She'd kept a careful watch on him since hearing it, but so far had seen no signs of it herself. She prayed he did not have it.

"I don't want to quarrel," she said. "Let's go to bed. I won't ask about your plans again. In that, I can't command you, either as a woman or the Archmage."

He turned his head and kissed her. "I don't want to quarrel, either."

Together, they went into the bedroom.

The next morning, a servant stopped by Gerin's rooms and relayed a message from Hollin. "He asks that you bring your sword, the Scepter of the King, and the Staff of Naragenth to the Warden of the Archive's private library," said the slender young man.

Gerin understood the reason for Hollin's request. Since their arrival, they'd been so focused on the Ammon Ekril that they completely neglected Gerin's achievement in creating Nimnahal and the discovery of the Varsae Estrikavis.

He had not forgotten them, however. Since being granted the dreams of the Telchan, he'd been thinking about how the *kalaya mithran* functioned. He had some ideas, but not yet had time to test them.

That time had come.

"The gods preserve me, I could sense your sword when you were down the hallway," said Kirin when Gerin entered the room. The Archmage, First Siege, and a number of the High Ministers were present as well, making the room feel crowded and small.

Gerin placed the sheathed weapon on the table and allowed the wizards to examine it. He demonstrated how the blade's silvery light brightened when he held it, recognizing in some way the power that created it. They asked him many questions about its creation and what inspired him. He enjoyed the way they showed interest over something new; it never would have occurred to them to create a magical weapon. Their thinking, in some respects, was far too rigid to see value in such an exercise.

They spent even more time examining the staff. Gerin described the Presence that at times communicated with him by implanting mages in his mind of what it wanted him to do. The images were accompanied by a great deal of pain; clearly there was some flaw in the method of communication. Either Naragenth had never perfected it, or he himself was missing some crucial bit of information.

"And you've found no extant writings about the creation of the staff?" asked Rahmdil.

"Nothing. The whole of the Varsae Estrikavis hasn't been cataloged yet, but we've found very little written by Naragenth himself."

When they were done with their questions, Gerin opened the box that contained the Scepter of the King.

"I can't believe the entrance to the Varsae Estrikavis is here in front of my eyes!" said Rahmdil Khazuzili. He rubbed his hands together like a child about to receive an apple tart.

"Indeed," said the Archmage. She looked at Gerin. "It seems you are destined to be a finder of lost relics."

Gerin smiled at the compliment. This was something he had discovered on his own, reasoned out with a great deal of thought. He explained how he'd come to the conclusion that only an enormous influx of amber magic would unlock all of the protections Naragenth had placed in the scepter.

"I fully expected it to turn to ash," said Hollin. "I admit I had little faith he was right."

"I wasn't too sure myself," Gerin admitted. "But there was only one way to know."

"You took a terrible risk," said the First Siege, with more than a trace of disapproval.

"Sometimes risks are necessary to achieve a goal," Gerin said. "Timidity very rarely wins anything."

"Risk taking seems endemic to your character."

"Enough, Sevaisan," said the Archmage. "This is King Gerin's moment of triumph. For once, stop being disagreeable."

"I have another idea I'm going to test now," Gerin said. "Don't fret, First Siege. This one entails no risk. At least no risk that I can foresee. But the reward if I'm right . . . "

"Gerin, what are you planning?" asked Hollin with some trepidation.

"Nothing dangerous, so stop worrying. It's just an idea. I'm going to open the door to the Varsae Estrikavis now." He glanced at the Archmage as he spoke.

He opened himself to magic, let amber power fill him, then directed it into the scepter.

The defensive spells within the scepter had not reset themselves after he'd first unlocked them. If Naragenth had a method for doing so, he had not found it, and would not reset them even if he could. There was no need.

The magic fed the spell at the heart of the scepter, an utterly strange power that drank his magic and unfolded like the edge of a knife, only sharper than the sharpest physical blade. This was a power intended to cut its way between worlds, slicing through the barriers that separated one plane of existence from another.

In a moment a door of dark wood with a gold handle appeared in the air before him, floating above the tiled floor. The sigil of Naragenth, an upright staff bisecting a rayed sun, was imprinted upon it. Below the sigil was a silver crescent. Several of the wizards gasped at the sight.

"This is the entrance to the Chamber of the Moon, which contains the Varsae Estrikavis," said Hollin.

Rahmdil ran his trembling fingers lightly across the wood. "It's almost a miracle that you found this."

Gerin was not looking at the door. He kept his gaze on the Archmage and wondered if his idea was correct.

A moment later his heart fluttered when the diamond in the Ammon Ekril began to shine with a warm, golden glow.

I was right, he thought.

* * *

"By the gods, what have you done?" said the First Siege.

"I've figured out how to activate the *kalaya mithran*," he said. He turned to the Archmage. "Has it ever done that before?"

"No. Never." She removed the circlet and placed it on the table.

"Gerin, please," said Hollin. "Enough with your secrecy. Tell us how you knew this would happen."

He quelled his excitement. "The dreams showed us that the *kalaya mithran* originated in another world. The Varsae Estrikavis *exists* in another world. I thought perhaps it needed the energy of another world to awaken."

"Remarkable," said Rahmdil.

Rahmdil started to create a complex incantation. Gerin could only follow a fraction of what he was doing, and was amazed at the old wizard's prowess. Rahmdil was doing something far more subtle than anything he himself could accomplish. Strength alone was no substitute for years—decades, lifetimes—of practice with magic.

Even though he could not understand all of what the Warden was doing, Gerin realized he was attempting to determine if there was a link of some kind between the door to the Chamber of the Moon and the Ammon Ekril. It was an astoundingly complex spell, the likes of which he had never seen before. Like a Seeing in some respects, only an order of magnitude more complicated. Gerin watched as dozens of threads of magic wove about the room, seeking fractures or holes in the very fabric of reality.

The other wizards remained still and silent, watching the Warden work his spell. The threads snaked about the room for several minutes, probing, searching. He wondered how Rahmdil was able to maintain control for so long. It was not a question of strength, but of concentration and will. Amber magic would not necessarily be any more suited to the task at hand than less powerful magic. He found himself admiring the old man immensely.

One of the threads brightened and formed a straight, rigid line between the door and the circlet.

"Ah!" said Rahmdil. "There you are." He made a gesture, and the other threads vanished. "This is what brought the Ammon Ekril to life."

"Is it a particular kind of magic?" asked Gerin.

"It's not magic at all. There is energy flowing from the Chamber of the Moon into the circlet." The Warden of the Archives made another gesture, and a line of pulses along the thread began to move from the door toward the diamond. "There. You can see the direction of the flow."

"What is that energy?" asked Kirin.

"I'm not sure," said Rahmdil. "It has no direct source that I can detect, but maybe we'll discover more once we enter the Varsae Estrikavis. It is a diffuse kind of power."

Kirin created an intricate Seeing spell that he peered at for a long moment. "I think it's simply the fabric of the other world where the library is hidden. It's like"—he waved his hand, grasping for the right words—"the air of that place. It's not coming from a specific *thing*. I'm not explaining this very well."

"I understand," said Gerin. "This power is a property of the *difference* between the two worlds."

"Yes, exactly."

"So the world where Naragenth hid the Varsae Estrikavis just happens to be the very world where the *kalaya mithran* came from?" asked Kirin. "That seems a rather large coincidence."

"Not necessarily," said Gerin. "Maybe that was an easy world for Naragenth to reach. Maybe there's something about it that makes it more accessible than others. We have no idea how he found it or how he created the Chamber of the Moon. But if it *is* a more accessible realm, perhaps the Atalari found the same path."

"Or all other worlds might create the same kind of energy when doors are opened between them," said Abaru.

"How would the Atalari have used the *kalaya mithran* if they needed to access another world first?" asked the Archmage. "That is certainly not an ability they were known to have."

"There's no way to know, Archmage," said Rahmdil. "What we did here may have no relation to how the Atalari used this."

They worked at least a dozen spells on the Ammon Ekril itself, attempting to determine the nature of the power causing the diamond to glow. Maddeningly, they could garner no clear insight into its properties. Even the source of the light proved elusive.

"This is absurd," said Marandra. "Is there nothing we can discover?"

"This power is so alien to our magic that I fear there may be little else we *can* know," said Rahmdil with a sigh.

"Perhaps it's time to be direct," she said. "Let's see if what we've awakened is in the mood to talk."

Rahmdil dispelled the thread of light extending from the door to the Ammon Ekril. The Archmage placed the circlet on her brow. "Did any of you see exactly how the *kalaya mithran* was used in your dreams?"

"No, Archmage," said Gerin. "We saw it in use, but not *how* it was used. Our viewpoint was always outside of the wearer."

She closed her eyes. "I sense nothing out of the ordinary. If the *kalaya mithran* is in here, it remains hidden from me."

"Try calling out to it with your mind," said Hollin.

A scowl of irritation flashed across her face. "I've already done that. And I've used magic as well. But it might as well be a lump of lead for all of the reaction I've provoked."

They decided to leave the Ammon Ekril for a while and explore the Varsae Estrikavis. Gerin, Hollin, and Abaru led the other wizards through Naragenth's library, pointing out unique volumes of lore or devices of magic. Gerin feared that Rahmdil might actually die of joy.

Later, Gerin returned to his rooms and stretched out on his bed, elated that his idea had proved to be right, but also frustrated because they'd made no further progress toward understanding how to use the power within the circlet.

He was almost asleep when someone pounded on his door. In the hallway stood one of his own Khedeshian soldiers, his face animated.

"Your Majesty, please, come quickly!" said the man. "Captain Vaules just arrived!"

26

Balandrıck was drainıng his third cup of water when Gerin swept into the room. "Balan!" he cried out as he hugged the captain. "By the gods, it's good to see you! Where have you been? What happened?"

Balan felt himself grinning like a fool. "It's good to see you too, Your Majesty. I was pretty sure I wouldn't see a familiar face ever again."

Elaysen and Hollin entered the drawing room. Elaysen threw her arms around his neck. "Oh, Balan, I thought you were dead!"

Hollin shook his hand warmly and welcomed him home. "You seem uninjured."

Images of his rape at the hands of Algariq flashed in his mind, but he angrily pushed them down. "I'm fine."

"Your disappearance was quite mysterious," said the wizard. "We were completely confounded."

"If everyone will be quiet for a bit, I'll explain."

"Please," said Gerin. "Go on."

They sat around a table and listened while Balandrick told them of his captivity at the hands of the soul stealer. Balan watched Gerin's face darken with anger. *He knows what I had to endure at her hands,* he thought. *I wonder if it's anything we'll ever speak about to each other?*

He was certainly not going to be the one to bring it up.

He felt overwhelmed once more with guilt and shame

when he admitted that he told Tolsadri everything they had
learned about the Words of Making. "I'm sorry, Your Majesty. I couldn't help myself. Her power. . ."

"I understand, Balan. I know there was nothing you could
do. Believe me, I understand."

Balandrick described Tolsadri's attempt to betray Algariq
after he'd raised her from the caste of the Harridan, her anticipation of his treachery, and their escape from the camp.

"Then she surprised me," he said. "She said she was sorry
if she'd hurt me and made me sleep. She said she wanted to
be merciful to me, the way you were to her, Your Majesty.
When I woke up she was gone, and I was no longer in her
power. I was myself again. I couldn't believe how good it felt
to simply raise my arm or clench a fist. Being trapped in my
body like that was a true nightmare."

"What can you tell us about the Havalqa army?" asked
Gerin.

"It's big, disciplined from what I could see, and it's on its
way here. After she released me, I made my way here as fast
as I could. I had to walk at first because I couldn't find a
damn horse to save my life! Finally, a few days later, I spied
a Havalqa scout and managed to relieve him of his mount.
Killed him before he knew what hit him."

"The Archmage must be warned at once." Hollin rose
from the table. "Balandrick, once again, it's good to have
you back."

They talked awhile longer, then a wizard arrived asking
Balandrick to come with him to tell the Archmage all he
could of the approaching army. He took his leave of Gerin
and Elaysen and followed the wizard to the Archmage's
manor house.

On his approach to the fortress earlier that day, he was as
impressed with its formidable defenses as he had been the
first time he'd sojourned here. This would not be an easy
place to siege. But he also knew the Havalqa had substantial
powers at their disposal. He wondered if Hethnost had ever
been besieged, and asked the wizard escorting him.

"No, it has not," said the wiry man.

"It looks like that's about to change."

"Any army foolish enough to attack us will break themselves against our might. We are not a warlike people, but we can and will defend ourselves with every means we have."

"I hope you're right."

They entered the manor house and made their way to the second floor. "Welcome, Captain," said the Archmage when he entered the room where she and the other rulers of Hethnost waited. "Hollin has told us that you have information about a Havalqa army that is even now marching to attack us."

"Yes, Archmage."

Sevaisan gave Balandrick a hostile stare. "I for one am skeptical of these powers that forced you to confess all you knew of the Words of Making to your enemies."

"I've already explained the soul stealer's powers to you, Sevaisan," said Hollin. "I experienced them myself. Shall we bring King Gerin in here to validate them to your satisfaction? Her powers *cannot* be broken. It is one of the most insidious abilities I've ever heard of, and I hope I never experience it again. Believe me when I tell you there is as much chance of breaking her powers as there is of you behaving reasonably and showing basic manners to a guest of Hethnost."

Sevaisan looked incensed. "That is outrageous! I am the First Siege—"

"No, Sevaisan, the only outrage is your inability to accept anything that doesn't conform to your rigid—"

"Enough!" shouted the Archmage. "Another outburst like that from either of you and I'll have you both thrown out." She looked toward Balandrick as the two wizards pointedly ignored each other. "Captain, my apologies for that . . . *unseemly* behavior. Our long lives do not always confer wisdom or maturity, unfortunately."

"It's quite all right, Archmage. I'm unhappy with myself about what I revealed, but I assure you there was no way to resist."

"I believe you, young man. I heard Gerin and Hollin both tell of this woman's powers. We won't question it again." She glanced at the First Siege.

Balandrick spent the next hour answering questions about the size and strength of the Havalqa army. He emphasized that he was with it for only a short period of time and that his attention had been dominated and controlled by Algariq.

"Still, what you have told us will be helpful," said the Archmage. "If you have nothing else to add, you are dismissed."

A servant showed him to rooms that had been prepared for him. Balan stretched out on the bed and closed his eyes, but sleep would not come. Finally he got up, pulled on his boots, and went for a walk.

He moved brusquely through the fortress, hoping to tire himself out. He decided to wander some of the garden paths, and then, if he still wasn't ready for sleep, to climb the long slope to the top of the Partition Rock. He noted a number of wizards and soldiers of the Sunrise Guard moving in and out of the Archmage's manor house, whose windows were now almost fully lit despite the late hour.

Balandrick turned a corner by a retaining wall and saw Zaephos seated on a bench nearby. The One God's messenger was staring up at the stars through an opening in the trees. He glanced at Balandrick, then returned his gaze to the sky.

"Hello, Captain," he said. "I heard you'd returned."

Balan went to the bench but did not sit. "You didn't somehow sense it on your own? I would have thought a divine being would know such things before anyone. In fact, I would have thought that you could have told them what happened to me when I disappeared."

"When not in the mortal realm, my vision is very different. Here, clothed in flesh, most of my power is veiled."

"Yes, you said that before. Near the Watchtowers. You said if you were to release your might, you could level mountains. I still find that hard to imagine. Perhaps the failing is mine."

"It is. Whether you can imagine such a thing or not is irrelevant. A conflict among beings of my rank could easily lay waste to this continent, or reshape it beyond recognition. Mountains leveled, forests turned to ash, rivers and lakes boiled away, the earth torn like parchment with new seas bubbling up from the depths. It happened once before, Balandrick. Long ago, eons before the coming of humankind, there was such a war. In its aftermath, the very laws of the universe were changed to make it far more difficult to ever wage a similar conflict again. I am bound by those laws."

"Is the Adversary?"

"Yes, though he is far more powerful than I."

"You said the laws were changed to make it far more difficult. That doesn't mean it's not impossible. It could happen again."

"It could, but the effort required to wage such a war is substantial. Far beyond any possible gains one side could make."

"So whoever changed the laws made it *impractical* for your type of being to come down and fight in our little corner of the universe."

"An interesting phrasing, but essentially correct."

"And who exactly changed the laws of the universe? And how? That must have been some trick."

"The Maker is the one who altered the rules of His creation."

"But how? Is that just part of His power? His nature? It seems to me that altering the rules once they're in place would be a lot harder than setting them up at the beginning. Did He alter the mortal realm, as you call it, or the divine place where you hail from, or both? I'm curious how something like that is done."

Zaephos cocked his head. "You are oddly perceptive, Captain. I can say only that the Maker has the power to alter His creations as He sees fit. Though it is never done lightly, or without cost."

"What about all these other worlds? Like the one where Naragenth's library is hidden? Did the Maker create all of those, too? Are some of them more real than others? How busy is He?"

"That is a topic I am forbidden to discuss."

Balandrick decided to drop that line of questioning. "So what does our mortal world look like to you now?"

"Much the same as it does to you. These eyes are no different from your own."

"But what you see now is not the same as when you come here without flesh, right? Like when you appeared to Gerin on the road to Hethnost."

"Yes. What I saw then was not only what was, but all of the possibilities of what might be. And if I bent my will to it, what once had been."

Balan tried to conceive what that type of vision might look like and failed miserably. He could not comprehend it. *How could anyone see not just one future but many of them? Did I step here, or there? Did I turn my head left or right? Did I cough or not? Do all of those little changes create a different path to the future?* It seemed to him there must be an almost infinite number of variations. How could any being comprehend that?

A basic question occurred to Balan that he didn't think anyone else had yet asked.

"What does the Adversary want? What is he trying to accomplish?"

"What he wants does not matter. The only thing we must concern ourselves with is stopping him."

"But if we know what he's after, maybe there's a way of thwarting his plans. Hit him indirectly, since it seems to me that we're woefully unprepared to battle a god. I think we could use as many plans of attack as possible."

"He and his goals are inextricably twined. One cannot be defeated without defeating the other."

"What does that mean? Is that some kind of riddle?"

Zaephos stood. "It is all I can say. Good night, Balandrick."

27

I t's time to begin your siege, General," said Vethiq aril Tolsadri.

"It is no such thing, Voice," said Lorem taril'na Ezqedir. He held a seeing-glass to his right eye and surveyed the fortress ahead of them while he spoke. "It's time to observe, and to plan."

He collapsed the seeing-glass and turned to an adjutant. "Have Tereen prepare my meal," he said. "Find Haavi and have him join me."

Tolsadri could not believe this insect of a general was ignoring him. He was positioning his army too far from the valley where the accursed wizards were hiding. Gerin Atreyano was most likely there as well. The mere thought of the man who had brought humiliation upon him caused blood to rush in his ears and his heart to race. He'd lost stature and standing that he had yet to regain because of the debacle on the island.

Behind him, members of the caste of Elqos the Worker labored to pitch the tents of Tolsadri, Ezqedir, and the other commanders. It galled Tolsadri that his tent was no larger than that of Ezqedir—the man was a general, not even a Sword!—but his machinations to obtain a larger tent befitting his station had been thwarted at every turn.

He fingered the Mark of Bariq the Wise. The medallion was a comfort to him, a reassurance that he served the greatest of the Powers and a reminder of his achievements in becoming both an Adept and Loremaster. He was the greatest of the Adepts and the Voice of the Exalted herself.

Yet all was now in jeopardy because of Gerin Atreyano. Tolsadro knew that the Dreamers were wary of him, and the Exalted had chided him for his loss of the captive. He knew the true fault lay with that wretch of the Harridan, a spawn of evil if ever he'd known one. He wondered where she had gone after delivering the location of the Words of Making. He shook his head in disgust. *She sullies my mind. Her task is done. Best not to think of her again.*

"I demand that you begin your siege," he said in a low voice to the general. "The Words of Making are within that fortress!"

"I *am* beginning my siege," said Ezqedir. He was taller than Tolsadri, something else Tolsadri did not like about the man. He was broad through the chest and shoulders, his legs thick and well-muscled, typical of the men in the Kledeen Valley where he'd been born. Barbarian giants, all of them. His black hair fell in snaking coils to his shoulders, brushing the top of glinting armor that almost seemed an extension of his bronze skin.

"Observing one's enemy to determine both weaknesses and strengths is the first part of any battle," Ezqedir continued.

"You need to attack!" hissed Tolsadri.

"I will attack when I am ready, Voice of the Exalted. And not a moment before."

"While you dawdle, they strengthen their defenses."

"There is nothing they can do now that will make a material difference. But if I attack before *I* am ready, we may suffer yet another disastrous defeat. One that I'm not sure even you're high reputation could endure."

Tolsadri could not be certain whether Ezqedir was mocking him. He did not know the man well enough to gauge if he was capable of such subtleties. *And I will never know him that well,* he vowed. *I will destroy him for his lack of proper respect, the way I destroyed Drugal.*

"The fortress is before you," said Tolsadri. "What more do

you need to see? We have the Loh'shree and the eunuchs as well as your Herolen! If that is not sufficient for the task at hand, you should fall on your sword for your incompetence and leave the siege to someone who will take action."

"Did you fall on your sword after your failure to hold the man you're now demanding I recapture? He not only escaped you—and took your life in the process—but escaped your stronghold as well. I have failed at nothing yet, Voice, and I don't intend to."

"You know nothing about—"

Ezqedir moved so close to Tolsadri that the Voice had to take a step back.

"The blockade of their capital city was destroyed by Gerin Atreyano. Nineteen ships drowned. Sword of the Exalted Drugal lost much of his army and his life to Gerin Atreyano before *his* siege could even begin." He pointed toward the fortress without taking his eyes from Tolsadri. "Gerin Atreyano is more than likely in that place. If you think I'm going to risk my men because of your impatience—brought about by your own incompetence—you'll be sorely disappointed. I suggest you revise your expectations accordingly, Voice."

"You forget yourself, Ezqedir. You are not the Sword. I *order* you to begin your siege, or I'll replace you with someone who will." As soon as spoke, he knew he'd made a mistake. He cursed his own anger. He usually did not let it get the best of him, did not let it make him speak when he should remain silent—but this was an error.

Ezqedir had the gall to grin. "It is you who forget yourself, Voice. You are right in one thing, and one thing only. I am not the Exalted's Sword—yet. But I have been charged by her to command this army and locate the Words of Making. I lead here in the ways of war, not you.

"I'll conduct this siege as I see fit, so that the victory will be mine. When that is done, I'll become the new Sword. I won't make the mistake Drugal made of underestimating your skill for treachery. The manner of his death has been questioned. There are whispers that he was murdered, that he did not perish in the conflagration set off upon the ridge.

There is no proof, of course, and no proof will ever come. But the whispers will remain, Voice, and cling to you like a foul vapor."

The general paused, as if waiting for a response, then went on. "Nothing to say? I'm surprised. You have a reputation for garrulousness. Perhaps that is one of many things exaggerated about you."

"You'll pay for your impertinence and slander."

Ezqedir shrugged. "We shall see about that. Is it not the role of the Voice to parley with our enemies? Perhaps you should knock on their gate and demand they turn over the Words to us."

Tolsadri stepped forward until his chest almost touched the general's. He was hoping that Ezqedir would step back, but the whoreson did not move.

"You overstep your place, General. Regardless of the whispers you claim exist, I am still the Voice of the Exalted, chosen by her to speak on her behalf. You will show me the respect owed to my station, regardless of your opinion of me, or I swear by Holvareh Himself, you will be punished. The laws of Aleith'aqtar are not forgotten because we are in a foreign land. Many things changed when Drugal died in battle and the blockade was broken, but not this."

There was another long pause; Ezqedir seemed to be holding his breath. Then he blinked a single time, stepped away from Tolsadri, bowed his head.

"I will not remind you again of your place," said Tolsadri.

"You're right in that many things changed when the Sword died," said Ezqedir. "What you may not have realized is that not all of those changes benefit you."

He turned away and vanished behind the fold of his tent flap.

28

One of Ezqedir's adjutants summoned Telothes var Nitendi to the general's tent. The commander of the Loremasters attached to this army carried himself as all Loremasters seemed to: with an air of aloof haughtiness, a sense of superiority and a disdain for anything unrelated to their caste or their work. Ezqedir had never met a Loremaster he liked, but Nitendi was at least tolerable compared to some of the others he'd dealt with.

He was aware that Nitendi had just spent the better part of an hour with the Voice, and was curious to see how much Tolsadri's presence might have affected him. He had no doubt that Tolsadri would do whatever he could to make his command of this siege as difficult as possible. The Voice was not so stupid as to want the siege to fail—he was far too eager to claim the Words of Making for himself. But he would do whatever he could to undermine his authority, and twist the smallest signs of weakness to his advantage.

Ezqedir had been under Drugal's command on several campaigns, and his opinion of the late Sword of the Exalted was that he was a brilliant field commander who did not have the ability—or perhaps the desire—to wage the games of intrigue demanded by members of the Court of Kalmanyikul. If Drugal had been more competent in that arena, he would have maneuvered himself into a position to kill Tolsadri, or at least destroy his power and influence, which in the end would have resulted in the same thing.

The general was certain that Tolsadri was involved in the murder of the Sword. He did not care about it personally; he felt no need to avenge Drugal. Indeed, it was the Sword's own indifference to the danger Tolsadri posed that led to his death, and Ezqedir felt only a mild contempt for someone who did not understand the nature of the threats he faced. The Sword played the games of intrigue poorly, and paid a heavy price for his failure. From what little he'd known of the man, Drugal placed a great deal of weight on the guiding hand of Herol.

Ezqedir believed in the Powers and the order they brought to the world, but in his view men needed to look after their own affairs and do everything they could to make themselves succeed, to seize their own destinies. The Powers would not step in to help them; that was not their role. They watched to see how well the men and women who served them did their tasks, and would reward them accordingly in the afterlife. But here, now . . . it was up to men to do what needed to be done. To be strong. To be smart. To accomplish things like conducting a siege, or ridding oneself of a hated and dangerous enemy.

Long before this campaign began—before they'd left Aleith'aqtar on that interminable sea voyage—the general had identified Tolsadri as the most dangerous man in Kalmanyikul. The Voice was exceptionally talented at covering his trail. He destroyed reputations, and sometimes lives, with devastating efficiency. It was his true talent, even more so than his abilities as a Voice or Loremaster. After someone's fall from grace—or execution, or murder—the halls were filled with whispers that guessed at Tolsadri's involvement. Ezqedir suspected that some of the whispers that pointed to the Voice were in fact started by Tolsadri himself to bolster his own reputation as a power not to be trifled with, and to intimidate those who would oppose him.

I'll trifle with him, and he'll be surprised at what a lowly soldier like me can do, and the knowledge I possess. Yes, he'll be surprised indeed.

Nitendi entered the tent, his graying beard impeccably combed and oiled. He glanced about with an expression of distaste, as if the very air associated with Ezqedir were somehow offensive, beneath him in some way.

Tolsadri has done his work with him, thought Ezqedir. Nitendi had been in his tent many times before, and his attitude had never been this openly arrogant.

He offered Nitendi wine, which the slender man declined with a wave of his hand. "I've come as you requested, General. What do you want?"

Ezqedir ignored the rudeness of the man's remark and poured himself some wine, which he sipped slowly while Nitendi waited with increasing impatience for him to speak.

"Loremaster Nitendi, tomorrow you will take your men and probe the defenses of the fortress. I need to know what powers are arrayed against us."

"I believe the demons of the eunuchs would be better suited for that task," said Nitendi.

"They are not. The demons cannot make reports of what they see, Nitendi. Besides, the eunuchs cannot hold their demons here for long. I must be sparing in their use. I need information, of the kind that only you and your fellow Loremasters can provide."

Nitendi glowered at him. "We are not common foot soldiers, General. It is not our duty to march in the vanguard, or to reconnoiter. Isn't a task like this what your precious Predor Company is for?"

"The wizards have power, Nitendi. The Predors have no means of detecting such things. This falls to you."

He straightened, defiant. "No."

"I'll not give my command again."

"Then you'll save me the trouble of refusing again. Find some other means to gather your information." He turned to leave.

"Meloqthes," called Ezqedir.

His first adjutant appeared at the entrance to the tent, blocking Nitendi's exit. "Yes, General."

"Arrest this dog for treason. Call the headsman and relieve him of the haughty lump between his shoulders. When he is dead, burn the body, then quarter it to prevent him from returning. Send his remains to the other Loremasters as a warning that I will not tolerate disobedience. Then have Olo'kidare brought to me. I believe he is second in line after Nitendi. We'll see if he is any better at obeying the will of the Exalted."

"At once, General." Meloqthes gestured. Four armed soldiers entered the tent and surrounded the Loremaster. Two of them gripped his upper arms and held him firmly.

"If he resists, beat him, but do not kill him. I'm curious if he will scream or cry before the axe falls."

"You can't do this!" shouted Nitendi. "I am an Adept and Loremaster of—"

Ezqedir punched him squarely in the face. Nitendi's head rocked back; blood poured from his broken nose. The Loremaster grunted, but the guards would not let him bring his hands to his face.

"No, Nitendi. You are no longer a Loremaster. You're a traitor who has disobeyed the will of she whom we all serve." Ezqedir produced a scroll with the seal of the Exalted upon it. "You know as well as I that the Exalted granted me absolute authority over this army. You and your fellow Loremasters are part of this army. To disobey me is to disobey her. I'll not waste time arguing with you. You obey me, or you will be executed. The choice is yours. I care nothing for your life—I only hope the one who follows you will have learned from your example. It would be a waste to have to kill all of you."

The soldiers began to drag him from the tent. "Wait! Wait! All right! Stop!" shouted Nitendi. His lips were slick and dark with blood, his voice congested from his smashed nose.

Ezqedir gestured for the guards to halt. "Don't think to try to bargain with me. I've given you my orders. I expect them to be obeyed. If you think you can convince me to change my mind, nothing will save you. This is your only chance to remain alive, Nitendi. Think well before you speak."

The soldiers released the Loremaster's arms. He brushed sweat from his brow, wiped the blood from his nose on his embroidered sleeve, and stared at the general with an almost dazed look upon his face. Ezqedir felt only contempt for the man's cowardice. *He did not face his death well,* he thought. *How quickly he folded! I expected more from a man of his station. Are all Adepts so craven?*

"We will probe the fortress's defenses, General."

"Have your men assemble behind the forward pickets an hour after sunrise. That is all."

Nitendi actually bowed his head before he left.

"Have him followed," Ezqedir said to Meloqthes. "I want to know if he runs to Tolsadri or back to his fellow Adepts."

"Yes, General."

"It's time, Honored Loremaster," said the captain of the company of horsemen who would protect the Adepts while they probed the defenses of the fortress.

"A moment, damn you!" shouted Telothes var Nitendi as he shifted in his saddle in a futile attempt to find a comfortable position. Despite the healing that Klaati had worked the night before, his nose was still tender and swollen. *I will find some way to repay Ezqedir a thousandfold for his attack upon me and his threats to my life.* He tried to push all thoughts of the general from his mind. He needed to concentrate on the task at hand—if he did not, it was quite possible he would be dead before the day was out. But the humiliation of the previous evening would not let go of his thoughts. They clung like a tenacious dog, jaws clamped tight. The image of the general's fist driving into his face—and the sudden, blinding pain that accompanied it—would not leave him no matter how hard he tried to make it go away.

The horse captain looked away pointedly. Nitendi thought he glimpsed a fleeting look of disdain in the man's dark eyes and fought back the urge to rail against him. It would do no good to antagonize the man charged with keeping Nitendi and his fellow Loremasters alive during this dangerous endeavor. He cursed Ezqedir once more, then turned his ire toward Tolsadri. The Voice of the Exalted had appeared briefly in the tent Nitendi shared with Klaati while Nitendi was still washing blood from his face and beard.

"The Harridan-damned general *assaulted* me!" he'd said.

Tolsadri regarded him with a blank expression, as if Nitendi had commented on the weather or the color of a flower. "You agreed to do as he asked?"

"I had no choice!" He coughed a thick glob of blood into a towel, which he flung at an Elqosi. "He was about to have me executed for treason to the Exalted!"

Tolsadri's mouth tugged downward at the corners and there was a tightening around his eyes. "Assuming you survive this venture, report your findings to me upon your return."

He left the tent. The Voice had taken his morning meal in private, and had not appeared to see his Adepts embark on their mission.

"Are you ready, Honored Loremaster?" the captain asked again.

Nitendi felt the weight of a hundred eyes upon him. "Yes. Let's see what these infidels have prepared for us."

"There's a company of cavalry leaving the forward lines, Archmage," said Abaru. He was peering through a Farseeing directed toward the Havalqa encampment. A number of wizards along the Hammdras were using Farseeings to watch their enemy. Each wizard was accompanied by at least one soldier of the Sunrise Guard. Many of the wizards carried magical devices designed for warfare, some plumbed from the dusty depths beneath the Varsae Sandrova, others from the Varsae Estrikavis.

Five wizards upon the wall-walk directed their powers into the many layers of defensive magic protecting the valley. When the Havalqa had first appeared, the Archmage ordered wizards to work in shifts day and night to keep the protections at their highest levels. "I want them to have to fight for every inch they move into our valley," she said.

The Archmage and Wardens of Hethnost were gathered upon the gate tower. Gerin, Balandrick, Zaephos, and Nyene were with them.

Elaysen elected to remain in her rooms. She had become increasingly withdrawn, spending most of her time either alone in her chambers or in the Varsae Sandrova. She spoke with Kirin often, but rebuffed Gerin's attempts to talk. She did not look well to him. She'd lost weight, and the redness he often saw in her eyes made him think she was crying. But when he asked her what was wrong—when she would even agree to see him, which was not often—she said she was fine. "I'm tired from trying to rebuild my supply of medicines."

The gods take me, I wish she would tell me what was wrong, Gerin thought while he watched the horsemen ride across the open plain toward them. It bothered him deeply that she was apparently confiding in the Warden of Healing and not him. In a moment of weakness after being rebuffed by Elaysen yet again, he had pleaded with Kirin to tell him what was going on with her.

The Warden refused. "It is not my place to tell you such things, Gerin," he'd said. "If she won't tell you, I can't help. I'm sorry."

And that is where things remained: broken between them. *How can I fix things if she won't tell me what's wrong?* He knew it was far more than a lost medicine pack that was troubling her.

Beside him, Nyene was shifting her knives from hand to hand with great skill, the motion so fast and fluid it was almost hypnotic. "I long to fight these dogs," she said.

"I hope you don't get the chance, at least not here," said Kirin. "I would greatly prefer that we defeat them or drive them off before they get close enough for you to use your knives on them."

Nyene laughed. "They'll never leave. You have what they want, and the only way this will end is with us or them wiped from the face of the earth."

"Who are those men in the center?" asked Kirin, pointing to the approaching horses.

Gerin peered through the Farseeing the Warden was using. "They're Loremasters, from the look of them."

"Have they come to offer terms?" asked the Archmage.

"I don't know, Archmage," said Gerin. "I would think Tolsadri would be among them if that was their purpose, since he is their leader's Voice in foreign lands. But I don't see him there."

The Archmage turned to Lord Commander Medril. "Are your men ready with the trebuchets?"

"Say the word, Archmage, and I'll signal for them to attack."

"Good. I want to withhold our magic until absolutely necessary."

"Yes, Archmage."

Gerin made his own Farseeing and watched the Loremasters. He gripped the Staff of Naragenth in his left hand; Nimnahal was a comforting weight along his hip.

Blood will be shed, he thought. *And soon.*

"Stop!" shouted Loremaster Wrotherqu Klaati. He'd been riding with his eyes closed, one hand gripping his reins, the other held out before him, fingers rigid and splayed. "There's power just ahead."

"Of what nature?" asked Nitendi.

Klaati moved his hand left and right as if caressing something invisible. "I don't know. It's completely unlike the Mysteries. I'm surprised I can sense it at all."

Nitendi invoked his own powers and projected forward with the Eyes of Drunn, the Mystery Klaati was using. He sensed nothing but emptiness before him. He strained harder; sweat burst from his brow and back. After more probing, he *thought* he felt the slightest trace of . . . *something* in their path, but it was as nebulous as the wind, and if he had not known something was there, he never would have discovered it.

Klaati was the most sensitive of the Loremasters, which was why he'd been placed in the lead, his powers sweeping the path before them. It nevertheless irked Nitendi that his subordinate Adept was more proficient at certain aspects of the Mysteries than he. It left the door open for Klaati to challenge his authority at some point, especially in light of the humiliation he'd received at the hand of the general.

The anger that surged through him destroyed his concentration, and the Eyes of Drunn collapsed entirely. He swore and let his powers recede.

"I sense a curtain of power just ahead," said Klaati.

"I feel it, too, though faintly," said Moktan.

"Can you discern its purpose?" asked Nitendi. "Can we pass through it?"

"It's not a physical barrier," said Klaati. "Other than that, I can't say."

"Does it activate traps when passed?" asked the captain.

"It's not your place to question us," snapped Nitendi.

"It's my place to keep you alive, Honored Loremaster," said the captain. "To do so, I will ask questions when I see fit. If you decide that our presence is no longer necessary, my men and I will return to the encampment and leave you to your work without the possibility of interruption."

Nitendi swallowed. *The entire world has turned against me today.* "No, Captain. Remain. Klaati, answer his question."

"I have no idea if the power is a trigger for something else. I've told you all I can."

The captain climbed down from his horse, picked up a rock and hurled it toward the fortress in a high arc. It landed and disappeared in the grass.

"Did that penetrate the barrier?" he asked. "Did I throw it far enough?"

Moktan nodded. "The rock crossed the power."

"That seems to confirm it does not trigger traps," said the captain as he swung back into his saddle.

"Then what is the damned thing for, sir?" asked a bowman.

A soldier rushed along the wall-walk and shouted up at the battlements atop the gate tower. "Archmage, Vesai Torndel says our defenses are being probed by the men in the field!"

Blades of ice moved through Archmage Marandra's bowels. *I must show no fear!* she chided herself. But the fact that *war* was about to descend upon Hethnost—for the first time in its history—was a thought so horrifying it threatened to send her to her knees.

One of the Havalqa horsemen dismounted and threw a rock toward them. *Probing our defenses indeed,* she thought.

"Lord Commander? Your recommendation?" she said with a calm, steady voice. Certainly much calmer than she felt.

"Can the defenses be moved forward? I don't think they'll willingly ride into them if they've realized they're there."

A grim smile touched Marandra's lips. "Yes. We'll see that it's done."

"Captain, should we send one of the horses through to see what happens?" suggested the archer.

"And if nothing happens to the horse, are you volunteering to go through next?"

"Me, sir? No, I was thinkin' more along the lines of—"

"It's moving toward us!" shouted Moktan. "Run! It's almost—"

Nitendi did not even have time to kick his heels into his mount before the heathen's power washed over them. His head rocked back as an overwhelming terror gripped him. He was going to die! He knew it as certainly as he knew his own name. A whimpering cry of horror escaped his lips, though he was scarcely aware of the sound. His heart would burst in his chest; his flesh would burst into flame; his organs would collapse; his very bones would turn to dust within him. He *knew* it would happen and felt himself drowning in panic.

Nitendi began to convulse. He barely noticed that the horsemen and his fellow Adepts were shrieking, clawing at their faces, their horses mad with terror. The captain had gouged out his eyes, which he'd flung away as if they were poisoned vipers. The black empty sockets wept thick streams of blood.

Nitendi's horse bucked beneath him, screaming in its own frenzied terror, its head whipping wildly back and forth. The Loremaster dropped the reins as his body was flung from the saddle. He arced sideways and landed hard on his left shoulder. His clavicle snapped cleanly in two, and his shoulder popped out of its socket. He opened his mouth to scream, but his thrashing horse stomped on his head with its hoof, almost tearing his jaw from his face. Hot blood filled his mouth and throat. He inhaled, choked on the blood, began to cough. He could not move, could not so much as roll over.

He lay convulsing on the grass, waiting to die.

"Let's test the accuracy of our trebuchets," said the Lord Commander. He turned to his adjutant. "Give the signal for the towers to attack the enemy."

"Yes, sir."

"What in the Harridan's name is happening to them?" muttered Ezqedir. He peered through his seeing-glass at the Loremasters and soldiers. All of them seemed to have gone insane, their horses included. Three of the animals had thrown their riders and dashed away. Nitendi himself was down and looked to be grievously injured. Captain Beurleh had blinded himself with his knife. Other soldiers had been crushed beneath their flailing horses.

So this is what their power can do, he thought. *Inspire madness in men. Make them hurt or kill themselves. The question is, how far does their arm reach?*

"Retrieve the Voice from his tent," said Ezqedir. "Maybe he can tell us what's happening down there."

Just then he heard the distant retorts of the hilltop trebuchets releasing their projectiles.

Gerin watched as the trebuchet at the Tower of Wind hurled its stone toward the valley. A few seconds later the trebuchet on the far side of the valley did the same. The stones tumbled through the air and smashed into the ground a few dozen yards from the writhing men and horses.

"Not bad for a first shot," said Balandrick. "What exactly did those spells do? Drive them crazy?"

"Not quite," said Gerin. Three of the Havalqa horses had thrown their riders and dashed beyond the reach of the spells. "Warden Khazuzili told me they're similar to the spells that were guarding the crypt where the materials of the Baryashin Order were stored."

"Ah, yes, Your Majesty. Back in your days of late night thievery and skulduggery."

Gerin ignored him. "I was so overwhelmed with fear I couldn't take another step toward the door. I needed to get the key amulet before I had any hope of getting in. The spells they put out there"—he waved his arm in the general direction of the field beyond the Hammdras—"are much stronger than the ones I experienced."

The trebuchets launched their second projectiles. The stone from the Tower of the Clouds struck squarely in the center of the Havalqa and rolled through them, crushing at least ten of the enemy. The other stone struck too far to the north and missed completely.

"Why not just use death spells, Your Majesty?" asked Balan. "Why bother making them crazy if you can just kill them outright?"

"Death spells take a lot more power to use, and they're directional—you can't just spread them along a defensive perimeter the way you can these terror spells. They also dissipate much more quickly, so you can't use them over long distances. A lot of reasons."

"At last those dogs are dying," said Nyene. She spat over the tower's crenellation. Beside her, Zaephos watched dispassionately. Two more projectiles smashed through the Havalqa ranks, killing most of the remaining enemy. One soldier with crushed legs was trying to crawl back to the encampment. Gerin did not think it would be long before he was dead, even if he did not get struck by another stone.

"What do you think of human warfare, god-man?" Nyene said to Zaephos.

"I believe it demonstrates the ultimate futility of your race. Your inability to recognize and embrace the differences between your cultures. Your passion for violence, for death."

Nyene glowered at him. "Bah. What do you know?"

"Halt the trebuchets," ordered Medril. A soldier ran to relay the order to the signalmen. "There's no point in wasting any more stones on them. They're finished."

* * *

Ezqedir realized he was grinding his teeth and forced himself to stop. Tolsadri had been slow to emerge from his tent even after being told his Loremasters were in grave danger. The Voice did not join the general and his commanders—he remained near his own tent with that worm of an aide, Enbrahel, who fussed about his master like a prattling old woman. Enbrahel disgusted him. Not only his flabby, flaccid body, his utter lack of courage and any kind of physical prowess, but also his obsessive, sycophantic desire to please Tolsadri to the point of sublimating all of his own desires and ambitions, as if a distinct, unique individual did not exist, only a vessel to please and fulfill the twisted needs of the Voice of the Exalted.

He lowered his seeing-glass. The Loremasters and Kulree Company had been annihilated. The wizards had driven the men to a maddened frenzy. *A power we can't see. Can it touch us here? Will we all kill each other at the bidding of the wizards?*

No. He did not believe they had such abilities. If they did, they would be the unequivocal masters of this continent. No one could stand against such might. They had limits. All such powers did, save for those of Holvareh Himself. He needed to find out what those limits were.

"Have Olo'kidare brought to me," said Ezqedir.

Ezqedir was conferring with Moliu Hu'mar, the designated commander of the mursaaba eunuchs, when Olo'kidare, the new leader of the cadre of Loremasters, was escorted into his tent. His normally red-hued skin was ashen, his lips squeezed into a thin pale line. His fingers moved constantly in an unconscious dance of agitation.

Hu'mar stepped away from the general as the Loremaster approached. Ezqedir offered the Loremaster wine, which Olo'kidare accepted with a trembling hand. He swallowed the contents of the goblet in three long gulps. Ezqedir raised an eyebrow at this uncharacteristic display, but made no comment on it.

"Can you shed any light on what transpired on the field

today?" asked the general. "What power was used against them? Is there a way to counteract it?"

"Ventro Gulethis was in contact with Klaati using the Mysteries, so we felt what they felt until . . . until their deaths. There are invisible barriers across the valley," said Olo'kidare. "When it struck Klaati and the others, Gulethis felt terror such as he has never experienced. It shattered their bond. Fear enough to drive them mad, to strip them of all reason or thought."

"What do you mean, it struck him?" asked Ezqedir. "You mean they didn't ride into it by accident?"

"No. They sensed its presence. That's why that horseman threw the rock—to see if the barrier was physical in some way. These wizards then moved their power forward enough to engulf our men."

Ezqedir folded his arms. "Is there anything else you can tell me? How is it created? Is it there all of the time? Do you know where the wizards are located who are controlling it? Are they in the fortress itself or the hilltop fortifications?"

"I cannot say, General. Its power is unlike the Mysteries in almost all respects. That Klaati was able to sense it at all is a testament to his abilities, may Ruren watch over him."

"If there's anything else you or the other Loremasters discover, you will come to me at once."

"Of course, General. I want nothing more than to punish these heathens for what they did to Nitendi and the rest. May the Harridan take them all."

29

Tyne felt a mingled sense of exhilaration and deep, stomach-churning dread when the dragon drew back on its haunches and sprang into the air with himself and Marrek harnessed to its neck. The sense of speed was fantastic. The wind on his face forced his eyes to close to the narrowest of slits, which, at the moment, was fine with him, since it prevented him from seeing the enormous volumes of empty air that were rapidly growing between him and the ground.

Behind him Marrek laughed and whooped as if he were having the grandest of times at the midsummer fair. *He must be insane,* thought Tyne, his grip on the harness straps so hard his fingers had already cramped. *How could he* enjoy *this?*

The first beat of the dragon's wings propelled them upward with even more velocity than the beast's initial leap. Marrek's laugh was nearly lost in the sound of the wind and the downward *whump* of the wings. They climbed into the sky at an alarming rate.

"This is incredible!" shouted Marrek. "I never could have imagined something like this!"

"Yes!" Tyne said. He hoped he sounded calm, assured. He wanted to betray no signs of his fear before Marrek.

It seemed that the dragon climbed almost vertically into the sky. Despite the hold of the leather harness, Tyne felt he would tumble off the beast's neck and plummet to his death far below.

It felt as if it took forever for this dragon to reach its brethren, though in truth it probably required less than a minute. When Tyne's dragon mercifully leveled out its flight, the others roared what sounded like approval. They whirled in a massive circle, waiting.

Tyne sent a command through the Stone for them to go to the east.

His dragon took the lead, the others falling into formation behind him like a flock of geese.

Now that they were flying level, some of Tyne's fear eased. It did not go away completely. He dared not look straight down, which made him light-headed and caused his stomach to clench, but if he kept his gaze toward the haze-shrouded horizon, which looked relatively stable, it reduced the sense of extreme height.

"Where are we going?" asked Marrek.

"Toward Khedesh. We have an appointment with the king."

They did not remain in the air for long before Tyne commanded them to land. His use of the Stone had exhausted him to the point where he was about to lapse into unconsciousness. He did not want to fall asleep in the air, even in the relatively secure harness. Perhaps once he grew more used to flying he would attempt to sleep on the dragon's neck, but not now.

He staggered from the harness and stumbled on the ground. Marrek's hand gripped his shoulder to steady him. "Are you all right?"

He nodded. "Just tired." He gave the dragons the freedom to hunt as they saw fit, but commanded that at least three of them remain close to protect him.

"Marrek, I need to sleep. I told you about this. I may be asleep for days. I don't know. I couldn't tell how long I slept when I was alone." It was an effort to push the words out.

"I understand. I'll watch over you."

"Stay away from me while I'm sleeping."

"But what if you need—"

"Stay away from me, Marrek. No matter what. I won't tell

you again. If you disobey me, you won't live long enough to regret it."

He staggered over to a small stand of trees, threw a cloak on the ground, and collapsed on it. Three of the dragons landed around them, their long tales whipping through the grass.

Just before he sank into sleep, he told the dragons, *If the other human gets near me, eat him.*

He wondered if he would see Marrek when he awoke.

The sun was high overhead when his eyes fluttered open. His mouth and throat were parched, his stomach empty. He reflexively reached for the Stone and found its comforting presence in his pocket.

He sat up slowly. His head swam; a wave of dizziness washed through him. He ran his hands through his hair.

"You're awake!" Marrek's voice was like the sound of shattering glass. Tyne winced.

"Don't come near me yet!" shouted Tyne. Marrek stopped dead in his tracks.

Tyne sent a command to the dragons rescinding his order to kill the other human if he approached him. *Do not harm him,* he thought through the connection.

"You can approach," he said then, and when Marrek did, asked, "How long was I asleep?"

"Four days. I can't believe you didn't starve to death, but I kept away like you asked."

I know you did, otherwise you'd be dead. "I need food and water. Now. Hurry. Bring whatever you have."

While Tyne ate, Marrek recounted what had happened while Tyne slept. The dragons had rotated the three on the ground who guarded him so all of them could hunt. The rest disappeared from the sky for most of the time, and did not return even at night to sleep. "I think they try to sleep right after they eat," said Marrek.

Two of the dragons had returned with arrows stuck through the tough leathery hide of their wings. Tyne ordered them to stretch out their wings so he and Marrek could pull them free.

"I bet whoever shot these didn't live to brag about it," said Marrek with a smile as he yanked out a yellow-feathered shaft and threw it to the ground.

"No one who tries to hurt my dragons will live long," muttered Tyne.

Tyne still hated the ascent into the sky, but he quickly grew used to steady, level flying—much more than he would have thought. He wondered if some power of the Stone, or something through the connection to the dragons themselves, was easing his fear.

It amazed him to view the world from such a height. Everything looked so *small*. The brown thread of the road, bumps of the hills, trees, streams and lakes, the occasional farmstead—all looked like toys to him.

In the distance he saw what looked like a small city on the horizon to the north. He decided in that moment to conquer it.

He commanded the dragons to fly toward it.

The city stretched along the shoulders of a long narrow lake with a dogleg bend in the middle. Trees rimmed the stony shore like a fringe of beard. Tyne could see several boats out on the still blue water. Farming fields stitched the landscape around the lake, with homesteads and a few small villages scattered about, linked by the slender threads of dirt roads.

A masonry wall, perhaps forty feet high, protected the city. There were a number of smaller settlements outside the city walls, with no clear design to the streets.

He commanded the dragons to swoop in lower. Defenders were running along the wall-walk toward the western side of the city. Tyne fought down a laugh when he spied the bows in their hands. Arrows could never pierce the scales that covered the dragons' underbellies. There were also a few small trebuchets atop the walls that the defenders were in the process of loading.

"Burn the walls," he said aloud. He felt the command reach his dragons through the Stone, which converted his words and thoughts into some language or power the dragons understood. He did not know how it worked, and did not care. All that mattered was that it *did* work, that his thoughts and words could control these powerful beasts.

The dragons dived headlong toward the city. Tyne gripped his harness in terror at the rapid descent, the overwhelming sense that they were destined to smash themselves to bits against the earth.

Two of the trebuchets flung their loads into the sky. The defenders had filled the buckets with bricks and small rocks and broken bits of glass that glinted wildly as they spun through the air. The two dragons closest to the projectiles easily veered away from them and continued their descent. Before the defenders could reload the trebuchets, the dragons unleashed streams of orange fire that set them ablaze. Burning men tumbled from the wall. Others fell where they stood, instantly overcome by the fire. The timbers of the weapons caught fire like dry kindling. The ropes burned through in seconds. The trebuchets collapsed on themselves, with portions tumbling inside the city and setting smaller fires below.

Volleys of arrows streaked toward them. Most missed entirely. A few bounced harmlessly off the dragons' scales, and even fewer managed to pierce a wing or two, with no real harm to the beasts.

The dragons washed the walls in fire. The defenders had no chance. Some flung themselves from the wall before facing certain death from the flames. They crashed onto the cobbled streets below or caromed off a tiled roof.

But most died in the fire, unable to escape the crisscrossing streams of flame that shot from the dragons' mouths. The fire had a sticky, almost tarlike element to it, so that it clung to everything it touched, even the stone of the wall.

"Look at 'em run!" shouted Marrek.

Tyne was about to respond when a needle of crimson light shot upward from the city and just missed the neck of one of the dragons. The light vanished before he could determine its source.

"Did you see that?" asked Marrek.

"Shut up and help me find where it came from!"

Another lance of red light shot toward a dragon. The light was about to strike its wing when it suddenly bent away from it. Tyne did not understand why it had veered off; all he knew was that his dragons were under attack by sorcery.

The light vanished quickly, but it was enough for Tyne to see where it had come from—a balcony near the summit of a tower a few streets behind the city wall. Tyne sent a furious command for the dragons to destroy the tower.

Several more needles of light shot at the dragons as they closed on the tower. None of them struck the beasts. All of them bent away, repelled by some unknown force.

Whoever was on the balcony did not retreat. Tyne ordered his dragon to descend so he could get a better look.

There was a woman on the balcony, her hair and cloak billowing in the wind. The crimson light was shooting from her hands.

The woman spotted Tyne on the dragon's neck and shot a lance of light toward him. The dragon lurched violently to the left even as the magic bent away from them. Tyne's harness bit into his flesh as he was thrown against the straps. Marrek cursed loudly as the light sizzled the air where it passed by them. *Kill her now!* he commanded through the Stone.

A moment later the dragons blasted the tower with fire.

The woman on the balcony made a gesture of some kind, pulled her cloak around her shoulders and lowered her head. A blast of fire that should have incinerated her bent around her body as if deflected by an invisible shield. Tyne realized she was using her sorcery to protect herself.

But she was not strong enough. Several other gouts of fire struck her magical barrier, which could not withstand the attack. It collapsed, and the fire engulfed her. Her clothing and hair burst into flames as if they'd been soaked in oil. She fell backward through a doorway and was lost to Tyne's sight.

The dragons circled the tower and continued to bathe the structure with fire until the stone itself started to slag. The slate roof collapsed inward as the wooden support structure burned away beneath it. The balcony tore away from the tower and broke apart as it fell toward the street below, leaving behind a gaping, fire-filled hole.

Tyne sent a command for them to stop.

The dragons rose upward to join the rest of their brethren. The tower continued to burn like a beacon, the stones charred black, the mortar dripping from the joints like thick dark wax.

Tyne needed to know about that woman. Were there more sorcerers in the city, waiting to attack him? He did not like the air-scorching lance of light the woman had hurled at them. It did not harm the dragons, but if she had managed to strike him instead . . .

Yes, he needed to find out more about who she was.

"Y-You sent for me, good sir?" said the thin man wearing a black wide-brimmed hat. He swept the hat off his head and turned it nervously in shaking hands.

"Are you in charge of this city?" asked Tyne.

"Y-Yes, good sir. I'm the mayor."

Tyne was seated in a folding chair a half mile from the main gate. He'd sent Marrek into the city to demand that whoever was in charge be brought to him at once, along with a chair and food and drink. Marrek returned with five trembling men carrying the chair, a table, and food that they placed upon it.

Tyne had told the men to remain, not because he needed them for anything, but because he could, and he liked exercising his power over others. Now that the mayor had arrived, he dismissed the men with a wave of his hand. They nearly fell over themselves as they rushed back toward the city.

"Well, Mayor, I have a question for you," said Tyne. "Who was the woman on that tower"—he pointed toward the smoking husk visible behind the city's walls—"who attacked us with sorcery? Are there more like her skulking somewhere inside? Don't lie to me. The price for lying is not only your death, but the death of your city. I'll unleash my dragons upon it until there's nothing left but ash and bones."

The thin man trembled so much he dropped his wide-brimmed hat. He froze for a moment, unsure whether he should stoop to pick it up. He decided to leave it where it was.

"I don't know her name, good sir, but she is a wizard from Hethnost." He'd managed to recover some strength in his voice. "They pass through here from time to time on their travels to the west, and on their return."

"Was she traveling alone?"

"I—I don't know, good sir. They often travel alone, but sometimes in pairs. Rarely more than two."

"You will find out if she had a companion. If she did, kill the— What did you call her? A wizard? Kill the wizard and bring me the head."

The mayor turned white. "You . . . uh . . . you . . . "

"The price for disobedience is the same as for lying."

The mayor swallowed heavily. "Yes, good sir. I'll see to it at once."

"You will *personally* tell me what you find. Do you understand?"

The mayor picked up his hat. Sweat dripped down his face, though the afternoon was cool. "Yes, good sir. I understand."

There were no other wizards in the city, according to the mayor. It was possible that the man was lying, or that any other wizards had been spirited away through other exits. But it was no matter to Tyne. He'd made his point. He spoke, and these people obeyed.

"Where is this Hethnost you spoke of?" asked Tyne.

"I've never been there, good sir. It's the home of wizards in these lands, is all I know. It lies northeast of here, in the Redhorn Hills, I believe."

The home of wizards. If they were a threat to him and his dragons, better to strike them first and take them by surprise rather than wait for them to attack him.

"You looked pleased," said Marrek.

"I am," said Tyne. "We're making a slight detour."

30

The Havalqa sent no one to recover the bodies on the field. The man with the broken legs had crawled less than fifty feet before falling still. Gerin was certain he was dead. He could almost hear the flies buzzing over the corpses, laying their eggs in the still warm bodies, crawling across open, drying eyes.

He descended the stairs in the gate tower to a small guard room where food had been laid out for them. The forward wall contained three arrow slits, all of which were manned with soldiers of the Sunrise Guard.

Gerin sat at the table, tore a loaf of bread in half and began to chew on it. He'd almost finished when Balandrick entered.

"Hello, Your Highness. Gods, I'm famished." Balan grabbed an apple and a handful of dried strips of beef, then dropped into a chair across the table from Gerin.

"Are our friends up to anything interesting?"

"They've started building siege towers, but that's the extent of what I could see," said Balan with a mouthful of apple. "Their commander must be worried about what kind of magic we can throw at them."

"Good. Let him worry."

"I don't think they sent their Loremasters with the expectation that they'd be slaughtered. I wonder what they'll do now that they know there are defenses across the valley? I can't see them sending troops to try to push their way through, but how else are they going to get those siege towers to the wall once they're built?"

Gerin knew better than to underestimate the Havalqa. So far they'd been lucky in their encounters with them, but the foreigners had powers they did not understand and a seemingly endless supply of soldiers. The Staff of Naragenth could not save them as it had before. That was a onetime manifestation of power he could not create again.

"They're resourceful. I think it's best not to feel too safe, or underestimate what they might do."

"Oh, not at all, Your Majesty. Still, without the Loremasters, I wonder who they have who can stand toe-to-toe against wizard magic."

"We saw creatures of some kind on the army's left flank," said Gerin. "Maybe they're just soldiers of a different species, but something tells me there's more to them than that."

"I guess we'll find out once the real fighting starts."

Gerin wondered what was happening back in Almaris. What kind of trouble were the nobles causing for Terl Enkelares because of his absence? His Minister of the Realm was a strong man, not easily intimidated, yet Gerin still worried about Sedifren Houday and those who followed his aunt's father. They thirsted to oust him from the throne with such ferocity that at times it astounded him to think of them as Khedeshians. They seemed more like enemies of the realm rather than the nobles sworn to obey the king and uphold the kingdom's laws and customs.

Terl will handle them, he thought. *He's well aware of what he's up against, and if need be he can throw the lot in the dungeon and wait for my return, if it makes life easier for him. I certainly won't object, and to Shayphim with any nobles who try to bully him.* The thought of Sedifren Houday and his haughty daughter Omara rotting in a rank, dark dungeon cell brought him far more pleasure than it should have.

"What are you grinning at?" asked Balan.

"Nothing."

"That wasn't nothing, Your Majesty. I know my grins, and there was a woman involved in there somewhere. Nyene's taken a fancy to you. Maybe you and she could . . . you know . . . in the name of improving relations between our two countries. She looks to be the type who might teach you a thing or two. Or even three."

Gerin let out a deep laugh. *The gods bless you, Balan. You do always know how to brighten my mood.*

"You get points for guessing right about a woman, but you lose the same number, and then some, for being completely wrong about the situation. I was imagining my lovely aunt Omara shackled in a cell below Vesparin's Hill."

"Ah, yes, I can see where that would have you grinning like Luro the Cat. Still, I like my idea better. You can't do anything about your aunt at the moment. Nyene, however . . . " He made a curvy gesture with his hands.

"Yes, Balan, I get the point. I think I'd be worried about cutting myself on one of her knives. She's probably got five or six hidden in that hair of hers alone."

"I'm sure you have spells that can ferret out her hidden weapons. Though, to be honest, if you have to resort to searching every nook and cranny on that bloody incredible body of hers with magic rather than doing it the old-fashioned way, then I'm afraid there's no hope for you. Your increasingly lengthy bachelorhood will just go on and on until the end of time."

"You do realize you're talking to your *king*, don't you?"

"Of course, Your Majesty. But seeing as it's my duty to protect you, I feel it necessary to tell you the unvarnished truth."

"I do seem to recall that a certain captain's bachelorhood is almost as long as mine . . . " As soon as he said it, he realized he might have made a mistake. Balan's feelings for his sister, and their desire to marry, might make his comment sound hurtful, which was not his intent.

Balandrick, however, showed no sign that the comment bothered him. "But the entire *kingdom* isn't waiting for me to marry."

"Please. They're not waiting for me, either."

"The many bets that have been placed in the Tirthaig alone would beg to contradict you."

"You're joking! No one's placed bets on when I'm going to marry!"

"Well, it's not just *when* you're going to marry, Your Highness. There are also bets on who, whether you bed her first or not, how pretty she'll be—a subjective notion, I know—whether she'll—"

Gerin threw an apple at Balan, which the captain caught deftly in his right hand.

"So what did *you* bet?" asked Gerin.

"Your Highness, that would be cheating! You might alter your plans for eternal bachelorhood in order to help fatten the purse of your dashing and charming captain if you were made privy to such secret and important information."

"The fact that you're pushing me toward Nyene's knife-laden arms wouldn't have anything to do with your predictions, would it?"

"Not at all. At least that I'm willing to admit."

"So what other kind of betting goes on in the palace right beneath my nose, and how come *I'm* never invited to participate?"

Balandrick gave him a look of mock exasperation. "Your Highness, be reasonable. Since you're the topic of most of the betting, it's hardly fitting to have you participate. Goes back to what I was saying about you tipping the scales, only this time it would be in *your* favor. Besides, you have the kingdom's treasury for a purse."

"It's not about the coin, Balan. It's about *winning*."

"Point taken, Your Highness."

"I want in on any bets you have about Claressa and her soon-to-be-born child. Offspring. Spawn. Whatever it is you call the product of a woman like Claressa when she gives birth."

Balan tapped his chin with his forefinger. "I might be able to get you in on a few things. On the side, you understand. And no one can know. You'd be bad for business. No one would bet against the king."

The mention of his sister made Gerin wonder how Therain and his new bride Laysa were getting along with Claressa in Tolthean. He envied them that they didn't have to shoulder the cares and burdens that fell to him as king. *They're probably having a grand time, lounging about, sailing, hunting. Therain, you lucky bastard.*

"Shayphim take me, I could murder Gerin for running off and leaving me with this mess," muttered Therain as he waited for Terl Enkelares to arrive in the council room. He picked up the parchment from the table and read it again, then threw it down in disgust. *Bloody dogs, that's what they are! I should have the lot of them arrested for . . . I don't know, indefensible meddlesomeness. I'm sure we can come up with an appropriate charge with a little thought.*

A servant ushered the Minister of the Realm into the room. "The message I received said you had an urgent matter to discuss with me, my lord."

Therain slid the parchment toward him. "Please sit, and read this. Try not to gag with the absurdity of it."

Enkelares took the parchment, hooked his spectacles behind his ears, and began to read. Therain was not surprised to see the older man's brow furrow deeply. "I'm not sure what to make of this, my lord."

"I know exactly what to make of it. That son of a bitch Baron Houday is angling to prop his idiot grandson Marell on the throne. It won't happen—I'll see my damned cousin executed for treason first—but I need to know if they have any legal recourse in the Assembly of Lords. He seems determined to cause me no end of grief. I want to cut him off at the knees before this gets out of hand."

Enkelares read the parchment again, then placed it on the table. Therain had read it so many times he'd practically memorized it. Just thinking about it made the blood pound in his skull. The audacity of it all!

Ten powerful nobles had signed the parchment, a missive that noted Gerin's unexplained absence from the realm during a time of war. It demanded that an Assembly of Lords be convened so the Minister of the Realm and the acting regent—Therain—could be questioned as to the king's present whereabouts.

> ... If a satisfactory answer cannot be provided, it will
> be the unfortunate but necessary duty of the Assembly
> to demand that the Regent be appointed King, or, if the
> Regent is unwilling or unable to assume this authority,
> that another member of the Royal Family be named
> King ...

The missive went on to state that this appointed king would remain in power only until such time as Gerin returned to assume his powers—but only *after* he made a satisfactory accounting of his absence to the Assembly.

One of the ten who signed the parchment was Sedifren Houday. Therain was certain he was the man behind the entire scheme.

"You see what they're going to try, don't you?" said Therain. He tried to remain calm, but he was practically shouting at poor Enkelares. "They'll arrange it so that no matter what Gerin says, his 'account' of his whereabouts won't be satisfactory to them, so they can leave their little puppet on the throne!" He thumped his fist on the table; the parchment jumped and fluttered across the surface a few inches from where the minister had placed it, like a bird learning to fly.

"Do I have to listen to them?" Therain continued. "Is there anything they can do to compel the Assembly, or am I free to ignore this rubbish?"

Enkelares rubbed his hands together, as he usually did when pondering an important question. "You could become the interim king, as they state in the letter. That would leave them no better off than they are now."

"I wondered why that was in the letter when I first read it, then I realized that I'm the brother of the king and next in the line of succession, so they *have* to allow that. I can be dense sometimes, but I'll get the point eventually."

"My lord? I don't understand. If you do that, you'll stop them before this grows out of hand, as you put it."

"Because I don't want to be king, for one thing! But I also don't think they have any intention of allowing that to come to pass. Mark my words, either I'll meet with an unfortunate accident that will render me unable to continue, or they'll weasel some other way to bypass me. Maybe they'll say that as the Warden of the Western Marches and Duke of Ailethon and Agdenor I'm needed there to protect the interests of the realm. I don't trust my aunt's father any further than I can throw the palace. He had a plan in place to cover all eventualities before the first word in that bloody letter was written."

"Baron Houday is ruthless and ambitious, I grant you that. But do you really think he would make an attempt on your life?"

Therain threw up his arms. "I don't know. Before this letter, I would have said probably not, but this"—he pointed a rigid finger at the parchment—"opened my eyes. The fact that it specifically mentions the regent being 'unable' to fulfill his duty is ominous. It's practically a threat, though a veiled one. One they can easily deny even if something *should* happen to me. The kingdom is beset on all sides, Terl. The Pelklanders, the Havalqa, even the bloody Threndish have spies here. It's an unsettled time. With so many enemies, it would be a fairly simple thing to deflect blame to one of them should anything unfortunate happen to me."

"I fervently hope you are wrong, my lord. But I also fear you are more right than not. We need to form a plan of action as well as ensure that you and your wife are well-protected."

Therain's remaining hand clenched into a fist so tight it cramped his fingers. "The gods themselves won't save anyone who tries to harm Laysa."

Therain stormed through the Tirthaig in a fury, his three personal guards trailing close behind. He was looking for his wife to tell her what the bloody scheming Baron of Lormenien was trying to do, and damned if he couldn't find her. It simultaneously annoyed and worried him. He was annoyed because she was almost never where she said she was going to be, as if she deliberately gave him false information just to throw him off balance and send him—or more usually, servants—on endless searches for her, which invariably ended with her in some remote location far, far from where she said she would be, with an explanation that was invariably the same. "I decided to go for a walk. Why is that such a problem for everyone?" she would say with a harried and exasperated look, as if the problem was with everyone else.

But this time he was worried as well. His concerns about the letter, and what Houday might try, had gotten to him, sending his thoughts to very dark places. *What if she's been kidnapped and spirited out of the castle, and one of the conditions of her return is that I make no claim to the throne? No, that would obviously tip their hand; our enemies wouldn't make such a condition. So what if she just disappears, and the devastation of her loss is supposed to wreck me and my ability to rule? What then?*

Damn the woman for disappearing like this. They were going to have a serious talk about it this time. It was no longer an amusing way for her to play with him. Things were growing dangerous. If he was going to have to live with an armed escort, then by Shayphim so was she.

A breathless servant appeared to tell him that the Lady Laysa and his sister Claressa were having tea on the covered balcony outside of Claressa's chambers. "I'll take you there at once, my lord."

"There's no need, I know the bloody way," muttered Therain. His worry evaporated and was replaced with a much stronger sense of annoyance.

"Laysa, what in the gods' names are you doing here?" he said as he stepped onto the balcony. His wife and sister were sitting in rocking chairs with a small table between them. *Shayphim take me, Claressa is positively huge. She looks ready to burst.* "You said you were going to be in the courtyard."

His wife flashed him her own look of annoyance, which shifted his mood from one of irritation to outright anger. He fought it back as best as he could. *She doesn't know about the letter or the danger it represents,* he told himself. *Don't take your own fears out on her.*

"I was in the courtyard, Therain, and then decided I wanted to stretch my legs a bit and visit your sister. Why are you so irritated by that?"

"Because something's happened that makes everything a lot more dangerous than it was, and I was worried about you."

Her expression softened instantly. She rose from her chair, kissed him, then hugged him close. "My brave husband, always worrying about me."

"What's happened?" asked Claressa. "What's dangerous?"

Therain explained about the letter. While he was speaking, the expression on Claressa's face grew stony, but at the same time he noticed her fighting not to smile.

"Do you find this amusing?" he asked her when he was done. His irritation had found a new target.

"Not at all. But I also don't think it's dangerous."

"And what makes you think that?"

She shrugged in an offhand way he knew all too well. "I just don't. Baron Houday isn't going to try to take the throne. He just wants to see certain changes made."

Therain straightened. "How would you know what the baron wants?" Though he already knew the answer.

"I'm just guessing. It seems reasonable."

"It doesn't seem reasonable at all." He shook his head in disbelief. "You were part of this. You knew about the letter. Admit it, Claressa. You've all but come out and said you spoke to him about this."

She stared at him coldly. "And what if I did? *Someone* has to save the kingdom before it's parceled off and we have nothing left. I gave the baron my assurance as an Atreyano that I would back his attempt to force changes in our policy by means of the Assembly of Lords."

"You *idiot*," said Therain. "He's using you. He's trying to steal the throne from us, and you gave him your seal of approval."

"You won't speak to me that way again, Therain!"

"I'll speak to you any damn way I please."

He took Laysa's hand. His wife was wide-eyed with horror over what Claressa had done. *She understands exactly what's going on,* he thought with more than a little pride. *Claressa is blinded by her vanity. She's still furious that we didn't charge to the rescue of her husband and his family. She thinks that's something she* deserves, *and that anything less is somehow an insult to her lofty station. Damn her arrogance! She may doom us all if I can't figure a way out of this mess.*

"You told me that Father would be ashamed of what I did to defend the kingdom," he said, "but I did it so we could get Baris and his parents back safely without destroying ourselves in the process. Maybe he *would* be ashamed, but I did what I did for you. So that your husband would live and your child would know its father. That you wouldn't become a widow before you became a mother."

He stepped forward. He could feel the look of fury on his face. Claressa drew back from him a little, frightened by what she saw. *Well, there's a first.*

"You thought the bargains I made with the Pelklanders were cowardly. So be it. I thought they were prudent, and so did the lords who approved them. But *you've* betrayed your *family.* Me. Gerin. Our heritage and birthright. If Father's ashamed of *me,* how do you think he feels about *you?*"

He did not wait for her reply. He feared he might lash out and strike that oh-so-smart mouth of hers if she dared to utter anything but the sincerest of apologies.

He and Laysa left the balcony. Claressa, mercifully, remained silent.

31

Gerin and Balandrick were still in the gate tower when they heard shouting from above. They took the stairs two at a time until they reached the roof.

"What's happening?" Gerin asked Hollin.

"Look there," said Hollin, pointing toward the sky above the Havalqa encampment.

Gerin saw a number of winged shapes rising into the air. While he watched, three more materialized above the army's left flank, conjured into this world by some dark power.

"Are those the things that attacked us near the Watchtowers?" asked Balandrick.

"Demons," said Hollin. "Yes, I think so."

"Damn," said the captain. "That's trouble."

Gerin created a Farseeing. It was difficult to keep the power trained on the shapes—they were moving very quickly—but it was clear they were the same demonic creatures they'd encountered in the Hollow.

We beat them there because of the power of the Telchan, Gerin thought. *We didn't do so well on our own. I hope the wizards are better prepared for this than we were.*

"Gods above, there are a lot of them," said Balan.

"They can break through Wardings," said Gerin, remembering how one of them had clawed its way through his magical protection.

"How are they conjured?" asked Warden Khazuzili.

"I have no idea, Warden," said Hollin. "We were running for our lives. The only effective power we had was a Word of Reflection."

"Wardens, send messages to the wizards along the walls to use Words of Reflection against this attack," said the Archmage. She glanced at Gerin's sword and staff. "Can those help us?"

"I'll do what I can, Archmage," he said. "But even my powers were of little use against them. I also don't know how to create a Word of Reflection."

"There's no time to teach you," said Kirin. "You haven't been properly trained to use that kind of power."

Gerin tightened his grip on Nimnahal and watched as the demons sped toward them like a flock of nightmarish birds. He could hear the faint sounds of their shrieking on the air.

"Gods, I forgot what an awful sound they make," muttered Balandrick. He'd sheathed his sword and nocked an arrow in a bow he had acquired from the Sunrise Guard.

Gerin could feel the Presence stir within the Staff of Naragenth. It had been a long time since he'd felt it, the voiceless entity that haunted Naragenth's greatest creation. He wondered what had awakened it. Did it sense the coming conflict? Was its true purpose as a weapon of war?

He projected his question at the staff with his thoughts. *Are you intended to be a weapon?* He felt the whisper of the Presence, like a chill moving back and forth within the staff; but he received no images from it, no answer to his question.

"Archers, when they're in range, fire at will!" shouted the Lord Commander. His command was relayed down the length of the Hammdras.

But they never got the chance. Before the demons got into range they split into two groups and veered sharply left and right. The sudden division and change of direction created a strangely beautiful geometric symmetry in Gerin's eyes. Their shapes cast fast moving shadows onto the plain far below.

Then he realized what they were about to do.

"They're going to attack the hilltops!" he shouted. He felt helpless as he watched the demons soar up toward the towers. The garrisons atop the hills were too far away for their magic to reach. The wizards at the far ends of the Hammdras might have some luck, but from where Gerin and the others stood at the center they were out of range.

"Warden, will our terror spells and other defenses stop these things?" asked the Archmage.

Khazuzili's mouth worked silently as he pondered her question. "I don't know, Archmage."

"They'll fly right over them," said Kirin. "The spells only reach about thirty feet off the ground. We don't have enough power to keep them in place if we make them taller."

The wizards at the ends of the Hammdras created Words of Reflection to combat the demons. Points of golden light appeared ahead of the demons' paths. Even at this distance, Gerin could feel the concussive force of the power when it inverted.

The vortices of energy engulfed a few of the demons, but not nearly enough. They veered away from the Words the moment they sensed them. Those trapped within the power struggled against it but could not break free. Within moments they winked out of existence as if they had never been. The Words vanished as soon as the demons within them were gone.

"Can you move the terror spells?" asked Balandrick. "Don't make them any larger, but lift them off the ground and place them between the hilltops and the demons? That would leave the fields in front of us exposed, but if you can move the spells around quickly enough, it won't matter."

Marandra turned to Abaru and Warden Khazuzili. "Is that possible?"

Abaru was nodding and stroking his chin. "I think so. But we can't move the entire web of spells. We'll have to split them apart, and that's going to take time."

"Then you'd better get started," she said.

"Yes, Archmage."

The archers upon the hilltops launched volley after fran-

tic volley against the demons, but even those few arrows
that found their targets did little harm. Through a Farseeing, Gerin watched one demon with three arrows sunk deep
into its chest yank them out and throw them away as if they
were a mere annoyance. Dark blood gushed from the wounds
for a moment before halting, as if the punctures had already
begun to heal.

Balandrick stepped close to Gerin. "Is there anything you
can do from here, Your Majesty?" he said in a low voice.

Gerin shook his head. "They're too far away."

The demons fell upon the garrisons.

They were too far to hear the screaming of the men who
were carried into the air by the demons and torn limb from
limb. Others were thrown over the walls, their bodies caroming off the rocky slope as they fell toward the plain far
below. One of the trebuchets launched a stone inadvertently.
It hurled through the air toward nothing, and sank into a soft
spot in the earth near the bodies of the Loremasters.

"Shayphim take the bloody things," muttered Balandrick.

Then it was over. All of the men on the hilltops were
dead.

The demons rose into the air above the hills. Their shrieks
echoed across the valley.

"Wizards, prepare to repel!" shouted the Archmage.
"Abaru, Rahmdil, if you can move the terror spells to protect
us, now would be the time!"

But the demons did not attack them. They hovered in the air,
wings beating rhythmically, and winked out of existence.

"What just happened?" asked Medril. He was visibly
shaken by the slaughter on the hills. "Why did those things
vanish?"

Warden Khazuzili rubbed his temples and faced them.
"The demons were returned to their native realm, Lord
Commander. They were pulled here, to our world, by some
power in that army, and when that power ceased, the demons
could no longer remain."

"Are they like sheffains?" asked Hollin.

"Yes, exactly. Though they seem to have more of a material form than the sheffains, who do not possess physical bodies, at least as we understand them."

Gerin saw the Archmage close her eyes and press her lips together in an attempt to rein in her impatience at Khazuzili's tendency to wander. The Ammon Ekril flashed in the sun.

"Warden, please. Is there anything you can tell us as to why they vanished before attacking us, or how we might defeat them?"

"I believe they vanished because whatever beings have called them here could no longer hold them. If you remember our own summoning of a sheffain, it was quite taxing. I tried to examine the amount of power needed to hold these demons here, and it was substantial. I would guess that those who summoned them will not be able to do so again for some time. But since we don't know how many can call demons, it does not necessarily mean a reprieve for us. They may have only used half of their numbers, or all of them, or a tenth. In which case more could be sent at us at any time."

"What of the devices of war we retrieved from Naragenth's library, and the Varsae Sandrova?" said the Archmage with irritation. "Surely *something* we have will provide us a measure of protection against these creatures."

"Those devices have been spread out along the Hammdras and in other areas of Hethnost, Archmage," said Kirin. "The ones from the Varsae Sandrova are potent, but they must be used at a much closer target."

"The weapons from Naragenth's library are better suited to repel a line of soldiers rather than creatures darting through the air, Archmage," said Hollin.

"Can we defeat them with something other than a Word of Reflection?" asked Kirin. "A single Word completely drains a wizard for hours. If we have to use them to defend against these demons, we won't be able to fight off anything else they send at us."

"I believe I can come up with alternatives," said Khazuzili. "Let me ponder this. I'll also need to consult books from my library."

"I'll send someone to retrieve whatever you need," said the Archmage.

"I'll make a list. I just hope they can find everything without making too much of a mess."

"Do you know how they were able to drive off your demons?" Ezqedir asked Moliu Hu'mar for the third time.

The leader of the mursaaba eunuchs was seated upon the floor of Ezqedir's tent, his huge body sunken into a number of velvet cushions whose plush tasseled shapes seemed to mirror the eunuch's own rounded, overweight physique. The eunuch was a native of Nurembi near the Vaas River in the far north of Aleith'aqtar, where winters were long and cold and filled with ice and snow. Ezqedir had seen snow and ice only a few times in his life, and would be content to never see them again. He was a creature of the desert down to his bones, and had no love for either wet or cold.

Hu'mar's pale skin, thin blond hair, and purple eyes bothered Ezqedir almost as much as the thought of a man bereft of his testicles. Ezqedir had lived most of his life among desert dwellers, men and women with a multitude of hues to their flesh. He had not seen white skin until he was thirty-three, at the Battle of Kohun-reh, and the sight had shocked him. He'd never imagined such a thing, men with skin so fair it seemed nearly translucent. He had loathed the sight of them at once.

There was something unnatural about Hu'mar as well, beyond the whiteness of his flesh. And about all of those like him. Their testicles were removed in ceremonies of power that imbued them with the ability to summon demons from another world.

He did not know how a child was chosen to become a mursaaba—if some hidden talent had to be discerned, or if any child could become one after being cut and undergoing the proper ceremonies. Ezqedir shivered and hoped it was the former. He did not like the idea that he could have been chosen to serve the Exalted in such a manner, and that only a chance of fate prevented such a doom from befalling him.

The ceremonies that imbued them with the power to summon demons had a deleterious and unavoidable side effect: it made the eunuchs insane.

Over the centuries, some of the greatest minds of the Steadfast had tried to understand why this occurred, with the hope of deriving some means of preventing it. Insanity in a being with the power to summon highly destructive demons was a dangerous liability. There had been numerous instances when the eunuchs, in one of their mad frenzies, wrought devastation among those they were sworn to serve. Once, nine hundred years ago, an Exalted himself had been slain by a mursaaba, which led to the prohibition against them coming within several miles of an Exalted, under pain of immediate death.

From what little Ezqedir had gleaned, those studying the insanity of the mursaabas had deduced that their madness was brought on by the fact that at times their minds existed in two worlds at once. Such an incongruity could not be understood by a human mind, and so it broke beneath the strain, splintered into fragments by the pressure of attempting to comprehend such vastly different worlds simultaneously. The incongruity was unavoidable.

Which meant that the insanity was also incurable. The very thing that brought them their power and gave them purpose was what drove them insane. To remove the insanity was to remove their usefulness.

Hu'mar, splayed upon the cushions, was at the moment in the throes of a fit of madness. He entire body trembled, the fat beneath his chin jiggling in a way that the general could not help but watch, eerily fascinated by the rhythmic vibration of the smooth white skin. The eunuch's eyes were rolled back into his head, showing only the thinnest sliver of pupil within the red-rimmed lids. A bit of froth bubbled from his mouth and dribbled down his chin.

Ezqedir held a knife in his hand, ready to slit Hu'mar's throat at the first sign that he was calling a demon. He would take no chances. The general was close enough to the eunuch to nearly decapitate him with a single stroke of his blade.

Ezqedir waited patiently for the madness to subside. He did not fear for his life since he knew exactly how long it took to summon a demon and was familiar with all of the attendant signs—the crackling in the air, the stench of dead meat, a sudden chill on the skin. At the slightest hint of any of them, Hu'mar's life was forfeit.

After all, they had more eunuchs, but there was only one Ezqedir.

"Do you know how these wizards were able to drive off your demons?" he said for the fourth time in a calm, soothing tone. He knew from experience that soft sounds could sometimes break the fits that came over the eunuchs. It did not always work, but it was better than sitting in silence, doing nothing.

Ezqedir's bodyguards waited outside. He saw no need for them to view Hu'mar in such a state. Sometimes in their fits, their bowels or bladders gave way. While he found the appearance of the mursaaba eunuchs repulsive, in some ways he liked Hu'mar, and saw no need to humiliate or embarrass him because of a condition he had no power to control. Certainly, Hu'mar was better company than Tolsadri or the Loremasters.

The eunuch's body shuddered and heaved; a huge sigh escaped his lips, along with a small river of frothy spittle. He jerked once, his eyes rolled down, and he looked at Ezqedir with dawning comprehension.

Hu'mar wiped the spittle away with the back of his arm and took a deep breath. "Regnel's curse?"

Ezqedir nodded. "For nearly half an hour."

He glanced at the general's blade. "Taking no chances, I see."

"I never do." Ezqedir sheathed the weapon and placed it on a table.

"Water," said Hu'mar. The general passed him a nearly full skin. "That came over me quickly. I usually know when it's about to take me."

"You stopped what you were saying and your eyes rolled into your head. I got you onto those cushions before you toppled into my supper."

"Thank you for that. I've broken my right arm twice and my left wrist once when the curse came upon me at inopportune times. Not that there are ever good times for such things, but you know what I mean."

"Of course. Better in your bed than strolling along the top of a cliff."

Hu'mar laughed and nearly choked on his water. "Yes, well, you will never find me taking such a stroll. Only a fool would do such a stupid thing. Anyway, what was I saying before the curse took me?"

"We were talking about what the wizards had done to your demons. I asked if you knew how they were able to send them away."

Hu'mar made a dismissive gesture. "Bah. They broke the connection between our minds and the demons. The very laws of the universe struggle to return the demons to their world. It's only our power, our force of will, that keeps them in ours. Whatever power these wizards have, they can sever our bonds. When that happens, the natural state of the universe asserts itself, and the demons vanish."

"So they yank them from your grasp."

Hu'mar thought for a moment. "Yes. And without us holding them, they cannot be here, cannot do our bidding."

"Can you prevent the wizards from breaking your grip? Did you learn anything about the nature of their power when they used it against you?"

"I have no idea, Ezqedir. Our powers are not subtle. The wizards' power was strong, I will grant them that. We can try to fight them off, but I can offer you no strategy other than that. For such things you need the Loremasters. Perhaps one of them can thwart the wizards. You must have *some* left. Surely you did not send all of the Voice's minions to their doom?"

"No, there are others. And I will use them as I must, but as weapons they are slippery and treacherous."

"And when have Adepts and Loremasters ever been anything else? Especially with their accursed Voice among them? You are not so blind as that, Ezqedir. If you are, I will need to reevaluate my opinion of you."

Ezqedir smiled. He had not realized how weary he was until now. "No, I'm not that blind."

"What will you do next?" asked Hu'mar. "That wall is high and strong. Be sure you do not break yourself upon it. You saw what they did to the Loremasters."

"I must think on that."

"Perhaps you should use the Loh'shree. As much as I loathe them, they have a formidable reputation."

Ezqedir said nothing. The truth be told, he had planned to hold the Loh'shree in reserve, preferring to use his Herolen to conduct the siege. But the deaths of Nitendi and the other Loremasters had given him pause. The wall of terror, as he'd come to think of the barrier the wizards had placed across the valley, thwarted his plans. They had no means to counter the power or cut off its source. A frontal assault against it would more than likely leave several thousand Herolen dead or incapacitated with terror—he did not put much hope that numbers alone might overwhelm the power, or that they could move quickly enough to pass through it before the madness took them completely. War was all about taking risks, but these passed beyond measured dangers into the realm of recklessness.

Fortunately, the barrier lay inside the range of the trebuchets they were constructing, so they would be able to hammer the fortress with their engines once they were built. But they would still be vulnerable to the trebuchets on the hilltops, assuming the wizards sent fresh troops to man them. He also did not know how far this wall of terror could expand. They had learned from the incident with the Loremasters that the wizards could move the location of the barrier forward when necessary. But how far? Certainly not enough to reach their encampment, or they would have already done so. But what if the Herolen moved their siege engines into position, only to have them swallowed by this invisible power that drove men insane with fear? And what other weapons were these wizards holding back?

He needed to adjust his plans. He could not see a way to use his Herolen to reach the fortress that did not end in disaster. He would have to find another solution.

It galled his Herolen pride to use the Loh'shree. His hope had been to hold them back, except perhaps to protect the encampment from attacks of power from the wizards. If he did not have to use them at all, so much the better.

Wars are nothing but constant adjustments of tactics, he reminded himself. *This is no different. I will do what I must to win. That goal is all that matters. We must take this place. We must have the Words of Making.*

"What is your command, General?" asked Hu'mar.

Ezqedir sighed. "Return to your companions for now. I will summon you when we begin this siege in earnest."

32

Gerin left the Hammdras to check on Elaysen, but she was not in her rooms. A few servants had seen her entering the Varsae Sandrova, but once inside, the few wizards and servants he came across did not know where she was. She was not in the section of the library devoted to the healing arts, which was her usual haunt. He wandered through several more floors and was about to give up when he heard a woman weeping. The sound was coming from one of the reading rooms.

He opened the dark paneled door and was shocked to find Elaysen on the floor, curled on her side, knees drawn up to her chest. She was crying uncontrollably.

"Elaysen, by the gods, what happened?" He knelt by her and tried to take her hand, but she pulled away from him.

"Leave me alone, please! I don't want you to see me like this!" She wept even harder.

"What is it? Are you ill?" He formed a Seeing, but a cursory glance revealed no obvious sickness.

"You don't understand! I need my medicines, but I can't make them here! I lost it all at the Watchtowers! I told you I needed my pack! Why didn't you listen?" She was screaming at him now, but the words were so slurred from her weeping that it was hard for him to understand them.

He could hear the footsteps of others approaching, and quickly created a spell of sleep. The magic washed over

Elaysen, and she slumped as the tension left her body, falling into a deep slumber.

Two servants appeared in the doorway. "What happened? We heard screaming," said one.

"She's ill," said Gerin. "I made her sleep, but I need to get her to her rooms and have someone watch over her." He picked her up, careful to cradle her head against his chest. She felt painfully thin and light.

"You," he said to the female servant. "Come with me."

Gerin carried Elaysen to her rooms in one of the women's halls. He placed her on her bed and told the servant to fetch food and water for her. "When she wakes, make sure she eats and drinks."

"Yes, my lord. What if she's still sick?"

"Fetch me if you can, or the closest available wizard if I'm occupied. I need to return to the Hammdras." He squeezed Elaysen's hand and kissed her forehead. She did not stir.

What's happened to her? he wondered as he made his way to the wall. She was scarcely the same woman he had met in her father's house on that long ago day in Almaris.

What medicine was it she needed? And why? She'd never spoken of it before, never hinted there was something she required. *Kirin knows what's happening with her, and this time he's going to tell me, by the gods. This isn't right! I want to help her!*

The Warden of Healing was not in the gate tower when he arrived. Nor were any of the other wizards. "Where's everyone gone?" Gerin asked Balandrick.

"They're all off on the wall somewhere, Your Majesty, relaying instructions," the captain said. "Apparently, Khazuzili figured out something else that might work against the demons and they're telling everyone what to do."

"Do you remember what it was?"

Balan shrugged. "I have no idea, Your Majesty. Some magical thing with an unpronounceable name. I swear, I have no idea how you remember what all your spells are called, let alone how to use them." His eyes widened and he snapped his fingers. "Bouncing Rings of Barley, or something like that. I think that's close."

"Binding Rings of Barados," said Gerin. "But that requires *andraleirazi* to bind the spirits," he murmured to himself. "How is he going to use that on demons that can fly?"

"See, that's what I mean. How in Shayphim's name can you say that? It sounds like you're talking with your mouth full of rocks."

"*Andraleirazi* is a kind of dust infused with power that can create prisons of magic, for want of a better term. It's used to hold beings of spirit, but that's usually when the spirits have been summoned by a wizard—the Binding Rings keep the spirit from escaping."

"You wizards should just name everything in Kelarin and be done with it, instead of 'gobbledegook spell' this and 'blah blah spell' that. It gives a man a headache."

"Not my decision to make, Balan. You'll have to take it up with the Archmage."

Hollin and a female wizard named Nenyal Fey appeared on the roof from the tower stair.

"What's this I hear about using the Binding Rings of Barados against the demons?" Gerin asked them.

"Our illustrious captain has misunderstood what he heard," said Nenyal, with a smile at Balandrick.

Balan held up his hands. "I was only trying to repeat what I heard and absolutely did not comprehend. I can't be held responsible if you wizards speak in gibberish half the time."

"The spell that Warden Khazuzili is teaching us works like the Binding Rings but does not use *andraleirazi*," said Nenyal. "He adapted another spell whose name now escapes me—"

"See!" said Balandrick. "I'm not the only one!"

"The Warden believes it will have the same effect on the demons as the Word of Reflection. It will sever the link that holds them here, but uses far less power than a Word."

"Will one of you teach me the spell?" asked Gerin.

"I will," said Nenyal. "Come, let's go inside. All of this sun is hurting my eyes."

* * *

The Warden's spell was relatively complex, but Gerin was able to learn it in less than an hour. When Nenyal was certain that he had a grasp of its nuances, they returned to the roof of the tower.

Nearly a dozen people had arrived in their absence. The Lord Commander and the Archmage were there, as well as Khazuzili and several other Wardens and high ministers.

Gerin spied Kirin looking through an embrasure at the enemy camp. He moved to the Warden's side and placed his hand on Kirin's shoulder.

"We need to talk about Elaysen," he said. "About what's happening to her."

"Gerin, please. She asked me specifically not to speak of this with you."

"I found her weeping uncontrollably in the Varsae Sandrova," he said angrily. "She was going on and on about her lost medicines and how she can't find what she needs here. I had to make her sleep so I could get her off the floor and take her to her rooms. Something is very wrong with her, Warden, and I need to know what it is."

Kirin's expression darkened. He stared off at nothing while he considered Gerin's demand.

"All right, I'll tell you. Her condition is worsening, and while there's nothing you can do for her, I do feel you should know what's happening."

"Is it something that can kill her?" he asked.

"Not directly, no. She has a disease of the mind, Gerin. Without her medicines, she becomes easily agitated and withdrawn. Her perceptions of the world become skewed, growing dark and menacing. I've seen some of them firsthand, as have you. In Almaris she said it's called Woman's Sadness."

Gerin had never heard of it. "Can you treat it? Isn't there anything we can do with our magic?"

"I've tried everything I can think of, but this particular affliction needs a more physical remedy. Unfortunately for all of us, the plants she needs to make her medicines are not native to these lands, and I don't have anything that can be substituted. Believe me, she and I have tried with the medicinal plants and herbs we have here, and nothing has helped. A few have even made things worse."

"You said it wasn't directly fatal. What did you mean by that?"

"The disease itself won't kill her, but it can drive someone to suicide. From what you've told me, she's taken a sudden and alarming downturn, which is why I decided to break my promise and share this with you. We all need to take care that she does not harm herself. Is someone watching her now?"

Gerin felt a great weight of helplessness settle on his chest. "Yes. I left a servant with orders to see that she eats when she awakens."

"Good. But we'll need to send additional instructions. She probably should not be left alone until her condition improves."

"Can it improve without her medicines?"

He shrugged. "Perhaps for a time. Even now her moods wax and wane, though the swings are sudden and extreme."

"What else can we do for her?"

"Get her back to Almaris so she can get the medicines we need. Other than that, there is little to be done other than ensuring she doesn't harm herself."

Gerin looked through the embrasure at the Havalqa. Several of their siege engines were almost complete. "Easier said than done with an army between us and the only way out of here."

The cloud-cloaked sun was near to setting behind the western rim of the valley. "I've never been in a war before," said Kirin. "Oh, in my travels I've come across the aftermath of many battles—camps of wounded soldiers, or the common folk displaced by the clashing of armies, banished from their homes to wander in a daze, wondering how they will rebuild their lives. I've found the victims of outlaws and brigands, sometimes alive, sometimes not, but in my long life this is the first I've experienced this kind of conflict directly. I confess, I thought I would find something exciting about it, something exhilarating, but after seeing what those demons did to the men of the Sunrise Guard, I realize there is nothing to enjoy in war and battle. It's abhorrent, a contest of atrocities."

"But there is something worthy in war," said Balandrick. "Yes, war is about death, but even more so, it's about *victory*. About vanquishing your enemy and proving your valor in the face of the very horrors you've witnessed for the first time. War is of course filled with blood and pain and death, but there is a purpose to it as well. It's a means for a man to take measure of himself and discover whether or not he is wanting."

"I would prefer to take my measure in other ways, thank you," said the Warden.

"Which is why you're not a soldier. I am not a wizard, so I do not profess to understand what it is you do, and so I would never think to disparage what I don't comprehend. But by the same token you are not a soldier, and likewise should not condemn it."

"Whether I choose to be a soldier or not, good captain, the fault with your comparison is that I am caught in a conflict of warriors not of my choice, and it seems my mettle will be tested in battle whether I desire it or not."

"True. My craft is inexact, and has a strong penchant for engulfing those who want no part in it. But to me, that's another reason to fight even harder—to protect those caught in a conflict through no fault of their own."

"The philosopher soldier has returned," said Hollin. "I was wondering when you would show your intellect again, Balan. I do believe it's as keen as your sword."

"I worry that may mean my sword is in dire need of sharpening."

Elaysen awoke slowly, her mind drifting up from the dense, dark sea of sleep that had taken her. Where was she? Still too tired to open her eyes—they resolutely refused to obey her command—she cast about with her hands to take note of her surroundings.

She was on a bed beneath a thin blanket. But how? The last thing she recalled was going to the Varsae Sandrova to see if there was something, *anything*, that might help her. Fueled by a heart-racing panic that she would die if she did not find something quickly to help her quell the storm that had swept across her thoughts, she'd dashed through the enormous library. She went to the room where she and Kirin had spent hours searching for spells that might help her, or alternatives to the herb-lore that she'd refined over the years in Almaris. She tried to concentrate on the first few volumes she examined, but her mind would not calm, and she knew— she *knew*—there was nothing to find. There was no hope. She was lost. Her hands trembled with anxiety; she found it impossible to sit still. If she remained in one place, the flood of panic would rise up and drown her. She remembered collapsing, crying . . . Gerin's voice . . . and then—

Her heart hammered suddenly when she heard a knock on the door.

"Who's there?" she said. With a heaving breath she at last mustered the strength to open her eyes and sit up. She was in her rooms in the women's hall. But again, how had she come here? She could not remember.

"Peylo Ossren, my lady," said a woman from the far side of the door.

She did not recognize either the name or the voice. Had that whore Nyene sent someone to kill her? *How did I get to my rooms? Where was Gerin?*

Then she remembered him finding her in the library. The horror of that memory struck her like a physical blow. *He saw me like this and now he's left me, fled into the arms of that knife-wielding whore. Oh, by the One God! I've lost him, lost him, lost him . . .*

"My lady, I was commanded to see that you eat and drink when you awoke," said Peylo Ossren. "May I come in?"

"No!" she shouted. "Stay away! I know who you are! I know who sent you!"

She scrambled out of bed and looked for a weapon. She needed to defend herself. She found a straight, long-bladed knife that Gerin had given her after they'd left the Watchtowers. She held it in front of her, the point aimed at the door as if the wood itself were somehow threatening her.

"My lady, please!" Peylo Ossren's voice was full of alarm. "King Gerin commanded me himself."

So much was lost to her. How long had it been since she'd seen her father? He would know how to comfort her. He always did, even when the Woman's Sadness—an idiotic name, as she had known men to suffer from the same affliction—had been at its worst. He told her that her mother suffered from it as well, and had devised several medicines that helped balance the volatility of her moods and confusion in her mind. Elaysen had taken what her mother started and honed it to a potent medicine: urlo, both leaf and root, the leaves dried and crushed to powder, the root kept moist and sliced into slivers, both placed in water over a fire until the water came to a raging boil; then morlenga juice, crushed pollur seeds, illned stems, a drop of tumarri oil, and ground teer leaves were added. The mixture was kept over the fire until it thickened to a paste. It was then removed from the fire, cooled, and the paste spooned into jars. A dab of paste the size of the tip of her little finger, applied to the back of the tongue each morning, kept the Woman's Sadness at bay.

But now she had none of her medicine and no ingredients with which to make more. What was wrong with these blasted lands that they didn't have such ordinary plants and herbs?

Or did they? Was Kirin lying to her, trying to keep her from getting well? Why would he do such a thing?

Was it easier for Gerin to break off his feelings for her if he could see her sick, know the truth of her illness? *He saw me in the library! He knows! He knows!*

A cry escaped her lips; a tear slid down her cheek. She dropped the knife and buried her face in her hands.

The door opened. A gray-haired woman entered. "My lady, what is wrong?"

If the woman was there to kill her, an assassin sent by

that whore Nyene, Elaysen no longer cared. All was lost.
Her world had become nothing but despair, swallowed in
darkness.

"I am no lady," she said. She lowered her hands to the
blanket and stared at them vacantly.

The woman knelt by her bed. "I'll fetch the wizards."

"No! No. I don't need them. There's nothing they can do
for me. We've already tried."

"Then you will at least take some food. I sent Rella an
age ago, but that girl is forever getting distracted. Please stay
calm, my lady. I'll be back soon." She gave Elaysen's hand a
reassuring squeeze, then left.

"I am no lady," Elaysen whispered after Peylo Ossren had
gone.

What would happen to her now? She could not return home
to her father, to her medicines, with an army on the doorstep
of Hethnost. She could find no solace here, or healing. There
was only despair. She yearned for Gerin, wanted him as she
had wanted no other, but he was so unattainable he might as
well have been on the far side of death.

She picked up her knife and a lamp, rose from her bed and
left her room. No one saw her. No one stopped her.

"There you are!"

Elaysen walked down the meandering flagstone path
that led to the statue *Death of a Son.* The garden in which
the statue was located was long and narrow, filled with old
trees. The bushes and flowers were wild, almost overgrown,
in contrast to the careful cultivation of the larger gardens
within the fortress, as if this particular place had been neglected or forgotten. *Forgotten, the way Gerin has forgotten
me,* she thought as she approached the bench where Zaephos
was seated.

He did not look at her. He kept his gaze upon the statue,
his brow furrowed, a mark of concentration she had rarely
seen upon his face. Despite herself, she followed his gaze
to the statue: the anguished father carrying the limp corpse
of his son. She hated it—hated the sorrow it evoked in her,

the sense of the inevitability and cruelty of death. It seemed almost to celebrate death with its terrible, aching beauty, and that was something she could not abide.

"I find myself strangely drawn to this work," said Zaephos, still without looking at her. "It is a keen representation of mortality." Finally, he looked at her. "Are you well, Elaysen?"

"I need my medicines," she said. "You have to help me."

"Have you spoken to the wizards?"

"Yes! Their spells can't help, and they don't have the ingredients I need. You have to help me. Use your power to make me well, or at least make the things I require to help myself."

"I'm sorry, Elaysen, but I cannot. I am not a healer, and my power is not such that I can conjure what you ask."

"Liar!" she screamed suddenly. If Zaephos was startled, he did not show it. His expression was as impassive as ever. "You've been lying to us all along! I know you have the power to help us! Why are you refusing? You could get rid of the Havalqa with a snap of your fingers! Why won't you? Are you secretly in league with them?"

"I am in league with all who oppose the Adversary, whoever they may be," he said in his infuriatingly calm voice.

"So if Hethnost falls to them, will you be spared? Have you made arrangements for your life? Have you sold us out to them?" It was so obvious now. His refusal to help them at the Watchtowers, his refusal here . . .

He was working with their enemy.

"I have made no arrangements with them, Elaysen. I have no need to. They oppose the Adversary in their own way. They need nothing from me."

"That's the real reason you don't fear death from them. Because they won't hurt you! I never believed you when you said you had stranded yourself here in the mortal realm without a means of defending yourself. I see I was right. You made deals with our enemies to keep yourself safe."

"I never said I was defenseless. I said that to use my powers would destroy you as well as your enemies. I could eradicate the army outside these walls, but I would also destroy Heth-nost utterly."

"But you would destroy your mortal form as well, if what you say is true."

"Yes. This body would perish if I were to release divine power here. Without the restrictions imposed upon me by this mortal body, my power is even greater—but then other laws bind me."

"What other laws?"

"I cannot deliberately kill. When I appeared to Gerin and your father, I did not possess a mortal body—they saw only a vision of what I wanted them to see, a perception bound within their thoughts. When I interact with this world in that manner, I am forbidden to kill. I can manipulate another to do my bidding if I desired, but I cannot directly stretch forth my hand and cause harm. It is an inviolable law of Creation. The servants of the Adversary are bound by the same laws."

"I don't believe you."

"It is irrelevant what you believe. I have told you the truth."

"How could the Adversary harm the world if what you said was true?"

"Because he is binding himself to the mortal sphere as I have, though his power is greater than mine to a degree that you cannot fathom. He is a wholly different being from me and my kin. But still there are laws that he cannot break. He cannot act upon Creation itself from outside of it. That is why he is manifesting himself here, within the world of mortals, so that he can be freed from those restrictions. Free to use his power to warp the will of the Maker. Unlike me, he is plac-ing all of his power here—a danger for him, but it is the only way to accomplish his goal."

"You said there are laws that govern Creation, but my father has long thought that Creation is broken, as do I. That the laws of which you speak have already been thrown down."

"It is flawed and bent from the original intent of the Maker by the will of the Adversary, but only to a small degree."

"Can it ever be made right? Can the world be healed of its

ills?" *Can I ever be healed? No, no. There is no hope for me. Gerin saw me as I truly am and fled!*

"It cannot be healed in the way you are thinking. There will always be pain and suffering. There must be. Mortals must have something to strive against. It is for you to make the world a better place from within, not the divine to do so from without."

She rubbed her temples. There was a storm once more in her mind. So many thoughts, swirling—

"Tell me what you meant when you told Gerin that even a prophet may not understand everything he is shown. What did you mean?"

"Those words were not for you or your father."

"I don't believe you." A quiet resolve had come over her. "You're not who you say you are. You've refused to help us, sowed doubts in our minds about my father's place as the Prophet. A servant of the One God would never do such things."

She slipped the knife from the pocket in her skirt and plunged it into Zaephos's chest, driving it in to the hilt. He looked up at her, his eyes wide.

"You're a servant of the Adversary. I know it in my heart."

He coughed a mist of blood. She felt the hot, coppery warmth of it on her face and neck, and wiped it with her hands.

He slid from the bench, the knife still in his chest. His body convulsed, flopping like a fish tossed into the bottom of a boat. Blood poured from his mouth, a dark river of it washing across the flagstones, rushing toward her feet.

Elaysen stepped around the widening pool of blood, knelt, and watched the life leave his eyes as he took a final, shuddering breath.

Then she stood, hands trembling. Filled with sudden horror at what she had done, she fled the garden, weeping, and wondering if she had made a terrible mistake.

33

Gerin was about to stretch out on a cot in one of the lower rooms of the gate tower for some much needed sleep when he felt a presence in the room. He turned his head and saw Zaephos standing in the corner, hands clasped in front of him, head bowed.

Gerin propped himself up on his elbows. Zaephos raised his head and stared blankly at a bare spot on the wall above Gerin's head. The messenger's mouth moved but no sound emerged. It was an eerie, unnerving sight.

"Zaephos, what's wrong?" Gerin sat up completely. He realized then that Zaephos was not physically present in the room. He could see the wall through the messenger's immaterial form. "What's happened?"

"Elaysen has slain my mortal body." The words were so faint as to be nearly inaudible, and did not match the movement of his lips.

"What?" He was on his feet. "Why would she do such a thing?"

"She believes I serve the Adversary. She is wrong, but her thoughts are unclear."

Gerin ran a hand through his hair, unsure of what to think or say. Elaysen had killed Zaephos? It made no sense. Why would she believe he served their enemy?

"I must go," said Zaephos. "It will be some time before I return to you again."

"Wait!"

But it was too late. Zaephos's form had vanished.

"Shayphim take me, what has she done?" Gerin muttered as he rushed from the room.

Balandrick was asleep in a room across the hall. Gerin shook his shoulder; the captain jerked awake, startled, and reached for his knife.

"Balan, calm down. It's me."

Balandrick blinked several times, then wiped his eyes. "Sorry, Your Majesty. I just drifted off a little while ago."

"I'm sorry to wake you. This isn't about the Havalqa." He told Balan what had happened with Zaephos. "I need you to help me look for her. I'm afraid she might try to hurt someone else, or perhaps herself."

Balandrick shook his head in dismay. "I can't imagine her harming anyone. She must truly be in a bad way."

"That's what scares me."

They made their way toward the dormitory where Gerin had left Elaysen earlier. He felt certain she was no longer there, but it was at least a place to start.

They found a servant who was frantic over Elaysen's disappearance. "I left her for just a little while to get her some food because that ninny Rella dawdled with her chores, blast her soul. She was gone when I came back. I've been looking everywhere."

"If you find her, get her to her room and make her stay there," said Gerin. "I don't care if you have to lock her in and sit on her."

He sent Balan to look through one of the nearby gardens while he returned to the Varsae Sandrova. He ran through the floors, frantic, asking anyone he came across if they'd seen her, but no one had. Filled with fury—though he was not sure exactly why he was furious, or at whom, which only served to anger him more—he left the library and went in search of Balandrick.

He was nearing the woman's dormitory when he saw Balan appear in the darkness. Elaysen was with him. He had his arm around her shoulders. She looked dazed, her eyes vacant. There was blood on her tunic and smeared across her face and hands.

"I found her wandering in one of the gardens," said Balan. There was a deep worry in his voice. "She barely acknowledged me."

Gerin gripped the sides of her head and looked into her eyes. "Elaysen, can you hear me? What happened with Zaephos?"

She blinked several times before finally focusing on him. Her face twisted into a rictus of horror. Tears spilled down her cheeks.

"Oh, oh, oh! Please, no! Don't see me like this! Not like this!" She tried to pull away from them both, but neither of them released her.

"Elaysen! Calm yourself! What happened to Zaephos?" He realized he was shouting and lowered his voice. "What did you do?"

She squeezed her eyes shut, as if that would somehow make them go away. "I killed him," she sobbed. "I thought he was our enemy, but now I don't know . . . I'm so confused. I need my medicines . . . "

"Let's get her to her rooms," he said to Balandrick. Elaysen was weeping, but allowed herself to be led to the dormitory.

"I'm sorry, I'm so sorry," she said as they made their way up the stairs. The servant woman they'd seen earlier saw them in the corridor and rushed to them.

"By the gods, there she is." The woman gasped and covered her mouth. "She's covered with blood!"

"It's not hers," said Gerin. "But she needs to be washed."

The woman nodded. "I'll get water."

Balan placed Elaysen on her bed. His face was filled with concern.

Gerin sat on the bed and held her hand. She squeezed it tightly, as if she feared to drown if she let go.

"I'm sorry," she said again. She had calmed a little, though she would not look at him. "I don't understand anything anymore. I never wanted you to see me like this, to know how broken I was. I need medicines to control these storms that sweep through my mind. I can't control it. My medicines gave me a normal life, but when they were destroyed near the Watchtowers, everything started to fall apart." She sniffled and wiped her eyes. "I am so in love with you, and I know you can't love me back because you're a king and I can offer you nothing as a wife, and now you know the awful truth about me . . . " She began to cry again, softly this time. She turned her head away from him and covered her eyes with her free hand.

"And then I see how you look at that Threndish whore and I just want to put a knife in her heart."

"Elaysen, no more talk of violence," Gerin said. "You've done enough."

"I know, I know. I'm so sorry."

The servant returned with a basin of water and several towels and began to wash her face and hands.

"You need to eat something," he said.

She shook her head. "I'm not hungry. I don't want anything."

He decided not to argue with her. "I'm going to make you sleep now. We'll talk more later."

She nodded, still not looking at him. He drew magic into himself and created the same spell he'd used earlier, only he made this one stronger. Immediately, she slipped into a deep sleep.

"Do *not* let her leave this room," Gerin said to the woman. "And make sure she eats when she wakens."

The woman nodded, abashed. "Yes, my lord. I'm sorry, I—"

"I'm not interested in your excuses. Just see that you do what I said."

Gerin descended the stairs so quickly that Balandrick had to run to keep up.

"Isn't there anything you can do?" Balan asked.

"No, there's not."

"Are you angry with her, Your Majesty?"

Gerin stopped at the bottom of the stairs and spun about

to face his captain. Balan's face was lost in shadows; the magefire sconces were behind him, so it seemed his head and shoulders were outlined with a halo of light.

Yes, he was angry; no, he was *furious*, even more so than in the library. He'd been unsure then of the object of his fury, but Balandrick was right—he was angry at Elaysen. Part of him knew he had no right to be, that she was suffering greatly and had been for some time. That these "storms" in her mind were beyond her ability to control.

But he could not help himself. She had killed Zaephos, and as maddening as the messenger of the One God often proved to be, he was nevertheless the only direct link they had to the world of the divine and, perhaps, the intentions of the One God toward both the world and him.

He also felt betrayed by her, that she had felt a need to conceal something so important as her illness from him. Had she not trusted him? Had she thought he wouldn't understand? He realized she did not want to appear "damaged" to him, but after her medicines were destroyed, why not confide in him? Why not trust him to try to help?

He did not know what to make of her proclamation of love for him, and her disparaging comments about Nyene. Were they the true feelings of her heart, or was it her illness speaking, corrupting her words, twisting them in unimaginable ways?

How could he ever trust her again?

34

"What will you do next, Ezqedir?" asked Tolsadri as he glanced around the general's tent with distaste. "You've succeeded so far in sending Loremasters to their deaths. Is this how you conduct yourself in a time of war? The Exalted will be very interested to hear about this campaign. I must admit, your strategy befuddles me."

"Then you will remain befuddled, Tolsadri," said Ezqedir with a practiced, offhand casualness. He was seated at his small desk, pretending to study a number of papers so he would appear to be ignoring the Voice. "I have neither the time nor the inclination to explain myself, any more than your desire to explain your many *successful* negotiations to me."

The Voice focused on the general. "You will refer to me by my title, Ezqedir. I will see that decorum is followed. And you may not choose to explain yourself to me, but you will have to make an accounting with the Exalted."

"I'll refer to you by title when you use mine, Tolsadri." He still did not look up from his papers, as if the Voice were not important enough to warrant his full attention. "I simply follow your lead in matters of decorum. As for explaining myself to the Exalted, I am relishing my return to Kalmanyikul when this campaign is concluded so I can personally tell her of our triumph here and deliver the Words of Making to her from my hand."

Ezqedir set down the paper he was holding and deigned to regard the Voice for the first time since the Loremaster had entered the tent.

"As for sending your Loremasters to their deaths, I assure you it was not needless, and the sacrifice of a few followers of Bariq was an acceptable loss, considering what I learned in return.

"Now, I have a siege to prepare. If you have nothing of substance to add to this conversation, or vital information to convey, you may go."

Tolsadri drew a hissing breath. "One such as you does not dismiss me!"

"In that you are wrong. It seems this campaign will provide many new experiences for you, Tolsadri. Leave, or I'll have you removed. And please do not bore me with threats of how you will tattle to the Exalted. I assure you, I'm not afraid of anything you might say to her. I've heard you've already fallen far in her eyes."

Tolsadri's face flashed with murderous anger. Without another word, he turned and left the tent.

"The Powers guide me, but would we all not be better off without that man?" Ezqedir muttered to himself.

He called his Elqosi and donned his armor. Once properly attired, he stepped outside. The day was clear and bright, the air still.

Ezqedir watched as the siege engines were moved into position. Four trebuchets were being arrayed across the face of the valley; more would follow. Once in place, he would begin to pound the defensive wall that sealed the mouth of the valley.

He had no idea what power the wizards would bring to bear on the weapons. He did not expect them to last long before being destroyed. They were faced with animal hides and soaked with water to prevent them from being set aflame, but those were defenses for a normal siege, not one such as this, where unseen powers would clash for supremacy.

But still, this was a siege, and certain conventions had to be followed. Four hundred horsemen and an equal number of infantry followed behind the slow-moving engines. A token number, but he was not willing to sacrifice more men in what would essentially be an empty gesture. The assault would provide some other advantages—it was not wholly without merit, or he would not have ordered it, conventions or not. He hoped to learn more about the defenses of the fortress, as well as provide a diversion for the Loh'shree. He wanted the wizards' attention fixed firmly on the siege engines and not the encampment.

In their part of the camp, the Loh'shree had begun their work. Ezqedir used his seeing-glass to watch the strange beings as they dug a series of concentric and overlapping circles in the earth. The first was about twenty feet in diameter; an unlit brazier had been placed at its center. The next circle was twice as wide. Others of similar diameter intersected the central circles by varying degrees.

The creatures worked with an odd, dispassionate efficiency. Other Loh'shree were setting up braziers at regular intervals within the rings.

Ezqedir hated the need for such dark power, but he had no choice.

"A good day for battle, sir," said Meloqthes.

Ezqedir lowered his glass and turned to his adjutant. Meloqthes had tied his thick black hair at the base of his neck, a change from his usual shock of unruly dark hair.

"Let's hope it ends as well as it begins," he said.

"Herol guides your hand, sir. We will not fail."

"Where is Hu'mar? Are the eunuchs ready?"

"He's with the other mursaaba, sir. He sent word that he would prefer to remain with them for this battle. I have signalmen ready. They'll summon their demons on your command."

"And the Loremasters?"

"Olo'kidare and his brethren are arrayed along the forward line as you asked. The Voice has not interfered. He returned to his tent as soon as he emerged from yours."

"Very good, Meloqthes. Our plans are in place. Time to let them unfold."

The siege engines had almost reached their positions. The bodies of the dead Loremasters and Herolen were finally removed from the field. Stakes had been pounded into the ground in a rough line running parallel to the fortress's curtain wall. The stakes marked their estimate of the location of the fear barrier. The siege engines would halt fifty feet before that line. Ezqedir had no idea if the barrier could move that far or if its location was more restricted. This was simple trial and error, and his decision had been to move his engines as close as he could.

"Meloqthes, you may send the signal to the field commanders to attack as soon as they are ready," he said.

"With pleasure, General."

"Archmage, their engines are in position," said Medril. "Can you reposition the fear spells to encompass them?"

"We'll try, Lord Commander. There is some room for them to move, as we did earlier, but that was only a short distance. This is much farther, and they may collapse."

Gerin could see Medril attempt to hide his frustration with the Archmage. *She doesn't understand war at all,* he thought. Her inability to think strategically and grasp the nature of the siege was beginning to wear on Medril, though he did his best not to show it.

"Archmage, do what you can to move those spells," he said, "even if you have to collapse them first and recreate them farther out."

"There are limits to what can be done with that kind of magic, Lord Commander. It may not be possible—"

Medril held up his hand in a highly uncharacteristic show of impatience. "Archmage, please. Just do what you can to get those fear spells over their siege engines."

Gerin was surprised that the Archmage did not give the Lord Commander so much as a harsh glare. "We'll do what we can," was all she said.

The Lord Commander turned to one of his lieutenants. "Give the order for the trebuchets to fire. I want their weapons destroyed."

"Yes, Lord Commander."

Gerin heard the distant retort of the first Havalqa siege engine launching its stone. Everyone turned to peer through the battlements. The stone landed short of the wall about two hundred feet to their left.

Gerin had a sudden, overwhelming urge to do something. He'd felt helpless and useless since this siege began, and he'd had enough. He'd sunk a Havalqa warship in the Gulf of Gedsuel, annihilated thousands of enemy soldiers marching on Almaris, and broken the sea blockade of the capital. He had *power* at his command, and by the gods, it was time to act!

He heard the distant grumble of a second Havalqa siege engine's throwing arm swinging through its arc. This boulder struck the face of the Hammdras directly. A spiderweb of cracks exploded across the white stone.

Gerin drew Nimnahal, aimed it through the embrasure, and released a blast of unshaped magic at the siege engine. He heard a collective gasp from the wizards and soldiers around him as the line of amber power raced across the field. Havalqa soldiers leaped out of its path before it struck his intended target.

Despite the amount of energy Gerin was pouring through Nimnahal, the distance was simply too great. His magic thinned and faded almost to nothing before it slammed into the wooden base of the weapon, where it did no damage.

He snarled in frustration and tried to increase the amount of magic flowing through the sword, tapping into the weapon's self-contained reservoir of power, but it did no good.

Furious, he relented.

Lord Commander Medril stepped in front of him, his expression severe. "You will not attack the enemy again without my expressed permission. You may be a king in your own country, but Hethnost is not Khedesh, and here, I am in charge of the defenses."

Gerin bristled at being talked to in such a way. "My goal was the defense of Hethnost."

Another Havalqa boulder slammed into the Hammdras. The impact was only a short distance from them, and the thunderous retort made them all flinch. A cloud of dust billowed across the roof of the gate tower.

"The only thing you've done is show them they're safe where they are because our magic can't reach them." Medril gestured through the embrasure. The Havalqa were cheering the failure of Gerin's attack. "You've boosted their morale after the slaughter of their Loremasters. Nothing more."

Gerin clenched his jaw. He wanted to argue, but did not. Medril was right. He'd acted out of turn, and if someone under his command had done the same thing, he would have been far less forgiving than Medril.

He bowed his head. "You're right, Lord Commander. Please accept my apology. It won't happen again."

"See that it doesn't."

"I'm not sure what I find more amazing, Your Majesty," said Balandrick. "That your attack failed, or your humble apology."

"Not now, Balan," said Gerin irritably. "I'm not in the mood."

Wizards stationed on the Hammdras erected overlapping Forbiddings to protect the gate tower. The Forbiddings were invisible to nonwizards, but Gerin could see the air shimmer as the spells took shape.

"I understand why you did it," said Balandrick. "I feel pretty useless standing around waiting for something to happen. It's maddening."

"Medril was right. Chain of command is everything. I'm not a king here, I'm a guest. I know better, and I shouldn't have done it."

Another boulder hurled toward them and smashed into the Forbiddings. Gerin saw the spells flex inward, and he sensed the backflow of magic toward the wizards maintaining them.

Balandrick ducked and swore loudly. "Bloody buggering Shayphim! What stopped that?"

"There are Forbiddings across this part of the Hammdras."

"Might be nice to know that," Balan muttered as he straightened. "Why not just use those all the time? This place would be impregnable."

"They need too much power and can't be held for very long before failing. The Archmage is going to have to rotate the wizards making them or they won't last. It's just not practical to protect the entire place with them."

In the Havalqa encampment, the jubilation over Gerin's failed attempt to destroy their siege engine died away. The sight of one of their projectiles striking an invisible wall in midair dumbfounded them.

A second stone struck the Forbiddings. This one was larger than the first, and the force of the impact caused the leftmost Forbidding to waver dangerously. Gerin saw wizards scrambling along the wall-walk, moving closer so they could help shore up the barriers.

"How long will they hold?" asked Balandrick.

"Awhile yet." He was not about to voice concerns about the Forbiddings to anyone, even Balandrick.

The air filled with nightmare shrieks. Gerin and Balandrick both swore and looked toward the Havalqa encampment.

Demons were appearing in the air. More than they had seen before.

Balandrick swore under his breath. "This isn't good."

35

Loremaster Olo'kidare finally managed to detect the wall of fear that had so unhinged Nitendi and his companions. It had not been easy to discover, this power that was so very different from the Mysteries of Bariq. But he had done it, an accomplishment that only reinforced his belief in his abilities and innate superiority over his fellow Adepts.

A clever thing, he admitted to himself. Eyes closed, he studied it as best as he could. It flickered in and out of his perception, as difficult to see as spying a single drop of rain in a downpour. He probed it with Leru's Eye, trying to discern some means of disrupting it. So far he had not succeeded. *Clever indeed. These accursed heathen wizards have some talents, I'll grant them that.*

He would make sure Dremjou knew what he had done here. The Wahtar of the Jade Temple would reward him accordingly—elevate his station and responsibilities, which in turn would grant him greater status, wealth, and power. His ultimate desire was to become the Voice of the Exalted. Tolsadri's obsessive desire to play the games of intrigue had served him well in his rise to power, and Olo'kidare had learned much from his veiled observations of Tolsadri; but in the end, Tolsadri's game playing would also prove to be his downfall. Already, his failures in this land had destroyed much of his capital with the Exalted and the court. Olo'kidare was somewhat surprised that Tolsadri managed to retain his position after returning to Kalmanyikul through the Path of Ashes. He had expected the Exalted to have him summarily executed for allowing Gerin Atreyano to slip from his grasp, a failure of gigantic proportions.

But the Loremaster was glad that Tolsadri had managed to elude disaster. Olo'kidare was not yet positioned to take his place, and the appointment of another Voice at this point in time would be a disastrous setback for him.

Sudden movement, a shifting . . . *The wall of fear is changing!* he realized with a start. New power was flowing into it, altering its fabric. It was maddeningly hard to see it from moment to moment—his body was sweating profusely from the demanding level of concentration.

The wall seemed to be . . . fluctuating, pulsing as its energy waxed and waned. What in the name of the Powers were these wizards up to?

Then the wall moved, and in an instant he understood their plan.

"They're going to swallow us with their power!" he shouted. Images of Nitendi's gruesome death filled his vision. He had to think! How could they counter the fear? Was there any Mystery that could combat it, or was this a hopeless endeavor, like trying to fight a fog bank with a spear?

He caught another glimpse of the wall of fear with Leru's Eye. The wall was unstable! He was sure of it! It either was not meant to be moved in such a manner, or was at the edge of its range, beyond which it flirted with collapse.

Another glimpse, another fluctuation, and he understood what they had to do.

"Loremasters!" he screamed. "Tireme's Seventh Mode! Send it toward the fortress! Now!"

His fellow Adepts looked at him with confusion. On the face of it, his command made no sense. Tireme's Seventh Mode—indeed, all modal Mysteries—had little to do with warfare, and certainly nothing with the present circumstances, in which they faced no combatants directly. It was a Mystery of occlusion, designed to cause confusion and chaos in the thoughts of others.

"*Now*, you imbeciles! Tireme's Seventh Mode, before it's too late!"

Olo'kidare invoked the Mystery and hurled it toward the invisible wall he knew was approaching them. He could no longer sense it directly—he had to drop Leru's Eye to create the mode. He did not know if he would feel anything when his own power intersected the wall of fear. They might simply slip past one another unchanged, powers so dissimilar they could not interact. Even if he was right and succeeded, he had no idea how or even if he would know, other than by the simple act of surviving.

But then there was something, a whisper, a breath of power that made the hair on his arms stand on end. The powers had touched! He felt pressure being exerted against the mode. The wizards' power of fear was confounded by what he had done! The occlusion had done what he thought it would: disrupt the ability of the other power to reach into the minds of its intended victims. That had been his insight—that the fear needed to penetrate a mind in order to carry out its task. And since Tireme's Seventh Mode was intended to occlude and confound, he'd hoped that it would do so to this "spell," as Tolsadri said the wizards' powers were named.

"Do not relent!" he bellowed. "Push with the mode until I give the order to stop!"

He took a terrible risk then. He allowed his own mode to drop so he could peer once again with Leru's Eye. He needed to *see*, to understand, if he could, what he had done. He could not, after all, properly articulate his triumph to Wahtar Dremjou if he did not comprehend it himself.

Olo'kidare swore as he searched once more for the slippery power of the wizards. At last he found it, though it immediately threatened to dance from his vision. He bore down on it with all of his thought and will, trying to understand—

Demons appeared in the air above their heads, their horrendous shrieks piercing his skull like slivers of glass. The demons took flight toward the fortress, compelled by the loathsome eunuchs. The arrival of the demons broke his concentration enough that he lost sight of the wall of fear.

He grasped for it once more, searching with the Eye, but he could not find it. He sensed the modes of his fellow—if lesser—Loremasters thrusting forward, and by following them tried to determine if they were still interacting with the wizards' power.

Ah! There it was! Writhing like a headless serpent, thrashing about madly. The wall flexed and rippled like a sail billowing in a maelstrom. It was withdrawing, moving back toward its original position. He was sure of it. The power calmed as it withdrew, becoming stronger and more coherent as it receded back toward its point of origin.

Olo'kidare laughed. Demons flew above him as the siege engines hurled boulders toward their enemy's stronghold. He did not care. He had beaten the wizards' power, forced it to retreat. A victory he could take to the Wahtar. He had seen, understood, acted, and won.

"Loremasters, to me!" he shouted. "I know how we can penetrate the wall of fear!"

"Venegreh preserve us," said the Archmage. "They're disrupting the terror spells."

"I thought their power couldn't harm yours?" said the Lord Commander. "That they were too dissimilar to interact."

"They are dissimilar, but perhaps not as much as we thought. They're doing something to cause the barrier to lose cohesion. We have to move it back."

Whatever Medril was about to say was cut off when demons began to appear above the Havalqa forward line. More than a score of the shrieking creatures were suddenly racing toward Hethnost, spread out along the length of the Hammdras. The Lord Commander bellowed for his archers and crossbowmen to shoot as soon as the creatures were in range.

"Will the Forbiddings stop them?" he asked the Archmage.

"Not for long. And we can't create enough to block them all."

"Then we'll have to pray that Warden Khazuzili's spell will work."

* * *

Gerin and Balan were on the far side of the gate tower roof from the Archmage and Lord Commander Medril. The two men watched the demons approach while the Havalqa siege engines continued to throw boulders at the fortress. Most were now striking the Hammdras directly. Others smashed against the Forbiddings and tumbled to the earth. Gerin could see the spells weakening with each impact and knew they would collapse before long, especially with the demons on their way. The wizards would have to divert their powers to fighting the creatures.

Balandrick drew his sword and inscribed a small circle in the air with its point, rotating his wrist to keep it loose.

"We need to get off this roof," said Gerin. "Archmage! Lord Commander!" he called out. "We should move to the Hammdras. Once the Forbiddings are down, we'll be vulnerable to those siege engines." At least on the wall they had room in which to avoid the incoming boulders.

Medril nodded his agreement and ushered the Archmage after them. They descended two flights of stairs and exited a door that led to the wall-walk of the Hammdras. Wizards and soldiers of the Sunrise Guard were rushing about, organizing themselves to face this new threat.

Hollin appeared before them. "Archmage, we can't hold the Forbiddings in place any longer. With the demons almost here—"

"I understand," she said. "Do as you must."

He turned to Gerin. "Come."

Gerin and Balandrick followed Hollin along the wall-walk as the older wizard shouted orders to allow the Forbiddings to collapse.

Hollin led them toward a cluster of wizards. Abaru and Kirin were among them. Nyene was present as well, angrily prowling the wall-walk like a caged cat, knives in both hands.

"When will these cowards send *men* to fight us?" she snarled. "I have no use for monsters or magic."

"I understand those sentiments more than you know," said Balandrick.

"Here they come!" shouted a soldier standing at the battlements.

Sword and staff in his hands, Gerin drew magic into himself and fashioned Khazuzili's spell.

Five demons dropped toward them from a dizzying height. Their shrieks set Gerin's teeth on edge. Balandrick swore, and Nyene's scowl deepened as she glared at the demons.

"I'll take the lead creature!" Gerin shouted. The other wizards claimed targets of their own so they would not waste their efforts attacking the same demons.

Gerin calmed his mind against the pain and distraction of the shrieking, then released the spell at the lead demon.

The creature's wings slammed tight to its body as if bound by invisible chains. Its trajectory changed very little—it had been dropping almost straight down, and Gerin's magic had little effect on its course.

He could see a translucent geometric shape encasing the demon. The planes in the shape rippled with energy. Gerin did not know if this was a power Balandrick could see. He could usually tell such things, but this spell was too strange for him to be certain.

The demon continued to fall, still writhing within the geometric shape.

By the gods, when will this bloody thing disappear? he wondered.

Then he and the others leapt aside as the demon slammed into the wall-walk. The impact shook the walk and cracked the stones beneath the demon. The thing's massive wings could not break through its prison, otherwise they all might have been swept from the walk by their frantic beating.

Another spell-trapped demon plunged past the outside of the wall and thudded on the ground far below.

The creature's appearance was horrific. Its skin was greenish-black, the color of fetid swamp water, and covered with scales. Its wide, slitlike eyes were squeezed shut as it struggled against the power holding it, so Gerin could not get a clear look at its gaze. Its shrieking had mercifully become more like strangled gasps, its fang-filled mouth gaping wide as if it was suffocating, its narrow tongue flicking in and out like a snake's.

Nyene stepped forward, amazingly fearless, and tried to bury her long-bladed knife in the creature's heart. But the spell turned her blade like a barrier of unbreakable glass. Furious, she pounded once on the barrier with the butt of the handle before turning away and shouting in frustration.

The next instant, the demon winked from existence with a flash of dark light. Whatever power connecting it to its master in the Havalqa encampment had been severed.

Another demon smashed into the wall-walk about thirty feet from them and tumbled into the practice field that lay inside the Hammdras. Gerin ignored it and looked skyward once more.

The other nearby demons were all encased in the geometric power devised by Warden Khazuzili. Two vanished in eruptions of dark light; a few seconds later the demon that had fallen inside Hethnost also vanished.

"Ghastly things," said Balandrick. "If it had gotten free before you made it disappear—"

"Bah," spat Nyene. "I would have gutted it like a fish before it could scratch that pretty face of yours."

Before Gerin could get them to shut up, more demons dropped toward them. Medril's archers and crossbowmen did what they could to pierce the creatures with arrows and bolts, but mundane weapons did them little harm. Once encased within the geometric spell, the soldiers' missiles could no longer reach them—they were deflected away just as Nyene's knife had been.

Gerin's knees buckled as an image flashed through his mind. The Staff of Naragenth was communicating with him. This was the first time the Presence had emerged since their arrival at Hethnost. He'd wondered if the sheer number of wizards somehow made it nervous, reluctant to show itself. Naragenth had lived in a time when wizards were highly suspicious and distrusting of one another, guarding their secrets jealously. And while Naragenth had indeed called a conclave of the greatest wizards of his time in order to propose that they gather their knowledge in a single location—what would become the Varsae Estrikavis—he nevertheless continued to distrust them, insofar as he never showed any of them his staff, his crowning achievement.

The prolonged absence of the Presence had made Gerin wonder if it somehow shared some of Naragenth's distrust of other wizards. Could the personality that resided within the staff have learned such a thing from its maker?

The image that flashed in his mind was of himself and the staff making not an enclosed geometric pattern of magic, but a broad shallow bowl between the wizards and the demons, as if Khazuzili's spell had been opened up and partially flattened. He had no idea how to fashion such a thing—Khazuzili's spell was very specific in its intent and execution, and Gerin could think of no way of altering its properties in such a drastic manner.

But creating a specific spell was not needed when using the staff. The Presence controlled the shaping of magic, communing silently with Gerin to understand his desires and needs. Gerin was largely passive in this process, little more than a conduit for magic once he had made his desires known.

Do what you showed me. He aimed his thoughts toward the staff, bending his mind to it with all of his will. *Create that spell between us and the demons.*

He felt a strong sense of jubilation from the staff. It was ecstatic to be used, to have a purpose—to serve.

The next instant, amber fire exploded from his body as the Presence drew magic from him to power the spell.

Balandrick, Nyene, and several other wizards leapt back in surprise at the sudden appearance of Gerin's aura. The amount of magic pouring through him was enormous. The Presence was drawing as much as it dared—any more and it threatened to burn out Gerin's *paru'enthred* forever.

He felt the Presence shaping the magic, an altered and massively more complicated form of Khazuzili's spell. The Presence worked so fast that Gerin could not follow the steps it took to create the curved surface of power.

Many of the attacking demons were already encased in Khazuzili's spell by other wizards, their trapped bodies tumbling through the air or writhing on the ground before winking out of existence.

But there were still many demons coming toward them who were as yet unmolested, and it was against these creatures that the Presence directed Gerin's power. It took his breath away to watch as the faceted surface expanded across the sky at an unbelievable rate. His heightened senses allowed him to hear wizards gasping in shock as they watched his spell unfold above them.

"What is going on?" shouted Nyene. "What are they pointing at?"

"No idea," said Balandrick. "But His Majesty is obviously doing something big. We just can't see it."

Gerin realized that the demons could not see the spell, either. They raced toward it headlong, varying in neither direction or speed as the faceted curvature of the spell rose suddenly in front of them like a cresting ocean wave.

He heard the wizards and soldiers around him shout as the demons smashed into the spell. The tremendous force of the impact stunned most of the creatures.

The Presence shifted the power—Gerin could feel its manipulation of magic through the staff itself.

At once, the curvature of the spell closed into a sphere, trapping all of the demons inside it. The closure was so fast it seemed instantaneous to Gerin, movement so rapid his eyes could not follow it.

The demons fell to the bottom of the sphere in a heap, unable to find purchase of any kind on the walls of the spell. They scrabbled over one another, clawing and tearing each other's wings in a desperate attempt to escape.

The Presence changed the spell again. Almost before Gerin realized what was happening, the sphere began to shrink. Within moments it had collapsed down to a point. The demons vanished instantly.

Then the Presence halted the flow of magic and ended the spell. Gerin's aura disappeared. A sudden light-headedness overcame him, and he leaned on the staff for support. Balandrick rushed to his side and gripped his elbow.

"Your Majesty, are you all right?"

Gerin nodded. "Just tired. That took a lot of magic to work."

"You're an astounding man, Gerin Atreyano," said Nyene.

"You can thank the staff," he said wearily. "It made the spell. I just provided the materials."

She frowned. "You mock me."

"I most certainly do not."

Before she could say anything more, he was swarmed by wizards asking him question after question about the spell he'd made.

Hollin forced his way to Gerin's side and angrily told the others to move back. "We need those Forbiddings back in place over us and the gate!" he shouted. "In case you haven't noticed, those siege engines are still throwing boulders at us!"

As if to make his point, a good-sized rock smashed into the battlements not far from them. The impact crushed the merlons completely and collapsed part of the wall-walk itself. The soldiers and wizards on that part of the wall were able to scramble out of the way just in time, but two servants who were moving across the inner yard were not so lucky and were crushed by the caroming boulder.

"Get those barriers up before we get hit!" bellowed Hollin.

Gerin sheathed Nimnahal and handed the staff to a surprised Balandrick, then leaned over, hands on his knees, to catch his breath. He was sweating profusely. *Gods above me, but that staff certainly knows how to drain my strength!*

Gerin could sense Forbiddings taking shape beyond the Hammdras. After the tumult of the demons and their terrible shrieking, the wall-walk seemed oddly hushed.

"That was a tremendous display of power," said Hollin quietly. "How did you manage such a thing?"

He took a deep breath, straightened, extended his arm toward Balan. The captain handed back the Staff of Naragenth without hesitation. *He doesn't like it,* thought Gerin. *He likes what it can do, its power; but he doesn't like the thing itself.* Balan had never said anything directly to him, but he didn't have to. Gerin knew him well enough: Balan's narrow-eyed glances at the staff when his friend thought he wasn't looking, the reluctance to touch it (which he tried to hide), his sometimes sarcastic comments about the "stick."

At first Gerin thought it was simply Balan's discomfort around anything related to wizardry—magic was something he could not defend against. Not a comforting thought for someone charged with the safety and well-being of the king. But Balandrick did not have the same sense of unease around Nimnahal, or some of the other artifacts of magic he and Hollin used. It was only the staff. Though the evidence had been accumulating in his mind for some time, Gerin only fully realized it now. He resolved to ask Balan about it when they had a private moment.

"Gerin?" Hollin said to him. "Are you all right?"

"I'm fine. Just tired." He took another deep breath. "But it wasn't me. It was the staff. It showed me what I could do, and I told it to do it. All I did was supply the magic."

"Astounding," said Hollin softly as he regarded it. "How did Naragenth create such a thing?"

Yes, thought Gerin. *How indeed?*

Khazuzili hobbled along the wall-walk toward them as fast as he could manage.

"Brilliant, young man!" he wheezed. He reached Gerin and gripped his forearm with bent, arthritic fingers. "I should have thought of that! I'm a doddering old fool for missing something so obvious." With his other hand, Khazuzili thumped his forehead like a woodpecker knocking against a tree.

"Warden, what did you miss?" asked the Archmage. "What was so obvious?"

"Why, contracting the spell! It forces the connection between demon and the summoner to sever! My method is much less efficient. It cripples the connection but has to wait for it to decay, which varies based on the strength of the connection itself. Stronger ones obviously take longer to completely die away. Gerin's method is more like slamming a door."

"Can you modify your spell to do that?" asked the Archmage.

"Well of course! Gerin can simply tell me what he did."

"I'm sorry, Warden. I can't," said Gerin. "I have no idea how it was done. The Presence within the staff fashioned the spell. I tried to follow along, but it was working too fast."

"The magic stick saves the day again," muttered Balandrick.

"Can you ask it to tell you what it did?" asked the Warden.

Gerin shook his head. "It doesn't work that way. It doesn't talk. It shows me images, and I tell it what I want. It doesn't use words."

"We know that it *can* be done because it *has* been done," said the Archmage. "Rahmdil, you will simply have to reason out the method on your own. I have the utmost confidence in your ability to do so."

Khazuzili regarded Naragenth's staff. "An object of legend appears and works miracles before my eyes. Who'd have thought I would live to see the day?"

Kirin approached the group. "We may have something new to worry about." He pointed toward the western flank of the enemy encampment. "Some power is building there. I don't know what it is, but it's already intense, and it doesn't look like they'll be done for hours."

Gerin made his way to the wall and managed to invoke a Farseeing. He aimed it toward the portion of the camp that Kirin had indicated. Balandrick and Nyene moved to either side of him so they could see as well.

This was the section of the encampment devoted to inhuman creatures they had not seen before this siege. When they'd first examined the camp, they took note of the beings immediately. They averaged a head taller than the humans around them and were broader through the shoulders and torso, though their proportions were subtly different. They wore a breastplate with pauldrons and vambraces on their forearms, but no armor below the waist, only a long leather skirt. Their skin was the color of clay, their hair often white or gray. Their faces were broad and flat, with prominent cheekbones and heavy foreheads. Their eyes were lost in shadows in the deep wells of their sockets, which made them look empty, giving their features a skull-like appearance.

The creatures had been inscribing interlocking circles into the earth, with glowing braziers set at intervals along the pattern. Two of them used heavy chains to drag a plowlike instrument across the ground. A third creature walked behind, ensuring that the plow remained steady and on course.

"I don't like the look of that at all," said Balandrick.

"Neither do I," said Nyene.

Despite his weariness, Gerin managed to create several Spells of Knowing and directed them at the circles. Kirin was right: there was immense power building, slowly organizing itself as it grew, though he had no idea how it would ultimately be used.

"Can you destroy it?" asked Nyene.

"No. It's too far."

"So what do we do?" asked Balan.

"Wait and see what this thing is. And hope we have a way to stop it."

36

"How did they stop you?" Ezqedir shouted at the mursaaba. The eunuch stood near the tent's entrance, head bowed, hands folded before him. Ezqedir had not and would not offer him a place to sit. "They snuffed out your demons like candles!"

"I apologize for my failure, General," said Hu'mar. "My life is forfeit if you so desire."

"I don't want your life—at least not yet. I want to know what went wrong."

The eunuch shifted his stance but still did not look at Ezqedir. "I can't explain it, General. The power they used was different than before. More efficient. I thought our numbers would overpower them, but they have proved . . . adaptable."

Ezqedir prowled about the tent, striding back and forth between the two center poles. He wanted to hit something, to lash out in his anger and frustration at how these heathen wizards were thwarting him at every turn. Was this entire land cursed? He'd heard some of his men whisper their belief that the Harridan held sway here, that the light of the Powers and Holvareh Himself were weak on this continent. He'd scoffed at their superstitions, but now felt uncertainty creep over him. It seemed his every thrust was turned from true. And if that was not the sign of the Harridan's foul influence, he did not know what was.

I beseech you, Herol, keep her from my battlefield! Ezqedir rarely prayed, but now felt the need to show at least some obsequiousness to the Power who governed his life. *Guide me so that I may claim this victory in your name.*

"What would you have us do?" asked Hu'mar.

"Nothing. These wizards have rendered you irrelevant. I can only hope the Loh'shree succeed where you failed."

Gerin removed himself to a guardhouse well inside the Hammdras and slept for a few hours. The Havalqa continued to hammer the wall with their siege engines, but the strength of the Hammdras itself, coupled with the Forbiddings that intercepted more than half of the boulders flung at them, meant that the damage was relatively light.

He awoke a short while before dawn and hurried to check on Elaysen. He found her already awake and sitting quietly in her room. She was outwardly calm—the extreme agitation that had gripped her earlier had melted away. But she was still not well. Sadness to the point of despair had enveloped her like a shroud. She would not look at him. She sat propped in bed, staring blankly out the window. Tears glistened in her eyes, and she sighed heavily with regret.

"I'm so sorry about Zaephos," she said. "What happened to his body?"

"The wizards gave him to the Releasing Fire. Kirin made the decision. He said it didn't seem right for a divine creature to be buried."

"I'm a healer. To think I killed a man . . . " Her breathing grew labored as she struggled to hold back a flood of tears.

"What's done is done. You weren't thinking clearly. I don't condone what you did, but neither will I condemn you for it."

She nodded. "I wish things were different. I wish I was well, and a woman you could love."

"Elaysen, please—"

"Hear me out." She looked down at her hands and absently picked at her nails. The cuticles were torn, and some had bled recently. "It's no secret any longer that I love you, and have for a long while. I know you don't love me in return, and never will. Even if I were of noble birth, you would never want someone as damaged as I am. I can't change the feelings in my heart, but I also can no longer be a part of your life. As soon as I'm able, I'll return home. You'll never have to see my again, or be reminded of how I shamed you with my behavior."

"Elaysen, stop. You've brought me no shame." He reached for her hand, but she drew it away and held it curled to her chest. "I don't profess to understand what's happened to you, or what you're enduring. I wish I could help you more than I have."

"Do you love me at all? I know it's a terrible thing to ask, but I can't help myself."

He did not know what to say. His feelings toward her had changed so drastically in recent days he did not understand them himself.

"I care about you and want you to be well." He turned toward the door. There was nothing else he could say. "I need to return to the Hammdras, but I'll check on you as I can."

His mind was fully occupied with Elaysen as he made his way toward the wall. How *did* he feel toward her? Did he, perhaps, still love her? He admitted to himself that he had at one time—loved her spirit, her passion. But she was nevertheless the daughter of an apostate priest who was considered a potential threat to the realm by the nobility. There was simply no possibility of her ever being accepted as queen. He would undermine his kingship in a fatal way were he to marry Elaysen.

That realization had cooled his feelings toward her. The weight of ruling Khedesh had so occupied his thoughts that he gave little consideration to her, or any other woman—he simply did not have time. He had still cared for her, perhaps deeply, but was able to push those feelings aside as matters of state took over nearly every waking moment.

Now he had this disease of the mind to consider. A problem that caused her to become so delusional she had murdered the living incarnation of a servant of the god she and her father followed. He shook his head as he walked, dismayed. He could not understand how a mind could become so unhinged.

Who else might she kill if she doesn't get better? he wondered. *Would she kill Balandrick, or Hollin, or even me? Is it possible for her to get well again after falling so far?*

He had no answers. The only hope for her appeared to be a swift return to Almaris so she could fashion the proper medicines, but it would be some time before they could get there.

He found Balandrick talking to a group of Sunrise Guards in the courtyard behind the gates.

"It's pretty quiet right now, Your Majesty," said the captain. "They stopped lobbing rocks at us a while ago. I think they ran out of boulders and need to get more."

"Any sign of demons?"

"None at all."

"What about those circles of power?"

Balan shrugged. "They've kept the braziers going and set up what look like a couple of small altars. Kirin's worried, I can tell you that." Balan glanced at the Staff of Naragenth. "Too bad your magic stick doesn't still have the power around it like it did at Almaris. You could take out those circles and most of that army in short order."

Despite his words, Balan's tone was filled with derision, and he regarded the staff itself with a faint expression of disgust.

"Why don't you like it?" asked Gerin. "It's obvious you hate the staff, but I have no idea why."

Balandrick stiffened like a boy who'd been caught sneaking a treat. "I don't hate it. Why do you think so?"

Gerin rolled his eyes. "I don't care if you do or don't, but it's plain you do, so don't deny it. I just want to know what bothers you so much."

Balandrick folded his arms. "All right. I admit it. I loathe the bloody thing. Not what it can do, which is pretty helpful in a pinch, but what it . . . *is*. That Presence, as you like to call it. Well, that's not really it, either. I don't hate the Presence, because from what you've said, it is trying to be helpful. Like some bloody beagle eager to please."

He stepped closer to Gerin and lowered his voice. "I'm telling you, Your Majesty, there's something wrong with it. Wrong like that bloody awful horn you blew when you were here before. Just looking at that stick makes my skin crawl. I don't know how to explain it any better than that."

Gerin stared hard at the staff. *What are you?* he projected toward the Presence. *How did you come to be? You must remember something of your origin. Tell me if you can. I need to know. I understand you may still have loyalty to Naragenth and his secrets, but he is long dead. Please. Tell me what you are.*

To his surprise, the staff answered.

A series of images of a young boy flashed across his vision, accompanied by a sharp pain in his temples. The boy was young, no more than five or six, with thick dark hair that fell in curls past his shoulders. First he was laughing, running; then other images came, of the boy sick and in bed, feverish and shaking, a woman weeping beside him.

Another image, a man bending over him. Gerin recognized him as Naragenth. A pained expression on his face; sorrow, grief, but also a grim determination, a hardened, almost cruel resolve.

More images flashed by, almost too quickly for him to see and comprehend:

Naragenth brandished a knife—

The atrium of the Varsae Estrikavis, galleries rising all around him—

Dizzying movement toward the marble pedestal on which they'd found the staff—

The pedestal open, its top somehow removed—

Naragenth placing a leather-bound book into the pedestal—

The young boy cold and dead, his wrist slit—

The vision ended. Gerin was soaked with sweat.

"What just happened?"

Gerin shook uncontrollably. Not all of it from the draining

power of the visions. *The gods above me, Naragenth, what did you do?*

Gerin turned and headed away from the Hammdras. Balandrick hurried to catch up.

"Your Majesty, where are you going?"

"To my rooms. I need the Scepter of the King. I need to get into the Varsae Estrikavis."

"Why? What just happened? You saw something—I know it. The Presence communicated to you again."

"Yes." He told Balan what he saw while they walked together.

Balandrick needed no prodding to reach the same conclusion.

"You think Naragenth murdered a boy to make the staff?"

"I'm afraid it might be true."

"But why did it show you that now? Why not tell you before?"

Gerin pondered Balan's question. "I never directly asked the Presence how it was made, at least that I can recall. But even if I did, maybe it didn't trust *me* until now. Maybe it had to get to know me well enough before it would reveal that secret."

"Is the dead boy the Presence? Is that how Naragenth got it to be alive?" Balan could not disguise the disgust he felt.

"As horrible as that sounds—as horrible as that *is*—yes, I think that's right."

They reached Gerin's rooms. He retrieved the box containing the Scepter of the King from the wardrobe where he kept it—safely behind several lock spells, shields, and Wards—and removed the ivory rod from it.

Do I really want to know what Naragenth did? he thought as he regarded the symbol of his kingship. But he knew the answer. Yes. He needed to know what happened. Especially if Naragenth had done the unspeakable and sacrificed a child in order to make his staff.

A finger of ice slid down his spine as he saw Naragenth standing over the child, knife in hand.

How could anyone do such a thing? He did not understand the cruelty that existed in some men's hearts. He saw once more the battle atop the Sundering and the murdered Eletheros children, whose only crime had been their race. An entire people, extinguished in a holocaust of blood.

He drew magic into himself, then flooded the scepter with power. The spells within it drank his magic and unfolded with great precision. The final spell, the one that worked like the keenest of knives, cut its way into the world where the Varsae Estrikavis existed.

A door marked with Naragenth's sigil and a silver crescent appeared in the room, floating a few inches off the floor.

Gerin wasted no time. He yanked open the door and hurried down the short hallway to the atrium of the Varsae Estrikavis, with the dome high above painted to mimic a sky at dusk.

The black marble pedestal was in the center of the atrium. It stood alone so that Naragenth's great staff would draw all eyes to it, a symbol he had incorporated into his personal sigil. That symbol survived his death and had been one of the few clues of the staff's existence. Wizards had long pondered if the staff bisecting a rayed sun was the staff whispered of in legend.

Gerin knelt by the pedestal and felt around its top. He could find no seam, no joint, no hidden lever or releasing mechanism. *How does the damn thing open?* he wondered.

Balandrick knelt across from him. "What exactly are we looking for, Your Majesty? In your vision, did you see how it opened?"

"Does it look like I know how it opens?" he snapped.

"Are there any opening spells you could try? Just a thought. It is a *magic* stick, after all."

Gerin created several unlocking and opening spells. They did not work. Next, he created a Seeing. At once, a hair-thin edge came into view about an inch down from the top. He moved slowly around the pedestal, examining the entire diameter with the Seeing—but despite finding the edge, he saw no latch or hinge.

He thought about how Naragenth had hidden the library itself. He'd used amber magic in such a fashion that no other wizard would ever be able to enter it even if they possessed the scepter.

Why should this be any different?

He placed his hand atop the pedestal and directed amber magic down through it, into the marble. He dispersed and diffused the power so it would not destroy the pedestal. He did not want to risk harm to the book he hoped it still contained.

He felt something within the marble drink in his magic.

The top of the pedestal rose up and swung outward on a silent hinge hidden inside the marble. He stopped the flow of magic and removed his hand, at which point the top ceased to move.

Gerin created a magefire spark above the pedestal and peered down into it. At first it looked empty, and his heart sank. Then he realized there was something wrapped in black velvet at the bottom.

He reached in and pulled out the book he'd seen in the vision.

It was surprisingly heavy. Preservation spells had been worked into it, so it looked virtually unchanged since the day it was placed there.

He felt a complex swirl of emotions from the Presence, stronger than anything he'd ever felt from it. Sorrow and exhilaration, anticipation mingled with fear and doubt, excitement and a sense of eagerness.

"So that's it?" asked Balandrick. "All of Naragenth's secrets?"

"I doubt this is all of them, but I would guess the important things are here. This explains why we never found writings of his elsewhere in the library."

"We should probably get back. Who knows what the bloody Havalqa are up to by now?"

Gerin opened the book and saw densely written Osirin scrawled in a neat, angular hand. *The achievements of Naragenth Ul-Darhel, amber wizard and King of Khedesh, as written in his own hand,* was scrawled at the top of the first page.

He considered himself a wizard first, before being a king, Gerin thought. *I wonder what the nobility of his era thought of him? But with so many wizards in the world back then, they probably saw it as a blessing and an honor to have such a powerful man on the throne.*

As much as he wanted to lose himself in Naragenth's book, he knew that Balandrick was right. They needed to get back.

Should he take it with him or leave it safely in the library? A part of him feared to take it from this place, worried that harm would somehow befall it. But he wanted to show it to Hollin and the other wizards as well, and he absolutely refused to carry the Scepter of the King with him while on the battlements. It was far too dangerous to risk damage to it simply to have easy access to the Varsae Estrikavis. Despite their studies of the scepter, so far they had failed to devise a means of duplicating its spells and properties. It was truly one of a kind. If it were damaged or destroyed, they would lose forever their means of entering the library.

He decided to take the book with him. He rewrapped it in the velvet and straightened. "All right. Let's go see what mischief our foreign friends have been making."

"So many?" asked Ezqedir when the Loh'shree commander, Arghen Helehba, told him how many men he would need.

The Loh'shree folded its arms and glared down at Ezqedir. The general forced himself to hold Helehba's gaze. The being's black eyes never failed to make the general uneasy, as if he were staring at two holes opening onto the Void, the realm of nonexistence where it was written in the *Yar'eleta* that all the enemies of Holvareh and the Powers would be cast on the Day of Doom.

"The fortress is strong, and not without powerful defenses," rumbled Helehba. His voice was dry, raspy, as if his vocal cords were stippled with sand. "If you wish to break it quickly, then we will need fifty men. Fewer, and you flirt with disaster yet again. How many men will you lose if you attempt a direct assault against these wizards? Our price is small, General. You should be grateful. Five hundred men would still be a bargain. Or have you forgotten already how the Loremasters and their escort perished before the walls?"

"I've not forgotten," Ezqedir snapped. "You'll have your men."

"Do not tally, General. Our power builds, but we cannot finish it without blood."

When the Loh'shree had gone, Meloqthes entered the tent. "What is your command, General?" He was troubled. Meloqthes knew quite well the price to be paid for using the power of the Loh'shree.

"They need fifty men. Choose them from the Ilmorr battalion. Line them up and pick every fifth man until you have what you need, then send them to the Loh'shree."

"Sir, we usually give them prisoners—"

"Helehba already inspected them and said they cannot use them. There is something in the blood of these foreigners that is at odds with their powers."

"Sir, if I may—"

"Now is not the time to argue with me, Meloqthes. I want those men to the Loh'shree within the hour."

"They may resist, sir."

"Then I expect you will go there with sufficient force to discourage any resistance. If they refuse to go willingly, tie them up and drag them. I don't like this any more than you, Lieutenant, but without the Loh'shree, we'll send thousands to their deaths with no guarantee they will ever pass the wall of fear these wizards have fashioned. As unpalatable as it may be, it is, in the end, for the good of the army and our mission.

"Send the battalion commander to me. I will explain to him the necessity of this action while you select the men. I plan to make it clear to him that if others under his command attempt to interfere, the first one to be hanged for insurrection will be him."

"Yes, sir. I understand."

While Ezqedir waited for the battalion commander to arrive, he sat and brooded. It was not that the lives of fifty men was so terrible a price. He'd sent thousands upon thousands of Herolen to their deaths in battle. That was their purpose in this world—to fight, and often to die, so that the light of Holvareh could shine where it otherwise did not.

But this is not battle, he thought. *There is no honor in this. They will be slaughtered like pigs for a feast. A shameful death.*

He had no choice. He hated the necessities of battle that forced his hand, but there was nothing else he could do.

The battalion commander was escorted into the tent. "You wished to see me, General?"

"Yes, Commander. Sit down. I have some unpleasant news to deliver."

37

A red dawn was bleeding into the eastern sky when Gerin and Balandrick returned to the Hammdras with Naragenth's book.

They found Hollin and Abaru napping in one of the guard rooms at the base of the gate tower. Gerin debated with himself whether he should wake the wizards or let them rest awhile longer. It only took him a moment to decide to leave them be. Who knew what they might face that day? They all needed whatever rest they could get.

As soon as he stepped onto the wall-walk he could sense a subtle alteration in the air, like the change that preceded violent storms in summer. The sky was clear of all but a few undernourished clouds, so he knew this was no ordinary storm building.

They found Warden Khazuzili, the Archmage, Kirin, and Lord Commander Medril looking out toward the Havalqa camp. "What's that I feel?" he asked them. "Is that coming from the circles they made?"

"Yes," said the Archmage. She looked worn, weary, to Gerin. "The Havalqa gave fifty of their soldiers to the creatures making the circles."

"What do you mean, 'gave'?" asked Balandrick. He peered out toward the encampment, but in the dim light and without a Farseeing, Gerin doubted he could make out any details.

"One group of soldiers chained fifty others and led them

to the creatures, then left them there," said Kirin. He looked down at the bundle Gerin carried. "What's that?"

"The staff showed me a vision of where Naragenth might have hidden some of his writings." He unwrapped the book. "We found this."

"Venegreh preserve us," muttered Khazuzili.

"I haven't had time to look at it, Warden. I have no idea what's here."

"But you have your suspicions," said Kirin.

"Yes." He described the vision the Presence showed him of a sick young boy and Naragenth approaching him with a knife.

"A dreadful discovery, if true," said Khazuzili.

"I feared such a thing when you first described the Presence," said Kirin. "I could think of no other way for intelligence to be imbued in an object. Damn his soul for practicing such foul magic. It's an abomination."

Medril was peering at the enemy camp with a looking glass. "I think you all need to see this."

Gerin created a Farseeing and directed it toward the flank of the camp where the creatures had inscribed their interlocking circles in the earth. They had finished their work and cleared the ground of any growth. Trees, bushes, shrubs, flowers—all were removed, leaving only grass they had shorn almost to the ground.

The fifty soldiers had been stripped to the waist and were being tied to the ground as Gerin and the others watched. Their arms were stretched over their heads, the shackles on their wrists tied to stakes pounded into the soil. Their ankles were similarly bound. Five men were staked near each of the braziers, which lit the area with an orange-red glow that reminded Gerin of descriptions of Shayphim's lair, an underhell where those captured by the dreaded spirit of evil were tormented before he deposited them into the Cauldron of Souls.

"What are they doing?" asked Balandrick as he looked through Gerin's Farseeing.

"I get the feeling they're to be sacrificed," said Abaru.

"Good riddance, I say, if they're going to start killing their own," said Balandrick.

"They won't kill them for no reason, Balan," said Gerin. "They're creating some power there, and if they're willing to kill their own men to complete it, it's not good news for us."

As the morning lengthened, they watched the creatures perform rituals within the circles. Various liquids, powders, and hunks of animal flesh were tossed onto the braziers; the smoke from them swirled upward on eddies of power. The columns bent inward and spiraled slowly until they met over the center of the inner ring, at which point a more massive column of smoke rose straight into the sky.

"That looks damn odd," said Balandrick.

Nyene had joined them sometime after sunrise. She regarded the happenings in the Havalqa camp with loathing and disgust. "We should go out and meet them on the field of battle," she said. "Enough of cowering behind walls. Enough of this cowardly magic that inflicts death with no honor. If I'm to die, I want to look into the eyes of my killer and curse him as my life leaves me."

"We'll do no such thing," said the Archmage. "My wish is that they'll batter themselves to death against our defenses, that not a single enemy will set foot inside Hethnost or any of us will set foot outside of it. I want no more of my people to die, and no more damage inflicted upon this great and ancient place. Though if you wish to go out and meet them on the field, young lady, I won't stop you. You're a guest here, not a prisoner, and your life is yours to do with as you will."

Nyene made a dismissive gesture and stalked off.

"She has fire, I'll give her that," said Kirin.

"Yet it's misplaced," said the Archmage. "She seems a woman intent on seeking her own death."

"I don't think she's seeking her own death," said Balandrick. "But she certainly is seeking *theirs*."

The central column of smoke continued to churn into the sky. A black cloud formed above the circles, fed by the column.

It grew at an alarming rate, and became so dark it seemed almost a solid thing floating in the air.

When the cloud had grown to twice the diameter of the cleared area beneath it, the creatures began to murder the soldiers they'd staked to the ground.

With methodical, dispassionate precision, they used curved daggers to cut the hearts from the men. The other soldiers began to struggle desperately against their bonds when they saw this, but could not break free.

The creatures threw the hearts onto the braziers. The bloody organs immediately flashed to ashes as the power concentrated there consumed them. The spiraling columns of smoke feeding the central column began to writhe like agitated snakes.

Every wizard along the Hammdras sensed immediately the power surging into the cloud. "Venegreh preserve us," muttered Kirin. "All that energy, and they still have more than forty to sacrifice."

"Have you figured out yet what that cloud is?" asked Balandrick.

Gerin shook his head. "All I can tell is that it's a receptacle for holding power, but I have no idea what they'll use it for."

"That's a bloody big receptacle," said Balan.

"This bodes ill for us," said the Archmage. She paused, then seemed to reach a decision. "Warden Khazuzili, have Ilyam's Lens brought here at once. I fear we will have need of it before this is done."

Khazuzili was aghast. "But Archmage, it cannot be used without causing the—"

"I'm well aware of its properties, Rahmdil. Please, don't argue."

"Yes, Archmage." Visibly shaken, he shuffled off.

Some of the Havalqa soldiers near the area of the circles were plainly distressed by the sight of their comrades being slaughtered in such a fashion. A number of them drew their weapons and ran toward that section of the camp, but were turned back by a perimeter guard of the creatures, heavily armored and brandishing spears. A number of officers were screaming at their men to fall back in an attempt to restore order. The soldiers were so far resisting the orders, but neither did they press forward.

"They may end up with a full-blown uprising over this," said Balandrick.

"We can only hope," said Gerin.

"I want order restored at once," said Ezqedir as he watched a skirmish threaten to erupt along the perimeter of the Loh'shree's section of the camp. "Any Herolen who refuses the order to fall back will be summarily executed."

"I'll relay the command immediately, sir." The adjutant bowed and raced off.

"I feared this would happen," said Meloqthes. "These sacrifices are an abomination."

"We obey whatever orders we are given, without question," snapped Ezqedir. "Armies cannot function if there is disobedience among the ranks."

Meloqthes took a step back and bowed his head. "Yes, General."

Tolsadri strode toward them from his tent, a smirk upon his face. "So you have need of the Loh'shree and their vile powers. I would have thought a man with as much pride as you would never resort to such a slaughter of your men."

Ezqedir did not deign to look at the Voice. "I would gladly sacrifice fifty to save the thousands who would break themselves upon the barriers of power the wizards have arrayed before us."

"Your Herolen think otherwise." He gestured toward the chaos along the Loh'shree perimeter. "I would have thought your soldiers better trained than this. A poor showing of their regard for your authority and the chain of command. Perhaps their confidence in you is not as high as you believe."

"Meloqthes, move the battalions into position," Ezqedir said, ignoring Tolsadri. "I want them ready when the Loh'shree deploy their power."

"Yes, General."

"And if the Voice questions my authority or the readiness of my men again, bind and gag him and throw him into the latrine. I'll not suffer insults to our proud warriors from one such as him."

"With pleasure, General."

Tolsadri snarled and left. Meloqthes and the other adjutants laughed.

Ezqedir did not smile. *The battle is about to begin in earnest. We need to break these wizards quickly, before they can bring more of their foul powers to bear on us. We need to wash over them like a tidal wave, leaving nothing standing in our wake.*

We'll kill them all. Only then will the Words of Making be ours.

Gerin watched with curiosity as a number of servants carried a wrought-iron oval up the steps to the wall-walk. The oval itself was about a yard high and mounted on a pedestal with a wide base. Nenyal Fey followed behind them, carrying two slender wooden cases whose lids bore silver plaques engraved with runic Osirin markings.

"What is that thing?" asked Balandrick. "It looks like a mirror whose glass has gone missing."

"I've never seen it before," said Gerin. "But I'll guess it's Ilyam's Lens. And before you ask me what it's used for, I have no idea."

"You're right about what it is," said Kirin. "It's a device for focusing the power of a single wizard in a very specific way to overcome the usual limitations of magic and distance. Pray that we do not have to use it."

The siege engines had been silent since the night before. Wagons had been hauling boulders to each of the weapons, but so far they merely piled them up near the throwing arms. Gerin wondered what they were waiting for, and feared the answer was linked to the ominous cloud growing over the enemy camp.

The sacrifices of the Havalqa soldiers continued. With each heart thrown onto a brazier, the power within the cloud grew. The column of smoke rising into it flashed and pulsed with crimson light.

The near uprising at the edge of the creatures' section of the encampment had unfortunately been averted. The Havalqa commanders were able to restore order before any fighting broke out.

More troubling, the Havalqa infantry were forming columns behind the siege engines. They were obviously preparing for a massive frontal assault—Gerin could see dozens of scaling ladders arrayed along the line.

"Looks like they're going to get serious," said Balandrick. "Nyene should be pleased."

Though he would never say such a thing aloud, Gerin almost welcomed action of some kind from the enemy. Waiting helplessly while their enemy plotted and prepared did his nerves no good. He understood Nyene's desire to at least *do* something.

The creatures sacrificed the last of the Havalqa soldiers. The killer straightened from its ghastly deed; blood from the heart ran down its arm and dripped to the ground. With a casual flourish, it threw the heart onto the brazier. The organ flared for an instant like a fiery eye opening among the coals before the power there consumed it.

The corpses of the dead men were left where they lay, the wounds in their chests gaping open like blood-drenched mouths.

Ten of the nonhuman beings arrayed themselves with the braziers. They wore mantles instead of armor—when he'd first seen them, Gerin thought of them as priests, though it appeared now they were also analogous to wizards, since they were the ones marshaling the power in the circles that created the massive black cloud.

The ten priestly beings began to speak in unison. Gerin could see their lips moving through the Farseeing but could not hear their words. He guessed it was a spell or ritual of some kind, designed to control the power they had created.

The light of the braziers began to throb: bright, dim, bright, dim, as if the hearts they'd devoured had begun to beat once more within the hell-red coals.

The Havalqa soldiers halted behind the line of the siege engines. The rear of the formations were still moving into position, but the forward lines were so still and quiet they might as well have been statues.

"Shayphim take me, I wish these bastards would get started already," said Balandrick.

From his hilltop vantage point, Ezqedir watched his army march into position, waiting for the Loh'shree to begin the attack.

"Now these wizards will understand what it means to awaken the wrath of the Havalqa," he said to no one in particular.

" 'The skies opened, and it was as a storm of rain and lightning and howling winds that Herol came to the field of battle. His enemies quaked with terror, and those who did not flee before his wrath were drowned in the tumult,' " he quoted from the *Herol-eilu Antaqar*.

He looked over at the cloud the Loh'shree had created. *Fashioned from the blood of my men,* he reminded himself.

The column feeding the cloud rippled with red light that pulsed in harmony with the glow from the braziers. Ezqedir had never seen a Loh'shree death cloud before and was impressed by the sight of it despite its gruesome origins.

He only hoped that it did what he was promised it would. That his men had not been slaughtered for nothing.

The braziers flared suddenly, the red coals spitting fire and sparks into the air. When the flare died back down, the central column of smoke feeding the cloud vanished.

" 'Those that did not flee were drowned in the tumult,' " he repeated softly. "Time to test the mettle of these wizards."

The cloud began to move.

38

It seemed to Gerin that all of the sounds in the world vanished for a lingering moment when the cloud began to slide toward them, a floating black mountain traveling upon unseen currents. That everyone and everything—wizard, servant, soldier, Havalqa, even the birds perched on the towers and battlements—held their breaths as the enormous black mass started to move.

"Archmage, it's not yet time for such drastic measures," pleaded Hollin.

Gerin turned, startled by the anguish in Hollin's voice, to see that Marandra had opened the cases brought by Nenyal. They contained serpentine spirals of black metal that she slid onto her forearms.

Hollin stepped closer, his face close to her ear. "Marandra, please, I beg you. Don't do this. This power should never be used."

Anger flashed across her face; then she took a deep breath and her anger vanished, replaced with a sad resignation.

"I will do what I must. Look at what is coming toward us." She pointed to the cloud, now halfway across the field separating the fortress from the Havalqa.

"What does Ilyam's Lens do?" Gerin asked Kirin. "What is the price of its power?"

"It directs the totality of a wizard's magic through that ring. All the power that she can draw through her *paru'enthred* will be released in an instant. It will allow her magic to reach the Havalqa camp."

"About bloody time," said Balandrick. "Why didn't we haul this thing out before now?"

Gerin considered the ramifications of the Warden's words. "*All* the magic? Won't that mean . . . "

Kirin looked at him gravely. "Yes. It will kill her. There is no way to survive using it."

"Oh," said Balandrick. "My apologies. I didn't know."

"Who made such a thing?" asked Gerin.

"Times were desperate during the Wars of Unification, when Helca's armies were commanded by some of the most powerful wizards of the day," said Kirin. "This was devised by a wizard enclave in Farad to defeat Maesur Entoch, the greatest of Helca's wizard generals. They succeeded in killing Maesur, but in the end the city fell and all of the wizards in that enclave were put to death."

"Gerin, come to me," said Marandra.

"Yes, Archmage."

She looked hard into his eyes, a lingering stare that made him feel naked and vulnerable but which he did not break. She was testing him in some way, trying to determine his worth. He had no desire to come up wanting.

"I don't know how this day will end," she said. Tears glistened in her eyes, and that more than anything filled him with a profound sense of dread. "But I must prepare for the worst. If I use this"—she gestured to the device—"I will forfeit my life. A sacrifice I'll gladly make to ensure the survival of Hethnost."

"Archmage, what are you saying?" He was keenly aware of Balandrick and the other wizards clustered around them, all of them hanging on the Archmage's every word.

"I will not be Archmage much longer. I have no power of Foretelling, I've had no premonitions or seen omens of death, but there is a darkness in my heart."

With great dignity and grace, she removed the Ammon Ekril and held it gently in both hands.

"This is no longer the symbol of my office. Upon my death,

it is my decree that Kirin succeed me until a new Archmage can be appointed. But this, Gerin, I give to you."

She held out the Ammon Ekril.

He looked at it, stunned by her actions, but made no move to take it.

"This grants you no office, title, or authority here," she said. "But if there truly is an Adversary, and if this contains the power to defeat him, then that great burden falls to you."

"Archmage, I—"

"Take it. We have little time. The cloud is almost upon us."

He took the circlet from her hands. "I will protect this with my life."

"See that you do." She removed the Alkaneiros and held it toward Kirin. "This is now the symbol of the office of Archmage, which you will assume in the event of my death."

Kirin took the ruby ring of Demos Thelar with a trembling hand. "I accept this great honor, Marandra. But I also fervently hope you do not need to use that awful power. *My* greatest wish is that I'll return this to you when this battle is done."

Sevaisan dashed up the stairs to the wall-walk. "Archmage, what is this? I just saw you hand the Ammon Ekril to Gerin and the Alkaneiros to Warden Zaeset!"

"There's no time to explain now, Sevaisan. The battle is upon us."

As she spoke, the shadow from the cloud slid across the Hammdras. It was as if twilight had fallen across them.

They heard the shrieks of the demons as they began to appear in the sky above the Havalqa army.

"Looks like they're throwing everything they have at us," said Balandrick.

Gerin was unsure what to do with the Ammon Ekril. He had no place to put it; the leather pouch tied to his belt was far too small for it.

"Put it on," said Hollin. His voice was tight.

"What?"

"*Put it on.* I can see you wrestling with what to do with it. She gave it to you. It's not sacrilege if you wear it."

Gingerly, Gerin placed the circlet on his head, sliding the braided gold band beneath his hair. The metal was cold, the diamond a dull weight on his forehead. He felt no power from it, no sense of the magic he had earlier awakened.

And then he had no time to consider it further.

A pillar of dark red light the width of an oak trunk shot down from the outer edge of the cloud. The column did not hit the Hammdras dead on or the entire section would have collapsed. The slight rotation of the cloud caused the column to hammer the rear section of the wall-walk instead of the outward-facing battlements.

The pillar of light completely pulverized the section of the wall it struck. Stone and mortar turned instantly to dust where the light touched it. The roar was deafening. The walk beneath Gerin's feet shook with the impact; two of the wizards near him lost their balance and fell to their knees.

Before anyone could react, two more pillars of light shot down from the cloud. One originated near its center, the other from the far rim. From what Gerin could see, the light could emerge from any point on the underbelly of the cloud.

The light itself made a bone-deep thrumming that was almost below the threshold of his hearing, a rumble so deep he felt it in his chest and teeth. Wizards and soldiers were shouting all around him; chaos erupted along the wall-walk. Balandrick swore about having no way to fight "all this bloody magic."

The cloud demolished one of the inner corners of the gate tower. The other struck within Hethnost itself, blasting down through the center of one of the courtyards. Thick black smoke belched out of the hole. Part of Gerin wondered how far down into the earth the power had reached, and what exactly was burning.

He realized they had to do something quickly or they would all die. He raised the staff toward the cloud and shouted wordlessly to the Presence, *Attack it! I don't care how, but disrupt the damn thing any way you can!*

He opened himself to magic just as the Presence reached
into him to draw his power so it could carry out his command. Gerin staggered as a river of energy poured through
his *paru'enthred*. Amber fire exploded from his body and
engulfed the staff. Balandrick and Hollin stepped away from
him. He felt the Presence shaping the magic into something
he'd never before experienced. It compressed raw and deadly
magic down to a small, dense point, then sheathed it within a
sphere of power designed to prevent the magic from expanding as it naturally wanted to do.

The Presence released five of the tiny spheres at the cloud,
spreading them out so they struck at different points. Just
after vanishing inside the cloud, Gerin felt the spherical
sheaths collapse. The compressed points of power exploded
outward violently, tearing out sections of the cloud, leaving
gaping holes in its surface.

The Presence was able to release four more of the explosive
spheres of magic when Balandrick waved his sword so close to
Gerin's face he thought his captain might cut off his nose.

"Demons!" screamed Balan, pointing behind Gerin.
"Demons!"

Gerin spun around to see the other wizards in a protective formation around the Archmage, each of them invoking
Khazuzili's spell. The Warden had not had time to modify
his original spell with the ability to "slam the door" on the
power connecting the demons to their masters in the Havalqa
army, so the spheres that caged the demons did not cause
them to vanish immediately. The creatures dropped from the
sky one by one as the wizards captured them, writhing in
torment as their connection was slowly choked off.

Three more demons were swooping toward them at a
fantastic speed. Before Gerin could properly formulate a
thought, the Presence created the altered version of Khazuzili's spell it had fashioned before. The careening creatures
smashed into the power they could not see and were trapped
within it helplessly. A second later the concave curvature of
the spell closed around them, contracted down to a point,
and forced the demons from this world.

Another pillar from the cloud destroyed the gate tower. The light smashed directly down through the roof and obliterated the portcullis and gate so thoroughly it was as if they'd never existed. Gerin could hear soldiers screaming as the tower began to collapse inward, no longer able to support its own weight.

Other demons were attacking along the wall and deeper into Hethnost. Gerin ignored them for the moment and turned his attention back to the cloud. *Do what you did before! We need to tear it apart!*

The Presence obeyed.

It drew staggering amounts of magic from him to create the condensed points of magic and the protective spheres enveloping them. A dozen more points shot from the end of the staff and ripped apart pieces of the deadly cloud, but despite the wounds in its underside, the damage appeared to have little effect on the cloud's ability to attack them.

Stop! he called out to the Presence. *You're drawing too much! This isn't working. We need to think of something else.*

He heard Balandrick curse and turned to see thousands of Havalqa charging across the field.

39

Gerin's aura vanished as soon as the Presence ceased drawing his power. A mingled sensation of relief and sudden fatigue filled him.

"What happened to the fear spells out in the valley?" asked Balandrick. "The Havalqa didn't miss a step."

"They must have collapsed," said Gerin between deep breaths. "The wizards who were holding them in place are probably fighting the cloud or the demons. They can't keep everything going at once."

The Sunrise Guard were shooting arrows and crossbow quarrels at the charging enemy as quickly as they could reload. Others fired the trebuchets positioned atop the Hammdras. A few of the wizards on the wall were attacking the Havalqa infantry with death spells now that they had advanced inside the effective range of their magic. Dozens of enemy soldiers tumbled dead of no cause their fellows could see, but the deaths did almost nothing to slow their advance. The fallen soldiers were trampled beneath the surge.

"I beg you not to do this!" shouted Hollin to the Archmage. "You'll die for nothing!"

She stepped close to Hollin and cupped his face in her hands.

"Hollin, please. Stop. I'm not throwing my life away on a gesture. I'm doing what I must to save Hethnost."

She kissed him, then drew him into a tight embrace. But

she did not hold it; she could not afford to. There was no time.

The cloud had destroyed several more sections of the Hammdras. The western half of the wall was mostly a shattered, smoking ruin. The bodies of dead wizards and soldiers lay broken on the ground.

The spinning cloud began to move deeper into Hethnost. The deep thrumming sound rumbled in Gerin's chest even from here. One of the gardens near the Varsae Sandrova erupted in flame. Servants were running deeper into the fortress in utter terror.

Marandra stepped away from Hollin, who could not contain his grief; tears spilled from his eyes, and though he fought to control it, his lower lip trembled. The Archmage whispered one last thing in his ear; he nodded and mouthed, *I know.*

Then she turned from him. "Step back, Hollin."

He stared at her hard, as if burning the image of her into his mind for all eternity—then did as she asked and moved away. Wind blew his hair; the shouts of the approaching Havalqa army and the shrieks of the demons filled the world, but Hollin seemed not to hear. His attention was consumed by the woman he had once loved, who was about to die.

Marandra gripped the oval of the device and closed her eyes in concentration. Gerin heard her begin the spell she had recently learned so she could use this dangerous and fatal device.

Balandrick grabbed his arm and tried to drag him down the wall-walk. "Forgive my impertinence, Your Majesty, but we have to get out from under that thing! Who knows when it might send that light down on top of us!"

Gerin looked up. They were still under the edge of the cloud, and would be for a little while longer even as it moved deeper into Hethnost. He flinched as another lance of crimson light drilled down through one of the towers of the Varsae Sandrova. Time seemed to slow. Gerin saw with great clarity flashes of light through the windows of the ancient library and realized he was seeing the books and scrolls and parchments bursting into flame as the cloud's power incinerated everything it touched.

The windows along that wall blasted outward. Shards of glass spun madly through the air. A woman running down a path alongside the library was sliced to bits by the glass. The force of the blast lifted her off her feet, but she was dead before she thumped to the grass in a bloody heap.

Nearly a third of the outer wall of the library collapsed, burying the dead woman and several other unfortunate servants under tons of rubble. Thousands of papers and parchments, many of them on fire, billowed outward from the ruins and fluttered slowly toward the earth like burning birds.

The gods take me, what would Reshel think of this? he thought as he watched the devastation. How much knowledge had just been eradicated from the world?

Khazuzili gasped in horror as he gazed at the devastation being done to the Varsae Sandrova.

"Your Majesty, please!" said Balandrick. "We need to move from here!"

Gerin followed Balan down the wall-walk, but only until they were out from beneath the rim of the cloud. He sensed other wizards creating Forbiddings and Wardings in front of the Hammdras to impede the approach of the Havalqa and block their arrows. He knew he should help, but he was transfixed by the sight of the cloud.

Another pillar of light blasted away the northeast corner of the library. A wall of smoke billowed across the structure, obscuring much of their view, but he could see fires taking hold within. The library had spells in place to protect against fire, both embedded in the books and scrolls to make them less prone to burning, as well as magic laced throughout the massive building's walls and floors and ceilings, designed to rid an area of air where a fire was detected, starving it of what it needed to burn.

But the harm done to its structure—another blast from the cloud ripped down through its center as he watched—was too great for the spells to prevent fires from breaking out everywhere.

If nothing was done, very soon what was not destroyed by the cloud would be consumed by fire.

"If Reshel were here to see that, she'd tear through that army like Shayphim's own Hounds," said Balandrick.

Gerin could feel the power gathering around the Archmage as the spell built toward its crescendo. Her aura had not come to life, though the amount of magic he sensed around her was more than enough to have caused it to ignite. He realized the power of the device was preventing it—the Archmage's magic was being contained within her, somehow building to levels that otherwise would have bled off in the form of an aura as raw, unshaped power.

Ilyam's Lens would direct this power in a single coherent burst of magic that was far greater than anything any single wizard—even Gerin—could produce alone. But the cost was the very life of the wizard using it. It truly was a weapon of desperation, as Kirin had said.

A demon swooped down toward them. Its shrieks tore through Gerin's head like a knife. It grabbed Nenyal Fey with its claws before she could react. It beat its wings fiercely and carried the screaming woman into the air. A second later her screams ceased as the thing ripped her head from her shoulders, then let her corpse fall to the ground far below.

The Archmage released her power.

The energy she unleashed was immense—far greater than any wizard with a golden flame should have been able to produce. Gerin felt a strange draw on his own power, as if Marandra stood at the center of a magical vortex or vacuum. It lasted the merest fraction of a second before there was a sudden burst of golden light from the device's ring, blinding in its intensity. There was no heat from it, no sound, no roar of fire—just light.

"Shayphim take me, I can't see a bloody thing," Gerin heard Balandrick say. He could not see much himself. He blinked and wiped his eyes to try to clear them.

As his vision slowly returned, Gerin saw Marandra lying in a heap on the wall-walk. Hollin knelt beside her, holding her lifeless hand to his face. The bands she'd wound about her forearms had burned into her flesh, leaving angry red weals along their edges. Wisps of dark smoke curled from her fingertips, eyes, and mouth.

"What did she do?" asked Balandrick.

"She attacked the beings who made the cloud," said Kirin. He pointed toward the Havalqa camp.

A long section of earth had been gouged out along one edge of the circles. Three of the braziers had been destroyed; of the rest, all but one had been thrown to the ground. At least a score of the beings lay dead or dying, burned to death by the power of the spell. The entire area was scorched. Small fires smoldered in the grass.

But the cloud was still present, Gerin saw to his dismay. It was growing smaller; so far it had lost almost half its size, its edges swirling chaotically as if the entire cloud were about to lose cohesion and be dispersed on the strengthening wind.

But then it stopped shrinking. Its boundaries calmed and stabilized themselves. It continued to rotate about its center as if driven by some strange clockwork mechanism, in defiance of the wind blowing across it.

"Did she kill the damn thing?" asked Balan. "The gods take me, but I hope that—"

His words were cut off by another bone-deep thrumming as a pillar of crimson light shot down from the cloud. The diameter of this one was smaller than the others, but its potency seemed undiminished as it obliterated a portion of the dining hall.

"Damn," muttered Balandrick. "Damn, damn, *damn*."

"Apparently she did not," said Kirin.

On the western side of the Hammdras, Havalqa soldiers were entering Hethnost through the broken ruins of the wall. Companies of the Sunrise Guard had moved into place to meet them. They set up a line of lancers just inside the wall, with archers a pace behind them. The Guard made the enemy's advance into Hethnost a costly one, killing scores as they poured through the gaps, the bodies piling up in the rubble. But the Havalqa were just too many, too determined—the

Sunrise Guard were forced to fall back, unable to hold the onslaught.

The eastern half of the wall was mostly intact, having missed the brunt of the attack from the cloud. The Havalqa infantry were being held back from the base of the Hammdras by a series of overlapping Forbiddings, Wardings, and shields, but those were beginning to collapse as the attacks from the demons intensified. Gerin used the staff to dispatch four more demons as they swooped down toward the wall-walk.

The surviving soldiers of the Sunrise Guard reformed their ranks in a line perpendicular to the wall in an attempt to prevent the Havalqa from driving behind the other half of the Hammdras and trapping those defenders still upon it. Despite additional companies rushing to shore up the line, Gerin did not think they would be able to hold for long.

"Your Majesty, we have to get down from here," said Balandrick. "We can't afford to be surrounded."

Gerin nodded. "Kirin—Archmage Zaeset—we need to abandon the wall." He pointed to the surge of Havalqa still pouring through the wreckage of the western side. "If they break through that line and get behind us, we have no chance."

"He's right," said Lord Commander Medril. "The entire Hammdras will soon be theirs. We need to fall back to a more defensible position."

"There is no more defensible position!" snapped Sevaisan. "Not with that cloud still above us."

"We need to reach the Kalabrendis Dhosa," said Medril. "From there we can use the escape tunnels into the Redhorn Hills."

"Abandon Hethnost?" said Sevaisan.

"You yourself just admitted we have no defensible position with that cloud above us. Marandra gave her life to defeat it, but she failed. We have no other recourse. If we don't flee, the Havalqa will kill or capture all of us."

Sevaisan opened his mouth to protest, but Kirin raised his hand. "If you respect what Marandra has done, you'll obey me now as Archmage. We'll fall back to the cliff and make our escape while the Sunrise Guard holds them back. Lord Commander, use as few of your men as necessary to form the rearguard. I doubt they will survive."

"Yes, Archmage."

Soldiers began to relay the order along the wall-walk to abandon the Hammdras and retreat to the base of the Partition Rock.

Hollin was kneeling by Marandra's body, still clutching her hand. Gerin grasped his shoulders. "Hollin, it's time," he said. "She made her choice, her sacrifice. For us. We have to honor that now."

Hollin kissed Marandra, ran his fingers along her cheek. Then he stood and wiped his eyes with the heels of his palms.

"For what it's worth, I'm sorry," said Gerin as they made their way to the stairs.

"It's worth a great deal, Gerin. Thank you."

Horns began to sound through Hethnost, calling the signal to fall back to the Kalabrendis Dhosa. Servants and wizards alike were dashing toward the rear of the fortress as the Sunrise Guard moved into position to defend the retreat. Demons still swooped over their heads, though their numbers had been depleted during the defense of the Hammdras.

Gerin saw Nyene among the Sunrise Guard, this time wielding a sword with great efficiency against her enemies.

"The woman's got talent with a weapon," said Balandrick.

"We should get her out of there," said Hollin. He halted and started to turn, but Gerin grabbed his arm and dragged him along.

"She's made her choice to fight," he said. "As Marandra did. Nyene's ways are different, but that doesn't mean her choices are any less valid. Leave her be."

"But she'll die . . . "

Gerin continued on. Hollin grunted and followed.

"She may, or she may fall back when she needs to. She's a smart woman, and as Balan said, a gifted fighter. But it's her choice to make, not ours."

40

Ezqedir surveyed the scene along the fortress wall and for the first time since arriving in this accursed place felt that victory was within his grasp. He knew that there was a price yet to pay in many, many lives of Herolen before their task was done. The wizards still had their magic, and while one wizard still lived, who knew what unseen dangers awaited his men?

The Herolen swarmed through the western half of the wall. Those attacking the eastern side were having difficulty reaching the wall itself—apparently the wizards had erected invisible barriers to impede their progress. But as Ezqedir watched, those barriers vanished as the defenders abandoned the wall and retreated.

His Herolen raised the first ladders. A few archers remained to harass his men with their arrows, but there were far too few to stop his soldiers from quickly reaching the battlements. Swords flashed, but the defenders were easily overrun.

"You finally breached the wall," said Tolsadri.

Ezqedir, focused on the battle through his seeing-glass, had not taken note of the Voice's approach. The fat oaf Enbrahel was with him.

"Of course you needed the Loh'shree to pave the way for you," said Tolsadri.

"I used the proper tools for the task at hand," said Ezqedir without looking at him. "I will commend the Exalted for her wise decision to send the Loh'shree with this army—a decision you objected to, I understand."

"Yet my Loremasters were slain by your incompetence," snapped Tolsadri. "Their deaths were needless, and solely your responsibility."

"Really, Tolsadri. Are you prepared to make such an argument in the Court of Kalmanyikul?" Ezqedir laughed, a rich, throaty sound. "By the Powers, I almost hope you do. You'll only expedite your own ruin, and for many it will not come soon enough. I for one cannot wait to see how far you'll sink before someone ends your miserable existence, since you don't have the courage to do so yourself. Your opinion of yourself, were it a natural resource that we could harness for the purpose of war, would be entirely without limits. A pity it cannot be used so."

He wondered if Tolsadri would take his bait. He doubted it. The Voice, for all his bluster and errors of late, was no fool, and had already diminished himself by uncharacteristically speaking in anger in his presence. Ezqedir did not think he would do so again. *But I must always hope. It is an amusing and rare thing to watch as one so high slowly destroys himself. With a little assistance from me, of course. His fall and ultimate ruin will be a thing of beauty to behold.*

"Honored Voice!" said Enbrahel in shock, obviously unaccustomed to having his superior spoken to in such a manner. "Will you—"

"Silence, Enbrahel." Tolsadri's tone was deadly. Ezqedir thought he could almost hear the sound of Enbrahel's teeth clacking together as he snapped his jaws closed.

No, he did not rise to the bait. A pity. "At least your servants are well-trained in obedience," said the general.

"Do not bother me with you inanities," said Tolsadri. "How will you contain any wizards you capture?"

"Since you and your remaining Loremasters have devised no means of containing their powers, we have no soul stealers among this army, and both the Loh'shree and the mursaaba have told me they do not believe they can hold a wizard captive, I've ordered my men to kill them all. They are to attempt to capture servants or members of the soldiering class, but even then they're to proceed with caution. Who knows if a wizard will disguise himself as a stable hand or archer to avoid death? What mischief could one cause if brought as a prisoner among us? He might even be able to kill *you* if you are unsuspecting."

His men were scaling the eastern part of the wall unchallenged at this point. All of the defenders had either been killed or had fallen back.

"You cannot kill them all!" protested Tolsadri. "We need some of them to tell us about the Words of Making!"

"Do you have a solution for me, Voice of the Exalted? Will you volunteer yourself or your Loremasters to oversee the interrogation of any wizards we capture? Will your followers guard them and ensure they don't escape or use their powers against us? Can you bind their magic? Answer me that, Tolsadri, and we'll see about a change of orders."

"If they all die and we cannot determine how to use the Words of Making—"

"That is the reason you and your brethren are along, Tolsadri. Once all the wizards are dead and the circlet is in our hands, it will be your task to determine how it functions."

"And what if the Loh'shree have destroyed the Words in their wanton destruction of the fortress?"

"That has always been a calculated risk. We knew before we set sail that whoever held the Words would not surrender them without a fight. There was a risk that whoever held the Words would destroy them outright rather than allow them to fall into our hands, and there is obviously the risk that they would be destroyed or damaged in any battle to take them. The Loh'shree were commanded to halt their pummeling once my Herolen breached the walls."

Ezqedir knew he was taking a risk by tweaking the nose of the Voice to such a degree, but he could not stop himself. Victory was almost his. Tolsadri's contributions to date had been nothing. Less than nothing. If he did not want to be remembered solely as an impediment on this campaign, he would have to step forward to avoid a complete personal disaster. Understanding how the Words of Making functioned seemed the only choice left to him.

He again felt a trace of unease about the use of the Loh'shree. The possibility that they would inadvertently destroy the Words of Making themselves had been another reason for holding them in reserve. But what choice did he have? The wizards' powers had all but made it impossible for him to conduct a proper siege. He would have gladly waited months to secure the fortress, starving them out or attempting to infect them with disease, but those options were taken from him by their infernal powers.

"Do we know what the circlet looks like?" asked Enbrahel.

"Do not speak again, Enbrahel!" said Tolsadri.

"I thought that's what your vaunted Mysteries were for?" said Ezqedir. "My Herolen will gather every circlet and headband we find, but the Words themselves are a matter of power, and such things fall to the followers of Bariq. How you will recognize it is not for me to say."

"The Mysteries are not for you or any other to know," said Tolsadri. "Not that one such as you could comprehend the sublime beauty of the power Bariq has bestowed to us."

"And I have no interest in them, I assure you. But if you cannot identify the Words, or discern with your 'sublime' power how to use them, then what use are you? Truly, why have you burdened yourself with this journey if you have nothing to contribute to this cause?"

"Gerin Atreyano, at least, should be taken alive."

"But if you cannot use your Mysteries to control captured wizards, surely you see my dilemma? They must all be killed, otherwise there will be chaos within our ranks. Besides, if you make them Havalqa, as by our laws you must, would they not be made followers of Bariq? Their magic is strong, Tolsadri. Would you want such creatures to learn the Mysteries as well? Though perhaps it might be a good thing to provide your caste with an infusion of fresh blood. Who knows? Perhaps one of them could rise far within the Jade Temple."

"Your taunts are wearisome, Ezqedir. I'll warn you again not to kill them all, at your own peril."

"And I will say to you once more that unless you provide a means of containing their magic, they are too dangerous to take as prisoners. My orders have already been given, and will not be rescinded unless you provide a compelling reason."

Meloqthes approached and spoke quietly. "General, there is something in the sky to the southwest."

Ezqedir turned and saw at once the dark blot on the sky. He aimed his seeing-glass at the blot, which resolved into several dozen winged lizards flying toward them at great speed.

"The Loh'shree don't know what they are, but they fear them," said Meloqthes.

It was never good news to hear that the Loh'shree feared something. What new problem was this accursed land about to throw at him? "Have the Nureen Regiment set their archers along that rise," said Ezqedir. Were these things allies of the wizards? "Can the Loh'shree do anything to attack these beasts?"

Meloqthes shook his head. "Since the wizards were able to damage their power, it's taking all of their strength to maintain the cloud over the fortress."

Ezqedir turned to Tolsadri. "Well, Voice? Can your Mysteries help us?"

"That depends on the method of their attack, assuming they are hostile to us."

"Who in this wretched land is not hostile to us? Is not the negotiation with those who do not know the light of the Powers within your purview? No matter. I doubt these creatures are ones to parley. Watch them, Voice, and do what you can."

41

There was chaos throughout Hethnost. The cloud was now stationary above the grassy triangle that lay between the Archmage's manor house, the bathhouse, and a squat storage tower; mercifully, it had not released its destructive light in several minutes.

Is it dead? Gerin wondered as he ran toward the dormitory where he'd left Elaysen. *Was the Archmage able to mortally wound it? Is that nothing but a corpse floating above us?* He hoped that was the case but could not shake a nagging feeling of dread that the slowly rotating mass was merely waiting, or perhaps pausing to regain its strength before commencing with the killing blow.

People were running all around them: servants, soldiers of the Sunrise Guard, wizards, even a few Havalqa who'd managed to penetrate this far into Hethnost. Gerin killed three enemy soldiers with death spells who were chasing down a group of serving women.

"I'll meet you at the women's dormitory," he said. "I need to get the Scepter of the King from my rooms."

"I'm coming with you, Your Majesty," said Balandrick. "Being as your protection is my sworn duty and all."

Gerin didn't have time to argue. "That's fine, but keep up." He dashed off into the growing gloom seeping through the fortress.

His rooms were not far. He dashed up the stairs, into his

apartments, and was retrieving the case that contained the scepter when Balandrick huffed his way into the room.

"No fair," he said. "I can't run that fast."

"I told you to keep up."

They reached Hollin and the others just as soldiers of the Sunrise Guard approached them. Nyene was with the soldiers, her face and clothes splattered with blood, though none of it seemed to be her own.

"I'm glad you're alive," said Balandrick.

"The bastards are coming through everywhere," she said as she wiped a drip of blood from her eyebrow. "I'm not such a fool as to want to die just yet, Captain."

"What in the gods' names is that?" said a soldier, pointing toward the southwestern sky.

Gerin looked where he was pointing and saw what appeared to be a flock of birds heading toward them.

But they were far too large to be birds. He created a Farseeing and felt his skin go cold the instant he understood what they were.

"Dragons," he said.

"What?" said Balan. "How can that be?" He moved to get a better view through the Farseeing. "Those same things we saw in the visions from the Watchtowers?"

"Apparently."

"But I thought they were all destroyed in the Last Battle of the Doomwar? They're supposed to be extinct!"

"Those creatures look very much alive to me," said Nyene. "And they are moving very fast."

"We need to get Elaysen," said Gerin. With a wave of his hand, the Farseeing vanished. He set off once more for the women's dormitory.

"Do you have a way to fight them?" asked Nyene.

"Not if the stories about them are true. They're resistant to our powers."

"Are these things allies of the Havalqa?"

"I don't know where they came from." Deep in his heart, Gerin feared Nyene was right. Who else could have brought them here? Dragons had been gone from Osseria for thousands and thousands of years. Now they suddenly reappeared at the location of an Havalqa army? It stretched credulity to believe the Havalqa were not in some way responsible. *Yet another weapon for them to use against us,* he thought bitterly. *As if that bloody damned cloud of theirs wasn't enough.*

They found Elaysen and Peylo Ossren on the path outside the dormitory, heading toward the Partition Rock. Elaysen seemed to have regained some of her composure. The serving woman was leaning on Elaysen's arm, cowering in fear over the ruinous events occurring around them. Her fear had apparently brought out some of Elaysen's natural abilities as both leader and comforter. *Maybe that's what she needs to help her,* Gerin thought. *To be engaged in a meaningful way.* He would have to consider how best to make that happen until they could get her the medicines she needed.

When Elaysen saw Gerin, she threw her arms around his neck. "I knew you'd come for me," she said, her face pressed against his throat.

He pulled her away from him. "We need to hurry."

"Why are you wearing that?" She gestured to the Ammon Ekril.

"The Archmage died defending Hethnost," he said. "Kirin is Archmage now, but Marandra wanted me to have this. I'll explain more later. Right now we need to move."

Before he could say anything else they heard a distant roar and saw a sudden brightening of the sky. Everyone turned to see two of the dragons belching long gouts of liquid fire toward something on the ground outside of Hethnost.

"Are those . . . dragons?" asked Elaysen.

"Yes," said Balandrick. "And it looks like they're attacking the Havalqa."

"This get stranger and stranger," said Hollin. "Do we have allies we don't know about?"

"The Telchan?" suggested Abaru.

The dragons were almost upon Hethnost itself. One of them—a black creature with long orange markings along its hide and wings—swooped down toward the Hammdras and unleashed a stream of fire across the battlements. The dragon continued inside the fortress and burned an entire company of Sunrise Guard that had turned to flee before it.

"I'd say we and the Havalqa have a common enemy," said Abaru's wife, Delarra.

They could not see the Havalqa camp from their location, but it was apparent that a number of the dragons were raining fire down upon it, circling the encampment like vultures above a dying animal. *Let the bastards burn,* thought Gerin.

More dragons had begun circling Hethnost itself, blasting fire upon anything that moved. "We need to find shelter!" said Kirin. "We'll never make it to the Partition Rock with those things up there, let alone reach the Kalabrendis Dhosa!"

The closest structure was the storage tower. "Is there a cellar in that thing?" asked Balandrick.

"Yes. Several, I believe," said Kirin.

"Then that's where we're going," said Balandrick.

"No!" shouted Hollin. "Not there! We'll be trapped. The dragons will either collapse the tower on our heads or the Havalqa will find us. We need to get to the Varsae Sandrova."

"We'll be just as trapped there," said Kirin.

"There's a safe place we can hide where we won't be found."

Two hundred yards behind them a dragon roared and burned a swath through the grass and into one of the walled gardens. Trees exploded as soon as they were touched by the dragon's fire. All of them could feel the heat of the flames on their backs. Peylo Ossren shrieked in terror and threw her hands over her head. Gerin thought she might faint, but Elaysen grasped her wrists and managed to calm the woman. *Yes, she needs to be helping others,* he thought. *Focusing on something other than her own troubles. That's where she draws her strength.*

"I hope Hollin knows what he's doing," muttered Balandrick.

"So do I," said Abaru.

The dragon's path carried it off to their left, but it was close enough that they could feel the wind of its passing and smell its rank, leathery hide and sulfurous reek.

Gerin fired a death spell from Nimnahal at the dragon. Before it hit the creature, the spell veered sharply away.

"What the . . . ?" he muttered.

"I saw that," said Abaru. "The gods take me, how is that possible?"

"I saw it, too," said Hollin. "It's just like those things that cut off your brother's arm. The dragons must have rezarim in their bodies."

"That's just great," said Balandrick. "That's the metal that's immune to magic, right? So you're saying you can't hurt these things with your powers?"

"It appears that way, yes. No wonder the Atalari had so much trouble fighting them."

"Quiet!" said Kirin. "We need to keep moving!"

They'd gone only a short distance when at least a hundred Havalqa appeared between them and the Varsae Sandrova. The enemy soldiers were fleeing the dragons, all thoughts of conquering the fortress apparently lost to them for the moment. They hadn't yet seen Gerin and the others, who hid themselves behind a pile of rubble blasted out from the ruins of a nearby building. The Havalqa huddled behind a stone retaining wall and seemed in no hurry to move.

"They're between us and the library!" said Balandrick.

"We can fight our way through them," said Abaru.

"We can, but I'm sure the fighting will draw the attention of the dragons to us," said Kirin. He faced Hollin. "What is this secret place?"

"There's an entrance in the library hidden by magic. It leads beneath the earth to an underground lake."

Kirin arched an eyebrow. "Indeed. And why have I never heard of this?"

"It's a secret known only to the Archmage."

"Then how do you know about it?" asked Nyene.

"That, young lady, is none of your concern. But if we can get to it, we'll be safe. At least safer than anyplace else."

A dragon unleashed a river of fire between them and the Havalqa. The enemy soldiers shot arrows at the beast but their missiles had no effect, bouncing harmlessly off the creature's tough hide.

The Havalqa cloud came to life once more, releasing another blast of red light down upon the Varsae Sandrova. At least a third of the structure collapsed upon itself.

"Hollin, forget the library," said Gerin. "We can't get there."

"Back to the tower," said Kirin. The cloud of dust from the Varsae Sandrova blew across them and turned the world an ashen gray. They coughed and wiped their eyes as the fine powder settled on them, insinuating itself in their hair and clothes.

The two-hundred-foot-tall tower was painted white, with pale blue bands encircling it at regular intervals. So far it had remained undamaged by either the Havalqa cloud or the dragons.

Balandrick shouldered open the heavy wooden door, stuck his head inside, then backed away so the others could enter. "Get in, quickly!" he yelled.

Kirin looked over his shoulder, drew a hissing breath through his teeth, then created a spark of magefire as he crossed the threshold to light their way. Balandrick slammed and barred the door behind him.

Gerin, too, created a spark of magefire above their heads. They were in a small antechamber filled with crates and storage shelves.

"This way," said Kirin. Outside, they heard another roar of a nearby dragon. The entire tower trembled; small streamers of dust and grit fell from the ceiling to mingle with the grime from the Varsae Sandrova.

Kirin led them through several short hallways until they reached another closed door. "The cellars are down here," he said as he opened the door and started down.

Gerin found himself descending a short staircase that ended in a low-ceilinged room. They passed through another door and another set of stairs before Kirin halted.

"Are we safe here?" asked Peylo Ossren.

"Safer than we were outside, that's for certain," said Elaysen.

They were quiet for a time, listening to the distant sounds of battle. There were only a few chairs in the room, which they offered to the women. Nyene chose to remain standing.

"Well, I'm going to sit if you will not," said Abaru as he sank his bulk into a chair that seemed in danger of collapsing beneath him. "Who knows how long we'll be down here."

"You're bleeding," said Delarra, touching a cut on Abaru's face.

"Bah," he said. "It's nothing. A scratch."

The men settled against the walls, their legs stretched out before them. The magefire sparks floated in the air near the ceiling. Beyond the short reach of their light, the room was lost in darkness and gloom.

"What brought the dragons here now?" asked Balandrick. "I mean, what kind of coincidence is it that we see a vision of them, things that haven't been in this world for who knows how many thousands of years, and then suddenly they show up here while we're in the middle of a siege? It feels like some power is behind it, some force we don't yet know."

"Not a force, but there is definitely some*one* responsible for the dragons," said Kirin. "Did you see the men riding the neck of one of the things?"

"What?" Gerin, Hollin, Balandrick, and a number of others all blurted out at the same time.

"There was someone *riding* a dragon?" said Gerin.

Kirin nodded solemnly. "I saw them just before we entered the tower. Two men in some kind of harness on the neck of one of the larger dragons."

"That's insane," said Nyene. "You're mistaken."

"I wish I was, but I'm certain of what I saw, and what it means."

"And what is that?" asked the Threndish woman.

"That the Commanding Stone, which was thought to have been destroyed in the Last Battle of the Doomwar, has been found."

42

The flying lizards were destroying Ezqedir's army before his eyes. He could only watch in stunned horror as the creatures breathed streamers of fire across the ranks of his Herolen, roasting them alive. Thousands had already died, their corpses still burning in the field. The Loh'shree had erected some measure of protection that repelled the fire the monsters breathed; a shimmering, translucent dome enveloped their part of the camp, but that defense was beginning to crumble. The fire the monsters breathed vaporized the barrier wherever it struck, leaving gaping holes the Loh'shree seemed unable to repair.

What in Herol's name are they? Ezqedir wondered as he watched the flying monsters begin to attack the Loh'shree's black cloud. They spewed their hateful fire at it. To his surprise, the cloud began to burn like a pitch-soaked torch. It seemed almost to solidify as it burned, shrinking on itself as if attempting to recoil from the heat. Chunks of it started to drop away, creating smoking streamers as they fell.

These creatures had not been summoned by the wizards; they were destroying the fortress with the same grim efficiency they were exercising on his army.

The Voice and his insipid adjutant had fled, unable to conjure any means of countering the malefic flames. The demons had vanished from the skies when three of the flying creatures washed their flames across the mursaaba tents, killing the eunuchs.

Victory was quickly slipping from his grasp. Not only would he lose his chance to capture the Words of Making, he was very likely going to lose his entire army unless he could drive these beasts off.

The Harridan truly rules these lands with a fist of iron. Nothing else can explain the degree to which the will of the Powers is undermined here. For the first time, he felt a twinge of sympathy for the late Sword Drugal, realizing the obstacles he must have faced.

"General, we must call for a retreat," said Meloqthes.

"And if these creatures pursue us rather than wage war against the wizards?"

"Then we will almost certainly die," said his adjutant flatly. "But we must retreat, and hope these Harridan spawn do not follow. To stay is certain death."

The cloud exploded from its core. The blast propelled thousands of chunks of burning black debris into the air.

He thought frantically for a way to fight back, to drive off these monsters while defending his men. But there was nothing he could do, no strategy he could employ that would save them. He had no means of fighting these beasts.

The enemy had won the day.

"Sound the retreat," said Ezqedir. He'd never felt so weary in all of his life.

"Everyone stay here," said Gerin. "I'm going back out."

"Do you want to die?" asked Nyene.

"I must respectfully and completely disagree with that course of action, Your Highness," said Balandrick. "It's crazy."

"This has to end. Maybe we can't hurt the dragons, but if there's a human controlling them, we can hurt or stop *him*."

Hollin stepped in front of him. "Gerin, the combined might of the Atalari couldn't destroy the first dragonlord. This is suicide."

"But whoever's controlling them now isn't an Atalari."

A tremendous boom shook the tower. Peylo Ossren screamed. A spidery crack appeared in the ceiling. More dust and dirt settled over them.

"It sounds like the whole place is coming down on our heads," said Balandrick.

"It may very well be," said Hollin.

An idea came to Gerin. *I'm a fool for not seeing this earlier,* he thought.

He drew magic into himself, flooded the Scepter of the King with amber magic, felt the spells within it awaken and cut a hole in the reality around them. The door to the Varsae Estrikavis appeared a moment later, floating above the floor.

"By all that is holy, what is that?" asked Nyene.

"It's the entrance to a secret library. You can all wait safely in there."

"Very clever," said Abaru.

"Go inside, all of you. Leave the door open so I can come back if I need to. If you hear Havalqa, or the dragons . . . close it."

Balandrick opened the door. Light from the magefire lamps in the antechamber spilled out into the cellar. The short hallway within the door extended past the wall behind it, creating a disorienting sense of skewed depth.

Nyene stepped up into the hallway.

Elaysen helped Peylo Ossren to her feet. "What is this?" asked the serving woman, her voice filled with anxiety.

"Someplace we can be safe," said Elaysen.

"I'll help you," said Hollin to Gerin.

"Me, too," said Balandrick. "And before you think to argue, we're not going to change our minds no matter what you say or how much you pout, so you'll just be wasting precious time that you could be putting to better use outside trying to avoid becoming a roasted snack for our flying lizard friends."

"A way with words, as always," said Hollin.

"All right, the two of you, but that's it," said Gerin.

Kirin remained at the door to the Varsae Estrikavis. "I'll wait for your return. Venegreh's luck to the three of you."

* * *

Tyne Fedron surveyed the devastation below him and
laughed. Gods, the power at his command! He was routing
an entire army before him! The tiny soldiers were running
for their lives, scared to death of him and his dragons!

He watched wizards use their power to try to repel the
soldiers laying siege to their fortress. He wondered who
the army was, and why it was attacking the wizards, but
in the end he didn't care. All that mattered was that word
of his victory this day would spread like a fire across these
southern nations. Kings would hear of him and tremble on
their thrones.

The strange black cloud hovering over the fortress startled
him by shooting a lance of red light down at the ground,
destroying a building beneath it. Behind him on his harness,
Marrek Drayke shouted, "The gods take me, did you see
that?"

"Of course. I'm not blind."

"What if that thing can shoot the light at us?" He had to
shout to be heard over the roar of the wind.

He has a point. Through the Commanding Stone, Tyne ordered the dragons to come around and attack the cloud. They
began to circle it, bathing it with their cleansing fire.

"We should move away until it's destroyed!" said Marrek.

Tyne clenched his jaw. He disliked the barrage of sugges-
tions that came from Marrek—they made him wonder if his
servant thought him too stupid to consider such things on
his own. And it annoyed him even more when the boy was
right.

Maybe I'll leave him behind soon, he thought. No, that
would do no good. Marrek knew about his need for long pe-
riods of rest, and if he felt betrayed, might try to turn that
knowledge against him. If he ever decided he no longer
wanted Marrek's company, the boy's life would have to end.
*The dragons are always hungry. He'll never even know what
happened.* That time had not come yet. Despite Marrek's an-
noying tendencies, Tyne still found he preferred company to
being alone.

Tyne commanded the dragon they were riding to swing back over the army camped outside the fortress. He did not acknowledge hearing Marrek's suggestion that they distance themselves from the cloud, and he issued that command silently, through the Stone. For all the boy knew, he'd made the decision to move away on his own.

They'd crossed over the large defensive wall of the fortress when there was a tremendous explosion behind them. Tyne flinched, hunching his shoulders and crouching down toward the dragon's neck. Marrek tensed and let out a yelp.

Tyne turned his head to see the ruins of the black cloud raining down on the fortress in streamers of fire and smoke. "It's good we moved away from it when we did!" said Marrek.

Tyne remained silent. One of the dragons had been too close. He caught sight of its tumbling body just before it smashed into a building. The dragon's body crushed the slate tiles, collapsed the roof and one side wall. It lay still in the wreckage. Tyne knew at once from the Stone that it was dead. He could feel the sadness and anger and sense of loss from the other dragons, the absolute knowledge that one of their own had been slain.

Like Rukee and Tremmel, he thought.

Strange inhuman creatures huddled together in one part of the camp, protected by a dome of magic. Tyne's dragons had made several attacks against the dome and destroyed portions of it, but had not yet finished it off.

It's time to get rid of them, he thought. His new empire would have no room for mongrel races. They would be hunted down and destroyed. When he was emperor, a day of reckoning would come.

Through the Stone, he issued a command for more dragons to join the attack on the dome. They roared and banked hard, their cries loud even over the din of battle, their wings outstretched and rigid as they brought around their massive bulk.

They flew in a circle around the dome, then blasted it with their fire.

Tyne could see the creatures doing whatever they could to maintain their sorcery, but their frantic actions were not enough to overcome the dragons' withering fire.

A final blast from one of the dragons and the remainder of the dome vanished in a sudden outrush of light.

Kill all of these creatures, but allow the others to leave.

With the protective ring destroyed, the dragons began to scorch everything in that part of the encampment. A cyclone of flames erupted from the center and quickly spread outward. The sight of it awed him, even after all of the incredible things he'd witnessed. A tornado of fire growing thicker, churning into the sky. *And I'm responsible. This is my doing, a projection of my will.*

It looked to Tyne as if the human contingent of the army was calling for a retreat. He saw soldiers lining up in formation and marching quickly away from the fortress. Some tents had been packed or thrown onto wagons, but others were left where they were pitched. He wanted to devastate the army, but not destroy it completely. He needed survivors to carry on the tale of the dragonrider who had so thoroughly defeated them and the wizards.

Time for Marrek to deliver another message.

43

"Hear me, people of Hethnost!" shouted the young boy who had passed through the ruins of the Hammdras and now stood near the ruins of the Varsae Sandrova. "The merciful Lord Tyne Fedron has spared your lives . . . for now. Swear fealty to him, follow him loyally, and you will live and prosper. Resist him, and you will die painful deaths in the jaws of his dragons."

Gerin, Balandrick, and Hollin were listening from behind a pile of rubble. "Who in Shayphim's bloody name is Tyne Fedron?" said Balan.

Both Gerin and Hollin shook their heads.

"I'm tempted to go out there and wring his scrawny little neck," whispered Balan.

"Resist your urge," said Hollin. "That boy is not the problem. It's his master we have to worry about."

The boy had been going on about the mercy Lord Fedron would show to those who followed him.

"A new Helcarean Empire is about to rise from the ashes of the old one!" he shouted. "An empire that will never die."

"He's a long way from home," said Balandrick

"Lord Fedron knows this is a place of wizards and magic," said the boy, who looked to Gerin to be no more than sixteen. Gerin could see servants and surviving soldiers of the Sunrise Guard watching the boy from their own hiding places.

He did not see any surviving Havalqa. They'd either retreated or been killed.

"Lord Fedron is seeking a particular man," called out the boy. "A wizard, so you may know of him. His name is Gerin Atreyano. If you know where we may find him, speak now."

"In the name of all that's holy—" Balandrick shook his head. "How are *you* involved in this?"

"I have no idea." Gerin created a Farseeing so he could gain a closer view of the boy's face, but he was certain he'd never seen him before.

He watched the other survivors murmur among one another, trying to decide what to do.

"Answer me!" shouted the boy, enraged by the silence that greeted him. "Ignore me, and my master will call his dragons down on you. Attempt to harm me, and this place will become nothing but ash and bones."

"King Gerin was here." A male servant, holding his arm. It looked broken. Blood was smeared across his tunic and down the side of his face. "During the attack."

The boy looked shocked. "He was here? In this place?" It was obviously not what he expected to hear.

The servant nodded. "Yes. Got here just before that army arrived."

"Is he still here?" The boy was almost breathless.

"I don't know. He may be dead. A lot of wizards died."

"If he's dead, bring me his body."

The servant's mouth worked soundlessly for a moment. "I—I can't. I'm hurt. I have no idea where he might be . . . "

"Then what good are you?"

The servant took a fearful step backward. He looked around as if deciding whether to run, but could not decide which direction.

"Come here," said the boy. "And tell me everything you know."

On the ridge outside the walls of the fortress, Tyne sat in a chair left behind by the fleeing army and waited for Marrek to return. He held the Stone in his hand and lost himself staring into its pearlescent depth.

Once he landed on the ground, the world had been surprisingly quiet. Without the sound of the wind in his ears or the roar of his dragons' flames, the shouts and screams of men and women running for their lives, the crashing of collapsing buildings, or the throaty rumble of the mammoth cyclone of fire he'd set in the army camp—a fire that was still burning, though it was now only a fraction of the size it had been—the world seemed an almost silent place, hushed like a graveyard.

He'd sent off most of the dragons to feed. Three were with him, a retinue to keep him safe and remind onlookers exactly where his strength and authority came from.

He saw movement along the front of the fortress and lifted his gaze. Marrek was coming out with a tall man walking a few steps ahead of him. He wondered who the man was and why Marrek was bringing him. He felt a tickle of concern at the back of his neck and rose from his seat, his fingers unconsciously tightening around the Stone.

When Marrek was within shouting distance, Tyne called out to him. "Who is with you and why are you bringing him here?"

"He's a servant who says he knows where we can find Gerin Atreyano." Marrek's voice echoed across the wide field.

"How would a servant know where he is?" shouted Tyne.

"He claims Gerin Atreyano was here not long ago."

Tyne started at them hard. The servant carried no weapons in his hands, He moved with his head down, his shoulders hunched, as if trying to disappear from view.

"Where is he now?" called Tyne.

"Somewhere in the fortress," said Marrek. "He may be dead."

Tyne pondered this turn of events. Gerin Atreyano was here! He'd hoped to find information on his whereabouts, since even with maps it was difficult to find his way in these foreign lands. He'd never expected to find the man himself.

Why was a king not in his own country? He had not yet

crossed the border into Khedesh, if the mayor of the last city was to be believed.

But Gerin was both a wizard and a king. Perhaps he was required to return to this place of wizards from—

A shadow fell across him. He turned to see the snarling face of Drexos mere inches from his own.

"You fool! That is no servant! He *is* Gerin Atreyano!"

"Come here," the boy had said to the blood-covered man. "And tell me everything you know."

The servant nearly fainted from fear.

"Enough of this," Gerin had growled, watching them. "Stay here. That's a direct command from your king, Captain. You too, Hollin."

"What are you—" Balandrick started, but it was too late. Gerin was already walking toward the boy.

"I'm Gerin Atreyano," he'd said. "If your master is so eager to meet me, let's not keep him waiting."

Though he kept his head down in an attempt to appear cowed, Gerin's gaze never wavered from the figure upon the ridge. Tyne Fedron. A name, nothing more. Who was he? And more important, how had he come to possess the Commanding Stone?

Soon, he would know. Or would be quickly incinerated by one of the dragons surrounding Tyne. Gerin was encased in protective spells, but even with the power of an amber wizard behind them, the protections would not hold for long—seconds at most—against a withering onslaught of dragonfire.

When he'd stepped from his hiding place, Tyne's young servant had gaped at him as if he were Shayphim himself.

Before the boy could react in any way, Gerin encased him in a Binding.

He moved in front of the boy and used his large presence to physically intimidate him. "I am Gerin Atreyano," he repeated. "I don't know what your master wants with me, and at the moment I don't care. What *I* want is for you to take me to him."

Balandrick and Hollin of course disobeyed him and rushed to his side. "We need to have a talk about discipline and following your king's commands, Captain," he told Balan.

"We need to have a talk about your sanity, Your Highness," Balan replied. "Begging your pardon, but this is madness."

"Here's what I'm going to do. Notice that I am *not* asking for permission from either of you."

He told them his idea. Balan objected strenuously, but as he'd told the captain, he wasn't asking permission, and in the end they agreed to do what they could to help.

Not that he was overjoyed by his plan. He was risking his life on a number of unproven assumptions. But when the boy said that this Tyne Fedron was personally interested in him, he knew he had to act. There was no other choice. Some greater force was at work here, and he needed to know what it was.

He had to be closer to Tyne to carry out his plan. He already was stretching his strength to the limits. Not only was he maintaining the powerful protective spells in front of him, but he'd also worked a Compulsion to force the boy to do his bidding. Compulsions were never to be used lightly, but in this instance even Hollin agreed it was warranted and had helped him create it.

Gerin watched as Tyne took note of their approach and rose from the folding chair in which he'd been sitting. He called out, "Who is with you and why are you bringing him here?"

Gerin spoke softly and with his head still lowered. "Tell him I'm a servant who knows where you can find Gerin Atreyano."

He felt the power of the Compulsion overwhelm the boy's resistance. Then the boy relayed Gerin's message to Tyne Fedron.

"How would a servant know where he is?" came Fedron's reply.

"Tell him that Gerin Atreyano was here in the fortress not long ago."

The boy obeyed. They continued to close the distance to

the ridge. From the corners of his eyes, Gerin watched the dragons as he walked. So far they had not moved in any threatening way. The smell of sulfur wafted on the breeze and made his eyes sting.

"And where is he now?" Tyne called.

"Tell him I'm in the fortress, and that I may be dead."

A moment after the boy relayed Gerin's words, a figure appeared on the ridge next to Tyne. Gerin faltered a step. Even wizards could not appear out of thin air as this man just had.

The stranger said something to Tyne, but Gerin was already reacting. He felt instinctively that his little charade was about to end.

Tyne thrust out his right hand. Gerin could see an object in it. It had to be the Commanding Stone.

The dragons reared back and roared. The stench of sulfur grew overpowering.

Gerin dropped the Compulsion so he could add that power to Tocca's Mirror and the Forbiddings he'd created.

With Gerin's power no longer holding him, the boy came out of his daze, yelled in rage, and threw himself at the wizard.

Gerin's protections did not extend behind him. He had no time for the distraction of a furious boy and kicked out viciously. His boot slammed into the boy's chest, shattering several ribs. The boy tumbled backward down the gentle slope of the ridge and lay still.

Gerin spread the fingers of his left hand and trapped Tyne in a Binding. He could see Tyne's arms snap to his sides as he closed his fist to contract the spell's power.

The dragons lowered their heads and blasted him with fire.

The spell called Tocca's Mirror caught the fire and reflected it back toward its source. The dragons thrashed and reared back as the streams of fire rushed at them. For a moment the attack halted.

The dragonfire was strong enough to disintegrate the mirror, but the spell held long enough to protect Gerin from the flames. The air became scorching hot, searing his lungs with each breath. Sweat broke out all over his body, spurred by the sudden heat as well as his exertions. It dripped into his eyes, making it hard to see.

He fashioned a Grasping and used his right hand to hurl the spell's power toward Tyne. Gerin could see the thin thread of magic fly out from his fingers. It took all of his concentration to keep his spells in place.

The dragons recovered from their shock at having their fire directed back at them. They spread their wings in anger and roared so loud and deep that Gerin could feel it in his bones.

The Grasping found and latched onto the Commanding Stone just as the dragons unleashed their fire for a second time. The Forbiddings held, but in moments would collapse. The air grew so hot Gerin thought he would black out. He could not draw a breath. It felt as if the fire were sucking all the air from the world.

He used his fading strength to draw back the Grasping. The Commanding Stone flew from Tyne's hand, encased in a cocoon of Gerin's magic.

The Stone slammed into his palm just as the Forbiddings collapsed.

Gerin threw himself backward as the dragonfire blasted through the last of his defenses. The heat was searing, agonizing. Flames licked across his body as he rolled backward down the slope. He could smell his hair burning and smacked at it wildly with his free hand.

Then the fire stopped.

The air remained witheringly hot. He had squeezed his eyes shut just before the Forbiddings collapsed, and now forced them open.

The dragons were sitting back on their haunches, their wings flexing in agitation. They seemed to be looking at him.

Gerin sat up and burned his hand on the scorched ground. He drew it back quickly and swore. The grass around him had been set on fire in places, and he moved to get away from the flames. Each breath he took hurt. He began to cough, which made his chest hurt even more.

The Binding holding Tyne remained intact. Gerin reached out toward the stranger standing beside Tyne with a Sensing, but the spell's power found nothing. As if he were no more than a mirage or illusion.

Where the stranger had been standing, Gerin caught a glimpse of something monstrous—a creature enfolded in leathery wings with a lizardlike tail lashing about behind it. It was wreathed in an almost living smoke that swirled around it in thick black tendrils.

Then it was gone.

Gerin looked down at the Stone in his hand. "What have we here?" he said quietly.

44

Gerin started up the hill toward Tyne, skirting by a wide margin the scorched and burning ground the dragonfire had washed over. The other boy was dead. He'd taken the full force of the dragonfire; there was little left except blackened bones and burned tatters of flesh.

The skin of Gerin's face and hands was painful to touch. His hair was brittle; some of it broke off and turned to ash when he ran his fingers through it.

His left leg gave out when he'd covered about half the distance to Tyne. He knelt on the ground, trying to draw a full breath, and waited for some strength to return. In the distance he heard Balandrick and Hollin running toward him, shouting his name.

He pushed himself to his feet and staggered the rest of the way up the slope. The Binding was still holding Tyne, but just barely. Once Hollin arrived, he would have the other wizard take over.

The dragons watched him but made no other movements. He could feel a power in the Commanding Stone, not unlike the power he felt in Naragenth's staff. He sensed a faint connection between the Stone and the dragons. He did not understand it and did not have the strength to probe it. That would have to wait.

His plan had been based on a faulty premise. He had hoped to take the Stone from Tyne and use it to Command the dragons himself. That, he now realized, was impossible. It would take time to learn to use the Stone.

But he'd been lucky. Apparently, mere physical possession of the Stone was enough to halt the attack against him. Perhaps there was some kind of imperative built into the Stone that prevented the dragons from harming it. There was no way to know until they could study it more.

Whatever the reason, it had saved his life.

Tyne's struggles against the Binding had caused him to lose balance and fall to the ground.

"You're younger than I thought you'd be," Gerin said. He wheezed when he spoke, and his voice was raspy. It sounded old and worn to his own ears.

He shifted the Binding so Tyne could speak. "Let me go!" he shrieked. "Give me back the Stone! It's mine! *Mine!* You have no right to it!" He spoke with a thick, Middle Plains accent.

"You'll never get this back, I'm afraid." Gerin knelt in the trampled grass. The looming presence of the dragons unnerved him a little. He concentrated on the Stone, bent all his thoughts and will toward it. *Go away. Join the others for now. Feed or rut or do whatever it is dragons do, but leave us.*

A sharp pain jabbed through his skull. He felt . . . something . . . travel through the connection to the dragons, a sliver of a thought perhaps, an echo of his command. The dragons stirred restlessly, like deer spooked by the scent of a hunter. Then one of them roared, a throaty noise with a surprisingly complex series of inflections.

The dragons leaped into the air, spread their wings and took flight. The wind of their passing cooled Gerin's burned skin.

"There, that's better." He turned his gaze back toward the young man. "What did you want with me, Tyne Fedron? I don't believe we've ever met."

"You called a demon that killed my brother, that's why!" He let loose a mindless howl of rage. "Let me go! The gods damn you, let me go!"

Gerin was too exhausted to get angry. He also couldn't raise his voice if he wanted to. Every swallow was painful.

"I don't believe I've ever called a demon. Certainly not in Helcarea, which seems to be your home. I've never been there. So I don't see how I could have done what you claimed."

"It was you! I know it! You called the bronze-skinned demon from its barrow and it killed my brother! *He* told me!"

A painful chill swept across Gerin's skin. *The Vanil? Could that be what he's talking about?*

He decided to address that possibility later. "Who is the one that told you? Was it that creature who appeared beside you? Who is he? *What* is he?"

Tyne clamped his mouth shut.

"No matter. We have means of discovering what we need to know."

"I swear I'll kill you."

"Perhaps. But not today."

Hollin fashioned a new Binding on Tyne Fedron, then worked several healing spells on Gerin's skin and lungs. "I can't do much about your scorched hair," he said. "But don't worry, it should grow back just fine."

Between his exhaustion and the effect of the healing spells, Gerin could not finish the return to Hethnost without Balandrick's help. He slung his arm over his captain's shoulders and allowed him to carry the bulk of his weight.

Unconsciousness tugged mercilessly at him as they passed through the wreckage of the Hammdras.

"I'm glad your plan worked," said Balan, his voice thick with emotion. "I thought for sure you were dead when those dragons blasted you."

Gerin nodded. "So did I."

Over the next week, they pieced together most of the story of how Tyne Fedron had found the Commanding Stone. It seemed he was indeed driven by a lust for revenge against the Vanil that Gerin had inadvertently awakened from its millennia-long slumber when he fashioned Nimnahal. Somehow, when Tyne was driven into Nirovai Deep by a band of Aidrel's more bloodthirsty followers, he'd stumbled across the resting place of the Stone.

"He claims the Stone called out to him," said Hollin after a long session questioning their prisoner. They were in the relatively intact manor house of the Archmage. "That it showed him its resting place and where to dig to find it."

"That fits with what we've learned of the Stone so far," said Kirin. "There is an entity alive within it."

They had no idea what the entity was or how it had been confined. They also discovered they had no means of harming the Stone. No spell, no hammer, no fire could so much as scratch it.

"If it survived the Last Battle of the Doomwar, it can probably survive anything," said Gerin.

The creature that had appeared with Tyne on the ridge troubled them all. Tyne told them its name was Drexos and that it was a divine servant of a god it would not name.

"A counterpart to Zaephos, perhaps," said Hollin.

"That sniveling little whelp said that this Drexos fiend is the one who told Tyne you'd killed his brothers," Balandrick said to Gerin. "I guess it's true since there's no other way he could know about you and the Vanil. But why was the creature after you?"

"Zaephos told me that the Adversary was growing in the world much faster than expected," said Gerin. "Maybe I'm a threat to him, and this was his way of getting rid of me."

"You truly have a knack for drawing unwanted attention," said Balandrick.

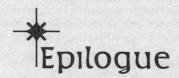

Epilogue

Gerin stared at the Commanding Stone, which rested on a velvet pillow that in turn was perched upon the Archmage's council table. The only light in the room came from a magefire lamp atop a tall decorative stand. It was early morning. The sun had not yet climbed above the eastern hills, though a diffuse, rosy glow was growing behind the gauzy curtains.

He heard footsteps in the hall, and the door open behind him. He recognized Nyene's scent before he saw her.

"What are you doing?" she asked.

"I'm wondering about the similarities between the Stone and Naragenth's staff." He tilted his head toward the staff, leaning in the corner.

He spoke softly. Hollin and Kirin had worked more healing spells on his skin and lungs, but his vocal cords had not taken as well to the spells and still felt raw.

"Then your eyesight is failing. One is a round jewel. The other is a long black stick."

He smiled. "The similarity of their power, not their shape. I used to want to do something like that to my sword. Make it alive, so it recognized me when I held it, or rejected anyone else who tried to use it."

She sat down beside him. "A worthy goal."

"Maybe. But not one I'm likely to achieve. I don't think it's possible to imbue an object with intelligence without causing far more harm than it's worth. To do such a thing to my sword, I'd have to sacrifice someone and force their mind into it. That's a price I'm not willing to pay."

"I'm surprised to find such compassion in a king. Certainly there is none in the stone heart of Threndellen's monarch."

They were silent for a time. Finally, she asked another question.

"Can you see the creature your wizards say lives in that thing?" She pointed at the Stone. The skepticism in her voice was obvious.

"No, I can't see it. But it's there. The more I hold the Stone, the more I can feel it. Whatever's in there, it's insane with rage."

"Yet your staff is not, if you are to be believed."

"I think that whatever's in the Stone was never a human being. It's something far more powerful and dangerous."

Gerin heard footsteps in the hall and immediately recognized Balandrick's long, heavy stride. Balan gave Nyene a knowing look as he came around the table.

"May I join you, Your Highness?"

"Of course, Balan. Sit."

The captain pointed to the Stone. "Have you decided what you're going to do with that yet? As much as I don't like the dragons, they would come in pretty handy against the Havalqa."

"I don't know."

"Bah," said Nyene. "It's a weapon, nothing more, and should be used against your enemies. Anything else is folly."

Balandrick craned his neck to look out the window toward the brightening sky.

"If I may ask, Your Highness, what's next for us?"

He thought of Elaysen and the medicines she needed. He wanted her whole again. Everything else could wait.

"We're going home."

Glossary and Pronunciation Guide

The pronunciation guide included in this glossary is in no way intended to be absolute, especially where Kelarin is concerned, which was a language of diverse regional dialects, accents, and vocabulary. The pronunciations of Kelarin words given here reflect the speech of central Khedesh, where in later years these accounts were compiled. For reasons of clarity and brevity, alternative pronunciations, even when they are known, are not included.

Osirin poses less of a difficulty since by Gerin's time it had long been a "dead" language and therefore mostly immune to the kinds of changes in vocabulary and pronunciation that affect a language used in everyday speech. The forms of Osirin had been fixed for centuries and had changed little since the time of the Empire, when it ceased its widespread use. Osirin became a largely ceremonial language, used by wizards in their rituals and spellmaking but for little else, not even record-keeping (at least not consistently), and even in Hethnost centuries had passed since it had been used for daily intercourse.

An accent after a syllable indicates stress (*af'ter*).

Ademel Caranis (*Ad'-eh-mel Ka'-ran-is*): Captain of the City Watch of Almaris.

398 *Glossary and Pronunciation Guide*

Aidrel Entraly (*Ay'-drel En'-trah-lee*): Member of Aunphar's Inner Circle.

akesh: A messenger of the Telchan.

Aleith'aqtar (*Ah-layth' Ak' -tar*): "Land of the Obedient," homeland of the Havalqa.

Alkaneiros (*Alk'-ah-nare'-ohs*): Ruby ring of Demos Thelar, worn by the Archmage of Hethnost.

Almaris (*Al-mare'-is*): Capital city of Khedesh.

andraleirazi (*an'-drah-lay-rah'-zee*): Magical powder that can be used to create the Binding Rings of Barados to imprison beings of spirit.

Archmage: The elected ruler of the wizards of Hethnost.

Arghen Helehba (*Ar'ghen Hel'-eh-ba*): Loh'shree commander attached to Ezqedir's army.

Arilek Levkorail (*Air'-ih-lek Lev'-kor-ail*): The Lord Commander and Governor General of the Taeratens of the Naege.

Aron Toresh (*Air'-on Tor'-esh*): Earl of Tolthean, knight lieutenant of the Realm.

Arsailen (*Ar-say'-len*): "Bringer of Oblivion," the name of a creature used for executions in the era of the Atalari Shining Nation.

Aunphar el'Turya (*On'far el-Toor'-ya*): Former priest of Telros, now the Prophet of the One God.

awaenjir (*Ah-wain-jeer'*): Device of magic used to Awaken a wizard's dormant powers.

Balandrick Vaules (*Bah-lan'-drick Vole'-es*): Youngest of the four sons of Earl Herenne Vaules of Carengil, and the captain of Gerin's personal guard.

Bariq the Wise (*Bar-eek'*): One of the Havalqa Powers, god of those who study the Mysteries.

Baris Toresh (*Bare'-is Tor'-esh*): Claressa's husband, son of Aron and Vaina Toresh.

Baryashin Order (*Bar'-yah-sheen*): A secret order of wizards who committed murders in an attempt to grant themselves eternal life. They originated within Hethnost but fled when they were discovered, and were later destroyed.

Chamber of the Moon: Location of the Varsae Estrikavis.

City Watch: Military order charged with enforcing the king's law in Almaris.

Cleave: Deepwater harbor bisecting part of Almaris.

dalar-aelom (*da-lahr' ay'-lom*): Name of the religion of the One God, an ancient Khedeshian phrase that means "holy path."

Demos Thelar (*Dem'ohs Thay'-lar*): Wizard who created the *methlenel* and *awaenjir*, and devised the Rituals of Discovery and Awakenings, among other accomplishments. Considered one of the greatest wizards who ever lived.

Donael Rundgar (*Don-ay'-il Rund'-gar*): Captain of Therain's personal guard.

Doomwar: Ancient war between the Atalari and a host of dragons that endured for decades and ended with the complete destruction of the Atalari Shining Nation.

Dreamers: Nonhuman entities with many mystical powers. Their exact numbers are not known; even their appearance is kept secret, under pain of death. They are the advisors of the Exalted of the Havalqa and wield enormous power.

Drufar (*Droo'-far*): "Silent servants," Loremasters of Bariq chosen to serve the Dreamers.

Elqos the Worker (*El'-kohs*): One of the Havalqa Powers, god of workers, laborers, and servants.

Enbrahel (*En'-bra-hel*): A Loremaster, assistant to Tolsadri.

Formale (*For'-mah-lay*): Region of Helcarea near the Bronze Demon Hills.

Gleso in'Palurq (*Gles'-oh in Pa-lurk'*): Founder of the Havalqa more than five and a half thousand years ago.

Hael Kouref (*Hail Koor'-ef*): A band of outlaws in Threndellen sworn to fight those who serve the Threndish king.

Hammdras (*Hahm'-dras*): Wall enclosing the Valley of Wizards, where Hethnost lies.

Havalqa (*Ha-val'-ka*): "The Steadfast," name of a people from beyond the Maurelian Sea who follow a multigod pantheon and whose society is organized into a rigid caste system.

Helion Spears (*Hee'-lee-on*): The soldiers and emissaries of Aidrel.

Herol-eilu Antaqar (*Hair'-ol eye'-loo An'-ta-kahr*): A holy book among the Herolen, describing some of the exploits of Herol the Soldier.

Herol the Soldier (*Hair'-ol*): One of the Havalqa Powers, god of warriors and mercenaries.

Hethnost (*Heth'-nost*): Fortress city in the Redhorn Hills, home of most of the remaining wizards in Osseria.

Holvareh (*Hohl-var'-eh*): God above the Havalqa Powers, the Father of All.

Huma endi Algariq (*Hyoo'-mah en-dee Al-gahr'-eek*): Son of Katel yalez Algariq.

Jade Temple: Training school in Kalmanyikul dedicated to the followers of Bariq the Wise.

Jaros Waklan (*Jar'-ohs Wahk'-lan*): Former Minister of the Realm of Khedesh.

Jurje Dremjou (*Jur'-jee Drem'-joo*): Wahtar of the Jade Temple.

Kalabrendis Dhosa (*Kal-ah-bren'-dis Doh'-sah*): The great meeting hall in Hethnost, where conclaves are held.

Kalmanyikul (*Kal-man'-yih-kool*): Capital city of the Havalqa.

kamichi (*ka-mee'-chee*): A Neddari sorcerer-priest.

Katel yalez Algariq (*Ka-tel' yah-leez Al-gahr'-eek*): A soul stealer, hunter, and follower of the Harridan.

Kelpa: Wild dog adopted by Therain.

Kua'tani (*Koo'-ah tahn'-ee*): King of Threndellen.

Kursil Rulhámad (*Kur'-seel Rool-ha'-mahd*): A maegosi, hunter and follower of the Harridan.

Leru's Eye (*Lair'-oo*): One of the Mysteries of Bariq, a sensing power.

Loesta Fedron (*Low-es'-ta*): Mother of Tyne, Tremmel, and Rukee.

Loh'shree: Nonhuman creatures of Aleith'aqtar who command mysterious powers.

Lorem taril'na Ezqedir (*Lor'-em ta-ril na Ez'-keh-deer*): General in the Havalqa military.

maegosi (*may-goh'-see*): A Havalqa sorcerer able to control quatans.

Magister's Palace: The seat of secular governmental authority in the holy city of Turen in Threndellen.

Marrek Drayke: Villager who becomes a companion of Tyne Fedron.

Medril: Lord Commander of the Sunrise Guard at Hethnost.

Metharog the Father (*Meh-thar'-og*): One of the Havalqa Powers, god of the ruling class.

methlenel (*meth'-leh-nel*): Device of magic used by wizards in the Ritual of Discovery to locate potential wizards.

Naragenth ul-Darhel (*Nare'ah-genth*): The first amber wizard. A king of Khedesh and creator of the Varsae Estrikavis.

Neddari (*Ned-dar'-ee*): Warrior society ruled by various clan chieftains.

Neddari War: Conflict caused by Asankaru, the undead Eletheros Storm King, who posed as a Neddari god in order to acquire the Horn of Tireon in an attempt to regain true life for himself and his people.

Nimnahal (*Nim'-na-hal*): Gerin's sword, originally called Glaros, rechristened as Nimnahal ("Starfire" in Osirin) after he infused it with magic.

Olo'kidare (*Oh'-lo kid-ahn'-eh*): Loremaster attached to Ezqedir's army.

Omara Atreyano (*Oh-mar'-ah At-ray-ahn'-oh*): Nellemar's wife.

Paérendras (*Pay-air'-en-dras*): Khedeshian god of the sea.

Pahjuleh Palace (*Pah'-joo-leh*): Imperial palace in the center of Kalmanyikul, home to the Exalted and the Dreamers.

paru'enthred (*par'-oo en'-thred*): "Inner eye" in Osirin, describing the ability of wizards to focus and shape the flow of magic through their bodies.

Pashti (*Pash'-tee*): Indigenous people of southern Osseria, conquered by Khedesh and his Raimen when they came to the southlands. Now mostly a servant class in the kingdom.

quatan (*kwah'-tan*): Creature from Aleith'aqtar whose body contains rezarim, making it immune from magic.

Raimen (*Ray'-ih-men*): The original followers of Khedesh, a nomadic warrior society from the distant south, beyond the borders of Osseria.

Regnel's curse: Name for the seizures that sometimes afflict a mursaaba eunuch, a by-product of their power.

Releasing Fire: Spell used by wizards to cremate the bodies of their dead.

rezarim (*reh-zar'-im*): A metallic substance that can nullify a wizard's magic. During the wars between the Atalari and Gendalos races, the Gendalos used rezarim weapons to give them an advantage in battle.

Ruren the Silent (*Rur'en*): One of the Havalqa Powers, god of the Underworld and Master of the Dead.

Sai'fen (*Sigh'-fen*): Elite, black-armored soldiers of the Steadfast entrusted with the physical safety of the Dreamers.

Scepter of the King: Ivory rod inlaid with gold, silver, and pearl filigrees that is the official symbol of the King of Khedesh. Its upper end is formed of gold in the shape of a gull, its sleek wings thrown forward so their tips nearly touch beyond the bird's beak.

Serpent Fangs: Name of the elite guards of the Pahjuhleh Palace in Kalmanyikul.

sharfaya (*shar-fay'-ah*): A garment worn by Havalqa noblewomen, fashioned from a long bolt of cloth wound loosely about the body.

Shayphim (*Shay'-fim*): Demonic figure of evil said to roam the southlands of Osseria with his Hounds Venga and Molok. He searches for wayward men and women whose spirits he captures and deposits in the Cauldron of Souls, where they are trapped forever, cut off from the light of the gods and unable to enter Velyol. The saying, "To Shayphim with him!" or "Shayphim take him!" is a curse that the dead will be denied the afterlife with the gods.

Sunrise Guard: Mortal soldiers entrusted with the protection of Hethnost.

taekrim (*tay'-krim*): "Vigilant," name of those who follow *dalar-aelom*.

Taeratens (*Tare'-ah-tens*): Elite fighter of Khedesh, marked with a circle-within-a-circle tattoos on the backs of their hands. They are trained in the fortress of the Naege in Almaris.

Tashqinni lumal Neyis (*Tash-keen'-nee loo'-mal Ney'-is*): the Exalted of the Havalqa.

tel'fan: A power in which an Adept of Bariq determines the caste assignment of one recently brought among the Steadfast.

Telros: Chief god of the Khedeshian pantheon.

Terl Enkelares (*Terl En-ke-lahr'-reez*): Gerin's Minister of the Realm.

tevosa (*teh-voh'-sa*): A rare disease that sometimes afflicts a wizard later in life. It causes them to lose the ability to separate the past from the present, and as it progresses destroys the mind.

Tulqan the Harridan (*Tool'-kwan*): One of the Powers of the Havalqa, goddess of the outcast. She at times is opposed to the wishes of the other gods, and her followers are often wicked for its own sake.

Urlos (*Er'-lohs*): Helcarean god of the dead.

Uron River (*Yoor'-on*): Small river flowing through the Helcarean region of Formale.

Vanil (*Van'-ihl*): Mysterious beings who inhabited Osseria before the coming of the Atalari. They were believed to have the power to devour the soul of a sentient being and thus deny it existence in the afterlife.

Varsae Estrikavis (*Var'-say Es-tri-kah'-vis*): Library of magical knowledge assembled by Naragenth and the great wizards of his age. It was hidden due to the outbreak of the Wars of Unification, and its location lost when Naragenth was killed in the siege of Almaris. Recently rediscovered by Gerin.

Varsae Sandrova (*Var'-say San-droh'-vah*): The library of Hethnost.

Velyol (*Vel'-yol*): The mansions of the dead where the god Bellon reins.

Ventro Gulethis (*Ven'-tro Goo-leth'-is*): Loremaster attached to Ezqedir's army.

Vethiq aril Tolsadri (*Veh-theek' air'-il Tol-sah'-dree*): Voice of the Exalted, Adept of Bariq the Wise, Loremaster of the Mysteries, and First of the sailing vessel *Kaashal*.

Wahtar: Title of the leader of the Jade Temple, and second to Tolsadri in rank among the followers of Bariq the Wise.

Word of Reflection: A very powerful and dangerous kind of magic.

Wrotherqu Klaati (*Row-thair'-kyoo Klay-ah'-tee*): Loremaster attached to Ezqedir's army.

Yar'el'eta (*Yar-el-et'-ah*): The holy book of the Havalqa, written by the Gleso in'Palurq and his son-in-law Meerta an-Distonyi.

Yendis the Mother (*Yen'-dis*): One of the Powers of the Havalqa, Spouse of Metharog; also called the Nurturer. Yendis is the goddess of older women and women who have given birth.

Zaephos (*Zay'-fohs*): Messenger of the Maker.

LEGENDS OF THE RIFTWAR

HONORED ENEMY

978-0-06-079284-8

by Raymond E. Feist & William R. Forstchen

In the frozen northlands of the embattled realm of Midkemia, Dennis Hartraft's Marauders must band together with their bitter enemy, the Tsurani, to battle *moredhel*, a migrating horde of deadly dark elves.

MURDER IN LAMUT

978-0-06-079291-6

by Raymond E. Feist & Joel Rosenberg

For twenty years the mercenaries Durine, Kethol, and Pirojil have fought other people's battles, defeating numerous deadly enemies. Now the Three Swords find themselves trapped by a winter's storm inside a castle teeming with ambitious, plotting lords and ladies, and it falls on the mercenaries to solve a series of cold-blooded murders.

JIMMY THE HAND

978-0-06-079299-2

by Raymond E. Feist & S.M. Stirling

Forced to flee the only home he's ever known, Jimmy the Hand, boy thief of Krondor finds himself among the rural villagers of Land's End. But Land's End is home to a dark, dangerous presence even the local smugglers don't recognize. And suddenly Jimmy's youthful bravado is leading him into the maw of chaos . . . and, quite possibly, his doom.

Visit www.AuthorTracker.com for exclusive information on your favorite HarperCollins authors.

LOR 0709

Available wherever books are sold or please call 1-800-331-3761 to order.

SAME GREAT STORIES, GREAT NEW FORMAT . . .
EOS TRADE PAPERBACKS

THE UNDEAD KAMA SUTRA
by Mario Acevedo
978-0-06-083328-2

GILL MEMORIAL LIBRARY
145 E. BROAD STREET
PAULSBORO, NJ 08066
(856) 423-5155

Visit www.AuthorTracker.com for exclusive
information on your favorite HarperCollins authors.

Available wherever books are sold or please call 1-800-331-3761 to order.

EOT 0409